Books by Isaac Bashevis Singer

NOVELS
THE MANOR

I. THE MANOR   II. THE ESTATE

THE FAMILY MOSKAT   THE MAGICIAN OF LUBLIN

SATAN IN GORAY   THE SLAVE

ENEMIES, A LOVE STORY

SHOSHA

STORIES
A FRIEND OF KAFKA   GIMPEL THE FOOL   SHORT FRIDAY

THE SÉANCE   THE SPINOZA OF MARKET STREET

A CROWN OF FEATHERS   PASSIONS

MEMOIRS
IN MY FATHER'S COURT

FOR CHILDREN
A DAY OF PLEASURE   THE FOOLS OF CHELM

MAZEL AND SHLIMAZEL OR THE MILK OF A LIONESS

WHEN SHLEMIEL WENT TO WARSAW   A TALE OF THREE WISHES

WHY NOAH CHOSE THE DOVE   ELIJAH THE SLAVE

JOSEPH AND KOZA OR THE SACRIFICE TO THE VISTULA

ALONE IN THE WILD FOREST   THE WICKED CITY

NAFTALI THE STORYTELLER AND HIS HORSE, SUS

COLLECTION
AN ISAAC BASHEVIS SINGER READER

AN
ISAAC
BASHEVIS
SINGER
READER

An Isaac Bashevis Singer Reader

Farrar, Straus and Giroux
NEW YORK

Author's Note

The contents of a Reader are always, at least from the writer's point of view, arbitrary. Nevertheless, anthologies have existed from the earliest times, even in religious literature. Their purpose is to give the reader a taste of and a desire for the writer's other works, and I hope that this will happen with at least some readers of the present collection.

Ordinarily a Reader does not contain material that has not appeared in book form before. My editor, Robert Giroux, and I decided to include four episodes from *In My Father's Court* that for technical reasons were omitted from the translation of that volume.

Though I write in Yiddish, I do most of the revisions of my writings after they have been translated into English by myself and a collaborator. Because of this, I can call myself a bilingual writer and say that English has become my "second original."

I.B.S.

Contents

Contents

STORIES

Gimpel
the
Fool

I am Gimpel the fool. I don't think myself a fool. On the contrary. But that's what folks call me. They gave me the name while I was still in school. I had seven names in all: imbecile, donkey, flax-head, dope, glump, ninny, and fool. The last name stuck. What did my foolishness consist of? I was easy to take in. They said, "Gimpel, you know the rabbi's wife has been brought to childbed?" So I skipped school. Well, it turned out to be a lie. How was I supposed to know? She hadn't had a big belly. But I never looked at her belly. Was that really so foolish? The gang laughed and hee-hawed, stomped and danced and chanted a good-night prayer. And instead of the raisins they give when a woman's lying in, they stuffed my hand full of goat turds. I was no weakling. If I slapped someone he'd see all the way to Cracow. But I'm really not a slugger by nature. I think to myself: Let it pass. So they take advantage of me.

I was coming home from school and heard a dog barking. I'm not afraid of dogs, but of course I never want to start up with them. One of them may be mad, and if he bites there's not a Tartar in the world who can help you. So I made tracks. Then I looked around and saw the whole market place wild with laughter. It was no dog at all but Wolf-Leib the Thief. How was I supposed to know it was he? It sounded like a howling bitch.

When the pranksters and leg-pullers found that I was easy to fool, every one of them tried his luck with me. "Gimpel, the Czar is coming to Frampol; Gimpel, the moon fell down in Turbeen; Gimpel, little Hodel Furpiece found a treasure behind the bathhouse." And I like a golem believed everyone. In the first place, everything is possible, as it is written in the Wisdom of the Fathers, I've forgotten just how. Second, I had to believe when the whole town came down on me! If I ever dared to say, "Ah, you're kidding!" there was trouble. People got angry. "What do you mean! You want to call everyone a liar?" What was I to do? I believed them, and I hope at least that did them some good.

I was an orphan. My grandfather who brought me up was already bent toward the grave. So they turned me over to a baker, and what a time they gave me there! Every woman or girl who came to bake a batch of noodles had to fool me at least once. "Gimpel, there's a fair in heaven; Gimpel, the rabbi gave birth to a calf in the seventh month; Gimpel, a cow flew over the roof and laid brass eggs." A student from the yeshiva came once to buy a roll, and he said, "You, Gimpel, while you stand here scraping with your baker's shovel the Messiah has come. The dead have arisen." "What do you mean?" I said. "I heard no one blowing the ram's horn!" He said, "Are you deaf?" And all began to cry, "We heard it, we heard!" Then in came Rietze the Candle-dipper and called out in her hoarse voice, "Gimpel, your father and mother have stood up from the grave. They're looking for you."

To tell the truth, I knew very well that nothing of the sort had happened, but all the same, as folks were talking, I threw on my wool vest and went out. Maybe something had happened. What did I stand to lose by looking? Well, what a cat music went up! And then I took a vow to believe nothing more. But that was no go either. They confused me so that I didn't know the big end from the small.

I went to the rabbi to get some advice. He said, "It is written, better to be a fool all your days than for one hour to be evil. You are not a fool. They are the fools. For he who causes his neighbor to feel shame loses Paradise himself." Nevertheless the rabbi's daughter took me in. As I left the rabbinical court she said, "Have you kissed the wall yet?" I said, "No; what for?" She answered, "It's the law; you've got to do it after every visit." Well, there didn't seem to be any harm in it. And she burst out laughing. It was a fine trick. She put one over on me, all right.

I wanted to go off to another town, but then everyone got busy matchmaking, and they were after me so they nearly tore my coat tails off. They talked at me and talked until I got water on the ear. She was no chaste maiden, but they told me she was virgin pure. She had a limp, and they said it was deliberate, from coyness. She had a bastard, and they told me the child was her little brother. I cried, "You're wasting your time. I'll never marry that whore." But they said indignantly, "What a way to talk! Aren't you ashamed of yourself? We can take you to the rabbi and have you fined for giving her a bad name." I saw then that I wouldn't escape them so easily and I thought: They're set on making me their butt. But when you're married the husband's the master, and if that's all right with her it's agreeable to me too. Besides, you can't pass through life unscathed, nor expect to.

I went to her clay house, which was built on the sand, and the whole gang, hollering and chorusing, came after me. They acted like bear-baiters. When we came to the well they stopped all the same. They were afraid to start anything with Elka. Her mouth would open as if it were on a hinge, and she had a fierce tongue. I entered the house. Lines were strung from wall to wall and clothes were drying. Barefoot she stood by the tub, doing the wash. She was dressed in a worn hand-me-down gown of plush. She had her hair put up in braids and pinned across her head. It took my breath away, almost, the reek of it all.

Evidently she knew who I was. She took a look at me and said, "Look who's here! He's come, the drip. Grab a seat."

I told her all; I denied nothing. "Tell me the truth," I said, "are you really a virgin, and is that mischievous Yechiel actually your little brother? Don't be deceitful with me, for I'm an orphan."

"I'm an orphan myself," she answered, "and whoever tries to twist you up, may the end of his nose take a twist. But don't let them think they can take advantage of me. I want a dowry of fifty guilders, and let them take up a collection besides. Otherwise they can kiss my you-know-what." She was very plainspoken. I said, "It's the bride and not the groom who gives a dowry." Then she said, "Don't bargain with me. Either a flat 'yes' or a flat 'no'—Go back where you came from."

I thought: No bread will ever be baked from *this* dough. But ours is not a poor town. They consented to everything and proceeded with the wedding. It so happened that there was a dysentery epidemic at the time. The ceremony was held at the cemetery gates, near the little corpse-washing hut. The fellows got drunk. While the marriage contract was being drawn up I heard the most pious high rabbi ask, "Is the bride a widow or a divorced woman?" And the sexton's wife answered for her, "Both a widow and divorced." It was a black moment for me. But what was I to do, run away from under the marriage canopy?

There was singing and dancing. An old granny danced opposite me, hugging a braided white *chalah*. The master of revels made a "God 'a mercy" in memory of the bride's parents. The schoolboys threw burrs, as on Tishe b'Av fast day. There were a lot of gifts after the sermon: a noodle board, a kneading trough, a bucket, brooms, ladles, household articles galore. Then I took a look and saw two strapping young men carrying a crib. "What do we need this for?" I asked. So they said, "Don't rack your brains about it. It's all right, it'll come in handy." I realized I was going to be rooked. Take it another way though, what did I stand to lose? I reflected: I'll see what comes of it. A whole town can't go altogether crazy.

2

At night I came where my wife lay, but she wouldn't let me in. "Say, look here, is this what they married us for?" I said. And she said, "My monthly has come." "But yesterday they took you to the ritual bath, and that's afterward, isn't it supposed to be?" "Today isn't yesterday," said she, "and yesterday's not today. You can beat it if you don't like it." In short, I waited.

Nor four months later she was in childbed. The townsfolk hid their laughter with their knuckles. But what could I do? She suffered intolerable pains and clawed at the walls. "Gimpel," she cried, "I'm going. Forgive me!" The house filled with women. They were boiling pans of water. The screams rose to the welkin.

The thing to do was to go to the House of Prayer to repeat Psalms, and that was what I did.

The townsfolk liked that, all right. I stood in a corner saying Psalms and prayers, and they shook their heads at me. "Pray, pray!" they told me. "Prayer never made any woman pregnant." One of the congregation put a straw to my mouth and said, "Hay for the cows." There was something to that too, by God!

She gave birth to a boy. Friday at the synagogue the sexton stood up before the Ark, pounded on the reading table, and announced, "The wealthy Reb Gimpel invites the congregation to a feast in honor of the birth of a son." The whole House of Prayer rang with laughter. My face was flaming. But there was nothing I could do. After all, I *was* the one responsible for the circumcision honors and rituals.

Half the town came running. You couldn't wedge another soul in. Women brought peppered chick-peas, and there was a keg of beer from the tavern. I ate and drank as much as anyone, and they all congratulated me. Then there was a circumcision, and I named the boy after my father, may he rest in peace. When all were gone and I was left with my wife alone, she thrust her head through the bed-curtain and called me to her.

"Gimpel," said she, "why are you silent? Has your ship gone and sunk?"

"What shall I say?" I answered. "A fine thing you've done to me! If my mother had known of it she'd have died a second time."

She said, "Are you crazy, or what?"

"How can you make such a fool," I said, "of one who should be the lord and master?"

"What's the matter with you?" she said. "What have you taken it into your head to imagine?"

I saw that I must speak bluntly and openly. "Do you think this is the way to use an orphan?" I said. "You have borne a bastard."

She answered, "Drive this foolishness out of your head. The child is yours."

"How can he be mine?" I argued. "He was born seventeen weeks after the wedding."

She told me then that he was premature. I said, "Isn't he a little too premature?" She said, she had had a grandmother who carried just as short a time and she resembled this grandmother of hers as one drop of water does another. She swore to it with such oaths that you would have believed a peasant at the fair if he had used them. To tell the plain truth, I didn't believe her; but when I talked it over next day with the school-master he told me that the very same thing had happened to Adam and Eve. Two they went up to bed, and four they descended.

"There isn't a woman in the world who is not the granddaughter of Eve," he said.

That was how it was; they argued me dumb. But then, who really knows how such things are?

I began to forget my sorrow. I loved the child madly, and he loved me too. As soon as he saw me he'd wave his little hands and want me to pick him up, and when he was colicky I was the only one who could pacify him. I bought him a little bone teething ring and a little gilded cap. He was forever catching the evil eye from someone, and then I had to run to get one of those abracadabras for him that would get him out of it. I worked like an ox. You know how expenses go up when there's an infant in the house. I don't want to lie about it; I didn't dislike Elka either, for that matter. She swore at me and cursed, and I couldn't get enough of her. What strength she had! One of her looks could rob you of the power of speech. And her orations! Pitch and sulphur, that's what they were full of, and yet somehow also full of charm. I adored her every word. She gave me bloody wounds though.

In the evening I brought her a white loaf as well as a dark one, and also poppyseed rolls I baked myself. I thieved because of her and swiped everything I could lay hands on: macaroons, raisins, almonds, cakes. I hope I may be forgiven for stealing from the Saturday pots the women left to warm in the baker's oven. I would take out scraps of meat, a chunk of pudding, a chicken leg or head, a piece of tripe, whatever I could nip quickly. She ate and became fat and handsome.

I had to sleep away from home all during the week, at the bakery. On Friday nights when I got home she always made an excuse of some sort. Either she had heartburn, or a stitch in the side, or hiccups, or headaches. You know what women's excuses are. I had a bitter time of it. It was rough. To add to it, this little brother of hers, the bastard, was growing bigger. He'd put lumps on me, and when I wanted to hit back she'd open her mouth and curse so powerfully I saw a green haze floating before my eyes. Ten times a day she threatened to divorce me. Another man in my place would have taken French leave and disappeared. But I'm the type that bears it and says nothing. What's one to do? Shoulders are from God, and burdens too.

One night there was a calamity in the bakery; the oven burst, and we almost had a fire. There was nothing to do but go home, so I went home. Let me, I thought, also taste the joy of sleeping in bed in mid-week. I didn't want to wake the sleeping mite and tiptoed into the house. Coming in, it seemed to me that I heard not the snoring of one but, as it were, a double snore, one a thin enough snore and the other like the snoring of a slaughtered ox. Oh, I didn't like that! I didn't like it at all. I went up to the bed, and things suddenly turned black. Next to Elka lay a man's form. Another in my place would have made an uproar, and enough noise to rouse the whole town, but the thought occurred to me that I might wake the child. A little thing like that —why frighten a little swallow, I thought. All right then, I went back to the bakery and stretched out on a sack of flour and till morning I never shut an eye. I shivered as if I had had malaria. "Enough of being a donkey," I said to myself. "Gimpel isn't going to be a sucker all his life. There's a limit even to the foolishness of a fool like Gimpel."

In the morning I went to the rabbi to get advice, and it made a great commotion in the town. They sent the beadle for Elka right away. She came, carrying the child. And what do you think she did? She denied it, denied everything, bone and stone! "He's out of his head," she said. "I know nothing of dreams or divinations." They yelled at her, warned her, hammered on the table, but she stuck to her guns: it was a false accusation, she said.

The butchers and the horse-traders took her part. One of the lads from the slaughterhouse came by and said to me, "We've got our eye on you, you're a marked man." Meanwhile the child started to bear down and soiled itself. In the rabbinical court there was an Ark of the Covenant, and they couldn't allow that, so they sent Elka away.

I said to the rabbi, "What shall I do?"

"You must divorce her at once," said he.

"And what if she refuses?" I asked.

He said, "You must serve the divorce. That's all you'll have to do."

I said, "Well, all right, Rabbi. Let me think about it."

"There's nothing to think about," said he. "You mustn't remain under the same roof with her."

"And if I want to see the child?" I asked.

"Let her go, the harlot," said he, "and her brood of bastards with her."

The verdict he gave was that I mustn't even cross her threshold—never again, as long as I should live.

During the day it didn't bother me so much. I thought: It was bound to happen, the abscess had to burst. But at night when I stretched out upon the sacks I felt it all very bitterly. A longing took me, for her and for the child. I wanted to be angry, but that's my misfortune exactly, I don't have it in me to be really angry. In the first place—this was how my thoughts went—

there's bound to be a slip sometimes. You can't live without errors. Probably that lad who was with her led her on and gave her presents and what not, and women are often long on hair and short on sense, and so he got around her. And then since she denies it so, maybe I was only seeing things? Hallucinations do happen. You see a figure or a mannikin or something, but when you come up closer it's nothing, there's not a thing there. And if that's so, I'm doing her an injustice. And when I got so far in my thoughts I started to weep. I sobbed so that I wet the flour where I lay. In the morning I went to the rabbi and told him that I had made a mistake. The rabbi wrote on with his quill, and he said that if that were so he would have to reconsider the whole case. Until he had finished I wasn't to go near my wife, but I might send her bread and money by messenger.

3

Nine months passed before all the rabbis could come to an agreement. Letters went back and forth. I hadn't realized that there could be so much erudition about a matter like this.

Meanwhile Elka gave birth to still another child, a girl this time. On the Sabbath I went to the synagogue and invoked a blessing on her. They called me up to the Torah, and I named the child for my mother-in-law —may she rest in peace. The louts and loudmouths of the town who came into the bakery gave me a going over. All Frampol refreshed its spirits because of my trouble and grief. However, I resolved that I would always believe what I was told. What's the good of *not* believing? Today it's your wife you don't believe; to-morrow it's God Himself you won't take stock in.

By an apprentice who was her neighbor I sent her daily a corn or a wheat loaf, or a piece of pastry, rolls or bagels, or, when I got the chance, a slab of pudding, a slice of honeycake, or wedding strudel—whatever came my way. The apprentice was a goodhearted lad, and more than once he added something on his own. He had formerly annoyed me a lot, plucking my nose and digging me in the ribs, but when he started to be a visitor to my house he became kind and friendly. "Hey, you, Gimpel," he said to me, "you have a very decent little wife and two fine kids. You don't deserve them."

"But the things people say about her," I said.

"Well, they have long tongues," he said, "and nothing to do with them but babble. Ignore it as you ignore the cold of last winter."

One day the rabbi sent for me and said, "Are you certain, Gimpel, that you were wrong about your wife?"

I said, "I'm certain."

"Why, but look here! You yourself saw it."

"It must have been a shadow," I said.

"The shadow of what?"

"Just of one of the beams, I think."

"You can go home then. You owe thanks to the Yanover rabbi. He found an obscure reference in Mai-monides that favored you."

I seized the rabbi's hand and kissed it.

I wanted to run home immediately. It's no small thing to be separated for so long a time from wife and child. Then I reflected: I'd better go back to work now, and go home in the evening. I said nothing to any-one, although as far as my heart was concerned it was like one of the Holy Days. The women teased and twitted me as they did every day, but my thought was: Go on, with your loose talk. The truth is out, like the oil upon the water. Maimonides says it's right, and therefore it is right!

At night, when I had covered the dough to let it rise, I took my share of bread and a little sack of flour and started homeward. The moon was full and the stars were glistening, something to terrify the soul. I hurried onward, and before me darted a long shadow. It was winter, and a fresh snow had fallen. I had a mind to sing, but it was growing late and I didn't want to wake the householders. Then I felt like whistling, but I remembered that you don't whistle at night because it brings the demons out. So I was silent and walked as fast as I could.

Dogs in the Christian yards barked at me when I passed, but I thought: Bark your teeth out! What are you but mere dogs? Whereas I am a man, the husband of a fine wife, the father of promising children.

As I approached the house my heart started to pound as though it were the heart of a criminal. I felt no fear, but my heart went thump! thump! Well, no drawing back. I quietly lifted the latch and went in. Elka was asleep. I looked at the infant's cradle. The shutter was closed, but the moon forced its way through the cracks. I saw the newborn child's face and loved it as soon as I saw it—immediately—each tiny bone.

Then I came nearer to the bed. And what did I see but the apprentice lying there beside Elka. The moon went out all at once. It was utterly black, and I trembled. My teeth chattered. The bread fell from my hands, and my wife waked and said, "Who is that, ah?"

I muttered, "It's me."

"Gimpel?" she asked. "How come you're here? I thought it was forbidden."

"The rabbi said," I answered and shook as with a fever.

"Listen to me, Gimpel," she said, "go out to the shed and see if the goat's all right. It seems she's been sick." I have forgotten to say that we had a goat. When I heard she was unwell I went into the yard. The nannygoat was a good little creature. I had a nearly human feeling for her.

With hesitant steps I went up to the shed and opened the door. The goat stood there on her four feet. I felt her everywhere, drew her by the horns, examined her udders, and found nothing wrong. She had probably eaten too much bark. "Good night, little goat," I said. "Keep well." And the little beast answered with a "Maa" as though to thank me for the good will.

I went back. The apprentice had vanished.

"Where," I asked, "is the lad?"

"What lad?" my wife answered.

"What do you mean?" I said. "The apprentice. You were sleeping with him."

"The things I have dreamed this night and the night before," she said, "may they come true and lay you low, body and soul! An evil spirit has taken root in you and dazzles your sight." She screamed out, "You hateful creature! You moon calf! You spook! You uncouth man! Get out, or I'll scream all Frampol out of bed!"

Before I could move, her brother sprang out from behind the oven and struck me a blow on the back of the head. I thought he had broken my neck. I felt that something about me was deeply wrong, and I said, "Don't make a scandal. All that's needed now is that

people should accuse me of raising spooks and *dybbuks*."
For that was what she had meant. "No one will touch
bread of my baking."

In short, I somehow calmed her.

"Well," she said, "that's enough. Lie down, and be
shattered by wheels."

Next morning I called the apprentice aside. "Listen
here, brother!" I said. And so on and so forth. "What
do you say?" He stared at me as though I had dropped
from the roof or something.

"I swear," he said, "you'd better go to an herb doctor
or some healer. I'm afraid you have a screw loose, but
I'll hush it up for you." And that's how the thing stood.

To make a long story short, I lived twenty years
with my wife. She bore me six children, four daughters
and two sons. All kinds of things happened, but I
neither saw nor heard. I believed, and that's all. The
rabbi recently said to me, "Belief in itself is beneficial. It is written that a good man lives by his faith."

Suddenly my wife took sick. It began with a trifle, a
little growth upon the breast. But she evidently was not
destined to live long; she had no years. I spent a fortune
on her. I have forgotten to say that by this time I had
a bakery of my own and in Frampol was considered to
be something of a rich man. Daily the healer came, and
every witch doctor in the neighborhood was brought.
They decided to use leeches, and after that to try
cupping. They even called a doctor from Lublin,
but it was too late. Before she died she called me to her
bed and said, "Forgive me, Gimpel."

I said, "What is there to forgive? You have been a
good and faithful wife."

"Woe, Gimpel!" she said. "It was ugly how I deceived you all these years. I want to go clean to my Maker, and so I have to tell you that the children are not yours."

If I had been clouted on the head with a piece of wood it couldn't have bewildered me more.

"Whose are they?" I asked.

"I don't know," she said. "There were a lot . . . but they're not yours." And as she spoke she tossed her head to the side, her eyes turned glassy, and it was all up with Elka. On her whitened lips there remained a smile.

I imagined that, dead as she was, she was saying, "I deceived Gimpel. That was the meaning of my brief life."

4

One night, when the period of mourning was done, as I lay dreaming on the flour sacks, there came the Spirit of Evil himself and said to me, "Gimpel, why do you sleep?"

I said, "What should I be doing? Eating *kreplach?*"

"The whole world deceives you," he said, "and you ought to deceive the world in your turn."

"How can I deceive all the world?" I asked him.

He answered, "You might accumulate a bucket of urine every day and at night pour it into the dough. Let the sages of Frampol eat filth."

"What about the judgment in the world to come?" I said.

"There is no world to come," he said. "They've sold you a bill of goods and talked you into believing you carried a cat in your belly. What nonsense!"

"Well then," I said, "and is there a God?"

He answered, "There is no God either."

"What," I said, "*is* there, then?"

"A thick mire."

He stood before my eyes with a goatish beard and horn, long-toothed, and with a tail. Hearing such words, I wanted to snatch him by the tail, but I tumbled from the flour sacks and nearly broke a rib. Then it happened that I had to answer the call of nature, and, passing, I saw the risen dough, which seemed to say to me, "Do it!" In brief, I let myself be persuaded.

At dawn the apprentice came. We kneaded the bread, scattered caraway seeds on it, and set it to bake. Then the apprentice went away, and I was left sitting in the little trench by the oven, on a pile of rags. Well, Gimpel, I thought, you've revenged yourself on them for all the shame they've put on you. Outside the frost glittered, but it was warm beside the oven. The flames heated my face. I bent my head and fell into a doze.

I saw in a dream, at once, Elka in her shroud. She called to me, "What have you done, Gimpel?"

I said to her, "It's all your fault," and started to cry.

"You fool!" she said. "You fool! Because I was false is everything false too? I never deceived anyone but myself. I'm paying for it all, Gimpel. They spare you nothing here."

I looked at her face. It was black; I was startled and waked, and remained sitting dumb. I sensed that everything hung in the balance. A false step now and I'd lose Eternal Life. But God gave me His help. I seized the long shovel and took out the loaves, carried them into the yard, and started to dig a hole in the frozen earth.

My apprentice came back as I was doing it. "What are you doing boss?" he said, and grew pale as a corpse.

"I know what I'm doing," I said, and I buried it all before his very eyes.

Then I went home, took my hoard from its hiding place, and divided it among the children. "I saw your mother tonight," I said. "She's turning black, poor thing."

They were so astounded they couldn't speak a word.

"Be well," I said, "and forget that such a one as Gimpel ever existed." I put on my short coat, a pair of boots, took the bag that held my prayer shawl in one hand, my stock in the other, and kissed the *mezzuzah*. When people saw me in the street they were greatly surprised.

"Where are you going?" they said.

I answered, "Into the world." And so I departed from Frampol.

I wandered over the land, and good people did not neglect me. After many years I became old and white; I heard a great deal, many lies and falsehoods, but the longer I lived the more I understood that there were really no lies. Whatever doesn't really happen is dreamed at night. It happens to one if it doesn't happen to another, tomorrow if not today, or a century hence if not next year. What difference can it make? Often I heard tales of which I said, "Now this is a thing that cannot happen." But before a year had elapsed I heard that it actually had come to pass somewhere.

Going from place to place, eating at strange tables, it often happens that I spin yarns—improbable things that could never have happened—about devils, magicians, windmills, and the like. The children run after me, calling, "Grandfather, tell us a story." Sometimes they ask for particular stories, and I try to please them. A fat young boy once said to me, "Grandfather, it's the same story you told us before." The little rogue, he was right.

So it is with dreams too. It is many years since I left Frampol, but as soon as I shut my eyes I am there again. And whom do you think I see? Elka. She is standing by the washtub, as at our first encounter, but her face is shining and her eyes are as radiant as the eyes of a saint, and she speaks outlandish words to me, strange things. When I wake I have forgotten it all. But while the dream lasts I am comforted. She answers all my queries, and what comes out is that all is right. I weep and implore, "Let me be with you." And she consoles me and tells me to be patient. The time is nearer than it is far. Sometimes she strokes and kisses me and weeps upon my face. When I awaken I feel her lips and taste the salt of her tears.

No doubt the world is entirely an imaginary world, but it is only once removed from the true world. At the door of the hovel where I lie, there stands the plank on which the dead are taken away. The gravedigger Jew has his spade ready. The grave waits and the worms are hungry; the shrouds are prepared—I carry them in my beggar's sack. Another *shnorrer* is waiting to inherit my bed of straw. When the time comes I will go joyfully. Whatever may be there, it will be real, without complication, without ridicule, without deception. God be praised: there even Gimpel cannot be deceived.

Translated by Saul Bellow

The
Mirror

I

There is a kind of net that is as old as Methuselah, as
soft as a cobweb and as full of holes, yet it has retained
its strength to this day. When a demon wearies of chasing after yesterdays or of going round in circles on a
windmill, he can install himself inside a mirror. There
he waits like a spider in its web, and the fly is certain to
be caught. God has bestowed vanity on the female, particularly on the rich, the pretty, the barren, the young,
who have much time and little company.

I discovered such a woman in the village of Krashnik.
Her father dealt in timber; her husband floated the logs
to Danzig; grass was growing on her mother's grave.
The daughter lived in an old house, among oaken cup-
boards, leather-lined coffers, and books bound in silk.

She had two servants, an old one that was deaf and a young one who carried on with a fiddler. The other Krashnik housewives wore men's boots, ground buckwheat on millstones, plucked feathers, cooked broths, bore children, and attended funerals. Needless to say, Zirel, beautiful and well-educated—she had been brought up in Cracow—had nothing to talk about with her small-town neighbors. And so she preferred to read her German song book and embroider Moses and Ziporah, David and Bathsheba, Ahasuereus and Queen Esther on canvas. The pretty dresses her husband brought her hung in the closet. Her pearls and diamonds lay in her jewel box. No one ever saw her silk slips, her lace petticoats, nor her red hair which was hidden under her wig, not even her husband. For when could they be seen? Certainly not during the day, and at night it is dark.

But Zirel had an attic which she called her boudoir, and where hung a mirror as blue as water on the point of freezing. The mirror had a crack in the middle, and it was set in a golden frame which was decorated with snakes, knobs, roses, and adders. In front of the mirror lay a bearskin and close beside it was a chair with armrests of ivory and a cushioned seat. What could be more pleasant than to sit naked in this chair, and rest one's feet on the bearskin, and contemplate oneself? Zirel had much to gaze at. Her skin was white as satin, her breasts as full as wineskins, her hair fell across her shoulders, and her legs were as slender as a hind's. She would sit for hours on end delighting in her beauty. The door fastened and bolted, she would imagine that it opened to admit either a prince or a hunter or a knight or a poet. For everything hidden must be revealed, each secret longs to be disclosed, each love yearns to be betrayed, everything sacred must be desecrated. Heaven and earth conspire that all good beginnings should come to a bad end.

Well, once I learned of the existence of this luscious little tidbit, I determined that she would be mine. All that was required was a little patience. One summer day, as she sat staring at the nipple on her left breast, she caught sight of me in the mirror—there I was, black as tar, long as a shovel, with donkey's ears, a ram's horns, a frog's mouth, and a goat's beard. My eyes were all pupil. She was so surprised that she forgot to be frightened. Instead of crying, "Hear, O Israel," she burst out laughing.

"My, how ugly you are," she said.

"My, how beautiful you are," I replied.

She was pleased with my compliment. "Who are you?" she asked.

"Fear not," I said. "I am an imp, not a demon. My fingers have no nails, my mouth has no teeth, my arms stretch like licorice, my horns are as pliable as wax. My power lies in my tongue; I am a fool by trade, and I have come to cheer you up because you are alone."

"Where were you before?"

"In the bedroom behind the stove where the cricket chirps and the mouse rustles, between a dried wreath and a faded willow branch."

"What did you do there?"

"I looked at you."

"Since when?"

"Since your wedding night."

"What did you eat?"

"The fragrance of your body, the glow of your hair, the light of your eyes, the sadness of your face."

"Oh, you flatterer!" she cried. "Who are you? What

are you doing here? Where do you come from? What is your errand?"

I made up a story. My father, I said, was a goldsmith and my mother a succubus; they copulated on a bundle of rotting rope in a cellar and I was their bastard. For some time I lived in a settlement of devils on Mount Seir where I inhabited a mole's hole. But when it was learned that my father was human I was driven out. From then on I had been homeless. She-devils avoided me because I reminded them of the sons of Adam; the daughters of Eve saw in me Satan. Dogs barked at me, children wept when they saw me. Why were they afraid? I harmed no one. My only desire was to gaze at beautiful women—to gaze and converse with them.

"Why converse? The beautiful aren't always wise."

"In Paradise the wise are the footstools of the beautiful."

"My teacher taught me otherwise."

"What did your teacher know? The writers of books have the brains of a flea; they merely parrot each other. Ask me when you want to know something. Wisdom extends no further than the first heaven. From there on everything is lust. Don't you know that angels are headless? The Seraphim play in the sand like children; the Cherubim can't count; the Aralim chew their cud before the throne of Glory. God himself is jovial. He spends his time pulling Leviathan by the tail and being licked by the Wild Ox; or else he tickles the Shekhinah, causing her to lay myriads of eggs each day, and each egg is a star."

"Now I know you're making fun of me."

"If that's not the truth may a funny bone grow on my nose. It's a long time since I squandered my quota of lies. I have no alternative but to tell the truth."

"Can you beget children?"

"No, my dear. Like the mule I am the last of a line. But this does not blunt my desire. I lie only with married women, for good actions are my sins; my prayers are blasphemies; spite is my bread; arrogance, my wine; pride, the marrow of my bones. There is only one other thing I can do besides chatter."

This made her laugh. Then she said: "My mother didn't bring me up to be a devil's whore. Away with you, or I'll have you exorcised."

"Why bother," I said. "I'll go. I don't force myself on anyone. *Auf wiedersehen.*"

I faded away like mist.

2

For seven days Zirel absented herself from her boudoir. I dozed inside the mirror. The net had been spread; the victim was ready. I knew she was curious. Yawning, I considered my next step. Should I seduce a rabbi's daughter? deprive a bridegroom of his manhood? plug up the synagogue chimney? turn the Sabbath wine into vinegar? give an elflock to a virgin? enter a ram's horn on Rosh Hashana? make a cantor hoarse? An imp never lacks for things to do, particularly during the Days of Awe when even the fish in the water tremble. And then as I sat dreaming of moon juice and turkey seeds, she entered. She looked for me, but could not see me. She stood in front of the mirror but I didn't show myself.

"I must have been imagining," she murmured. "It must have been a daydream."

She took off her nightgown and stood there naked. I knew that her husband was in town and that he had been with her the night before although she had not gone to the ritual bath—but as the Talmud puts it, "a woman would rather have one measure of debauchery than ten of modesty." Zirel, daughter of Roize Glike, missed me, and her eyes were sad. She is mine, mine, I thought. The Angel of Death stood ready with his rod; a zealous little devil busied himself preparing the cauldron for her in hell; a sinner, promoted to stoker, collected the kindling wood. Everything was prepared—the snow drift and the live coals, the hook for her tongue and the pliers for her breasts, the mouse that would eat her liver and the worm that would gnaw her bladder. But my little charmer suspected nothing. She stroked her left breast, and then her right. She looked at her belly, examined her thighs, scrutinized her toes. Would she read her book? trim her nails? comb her hair? Her husband had brought her perfumes from Lenczyc, and she smelled of rosewater and carnations. He had presented her with a coral necklace which hung around her neck. But what is Eve without a serpent? And what is God without Lucifer? Zirel was full of desire. Like a harlot she summoned me with her eyes. With quivering lips she uttered a spell:

> Swift is the wind,
> Deep the ditch,
> Sleek black cat,
> Come within reach.
> Strong is the lion,
> Dumb the fish,
> Reach from the silence,
> And take your dish.

As she uttered the last word, I appeared. Her face lit up.

"So you're here."

"I was away," I said, "but I have returned."

"Where have you been?"

"To never-never land. I was at Rahab the Harlot's palace in the garden of the golden birds near the castle of Asmodeus."

"As far as that?"

"If you don't believe me, my jewel, come with me. Sit on my back, and hold on to my horns, and I'll spread my wings, and we'll fly together beyond the mountain peaks."

"But I don't have a thing on."

"No one dresses there."

"My husband won't have any idea where I am."

"He'll learn soon enough."

"How long a trip is it?"

"It takes less than a second."

"When will I return?"

"Those who go there don't want to return."

"What will I do there?"

"You'll sit on Asmodeus' lap and plait tresses in his beard. You'll eat almonds and drink porter; evenings you'll dance for him. Bells will be attached to your ankles, and devils will whirl with you."

"And after that?"

"If my master is pleased with you, you will be his. If not, one of his minions will take care of you."

"And in the morning?"

"There are no mornings there."

"Will you stay with me?"

"Because of you I might be given a small bone to lick."

"Poor little devil, I feel sorry for you, but I can't go. I have a husband and a father. I have gold and silver and dresses and furs. My heels are the highest in Krash-nik."

"Well, then, good-by."

"Don't hurry off like that. What do I have to do?"

"Now you are being reasonable. Make some dough with the whitest of flour. Add honey, menstrual blood, and an egg with a bloodspot, a measure of pork fat, a thimbleful of suet, a goblet of libatory wine. Light a fire on the Sabbath and bake the mixture on the coals. Now call your husband to your bed and make him eat the cake you have baked. Awaken him with lies and put him to sleep with profanity. Then when he begins to snore, cut off one half of his beard and one earlock, steal his gold, burn his promissory notes, and tear up the marriage contract. After that throw your jewels under the pig butcher's window—this will be my engagement gift. Before leaving your house, throw the prayer book into the rubbish and spit on the *mezuzah*, at the precise spot where the word *Shadai* is written. Then come straight to me. I'll bear you on my wings from Krashnik to the desert. We'll fly over fields filled with toadstools, over woods inhabited by werewolves, over the ruins of Sodom where serpents are scholars, hyenas are sing-ers, crows are preachers, and thieves are entrusted with the money for charity. There ugliness is beauty, and crooked is straight; tortures are amusement, and mock-ery, the height of exaltation. But hurry, for our eternity is brief."

"I'm afraid, little devil, I'm afraid."

"Everyone who goes with us is."

She wished to ask questions, to catch me in contradic-tions, but I made off. She pressed her lips against the mirror and met the end of my tail.

3

Her father wept; her husband tore his hair; her servants searched for her in the woodshed and in the cellar; her mother-in-law poked with a shovel in the chimney; carters and butchers hunted for her in the woods. At night, torches were lit and the voices of the searchers echoed and re-echoed: "Zirel, where are you? Zirel! Zirel!" It was suspected that she had run off to a convent, but the priest swore on the crucifix that this was not so. A wonder worker was sent for, and then a sorceress, an old Gentile woman who made wax effigies, and finally a man who located the dead or missing by means of a black mirror; a farmer lent them his blood hounds. But when I get my prey, it is reprieved by no one. I spread my wings and we were off. Zirel spoke to me, but I did not answer. When we came to Sodom, I hovered a moment over Lot's wife. Three oxen were busy licking her nose. Lot lay in a cave with his daughters, drunk as always.

In the vale of shadow which is known as the world everything is subject to change. But for us time stands still! Adam remains naked, Eve lustful, still in the act of being seduced by the serpent. Cain kills Abel, the flea lies with the elephant, the flood falls from heaven, the Jews knead clay in Egypt, Job scratches at his sore-covered body. He will keep scratching until the end of time, but he will find no comfort.

She wished to speak to me, but with a flutter of wings I disappeared. I had done my errand. I lay like a bat blinking sightless eyes on a steep cliff. The earth brown, the heavens yellow. Devils stood in a circle wiggling their tails. Two turtles were locked in an embrace, and a male stone mounted a female stone. Shabriri and Bariri appeared. Shabriri had assumed the shape of a squire. He wore a pointed cap, a curved sword; he had the legs of a goose and a goat's beard. On his snout were glasses, and he spoke in a German dialect. Bariri was ape, parrot, rat, bat, all at once. Shabriri bowed low and began to chant like a jester at a wedding:

Argin, margin,
Here's a bargain.
A pretty squirrel,
Name of Zirel.
Open the door,
To love impure.

He was about to take her in his arms when Bariri screamed, "Don't let him touch you. He has scabs on his head, sores on his legs, and what a woman needs he doesn't have. He acts the great lover, but a capon is more amorous. His father was like that also, and so was his grandfather. Let me be your lover. I am the grandson of the Chief Liar. In addition I am a man of wealth and good family. My grandmother was lady-in-waiting to Machlath, daughter of Naama. My mother had the honor to wash Asmodeus' feet. My father, may he stay in hell forever, carried Satan's snuffbox."

Shabriri and Bariri had grasped Zirel by the hair, and each time they pulled they tore out a tuft. Now Zirel saw how things were and she cried out, "Pity, pity!"

"What's this we have here?" asked Ketev Mariri.

"A Krashnik coquette."

"Don't they have better than that?"

"No, it's the best they've got."

"Who dragged her in?"

"A little imp."

"Let's begin."

"Help, help," Zirel moaned.

"Hang her," Wrath, the Son of Anger, screamed. "It won't help to cry out here. Time and change have been left behind. Do what you are told; you're neither young nor old."

Zirel broke into lamentations. The sound roused Lilith from her sleep. She thrust aside Asmodeus' beard and put her head out of the cave, each of her hairs, a curling snake.

"What's wrong with the bitch?" she asked. "Why all the screaming?"

"They're working on her."

"Is that all? Add some salt."

"And skim the fat."

This fun has been going on for a thousand years, but the black gang does not weary of it. Each devil does his bit; each imp makes his pun. They pull and tear and bite and pinch. For all that, the masculine devils aren't so bad; it's the females who really enjoy themselves, commanding: Skim boiling broth with bare hands! Plait braids without using the fingers! Wash the laundry without water! Catch fish in hot sand! Stay at home and walk the streets! Take a bath without getting wet! Make butter from stones! Break the cask without spilling the wine! And all the while the virtuous women in Paradise gossip; and the pious men sit on golden chairs, stuffing themselves with the meat of Leviathan, as they boast of their good deeds.

Is there a God? Is He all merciful? Will Zirel ever find salvation? Or is creation a snake primeval crawling with evil? How can I tell? I'm still only a minor devil. Imps seldom get promoted. Meanwhile generations come and go, Zirel follows Zirel, in a myriad of reflections—a myriad of mirrors.

Translated by Norbert Guterman

The
Unseen

I
Nathan and Temerl

They say that I, the evil spirit, after descending to earth in order to induce people to sin, will then ascend to heaven to accuse them. As a matter of fact, I am also the one to give the sinner the first push, but I do this so cleverly that the sin appears to be an act of virtue; thus, other infidels, unable to learn from the example, continue to sink into the abyss.

But let me tell you a story. There once lived a man in the town of Frampol who was known for his wealth and lavish ways. Named Nathan Jozefover, for he was born in Little Jozefov, he had married a Frampol girl and settled there. Reb Nathan, at the time of this story, was sixty, perhaps a bit more. Short and broad-boned, he had, like most rich people, a large paunch. Cheeks red as wine showed between the clumps of short black beard. Over small twinkling eyes his eyebrows were thick and shaggy. All his life, he had eaten, drunk, and made merry. For breakfast, his wife served him cold chicken and raisin bread, which, like a great landowner, he washed down with a glass of mead. He had a preference for dainties such as roast squab, necks stuffed with chopped milt, pancakes with liver, egg noodles with broth, etc. The townspeople whispered that his wife, Roise-Temerl, prepared a noodle-pudding for him every day, and if he so desired made a Sabbath dinner in the middle of the week. Actually, she too liked to indulge.

Having plenty of money and no children, husband and wife apparently believed that good cheer was in order. Both of them, therefore, became fat and lazy. After their lunch, they would close the bedroom shutters and snore in their featherbeds as though it were midnight. During the winter nights, long as Jewish exile, they would get out of bed to treat themselves to gizzard, chicken livers, and jam, washed down with beet soup or apple juice. Then, back to their canopied beds they went to resume their dreams of the next day's porridge.

Reb Nathan gave little time to his grain business, which ran itself. A large granary with two oaken doors stood behind the house he had inherited from his father-in-law. In the yard there were also a number of barns, sheds, and other buildings. Many of the old peasants in the surrounding villages would sell their grain and flax to Nathan alone, for, even though others might offer them more, they trusted Nathan's honesty. He never sent anyone away empty-handed, and sometimes even advanced money for the following year's crop. The simple peasants, in gratitude, brought him wood from the forest, while their wives picked mushrooms and berries for him. An elderly servant, widowed in her youth, looked after the house and even assisted in the business. For the entire week, with the exception of market day, Nathan did not have to lift a finger.

He enjoyed wearing fine clothes and telling yarns. In the summer, he would nap on a bed among the trees of his orchard, or read either the Bible in Yiddish, or simply a story book. He liked, on the Sabbath, to listen to the preaching of a *magid*, and occasionally to invite a poor man to his house. He had many amusements: for example, he loved to have his wife, Roise Temerl, tickle his feet, and she did this whenever he wished. It was rumored that, he and his wife would bathe together in his own bathhouse, which stood in his yard. In a silk dressing gown embroidered with flowers and leaves, and wearing pompommed slippers, he would step out on his porch in the afternoon, smoking a pipe with an amber bowl. Those who passed by greeted him, and he responded in a friendly fashion. Sometimes he would stop a passing girl, ask her this and that, and then send her off with a joke. After the reading of the *Perek* on Saturday, he would sit with the women on the bench, eating nuts or pumpkin seeds, listening to gossip, and telling of his own encounters with landowners, priests, and rabbis. He had traveled widely in his youth, visiting Cracow, Brody, and Danzig.

Roise Temerl was almost the image of her husband. As the saying goes: when a husband and wife sleep on one pillow finally they have the same head. Small and plump, she had cheeks still full and red despite her age, and a tiny talkative mouth. The smattering of Hebrew, with which she just found her way through the prayer books, gave her the right to a leading role in the women's section of the Prayer House. She often led a bride to the synagogue, was sponsor at a circumcision, and occasionally collected money for a poor girl's trousseau. Although a wealthy woman, she could apply cups to the sick, and would adroitly cut out the pip of a chicken. Her skills included embroidery and knitting. She possessed numerous jewels, dresses, coats, and furs, all of which she kept in oaken chests as protection against moths and thieves.

Because of her gracious manner, she was welcomed at the butcher's, at the ritual bath, and wherever else she went. Her only regret was that she had no children. To make up for this, she gave charitable contributions and engaged a pious scholar to pray in her memory after her death. She took pleasure in a nest-egg she had managed to save over the years, kept it hidden somewhere in a bag, and now and then enjoyed counting the gold pieces. However, since Nathan gave her everything she needed, she had no idea of how to spend the money. Although he knew of her hoard, he pretended ignorance, realizing that "stolen water is sweet to drink," and did not begrudge her this harmless diversion.

2

Shifra Zirel the Servant

One day their old servant became ill and soon died. Nathan and his wife were deeply grieved, not only because they had grown so accustomed to her that she was almost a blood relative, but she had also been honest, industrious, and loyal, and it would not be easy to replace her. Nathan and Roise Temerl wept over her grave, and Nathan said the first *kaddish*. He promised that after the thirty day mourning period, he would drive to Janow to order the tombstone she deserved. Nathan, actually did not come out a loser through her death. Having rarely spent any of her earnings, and being without a family, she had left everything to her employers.

Immediately after the funeral, Roise Temerl began to look for a new servant, but could not find any that compared to the first. The Frampol girls were not only lazy, but they could not bake and fry to Roise Temerl's satisfaction. Various widows, divorced women, and deserted wives were offered her, but none had the qualifications that Roise Temerl desired. Of every candidate presented at her house, she would make inquiries on how to prepare fish, marinate borscht, bake pastry, struddle, egg cookies, etc.; what to do when milk and borscht sour, when a chicken is too tough, a broth too fat, a Sabbath pudding overdone, a porridge too thick or too thin, and other tricky questions. The bewildered girl would lose her tongue and leave in embarrassment. Several weeks went by like this, and the pampered Roise Temerl, who had to do all the chores, could clearly see that it was easier to eat a meal than prepare one.

Well, I, the Seducer, could not stand by and watch Nathan and his wife starve; I sent them a servant, a wonder of wonders.

A native of Zamosc, she had even worked for wealthy families in Lublin. Although at first she had refused— even if she were paid her weight in gold—to go to an insignificant spot like Frampol, various people had intervened, Roise Temerl had agreed to pay a few gulden more than she had paid previously, and the girl, Shifra Zirel, decided to take the job.

In the carriage that had to be sent to Zamosc for her and her extensive luggage, she arrived with suitcases, baskets, and knapsacks, like a rich bride. Well along in her twenties, she seemed no more than eighteen or nineteen. Her hair was plaited in two braids coiled at the sides of her head; she wore a checkered shawl with tassels, a cretonne dress, and narrow heeled shoes. Her chin had a wolf-like sharpness, her lips were thin, her eyes shrewd and impudent. She wore rings in her ears and around her throat a coral necklace. Immediately, she found fault with the Frampol mud, the clay taste of the well water, and the lumpy home-made bread. Served over-cooked soup by Roise Temerl on the first day, she took a drop of it with her spoon, made a face, and complained, "It's sour and rancid!"

She demanded a Jewish or Gentile girl as an assistant, and Roise Temerl, after a strenuous search, found a Gentile one, the sturdy daughter of the bath attendant. Shifra Zirel began to give orders. She told the girl to scrub the floors, clean the stove, sweep the cobwebs in corners, and advised Roise Temerl to get rid of the superfluous pieces of furniture, various rickety chairs, stools, tables, and chests. The windows were cleaned, the dusty curtains removed, and the rooms became lighter and more spacious. Roise Temerl and Nathan were amazed by her first meal. Even the emperor could ask for no better cook. An appetizer of calves' liver and lungs, partly fried and partly boiled, was served before the broth, and its aroma titillated their nostrils. The soup was seasoned with herbs unobtainable at Frampol, such as paprika and capers, which the new servant had apparently brought from Zamosc. Dessert was a mixture of applesauce, raisins, and apricots, flavored with cinnamon, saffron, and cloves, whose fragrance filled the house. Then, as in the wealthy homes of Lublin, she served black coffee with chicory. After lunch, Nathan and his wife wanted to nap as usual, but Shifra Zirel warned them that it was unhealthful to sleep immediately after eating, because the vapors mount from the stomach to the brain. She advised her employers to walk back and forth in the garden a few times. Nathan was brimful of good food, and the coffee had gone to his head. He reeled and kept repeating, "Well, my dear wife, isn't she a treasure of a servant?"

"I hope no one will take her away," Roise Temerl said. Knowing how envious people were, she feared the Evil Eye, or those who might offer the girl better terms.

There is no sense going into detail about the excellent dishes Shifra Zirel prepared, the babkas and macaroons she baked, the appetizers she introduced. The neighbors found Nathan's rooms and his yard unrecognizable. Shifra Zirel had whitewashed the walls, cleaned the sheds and closets, and hired a laborer to weed the garden and repair the fence and railing of the porch. Like the mistress of the house rather than its servant, she supervised everything. When Shifra Zirel, in a woolen dress and pointed shoes, went for a stroll on Saturdays, after the pre-cooked *cholent* dinner, she was stared at not only by common laborers and poor girls, but by young men and women of good families as well. Daintily holding up her skirt, she walked, her head high. Her assistant, the bathhouse attendant's daughter, followed, carrying a bag of fruit and cookies, for Jews could not carry parcels on the Sabbath. From the benches in front of their houses women observed her and shook their heads. "She's as proud as a landowner's wife!" they would comment, predicting that her stay in Frampol would be brief.

3
Temptation

One Tuesday, when Roise Temerl was in Janow visiting her sister, who was ill, Nathan ordered the Gentile girl to prepare a steam bath for him. His limbs and bones had been aching since morning, and he knew that the only remedy for this was to perspire abundantly. After putting a great deal of wood in the stove around the bricks, the girl lighted the fire, filled the vat with water, and returned to the kitchen.

When the fire had burnt itself out, Nathan undressed and then poured a bucket of water on the red hot bricks. The bathhouse filled with steam. Nathan, climbing the stairs to the high shelf where the steam was hot and dense, whipped himself with a twig broom that he had prepared previously. Usually Roise Temerl helped him with this. When he perspired she poured the buckets of water, and when she perspired he poured. After they had flogged each other with twig brooms, Roise Temerl would bathe him in a wooden tub and comb him. But this time Roise Temerl had had to go to Janow to her sick sister, and Nathan did not think it wise to wait for her return, since his sister-in-law was very old and might die and then Roise Temerl would have to stay there seven days. Never before had he taken his bath alone. The steam, as usual, soon settled. Nathan wanted to go down and pour more water on the bricks, but his legs felt heavy and he was lazy. With his belly protruding upward, he lay on his back, flogging himself with the broom, rubbing his knees and ankles, and staring at the bent beam on the smoke-blackened ceiling. Through the crack, a patch of clear sky stared in. This was the month of Elul, and Nathan was assailed by melancholy. He remembered his sister-in-law as a young woman full of life, and now she was on her deathbed. He too would not eat marchpanes nor sleep on eiderdown forever, it occurred to him, for some day he would be placed in a dark grave, his eyes covered with shards, and worms would consume the body that Roise Temerl had pampered for the nearly fifty years that she had been his wife.

Probing his soul, Nathan lay there, belly upward, when he suddenly heard the chain clank, the door creak. Looking about, he saw to his amazement, that Shifra Zirel had entered. Barefoot, with a white kerchief around her head, she was dressed only in a slip. In a choking voice, he cried out, "No!" and hastened to cover himself. Upset, and shaking his head, he beckoned her to leave, but Shifra Zirel said, "Don't be afraid, master, I won't bite you."

She poured a bucket of water over the hot bricks. A hissing noise filled the room, and white clouds of steam quickly rose, scalding Nathan's limbs. Then Shifra Zirel climbed the steps to Nathan, grabbed the twig broom, and began to flog him. He was so stunned, he became speechless. Choking, he almost rolled off the slippery shelf. Shifra Zirel, meanwhile, continued diligently to whip him and to rub him with a cake of soap she had brought. Finally, having regained his composure, he said, hoarsely, "What's the matter with you? Shame on you!"

"What's there to be ashamed about?" the servant asked airily, "I won't harm the master . . ."

For a long time she occupied herself combing and massaging him, rubbing him with soap, and drenching him with water, and Nathan was compelled to acknowledge that this devilish woman was more accomplished than Roise Temerl. Her hands, too, were smoother; they tickled his body and aroused his desire. He soon forgot that this was the month of Elul, before the Days of Awe, and told the servant to lock the wooden latch of the door. Then, in a wavering voice, he made a proposition.

"Never, uncle!" she said resolutely, pouring a bucket of water on him.

"Why not?" he asked, his neck, belly, head, all his limbs dripping.

"Because I belong to my husband."

"What husband?"

"The one I'll have some day, God willing."

"Come on, Shifra Zirel," he said, "I'll give you something—a coral necklace, or a brooch."

"You're wasting your breath," she said.

"A kiss at least!" he begged.

"A kiss will cost twenty-five coins," Shifra Zirel said.

"Groszy or threepence pieces?" Nathan asked, efficiently, and Shifra Zirel answered, "Gulden."

Nathan reflected. Twenty-five gulden was no trifle. But I, the Old Nick, reminded him that one does not live forever, and that there was no harm in leaving a few gulden less behind. Therefore, he agreed.

Bending over him, placing her arms about his neck, Shifra Zirel kissed him on the mouth. Half kiss and half bite, it cut his breath. Lust arose in him. He could not climb down, for his arms and legs were trembling, and Shifra Zirel had to help him down and even put on his dressing gown. "So that's the kind you are . . ." he murmured.

"Don't insult me, Reb Nathan," she admonished, "I'm pure."

"Pure as a pig's knuckle," Nathan thought. He opened the door for her. After a moment, glancing anxiously about to make sure he was not seen, he left also. "Imagine such a thing happening!" he murmured. "What impudence! A real whore!" He resolved never again to have anything to do with her.

4
Troubled Nights

Nathan lay at night on his eiderdown mattress, wrapped in a silken blanket, his head propped up by three pillows, but he was robbed of sleep by my wife Lilith and her companions. He had droused off, but was awake; he began to dream something, but the vision frightened him, and he rose with a start. Someone invisible whispered something into his ear. He fancied, for a moment, that he was thirsty. Then his head felt feverish. Leaving his bed, he slipped into his slippers and dressing gown, and went to the kitchen to scoop up a mug of water. Leaning over the barrel, he slipped and almost fell in. Suddenly he realized that he craved Shifra Zirel with the craving of a young man. "What's the matter with me?" he murmured, "This can only be a trick of the devil." He started to walk to his own room, but found himself going to the little room where the servant slept. Halting at the doorway, he listened. A rustling came from behind the stove, and in the dry wood something creaked.

The pale glow of a lantern flashed outside; there was a sigh. Nathan recalled that this was Elul, that God-fearing Jews rise at dawn for the *Selichot* prayers. Just as he was about to turn back, the servant opened the door and asked in an alert tone, "Who's there?"

"I am," Nathan whispered.

"What does the master wish?"

"Don't you know?"

She groaned and was silent, as though wondering what to do. Then she said, "Go back to bed, master. It's no use talking."

"But I can't sleep," Nathan complained in a tone he sometimes used with Roise Temerl, "Don't send me away!"

"Leave, master," Shifra Zirel said in an angry voice, "or I'll scream!"

"Hush. I won't force you, God forbid. I'm fond of you. I love you."

"If the master loves me then let him marry me."

"How can I? I have a wife!" Nathan said, surprised.

"Well, what of it? What do you think divorce is for?" she said and sat up.

"She's not a woman," Nathan thought, "but a demon." Frightened by her and her talk he remained in the doorway, heavy, bewildered, leaning against the jamb. The Good Spirit, who is at the height of his power during the month of Elul, reminded him of *The Measure of Righteousness*—which he had read in Yiddish—stories of pious men, tempted by landowners' wives, she-demons, whores, but who had refused to succumb to the temptation. "I'll send her away at once, tomorrow, even if I must pay her wages for a year," Nathan decided. But he said, "What's wrong with you? I've lived with my wife for almost fifty years! Why should I divorce her now?"

"Fifty years is sufficient," the brazen servant answered.

Her insolence, rather than repelling him, attracted him the more. Walking to her bed, he sat on the edge. A vile warmth arose from her. Seized by a powerful desire, he said, "How can I divorce her? She won't consent."

"You can get one without her consent," said the servant, apparently well-informed.

Blandishments and promises would not change her mind. To all Nathan's arguments, she turned a deaf ear. Day was already breaking when he returned to his bed. His bedroom walls were gray as canvas. Like a coal glowing on a heap of ashes, the sun arose in the east, casting a light, scarlet as the fire of hell. A crow, alighting on the windowsill, began to caw with its curved black beak, as though trying to announce a piece of bad news. A shudder went through Nathan's bones. He felt that he was his own master no longer, that the Evil Spirit, having seized the reins, drove him along an iniquitous path, perilous and full of obstacles.

From then on Nathan did not have a moment's respite.

While his wife, Roise Temerl, observed the mourning period for her sister in Janow, he was roused each night, and driven to Shifra Zirel, who, each time, rejected him.

Begging and imploring, he promised valuable gifts, offered a rich dowry and inclusion in his will, but nothing availed him. He vowed not to return to her, but his vow was broken each time. He spoke foolishly, in a manner unbecoming to a respectable man, and disgraced himself. When he woke her, she not only chased him away, but scolded him. In passing from his room to hers

in the darkness, he would stumble against doors, cup-
boards, stoves, and he was covered with bruises. He ran
into a slop basin and spilled it. He shattered glassware.
He tried to recite a chapter of the Psalms that he knew
by heart and implored God to rescue him from the net
I had spread, but the holy words were distorted on
his lips and his mind was confused with impure
thoughts. In his bedroom there was a constant buzz and
hum from the glowworms, flies, moths, and mosquitoes
with which I, the Evil One, had filled it. With eyes
open and ears intent, Nathan lay wide awake, listening
to each rustle. Roosters crowed, frogs croaked in the
swamps, crickets chirped, flashes of lightning glowed
strangely. A little imp kept reminding him: Don't be
a fool, Reb Nathan, she's waiting for you; she wants
to see if you're a man or a mouse. And the imp
hummed: Elul or no Elul, a woman's a woman, and if
you don't enjoy her in this world it's too late in the
next. Nathan would call Shifra Zirel and wait for her to
answer. It seemed to him that he heard the patter of
bare feet, that he saw the whiteness of her body or of
her slip in the darkness. Finally, trembling, afire, he
would rise from his bed to go to her room. But she remained stubborn. "Either I or the mistress," she would
declare. "Go, master!"

And grabbing a broom from the pile of refuse, she
would smack him across the back. Then Reb Nathan
Jozefover, the richest man in Frampol, respected by
young and old, would return defeated and whipped to
his canopied bed, to toss feverishly until sunrise.

5
Forest Road

Roise Temerl, when she returned from Janow and saw her husband, was badly frightened. His face was ashen; there were bags under his eyes; his beard, which until recently had been black, was now threaded with white; his stomach had become loose, and hung like a sack. Like one dangerously ill, he could barely drag his feet along. "Woe is me, even finer things than this are put in the grave!" she exclaimed. She began to question him, but since he could not tell her the truth, he said he was suffering from headaches, heartburn, stitches, and similar ailments. Roise Temerl, though she had looked forward to seeing her husband and had hoped to enjoy herself with him, ordered a carriage and horses and told him to see a doctor in Lublin. Filling a suitcase with cookies, jams, juices, and various other refreshments, she urged him not to spare money, but to find the best of doctors and to take all the medication he prescribed. Shifra Zirel too, saw her master depart, escorting the carriage on foot as far as the bridge, and wishing him a speedy recovery.

Late at night, by the light of the full moon, while the carriage drove along a forest road and shadows ran ahead, I, the Evil Spirit, came to Reb Nathan and asked, "Where are you going?"

"Can't you see? To a doctor."

"Your ailment can't be cured by a doctor," I said.

"What shall I do then? Divorce my old wife?"

"Why not?" I said to him, "Did not Abraham drive his bondwoman, Hagar, into the wilderness, with nothing but a bottle of water, because he preferred Sarah?

And later, did he not take Keturah and have six sons with her? Did not Moses, the teacher of all Jews, take, in addition to Zipporah, another wife from the land of Kush; and when Miriam, his sister, spoke against him, did she not become leprous? Know ye, Nathan, you are fated to have sons and daughters, and according to the law, you should have divorced Roise Temerl ten years after marrying her? Well, you may not leave the world without begetting children, and Heaven, therefore, has sent you Shifra Zirel to lie in your lap and become pregnant and bear healthy children, who after your death, will say *kadish* for you and will inherit your possessions. Therefore do not try to resist, Nathan, for such is the decree of Heaven, and if you do not execute it, you will be punished, you will die soon, and Roise Temerl will be a widow anyway and you will inherit hell."

Hearing these words, Nathan became frightened. Shuddering from head to foot, he said, "If so, why do I go to Lublin? I should, rather, order the driver to return to Frampol."

And I replied, "No, Nathan. Why tell your wife what you're about to do? When she learns you plan to divorce her and take the servant in her place, she will be greatly grieved, and may revenge herself on you or the servant. Rather follow the advice Shifra Zirel gave you. Get divorce papers in Lublin and place them secretly in your wife's dresses; this will make the divorce valid. Then tell her that doctors had advised you to go to Vienna for an operation since you have an internal growth. And before leaving, collect all the money and take it along with you, leaving your wife only the house and the furniture and her personal belongings. Only when you are far from home, and Shifra Zirel with you, you may inform Roise Temerl that she is a divorcee. In this way you will avoid scandal. But do not delay, Nathan, for Shifra Zirel won't tarry, and if she leaves you, you might be punished and perish and lose this world as well as the next."

I made more speeches, pious and impious, and at daybreak, when he fell asleep, I brought him Shifra Zirel, naked, and showed him the images of the children she would bear, male and female, with side whiskers and curls, and I made him eat imaginary dishes she had prepared for him: they tasted of Paradise. He awoke from these visions, famished, and consumed with desire. Approaching the city, the carriage stopped at an inn, where Nathan was served breakfast and a soft bed prepared for him. But on his palate there remained the savor of the pancake he had tasted in his dream. And on his lips he could almost feel Shifra Zirel's kisses. Overcome with longing, he put on his coat again, and told his hosts he must hurry to meet merchants.

In a back alley where I led him, he discovered a miserly scribe, who for five gulden, wrote the divorce papers and had them signed by witnesses, as required by law. Then Nathan, after purchasing numerous bottles and pills from an apothecary, returned to Frampol. He told his wife he had been examined by three doctors, that they had all found he had a tumor in his stomach, and that he must go at once to Vienna to be treated by great specialists or he would not last the year. Shaken by the story, Roise Temerl said, "What's money? Your health means far more to me." She wanted to accompany him, but Nathan reasoned with her and argued, "The trip will cost double; moreover, our business here must be looked after. No, stay here, and God willing, if everything goes well, I'll be back, we'll be happy together." To make a long story short, Roise Temerl agreed with him and stayed.

The same night, after Roise Temerl had fallen asleep, Nathan rose from bed and quietly placed the divorce papers in her trunk. He also visited Shifra Zirel in her room to inform her of what he had done. Kissing and embracing him, she promised to be a good wife and faithful mother to his children. But in her heart, jeering, she thought: You old fool, you'll pay dearly for falling in love with a whore.

And now starts the story of how I and my companions forced the old sinner, Nathan Jozefover, to become a man who sees without being seen, so that his bones would never be properly buried, which is the penalty for lechery.

6
Nathan Returns

A year passed, Roise Temerl now had a second husband, having married a Frampol grain dealer, Moshe Mecheles, who had lost his wife at the same time as she had been divorced. Moshe Mecheles was a small red-bearded man, with heavy red eyebrows and piercing yellow eyes. He often disputed with the Frampol rabbi, put on two pairs of phylacteries while praying, and owned a water mill. He was always covered with white flour dust. He had been rich before, and after his marriage to Roise Temerl, he took over her granaries and customers and became a magnate.

Why had Roise Temerl married him? For one thing, other people intervened. Secondly, she was lonely, and thought that another husband might at least partially replace Nathan. Third, I, the Seducer, had my own reasons for wanting her married. Well, after marrying, she realized she had made a mistake. Moshe Mecheles had odd ways. He was thin, and she tried to fatten him, but he would not touch her dumplings, pancakes, and chickens. He preferred bread with garlic, potatoes in their skins, onions and radishes, and once a day, a piece of lean boiled beef. His stained caftan was never buttoned; he wore a string to hold up his trousers, refused to go to the bath Roise Temerl would heat for him, and had to be forced to change a shirt or a pair of underpants. Moreover he was rarely at home; he either traveled for business or attended community meetings. He went to sleep late, and groaned and snored in his bed. When the sun rose, so did Moshe Mecheles, humming like a bee. Although close to sixty, Roise Temerl still did not disdain what others like, but Moshe Mecheles came to her rarely, and then it was only a question of duty. The woman finally conceded that she had blundered, but what could be done? She swallowed her pride and suffered silently.

One afternoon around Elul time, when Roise Temerl went to the yard to pour out the slops, she saw a strange figure. She cried out; the basin fell from her hands, the slops spilled at her feet. Ten paces away stood Nathan, her former husband. He was dressed like a beggar, his caftan torn, a piece of rope around his loins, his shoes in shreds, and on his head only the lining of a cap. His once pink face was now yellow, and the clumps of his beard were gray; pouches hung from his eyes. From his disheveled eyebrows he stared at Roise Temerl. For a moment it occurred to her that he must have died, and this was his ghost before her. She almost called out: Pure Soul, return to your place of rest! But since this

was happening in broad daylight, she soon recovered
from her shock and asked in a trembling voice:

"Do my eyes deceive me?"

"No," said Nathan, "It is I."

For a long time husband and wife stood silently gazing at each other. Roise Temerl was so stunned that she
could not speak. Her legs began to shake, and she had to
hold on to a tree to keep from falling.

"Woe is me, what has become of you?" she cried.

"Is your husband at home?" Nathan asked.

"My husband?" she was bewildered, "No . . ."

About to ask him in, Roise Temerl remembered that
according to law, she was not permitted to stay under
the same roof with him. Also, she feared that the servant might recognize him. Bending, she picked up the
slop basin.

"What happened?" she asked.

Haltingly, Nathan told her how he had met Shifra
Zirel in Lublin, married her, and been persuaded by
her to go to her relatives in Hungary. At an inn near the
border, she deserted him, stealing everything, even his
clothes. Since then, he had wandered all over the country, slept in poorhouses, and like a beggar, made the
rounds of private homes. At first he had thought he
would obtain a writ signed by one hundred rabbis,
enabling him to remarry, and he had set out for Frampol. Then he had learned that Roise Temerl had married again, and he had come to beg her forgiveness.

Unable to believe her eyes, Roise Temerl kept staring
at him. Leaning on his crooked stick, as a beggar
might, he never lifted his eyes. From his ears and nostrils, thatches of hair protruded. Through his torn coat,
she saw the sackcloth, and through a slit in it, his flesh.
He seemed to have grown smaller.

"Have any of the townspeople seen you?" she asked.

"No. I came through the fields."

"Woe is me. What can I do with you now?" she exclaimed, "I am married."

"I don't want anything from you," Nathan said, "Farewell."

"Don't go!" Roise Temerl said, "Oh, how unlucky I am!"

Covering her face with her hands, she began to sob. Nathan moved aside.

"Don't mourn for me," he said, "I haven't died yet."

"I wish you had," she replied, "I'd be happier."

Well, I, the Destroyer, had not yet tried all my insidious tricks. The scale of sins and punishment was not yet balanced. Therefore, in a vigorous move, I spoke to the woman in the language of compassion, for it is known that compassion, like any other sentiment, can serve evil as well as good purposes. Roise Temerl, I said, he is your husband; you lived with him for fifty years, and you cannot repudiate him, now that he has fallen. And when she asked, "What shall I do? After all, I cannot stand here and expose myself to derision," I made a suggestion. She trembled, raised her eyes, and beckoned Nathan to follow her. Submissively, he walked behind her, like any poor visitor who does everything that the lady of the house tells him to do.

7
The Secret of the Ruin

In the yard, behind the granary, near the bathhouse, stood a ruin in which many years before, Roise Temerl's parents had lived. Unoccupied now, its ground floor windows were boarded, but on the second floor there were still a few well preserved rooms. Pigeons perched on the roof, and swallows had nested under the gutter. A worn broom had been stuck in the chimney. Nathan had often said the building should be razed, but Roise Temerl had insisted that while she was alive her parents' home would not be demolished. The attic was littered with old rubbish and rags. Schoolboys said that a light emanated from the ruin at midnight, and that demons lived in the cellar. Roise Temerl led Nathan there now. It was not easy to enter the ruin. Weeds that pricked and burned obstructed the path. Roise Temerl's skirt caught on thorns sharp as nails. Little mole-hills were everywhere. A heavy curtain of cobwebs barred the open doorway. Roise Temerl swept them away with a rotten branch. The stairs were rickety. Her legs were heavy and she had to lean on Nathan's arm. A thick cloud of dust arose, and Nathan began to sneeze and cough.

"Where are you taking me?" he asked, bewildered.

"Don't be afraid," Roise Temerl said, "It's all right."

Leaving him in the ruin, she returned to the house. She told the servant to take the rest of the day off, and the servant did not have to be told twice. When she had gone, Roise Temerl opened the cabinets that were still filled with Nathan's clothes, took his linen from the chest, and brought everything to the ruin. Once more she left, and when she returned it was with a basket containing a meal of rice and pot roast, tripe with calves' feet, white bread, and stewed prunes. After he had gobbled his supper and licked off the prune plate, Roise Temerl drew a bucket of water from the well and told him to go to another room to wash. Night was falling, but the twilight lingered a long time. Nathan did as Roise Temerl instructed, and she could hear him splash and sigh in the next room. Then he changed his clothes. When Roise Temerl saw him, tears streamed from her eyes. The full moon that shone through the window made the room bright as daylight, and Nathan, in a clean shirt, his dressing gown embroidered with leaves and flowers, in his silken cap and velvet slippers, once again seemed his former self.

Moshe Mecheles happened to be out of town, and Roise Temerl was in no hurry. She went again to the house and returned with bedding. The bed only needed to be fitted with boards. Not wanting to light a candle, lest someone notice the glow, Roise Temerl went about in the dark, climbed to the attic with Nathan, and groped until she found some old slats for the bed. Then she placed a mattress, sheets, and pillow on it. She had even remembered to bring some jam and a box of cookies so that Nathan could refresh himself before going to sleep. Only then did she sit down on the unsteady stool to rest. Nathan sat on the edge of the bed.

After a long silence, he said, "What's the use? Tomorrow I must leave."

"Why tomorrow?" said Roise Temerl, "Rest up. There's always time to rot in the poorhouse."

Late into the night they sat, talking, murmuring. Roise Temerl cried and stopped crying, began again and was calm again. She insisted that Nathan confess everything to her, without omitting details, and he told her again how he had met Shifra Zirel, how they had married, how she had persuaded him to go with her to Pressburg, and how she had spent the night full of sweet talk and love play with him at an inn. And at daybreak, when he fell asleep, she had arisen and untied the bag from his neck. He also told Roise Temerl how he had been forced to discard all shame, to sleep in beggars' dormitories, and eat at strangers' tables. Although his story angered her, and she called him blockhead, stupid fool, ass, idiot, her heart almost dissolved with pity.

"What is there to do now?" she kept murmuring to herself, over and over again. And I, the Evil Spirit, answered: Don't let him go. The beggar's life is not for him. He might die of grief or shame. And when Roise Temerl argued that because she was a married woman she had no right to stay with him, I said: Can the twelve lines of a bill of divorcement separate two souls who have been fused by fifty years of common life? Can a brother and sister be transformed by law into strangers? Hasn't Nathan become part of you? Don't you see him every night in your dreams? Isn't all your fortune the result of his industry and effort? And what is Moshe Mecheles? A stranger, a lout. Wouldn't it be better to fry with Nathan in hell, rather than serve as Moshe Mecheles' footstool in Heaven? I also recalled to her an incident in a story book, where a landowner, whose wife had eloped with a bear tamer, later forgave her and took her back to his manor.

When the clock in the Frampol church chimed eleven, Roise Temerl returned home. In her luxurious, canopied bed, she tossed, like one in a fever. For a long time, Nathan stood beside his window, looking out. The Elul sky was full of stars. The owl on the roof of the synagogue screeched with a human voice. The caterwauling of cats reminded him of women in labor. Crickets chirped, and unseen saws seemed to be buzzing through tree trunks. The neighing of horses that had grazed all night came through the fields with the calls of shepherds. Nathan, because he stood on an upper floor, could see the whole little town at a glance, the synagogue, the church, the slaughterhouse, the public bathhouse, the market, and the side streets where Gentiles lived. He recognized each shed, shack, and board in his own yard. A goat stripped some bark from a tree. A field mouse left the granary to return to its nest. Nathan watched for a long time. Everything about him was familiar and yet strange, real and ghostly, as though he were no longer among the living—only his spirit floated there. He recalled that there was a Hebrew phrase which applied to him, but he could not remember it exactly. Finally, after trying for a long time, he remembered: *one who sees without being seen.*

8
One Who Sees Without Being Seen

In Frampol the rumor spread that Roise Temerl, having quarreled with her maid, had dismissed her in the middle of her term. This surprised the housewives, because the girl was reputedly industrious and honest. Actually, Roise Temerl had dismissed the girl to keep her from discovering that Nathan lived in the ruin. As always, when I seduce sinners, I persuaded the couple that all this was provisional, that Nathan would stay only until he had recovered from his wandering. But I made certain that Roise Temerl welcomed the presence of her hidden guest and that Nathan enjoyed being where he was. Even though they discussed their future separation each time they were together, Roise Temerl gave Nathan's quarters an air of permanency. She resumed her cooking and frying for him, and once more brought him her tasty dishes. After a few days, Nathan's appearance changed remarkably. From pastries and puddings, his face became pink again, and once more, like that of a man of wealth, his paunch protruded. Once more he wore embroidered shirts, velvet slippers, silken dressing gowns, and carried batiste handkerchiefs. To keep him from being bored by his idleness, Roise Temerl brought him a Bible in Yiddish, a copy of the *Inheritance of the Deer*, and numerous story books. She even managed to procure some tobacco for his pipe, for he enjoyed smoking one, and she brought from the cellar bottles of wine and mead that Nathan had stored for years. The divorced couple had banquets in the ruin.

I made certain that Moshe Mecheles was seldom at home; I sent him to all kinds of fairs, and even recommended him as arbiter in disputes. It did not take long for the ruin behind the granary to become Roise Temerl's only comfort. Just as a miser's thoughts constantly dwell on the treasure he has buried far from sight, so Roise Temerl thought only of the ruin and the secret in her heart. Sometimes she thought that Nathan had died and she had magically resurrected him for a while; at other times, she imagined the whole thing a dream. Whenever she looked out of her window at the moss-covered roof of the ruin, she thought: No! It's inconceivable for Nathan to be there; I must be deluded. And immediately, she had to fly there, up the rickety stairs, to be met half-way by Nathan in person, with his familiar smile and his pleasant odor. "Nathan, you're here?" she would ask, and he would respond, "Yes, Roise Temerl, I'm here and waiting for you."

"Have you missed me?" she would ask, and he would answer:

"Of course. When I hear your step, it's a holiday for me."

"Nathan, Nathan," she would continue, "Would you have believed a year ago that it would end like this?"

And he would murmur, "No, Roise Temerl, it is like a bad dream."

"Oh Nathan, we have already lost this world, and I'm afraid we'll lose the other also," Roise Temerl said.

And he replied, "Well, that's too bad, but hell too is for people, not for dogs."

Since Moshe Mecheles belonged to the Hassidim, I, Old Rebel, sent him to spend the Days of Awe with his rabbi. Alone, Roise Temerl bought Nathan a prayer shawl, a white robe, a prayer book, and prepared a holiday meal for him. Since on Rosh Hashona, there is no moon, he ate the evening meal in darkness, blindly dunked a slice of bread in honey, and tasted an apple, a carrot, the head of a carp, and offered a blessing for the first fruit, over a pomegranate. He stood praying during the day in his robe and prayer shawl. The sound of the ram's horn came faintly to his ears from the synagogue. At the intermission between the prayers, Roise Temerl visited him in her golden dress, her white, satin-lined coat, and the shawl embroidered with silver threads, to wish him a happy new year. The golden chain he had given her for their betrothal hung around her neck. A brooch he had brought to her from Danzig, quivered on her breast, and from her wrist dangled a bracelet he had bought her at Brody. She exhuded an aroma of honey cake and the women's section of the synagogue. On the evening before the Day of Atonement, Roise Temerl brought him a white rooster as a sacrificial victim and prepared for him the meal to be eaten

before commencing the fast. Also, she gave the synagogue a wax candle for his soul. Before leaving for the
Minchah prayer at the synagogue, she came to bid him
good-by, and she began to lament so loudly that Nathan
feared she would be heard. Falling into his arms, she
clung to him and would not be torn away. She drenched
his face with tears and howled as though possessed. "Nathan, Nathan," she wailed, "may we have no more
unhappiness," and other things that are said when a member of a family dies, repeating them many times. Fearing she might faint and fall, Nathan had to escort her
downstairs. Then, standing at the window, he watched
the people of Frampol on their way to the synagogue.
The women walked quickly and vigorously, as though
hurrying to pray for someone on his deathbed; they held
up their skirts, and when two of them met, they fell into
each other's arms and swayed back and forth as if in
some mysterious struggle. Wives of prominent citizens
knocked at doors of poor people and begged to be forgiven. Mothers, whose children were ill, ran with arms
outstretched, as though chasing someone, crying like
madwomen. Elderly men, before leaving home, removed their shoes, put on white robes, prayer shawls,
and white skull caps. In the synagogue yard, the poor sat
with alms' boxes on benches. A reddish glow spread
over the roofs, reflecting in the window panes, and illuminating pale faces. In the west, the sun grew enormous; clouds around it caught fire, until half the sky
was suffused with flames. Nathan recalled the River of
Fire, in which all souls must cleanse themselves. The
sun sank soon below the horizon. Girls, dressed in white,
came outside and carefully closed shutters. Little flames
played on the high windows of the synagogue, and inside, the entire building seemed to be one great flicker.

A muted hum arose from it, and bursts of sobbing. Removing his shoes, Nathan wrapped himself in his shawl and robe. Half reading and half remembering, he chanted the words of Kol Nidre, the song that is recited not only by the living but by the dead in their graves. What was he, Nathan Jozefover, but a dead man, who instead of resting in his grave, wandered about in a world that did not exist?

9
Footprints in the Snow

The High Holidays were over. Winter had come. But Nathan was still in the ruin. It could not be heated, not only because the stove had been dismantled, but because smoke, coming from the chimney, would make people suspicious. To keep Nathan from freezing, Roise Temerl provided him with warm clothes and a coal pot. At night he covered himself with two feather quilts. During the day he wore his fox fur and had felt boots on his feet. Roise Temerl also brought him a little barrel of spirits with a straw in it, which he sipped each time he felt cold, while eating a piece of dried mutton. From the rich food with which Roise Temerl plied him, he grew fat and heavy. In the evenings he stood at the window watching with curiosity the women who went to the ritual bath. On market days he never left the window. Carts drove into the yard and peasants unloaded sacks of grain. Moshe Mecheles, in a cotton padded jacket, ran back and forth, crying out hoarsely. Although it pained Nathan to think that this ridiculous fellow disposed of his possessions and lay with his wife, Moshe Mecheles' appearance made him laugh, as though the whole thing were a kind of prank that he, Nathan, had played on his competitor. Sometimes he felt like calling to him: Hey, there, Moshe Mecheles! while throwing him a bit of plaster or a bone.

As long as there was no snow, Nathan had everything he needed. Roise Temerl visited him often. At night Nathan would go out for a walk on a path that led to the river. But one night a great deal of snow fell, and the next day Roise Temerl did not visit him, for she was afraid someone might notice her tracks in the snow. Nor could Nathan go out to satisfy his natural needs. For two days he had nothing warm to eat, and the water in the pail turned to ice. On the third day Roise Temerl hired a peasant to clear the snow between the house and the granary and she also told him to clear the snow between the granary and the ruin. Moshe Mecheles, when he came home was surprised and asked, Why?", but she changed the subject, and since he suspected nothing, he soon forgot about it.

Nathan's life, from then on, became increasingly difficult. After each new snowfall, Roise Temerl cleared the path with a shovel. To keep her neighbors from seeing what went on in the yard, she had the fence repaired. And as a pretext for going to the ruin, she had a ditch for refuse dug close to it. Whenever she saw Nathan, he said it was time for him to take his bundle and leave, but Roise Temerl prevailed on him to wait. "Where will you go?" she asked. "You might, God forbid, drop from exhaustion." According to the almanac, she argued, the winter would be a mild one, and summer would begin early, weeks before Purim, and he only had to get through half the month of Kislev, besides Teveth and Shevat. She told him other things. At times, they did not even speak, but sat silently, holding hands and weeping. Both of them were actually losing strength each day. Nathan grew fatter, more blown up; his belly was full of wind; his legs seemed leaden; and his sight was dimming. He could no longer read his story books. Roise Temerl grew thin, like a consumptive, lost her appetite, and could not sleep. Some nights she lay awake, sobbing. And when Moshe Mecheles asked her why, she said it was because she had no children to pray for her after she was gone.

One day a downpour washed away the snow. Since Roise Temerl had not visited the ruin for two days, Nathan expected her to arrive at any moment. He had no food left; only a bit of brandy remained at the bottom of the barrel. For hours on end he stood waiting for her at the window, which was misted over with frost, but she did not come. The night was pitch black and icy. Dogs barked, a wind blew. The walls of the ruin shook; a whistling sound ran through the chimney, and the eaves rattled on the roof. In Nathan's house, now the house of Moshe Mecheles, several lamps seemed to have been lighted; it seemed extraordinarily bright, and the light made the surrounding darkness thicker. Nathan thought he heard the rolling of wheels, as though a carriage had driven to the house. In the darkness, someone drew water from the well, and someone poured out the slops. The night wore on, but despite the late hour, the shutters remained open. Seeing shadows run back and forth, Nathan thought important visitors might have come and were being treated to a banquet. He remained staring into the night until his knees grew weak, and with his last bit of strength, he dragged himself to his bed and fell into a deep sleep.

The cold awoke him early next morning. With stiff limbs he arose and barely propelled himself to the window. More snow had fallen during the night, and a heavy frost had set in. To his amazement, Nathan saw a group of men and women standing around his house. He wondered, anxiously, what was going on. But he did not have to wonder long, for suddenly the door swung open, and four men carried out a coffin hearse covered with a black cloth. "Moshe Mecheles is dead!" Nathan thought. But then he saw Moshe Mecheles following the coffin. It was not he, but Roise Temerl who had died.

Nathan could not weep. It was as though the cold had frozen his tears. Trembling and shaking, he watched the men carrying the coffin, watched the beadle rattling his alms box and the mourners wading through deep snowdrifts. The sky, pale as linen, hung low, meeting the blanketed earth. As though drifting on a flood, the trees in the fields seemed to be afloat in whiteness. From his window, Nathan could see all the way to the cemetery. The coffin moved up and down; the crowd, following it, thinned out and at times vanished entirely, seemed to sink into the ground and then emerge again. Nathan fancied for a moment that the cortege had stopped and no longer advanced, and then, that the people, as well as the corpse, were moving backward. The cortege grew gradually smaller, until it became a black dot. Because the dot ceased to move, Nathan realized that the pall bearers had reached the cemetery, and that he was watching his faithful wife being buried. With the remaining brandy, he washed his hands, for the water in his pail had turned to ice, and he began to murmur the prayer for the dead.

10
Two Faces

Nathan had intended to pack his things and leave during the night, but I, the Chief of the devils, prevented him from carrying out his plan. Before sunrise he was seized with powerful stomach cramps; his head grew hot and his knees so weak that he could not walk. His shoes had grown brittle; he could not put them on; and his legs had become fat. The Good Spirit counseled him to call for help, to shout until people heard and came to rescue him, because no man may cause his own death, but I said to him: Do you remember the words of King David: "Let me rather fall into God's hands, than into the hands of people?" You don't want Moshe Mecheles and his henchmen to have the satisfaction of revenging themselves on you and jeering. Rather die like a dog. In short, he listened to me, first, because he was proud, and second, because he was not fated to be buried according to law.

Gathering together his last remnants of strength, he pushed his bed to the window, to lie there and watch. He fell asleep early and awoke. There was day, and then night. Sometimes he heard cries in the yard. At other times he thought someone called him by name. His head, he fancied, had grown monstrously large and burdensome, like a millstone carried on his neck. His fingers were wooden, his tongue hard; it seemed bigger than the space it occupied. My helpers, goblins, appeared to him in dreams. They screamed, whistled, kindled fires, walked on stilts, and carried on like Purim players. He dreamed of floods, then of fires, imagined the world had been destroyed, and then that he hovered in the void with bats' wings. In his dreams he also saw pancakes, dumplings, broad noodles with cheese, and when he awoke his stomach was as full as though he had actually eaten; he belched and sighed, and touched his belly that was empty and aching all over.

Once, sitting up, he looked out of the window, and saw to his surprise that people were walking backward, and marveled at this. Soon he saw other extraordinary things. Among those who passed, he recognized men who had long been dead. "Do my eyes deceive me?" he wondered, "Or has Messiah come, and has he resurrected the dead?" The more he looked the more astonished he became. Entire generations passed through the town, men and women with packs on their shoulders and staffs in their hands. He recognized, among them, his father and grandfather, his grandmothers and great-aunts. He watched workers build the Frampol synagogue. They carried bricks, sawed wood, mixed plaster, nailed on eaves. Schoolboys stood about, staring upward and calling a strange word he could not understand, like something in a foreign tongue. As in a dance around the Torah, two storks circled the building. Then the building and builders vanished, and he saw a group of people, barefooted, bearded, wild-eyed, with crosses in their hands, lead a Jew to the gallows. Though the black-bearded young man cried heart-rendingly, they dragged him on, tied in ropes. Bells were ringing; the people in the streets ran away and hid. It was midday, but it grew dark as the day of an eclipse of the sun. Finally, the young man cried out: "Shema Yisroel, the Lord our God, the Lord is One," and was left hanging, his tongue lolling out. His legs swayed for a long time, and hosts of crows flew overhead, cawing hoarsely.

On his last night, Nathan dreamed that Roise Temerl and Shifra Zirel were one woman with two faces. He was overjoyed at her appearance. "Why have I not noticed this before?" he wondered. "Why did I have to go through this trouble and anxiety?" He kissed the two-faced female, and she returned his kisses with her doubled lips, pressing against him her two pairs of breasts. He spoke words of love to her, and she responded in two voices. In her four arms and two bosoms, all his questions were answered. There was no longer life and death, here nor there, beginning nor end. "The truth is two-fold," Nathan exclaimed, "This is the mystery of all mysteries!"

Without a last confession of his sins, Nathan died that night. I at once transported his soul to the nether abyss. He still wanders to this day in desolate spaces, and has not yet been granted admittance to hell. Moshe Mecheles married again, a young woman this time. She made him pay dearly, soon inherited his fortune, and squandered it. Shifra Zirel became a harlot in Pressburg and died in the poorhouse. The ruin still stands as before, and Nathan's bones still lie there. And, who can tell, perhaps another man, who sees without being seen, is hiding in it.

Translated by Norbert Guterman
and Elaine Gottlieb

The
Spinoza
of
Market
Street

Dr. Nahum Fischelson paced back and forth in his garret room in Market Street, Warsaw. Dr. Fischelson was a short, hunched man with a grayish beard, and was quite bald except for a few wisps of hair remaining at the nape of the neck. His nose was as crooked as a beak and his eyes were large, dark, and fluttering like those of some huge bird. It was a hot summer evening, but Dr. Fischelson wore a black coat which reached to his knees, and he had on a stiff collar and a bow tie. From the door he paced slowly to the dormer window set high in the slanting room and back again. One had to mount several steps to look out. A candle in a brass holder was burning on the table and a variety of insects buzzed around the flame. Now and again one of the creatures would fly too close to the fire and sear its wings, or one would ignite and glow on the wick for an instant. At such moments Dr. Fischelson grimaced. His wrinkled face would twitch and beneath his disheveled moustache he would bite his lips. Finally he took a handkerchief from his pocket and waved it at the insects.

"Away from there, fools and imbeciles," he scolded. "You won't get warm here; you'll only burn yourself."

The insects scattered but a second later returned and once more circled the trembling flame. Dr. Fischelson wiped the sweat from his wrinkled forehead and sighed, "Like men they desire nothing but the pleasure of the moment." On the table lay an open book written in Latin, and on its broad-margined pages were notes and comments printed in small letters by Dr. Fischelson. The book was Spinoza's *Ethics* and Dr. Fischelson had been studying it for the last thirty years. He knew every proposition, every proof, every corollary, every note by heart. When he wanted to find a particular passage, he generally opened to the place immediately without having to search for it. But, nevertheless, he continued to study the *Ethics* for hours every day with a magnifying glass in his bony hand, murmuring and nodding his head in agreement. The truth was that the more Dr. Fischelson studied, the more puzzling sentences, unclear passages, and cryptic remarks he found. Each sentence contained hints unfathomed by any of the students of Spinoza. Actually the philosopher had anticipated all of the criticisms of pure reason made by Kant and his followers. Dr. Fischelson was writing a commentary on the *Ethics*. He had drawers full of notes and drafts, but it didn't seem that he would ever be able to complete his work. The stomach ailment which had plagued him for years was growing worse from day to day.

Now he would get pains in his stomach after only a few mouthfuls of oatmeal. "God in Heaven, it's difficult, very difficult," he would say to himself using the same intonation as had his father, the late Rabbi of Tishevitz. "It's very, very hard."

Dr. Fischelson was not afraid of dying. To begin with, he was no longer a young man. Secondly, it is stated in the fourth part of the *Ethics* that "a free man thinks of nothing less than of death and his wisdom is a meditation not of death, but of life." Thirdly, it is also said that "the human mind cannot be absolutely destroyed with the human body but there is some part of it that remains eternal." And yet Dr. Fischelson's ulcer (or perhaps it was a cancer) continued to bother him. His tongue was always coated. He belched frequently and emitted a different foul-smelling gas each time. He suffered from heartburn and cramps. At times he felt like vomiting and at other times he was hungry for garlic, onions, and fried foods. He had long ago discarded the medicines prescribed for him by the doctors and had sought his own remedies. He found it beneficial to take grated radish after meals and lie on his bed, belly down, with his head hanging over the side. But these home remedies offered only temporary relief. Some of the doctors he consulted insisted there was nothing the matter with him. "It's just nerves," they told him. "You could live to be a hundred."

But on this particular hot summer night, Dr. Fischelson felt his strength ebbing. His knees were shaky, his pulse weak. He sat down to read and his vision blurred. The letters on the page turned from green to gold. The lines became waved and jumped over each other, leaving white gaps as if the text had disappeared in some mysterious way. The heat was unbearable, flowing down directly from the tin roof; Dr. Fischelson felt he was inside of an oven. Several times he climbed the four steps to the window and thrust his head out into the cool of the evening breeze. He would remain in that position for so long his knees would become wobbly. "Oh it's a fine breeze," he would murmur, "really delightful," and he would recall that according to Spinoza, morality and happiness were identical, and that the most moral deed a man could perform was to indulge in some pleasure which was not contrary to reason.

2

Dr. Fischelson, standing on the top step at the window and looking out, could see into two worlds. Above him were the heavens, thickly strewn with stars. Dr. Fischelson had never seriously studied astronomy but he could differentiate between the planets, those bodies which like the earth, revolve around the sun, and the fixed stars, themselves distant suns, whose light reaches us a hundred or even a thousand years later. He recognized the constellations which mark the path of the earth in space and that nebulous sash, the Milky Way. Dr. Fischelson owned a small telescope he had bought in Switzerland where he had studied and he particularly enjoyed looking at the moon through it. He could clearly make out on the moon's surface the volcanoes bathed in sunlight and the dark, shadowy craters. He never wearied of gazing at these cracks and crevasses. To him they seemed both near and distant, both substantial and insubstantial. Now and then he would see a shooting star trace a wide arc across the sky and disappear, leaving a fiery trail behind it. Dr. Fischelson would know then that a meteorite had reached our atmosphere, and perhaps some unburned fragment of it had fallen into the ocean or had landed in the desert or perhaps even in some inhabited region. Slowly the stars which had appeared from behind Dr. Fischelson's roof rose until they were shining above the house across the street. Yes, when Dr. Fischelson looked up into the heavens, he became aware of that infinite extension which is, according to Spinoza, one of God's attributes. It comforted Dr. Fischelson to think that although he was only a weak, puny man, a changing mode of the absolutely infinite Substance, he was nevertheless a part of the cosmos, made of the same matter as the celestial bodies; to the extent that he was a part of the Godhead, he knew he could not be destroyed. In such moments, Dr. Fischelson experienced the *Amor Dei Intellectualis* which is, according to the philosopher of Amsterdam, the highest perfection of the mind. Dr. Fischelson breathed deeply, lifted his head as high as his stiff collar permitted and actually felt he was whirling in company with the earth, the sun, the stars of the Milky Way, and the infinite host of galaxies known only to infinite thought. His legs became light and weightless and he grasped the window frame with both hands as if afraid he would lose his footing and fly out into eternity.

When Dr. Fischelson tired of observing the sky, his glance dropped to Market Street below. He could see a long strip extending from Yanash's market to Iron Street with the gas lamps lining it merged into a string of fiery dots. Smoke was issuing from the chimneys on the black, tin roofs; the bakers were heating their ovens, and here and there sparks mingled with the black smoke. The street never looked so noisy and crowded as on a summer evening. Thieves, prostitutes, gamblers, and fences loafed in the square which looked from above like a pretzel covered with poppy seeds. The young men laughed coarsely and the girls shrieked. A peddler with a keg of lemonade on his back pierced the general din with his intermittent cries. A watermelon vendor shouted in a savage voice, and the long knife which he used for cutting the fruit dripped with the blood-like juice. Now and again the street became even more agitated. Fire engines, their heavy wheels clanging, sped by; they were drawn by sturdy black horses which had to be tightly curbed to prevent them from running wild. Next came an ambulance, its siren screaming. Then some thugs had a fight among themselves and the police had to be called. A passerby was robbed and ran about shouting for help. Some wagons loaded with firewood sought to get through into the courtyards where the bakeries were located but the horses could not lift the wheels over the steep curbs and the drivers berated the animals and lashed them with their whips. Sparks rose from the clanging hoofs. It was now long after seven, which was the prescribed closing time for stores, but actually business had only begun. Customers were led in stealthily through back doors. The Russian policemen on the street, having been paid off, noticed nothing of this. Merchants continued to hawk their wares, each seeking to outshout the others.

"Gold, gold, gold," a woman who dealt in rotten oranges shrieked.

"Sugar, sugar, sugar," croaked a dealer of overripe plums.

"Heads, heads, heads," a boy who sold fishheads roared.

Through the window of a *Chassidic* study house across the way, Dr. Fischelson could see boys with long sidelocks swaying over holy volumes, grimacing and studying aloud in singsong voices. Butchers, porters, and fruit dealers were drinking beer in the tavern below. Vapor drifted from the tavern's open door like steam from a bathhouse, and there was the sound of loud music. Outside of the tavern, streetwalkers snatched at drunken soldiers and at workers on their way home from the factories. Some of the men carried bundles of wood on their shoulders, reminding Dr. Fischelson of the wicked who are condemned to kindle their own fires in Hell. Husky record players poured out their raspings through open windows. The liturgy of the high holidays alternated with vulgar vaudeville songs.

Dr. Fischelson peered into the half-lit bedlam and cocked his ears. He knew that the behavior of this rabble was the very antithesis of reason. These people were immersed in the vainest of passions, were drunk with emotions, and, according to Spinoza, emotion was never good. Instead of the pleasure they ran after, all they succeeded in obtaining was disease and prison, shame and the suffering that resulted from ignorance. Even the cats which loitered on the roofs here seemed more savage and passionate than those in other parts of the town. They caterwauled with the voices of women in labor, and like demons scampered up walls and leaped onto eaves and balconies. One of the toms paused at Dr. Fischelson's window and let out a howl which made Dr. Fischelson shudder. The doctor stepped from the window and, picking up a broom, brandished it in front of the black beast's glowing, green eyes. "Scat, begone, you ignorant savage!"—and he rapped the broom handle against the roof until the tom ran off.

3

When Dr. Fischelson had returned to Warsaw from Zurich where he had studied philosophy, a great future had been predicted for him. His friends had known that he was writing an important book on Spinoza. A Jewish Polish journal had invited him to be a contributor; he had been a frequent guest at several wealthy households and he had been made head librarian at the Warsaw synagogue. Although even then he had been considered an old bachelor, the matchmakers had proposed several rich girls for him. But Dr. Fischelson had not taken advantage of these opportunities. He had wanted to be as independent as Spinoza himself. And he had been. But because of his heretical ideas he had come into conflict with the rabbi and had had to resign his post as librarian. For years after that, he had supported himself by giving private lessons in Hebrew and German. Then, when he had become sick, the Berlin Jewish community had voted him a subsidy of five hundred marks a year. This had been made possible through the intervention of the famous Dr. Hildesheimer with whom he corresponded about philosophy. In order to get by on so small a pension, Dr. Fischelson had moved into the attic room and had begun cooking his own meals on a kerosene stove. He had a cupboard which had many drawers, and each drawer was labelled with the food it contained—buckwheat, rice, barley, onions, carrots, potatoes, mushrooms. Once a week Dr. Fischelson put on his widebrimmed black hat, took a basket in one hand and Spinoza's *Ethics* in the other, and went off to the market for his provisions. While he was waiting to be served, he would open the *Ethics*. The merchants knew him and would motion him to their stalls.

"A fine piece of cheese, Doctor—just melts in your mouth."

"Fresh mushrooms, Doctor, straight from the woods."

"Make way for the Doctor, ladies," the butcher would shout. "Please don't block the entrance."

During the early years of his sickness, Dr. Fischelson had still gone in the evening to a café which was frequented by Hebrew teachers and other intellectuals. It had been his habit to sit there and play chess while drinking a half a glass of black coffee. Sometimes he would stop at the bookstores on Holy Cross Street where all sorts of old books and magazines could be purchased cheap. On one occasion a former pupil of his had arranged to meet him at a restaurant one evening. When Dr. Fischelson arrived, he had been surprised to find a group of friends and admirers who forced him to sit at the head of the table while they made speeches about him. But these were things that had happened long ago. Now people were no longer interested in him. He had isolated himself completely and had become a forgotten man. The events of 1905 when the boys of Market Street had begun to organize strikes, throw bombs at police stations, and shoot strike breakers so that the stores were closed even on weekdays had greatly increased his isolation. He began to despise everything associated with the modern Jew—Zionism, socialism, anarchism. The young men in question seemed to him nothing but an ignorant rabble intent on destroying society, society without which no reasonable existence was possible. He still read a Hebrew magazine occasionally, but he felt contempt for modern Hebrew which had no roots in the Bible or the Mishnah. The spelling of Polish words had changed also. Dr. Fischelson concluded that even the so-called spiritual men had abandoned reason and were doing their utmost to pander to the mob. Now and again he still visited a library and browsed through some of the modern histories of philosophy, but he found that the professors did not understand Spinoza, quoted him incorrectly, attributed their own muddled ideas to the philosopher. Although Dr. Fischelson was well aware that anger was an emotion unworthy of those who walk the path of reason, he would become furious, and would quickly close the book and push it from him. "Idiots," he would mutter, "asses, upstarts." And he would vow never again to look at modern philosophy.

4

Every three months a special mailman who only delivered money orders brought Dr. Fischelson eighty rubles. He expected his quarterly allotment at the beginning of July but as day after day passed and the tall man with the blond moustache and the shiny buttons did not appear, the Doctor grew anxious. He had scarcely a groshen left. Who knows—possibly the Berlin Community had rescinded his subsidy; perhaps Dr. Hildesheimer had died, God forbid; the post office might have made a mistake. Every event has its cause, Dr. Fischelson knew. All was determined, all necessary, and a man of reason had no right to worry. Nevertheless, worry invaded his brain, and buzzed about like the flies. If the worst came to the worst, it occurred to him, he could commit suicide, but then he remembered that Spinoza did not approve of suicide and compared those who took their own lives to the insane.

One day when Dr. Fischelson went out to a store to purchase a composition book, he heard people talking about war. In Serbia somewhere, an Austrian Prince had been shot and the Austrians had delivered an ultimatum to the Serbs. The owner of the store, a young man with a yellow beard and shifty yellow eyes, announced, "We are about to have a small war," and he advised Dr. Fischelson to store up food because in the near future there was likely to be a shortage.

Everything happened so quickly. Dr. Fischelson had not even decided whether it was worthwhile to spend four groshen on a newspaper, and already posters had been hung up announcing mobilization. Men were to be seen walking on the street with round, metal tags on their lapels, a sign that they were being drafted. They were followed by their crying wives. One Monday when Dr. Fischelson descended to the street to buy some food with his last kopecks, he found the stores closed. The owners and their wives stood outside and explained that merchandise was unobtainable. But certain special customers were pulled to one side and let in through back doors. On the street all was confusion. Policemen with swords unsheathed could be seen riding on horseback. A large crowd had gathered around the tavern where, at the command of the Tsar, the tavern's stock of whiskey was being poured into the gutter.

Dr. Fischelson went to his old café. Perhaps he would find some acquaintances there who would advise him. But he did not come across a single person he knew. He decided, then, to visit the rabbi of the synagogue where he had once been librarian, but the sexton with the six-sided skull cap informed him that the rabbi and his family had gone off to the spas. Dr. Fischelson had other old friends in town but he found no one at home. His feet ached from so much walking; black and green spots appeared before his eyes and he felt faint. He stopped and waited for the giddiness to pass. The passers-by jostled him. A dark-eyed high school girl tried to give him a coin. Although the war had just started, soldiers eight abreast were marching in full battle dress—the men were covered with dust and were sunburnt. Canteens were strapped to their sides and they wore rows of bullets across their chests. The bayonets on their rifles gleamed with a cold, green light. They sang with mournful voices. Along with the men came cannons, each pulled by eight horses; their blind muzzles breathed gloomy terror. Dr. Fischelson felt nauseous. His stomach ached; his intestines seemed about to turn themselves inside out. Cold sweat appeared on his face.

"I'm dying," he thought. "This is the end." Nevertheless, he did manage to drag himself home where he lay down on the iron cot and remained, panting and gasping. He must have dozed off because he imagined that he was in his home town, Tishvitz. He had a sore throat and his mother was busy wrapping a stocking stuffed with hot salt around his neck. He could hear talk going on in the house; something about a candle and about how a frog had bitten him. He wanted to go out into the street but they wouldn't let him because a a Catholic procession was passing by. Men in long robes, holding double edged axes in their hands, were intoning in Latin as they sprinkled holy water. Crosses gleamed; sacred pictures waved in the air. There was an odor of incense and corpses. Suddenly the sky turned a burning red and the whole world started to burn. Bells were ringing; people rushed madly about. Flocks of birds flew overhead, screeching. Dr. Fischelson awoke with a start. His body was covered with sweat and his throat was now actually sore. He tried to meditate about his extraordinary dream, to find its rational connection with what was happening to him and to comprehend it *sub specie eternitatis*, but none of it made sense. "Alas, the brain is a receptacle for nonsense," Dr. Fischelson thought. "This earth belongs to the mad."

And he once more closed his eyes; once more he dozed; once more he dreamed.

5

The eternal laws, apparently, had not yet ordained Dr. Fischelson's end.

There was a door to the left of Dr. Fischelson's attic room which opened off a dark corridor, cluttered with boxes and baskets, in which the odor of fried onions and laundry soap was always present. Behind this door lived a spinster whom the neighbors called Black Dobbe. Dobbe was tall and lean, and as black as a baker's shovel. She had a broken nose and there was a mustache on her upper lip. She spoke with the hoarse voice of a man and she wore men's shoes. For years Black Dobbe had sold breads, rolls, and bagels which she had bought from the baker at the gate of the house. But one day she and the baker had quarreled and she had moved her business to the market place and now she dealt in what were called "wrinklers" which was a synonym for cracked eggs. Black Dobbe had no luck with men. Twice she had been engaged to baker's apprentices but in both instances they had returned the engagement contract to her. Some time afterwards she had received an engagement contract from an old man, a glazier who claimed that he was divorced, but it had later come to light that he still had a wife. Black Dobbe had a cousin in America, a shoemaker, and repeatedly she boasted that this cousin was sending her passage, but she remained in Warsaw. She was constantly being teased by the women who would say, "There's no hope for you, Dobbe. You're fated to die an old maid." Dobbe always answered, "I don't intend to be a slave for any man. Let them all rot."

That afternoon Dobbe received a letter from America. Generally she would go to Leizer the Tailor and have him read it to her. However, that day Leizer was out and so Dobbe thought of Dr. Fischelson whom the other tenants considered a convert since he never went to prayer. She knocked on the door of the doctor's room but there was no answer. "The heretic is probably out," Dobbe thought but, nevertheless, she knocked once more, and this time the door moved slightly. She pushed her way in and stood there frightened. Dr. Fischelson lay fully clothed on his bed; his face was as yellow as wax; his Adam's apple stuck out prominently; his beard pointed upward. Dobbe screamed; she was certain that he was dead, but—no—his body moved. Dobbe picked up a glass which stood on the table, ran into the corridor, filled the glass with water from the faucet, hurried back, and threw the water into the face of the unconscious man. Dr. Fischelson shook his head and opened his eyes.

"What's wrong with you?" Dobbe asked. "Are you sick?"

"Thank you very much. No."

"Have you a family? I'll call them."

"No family," Dr. Fischelson said.

Dobbe wanted to fetch the barber from across the street but Dr. Fischelson signified that he didn't wish the barber's assistance. Since Dobbe was not going to the market that day, no "wrinklers" being available, she decided to do a good deed. She assisted the sick man to get off the bed and smoothed down the blanket. Then she undressed Dr. Fischelson and prepared some soup for him on the kerosene stove. The sun never entered Dobbe's room, but here squares of sunlight shimmered on the faded walls. The floor was painted red. Over the bed hung a picture of a man who was wearing a broad frill around his neck and had long hair. "Such an old fellow and yet he keeps his place so nice and clean," Dobbe thought approvingly. Dr. Fischelson asked for the *Ethics*, and she gave it to him disapprovingly. She was certain it was a gentile prayer book. Then she began bustling about, brought in a pail of water, swept the floor. Dr. Fischelson ate; after he had finished, he was much stronger and Dobbe asked him to read her the letter.

He read it slowly, the paper trembling in his hands. It came from New York, from Dobbe's cousin. Once more he wrote that he was about to send her a "really important letter" and a ticket to America. By now, Dobbe knew the story by heart and she helped the old man decipher her cousin's scrawl. "He's lying," Dobbe said. "He forgot about me a long time ago." In the evening, Dobbe came again. A candle in a brass holder was burning on the chair next to the bed. Reddish shadows trembled on the walls and ceiling. Dr. Fischelson sat propped up in bed, reading a book. The candle threw a golden light on his forehead which seemed as if cleft in two. A bird had flown in through the window and was perched on the table. For a moment Dobbe was frightened. This man made her think of witches, of black mirrors and corpses wandering around at night and terrifying women. Nevertheless, she took a few steps toward him and inquired, "How are you? Any better?"

"A little, thank you."

"Are you really a convert?" she asked although she wasn't quite sure what the word meant.

"Me, a convert? No, I'm a Jew like any other Jew," Dr. Fischelson answered.

The doctor's assurances made Dobbe feel more at home. She found the bottle of kerosene and lit the stove, and after that she fetched a glass of milk from her room and began cooking kasha. Dr. Fischelson continued to study the *Ethics*, but that evening he could make no sense of the theorems and proofs with their many references to axioms and definitions and other theorems. With trembling hand he raised the book to his eyes and read, "The idea of each modification of the human body does not involve adequate knowledge of the human body itself. . . . The idea of the idea of each modification of the human mind does not involve adequate knowledge of the human mind."

6

Dr. Fischelson was certain he would die any day now. He made out his will, leaving all of his books and manuscripts to the synagogue library. His clothing and furniture would go to Dobbe since she had taken care of him. But death did not come. Rather his health improved. Dobbe returned to her business in the market, but she visited the old man several times a day, prepared soup for him, left him a glass of tea, and told him news of the war. The Germans had occupied Kalish, Bendin, and Cestechow, and they were marching on Warsaw. People said that on a quiet morning one could hear the rumblings of the cannon. Dobbe reported that the casualties were heavy. "They're falling like flies," she said. "What a terrible misfortune for the women."

She couldn't explain why, but the old man's attic room attracted her. She liked to remove the gold-rimmed books from the bookcase, dust them, and then air them on the window sill. She would climb the few steps to the window and look out through the telescope. She also enjoyed talking to Dr. Fischelson. He told her about Switzerland where he had studied, of the great cities he had passed through, of the high mountains that were covered with snow even in the summer. His father had been a rabbi, he said, and before he, Dr. Fischelson, had become a student, he had attended a yeshiva. She asked him how many languages he knew and it turned out that he could speak and write Hebrew, Russian, German, and French, in addition to Yiddish. He also knew Latin. Dobbe was astonished that such an educated man should live in an attic room on Market Street. But what amazed her most of all was that although he had the title "Doctor," he couldn't write prescriptions. "Why don't you become a real doctor?" she would ask him. "I am a doctor," he would answer. "I'm just not a physician." "What kind of a doctor?" "A doctor of philosophy." Although she had no idea of what this meant, she felt it must be very important. "Oh my blessed mother," she would say, "where did you get such a brain?"

Then one evening after Dobbe had given him his crackers and his glass of tea with milk, he began questioning her about where she came from, who her parents were, and why she had not married. Dobbe was surprised. No one had ever asked her such questions. She told him her story in a quiet voice and stayed until eleven o'clock. Her father had been a porter at the kosher butcher shops. Her mother had plucked chickens in the slaughterhouse. The family had lived in a celler at No. 19 Market Street. When she had been ten, she had become a maid. The man she had worked for had been a fence who bought stolen goods from thieves on the square. Dobbe had

had a brother who had gone into the Russian army and had never returned. Her sister had married a coachman in Praga and had died in childbirth. Dobbe told of the battles between the underworld and the revolutionaries in 1905, of blind Itche and his gang and how they collected protection money from the stores, of the thugs who attacked young boys and girls out on Saturday afternoon strolls if they were not paid money for security. She also spoke of the pimps who drove about in carriages and abducted women to be sold in Buenos Aires. Dobbe swore that some men had even sought to inveigle her into a brothel, but that she had run away. She complained of a thousand evils done to her. She had been robbed; her boy friend had been stolen; a competitor had once poured a pint of kerosene into her basket of bagels; her own cousin, the shoemaker, had cheated her out of a hundred rubles before he had left for America. Dr. Fischelson listened to her attentively. He asked her questions, shook his head, and grunted.

"Well, do you believe in God?" he finally asked her.

"I don't know," she answered. "Do you?"

"Yes, I believe."

"Then why don't you go to synagogue?" she asked.

"God is everywhere," he replied. "In the synagogue. In the marketplace. In this very room. We ourselves are parts of God."

"Don't say such things," Dobbe said. "You frighten me."

She left the room and Dr. Fischelson was certain she had gone to bed. But he wondered why she had not said "good night." "I probably drove her away with my philosophy," he thought. The very next moment he heard her footsteps. She came in carrying a pile of clothing like a peddler.

"I wanted to show you these," she said. "They're my trousseau." And she began to spread out, on the chair, dresses—woolen, silk, velvet. Taking each dress up in turn, she held it to her body. She gave him an account of every item in her trousseau—underwear, shoes, stockings.

"I'm not wasteful, she said. "I'm a saver. I have enough money to go to America."

Then she was silent and her face turned brick-red. She looked at Dr. Fischelson out of the corner of her eyes, timidly, inquisitively. Dr. Fischelson's body suddenly began to shake as if he had the chills. He said, "Very nice, beautiful things." His brow furrowed and he pulled at his beard with two fingers. A sad smile appeared on his toothless mouth and his large fluttering eyes, gazing into the distance through the attic window, also smiled sadly.

7

The day that Black Dobbe came to the rabbi's chambers and announced that she was to marry Dr. Fischelson, the rabbi's wife thought she had gone mad. But the news had already reached Leizer the Tailor, and had spread to the bakery, as well as to other shops. There were those who thought that the "old maid" was very lucky; the doctor, they said, had a vast hoard of money. But there were others who took the view that he was a run-down degenerate who would give her syphilis. Although Dr. Fischelson had insisted that the wedding be a small, quiet one, a host of guests assembled in the rabbi's rooms. The baker's apprentices who generally went about barefoot, and in their underwear, with paper bags on the tops of their heads, now put on light-colored suits, straw hats, yellow shoes, gaudy ties, and they brought with them huge cakes and pans filled with cookies. They had even managed to find a bottle of vodka although liquor was forbidden in wartime. When the bride and groom entered the rabbi's chamber, a murmur arose from the crowd. The women could not believe their eyes. The woman that they saw was not the one they had known. Dobbe wore a wide-brimmed hat which was amply adorned with cherries, grapes, and plumes, and the dress that she had on was of white silk and was equipped with a train; on her feet were high-heeled shoes, gold in color, and from her thin neck hung a string of imitation pearls. Nor was this all: her fingers sparkled with rings and glittering stones. Her face was veiled. She looked almost like one of those rich brides who were married in the Vienna Hall. The bakers' apprentices whistled mockingly. As for Dr. Fischelson, he was wearing his black coat and broad-toed shoes. He was scarcely able to walk; he was leaning on Dobbe. When he saw the crowd from the doorway, he became frightened and began to retreat, but Dobbe's former employer approached him saying, "Come in, come in, bridegroom. Don't be bashful. We are all brethren now."

The ceremony proceeded according to the law. The rabbi, in a worn satin gabardine, wrote the marriage contract and then had the bride and groom touch his handkerchief as a token of agreement; the rabbi wiped the point of the pen on his skullcap. Several porters who had been called from the street to make up the quorum supported the canopy. Dr. Fischelson put on a white robe as a reminder of the day of his death and Dobbe walked around him seven times as custom required. The light from the braided candles flickered on the walls. The shadows wavered. Having poured wine into a goblet, the rabbi chanted the benedictions in a sad melody. Dobbe uttered only a single cry. As for the other women, they took out their lace handkerchiefs and stood with them in their hands, grimacing. When the baker's boys began to whisper wisecracks to each other, the rabbi put a finger to his lips and murmured, "*Eh nu oh,*" as a sign that talking was forbidden. The moment came to slip the wedding ring on the

bride's finger, but the bridegroom's hand started to tremble
and he had trouble locating Dobbe's index finger. The next
thing, according to custom, was the smashing of the glass, but
though Dr. Fischelson kicked the goblet several times, it remained unbroken. The girls lowered their heads, pinched
each other gleefully, and giggled. Finally one of the apprentices struck the goblet with his heel and it shattered. Even
the rabbi could not restrain a smile. After the ceremony the
guests drank vodka and ate cookies. Dobbe's former employer
came up to Dr. Fischelson and said, "*Mazel tov*, bridegroom.
Your luck should be as good as your wife." "Thank you,
thank you," Dr. Fischelson murmured, "but I don't look forward to any luck." He was anxious to return as quickly as
possible to his attic room. He felt a pressure in his stomach
and his chest ached. His face had become greenish. Dobbe
had suddenly become angry. She pulled back her veil and
called out to the crowd, "What are you laughing at? This
isn't a show." And without picking up the cushion-cover in
which the gifts were wrapped, she returned with her husband
to their rooms on the fifth floor.

Dr. Fischelson lay down on the freshly made bed in his
room and began reading the *Ethics*. Dobbe had gone back to
her own room. The doctor had explained to her that he was
an old man, that he was sick and without strength. He had
promised her nothing. Nevertheless she returned wearing a
silk nightgown, slippers with pompoms, and with her hair
hanging down over her shoulders. There was a smile on her
face, and she was bashful and hesitant. Dr. Fischelson trembled and the *Ethics* dropped from his hands. The candle went
out. Dobbe groped for Dr. Fischelson in the dark and kissed
his mouth. "My dear husband," she whispered to him, "*Mazel
tov*."

What happened that night could be called a miracle. If Dr.

Fischelson hadn't been convinced that every occurrence is in accordance with the laws of nature, he would have thought that Black Dobbe had bewitched him. Powers long dormant awakened in him. Although he had had only a sip of the benediction wine, he was as if intoxicated. He kissed Dobbe and spoke to her of love. Long forgotten quotations from Klopfstock, Lessing, Goethe, rose to his lips. The pressures and aches stopped. He embraced Dobbe, pressed her to himself, was again a man as in his youth. Dobbe was faint with delight; crying, she murmured things to him in a Warsaw slang which he did not understand. Later, Dr. Fischelson slipped off into the deep sleep young men know. He dreamed that he was in Switzerland and that he was climbing mountains—running, falling, flying. At dawn he opened his eyes; it seemed to him that someone had blown into his ears. Dobbe was snoring. Dr. Fischelson quietly got out of bed. In his long nightshirt he approached the window, walked up the steps and looked out in wonder. Market Street was asleep, breathing with a deep stillness. The gas lamps were flickering. The black shutters on the stores were fastened with iron bars. A cool breeze was blowing. Dr. Fischelson looked up at the sky. The black arch was thickly sown with stars—there were green, red, yellow, blue stars; there were large ones and small ones, winking and steady ones. There were those that were clustered in dense groups and those that were alone. In the higher sphere, apparently, little notice was taken of the fact that a certain Dr. Fischelson had in his declining days married someone called Black Dobbe. Seen from above even the Great War was nothing but a temporary play of the modes. The myriads of fixed stars continued to travel their destined courses in unbounded space. The comets, planets, satellites, asteroids kept circling these shining centers. Worlds were born and died in cosmic upheavals. In the chaos of nebulae, primeval matter was being formed. Now and again a star tore loose, and swept across the sky, leaving behind it a fiery streak. It was the month of August when there are showers of meteors. Yes, the divine substance was extended and had neither beginning nor end; it was absolute, indivisible, eternal, without duration, infinite in its attributes. Its waves and bubbles danced in the universal cauldron, seething with change, following the unbroken chain of causes and effects, and he, Dr. Fischelson, with his unavoidable fate, was part of this. The doctor closed his eyelids and allowed the breeze to cool the sweat on his forehead and stir the hair of his beard. He breathed deeply of the midnight air, supported his shaky hands on the window sill and murmured, "Divine Spinoza, forgive me. I have become a fool."

Translated by
Martha Glicklich and
Cecil Hemley

The
Black
Wedding

Aaron Naphtali, Rabbi of Tzivkev, had lost three-fourths of his followers. There was talk in the rabbinical courts that Rabbi Aaron Naphtali alone had been responsible for driving away his Chassidim. A rabbinical court must be vigilant, more adherents must be acquired. One has to find devices so that the following will not diminish. But Rabbi Aaron Naphtali was apathetic. The study house was old and toadstools grew unmolested on the walls. The ritual bath fell to ruin. The beadles were tottering old men, deaf and half-blind. The rabbi passed his time practicing miracle-working cabala.

It was said that Rabbi Aaron Naphtali wanted to imitate the feats of the ancient ones, to tap wine from the wall and create pigeons through combinations of holy names. It was even said that he molded a golem secretly in his attic. Moreover, Rabbi Naphtali had no son to succeed him, only one daughter named Hindele. Who would be eager to follow a rabbi under these circumstances? His enemies contended that Rabbi Aaron Naphtali was sunk in melancholy, as were his wife and Hindele. The latter, at fifteen, was already reading esoteric books and periodically went into seclusion like the holy men. It was rumored that Hindele wore a fringed garment underneath her dress like that worn by her saintly grandmother after whom she had been named.

Rabbi Aaron Naphtali had strange habits. He shut himself in his chamber for days and would not come out to welcome visitors. When he prayed, he put on two pairs of phylacteries at once. On Friday afternoons, he read the prescribed section of the Pentateuch—not from a book but from the parchment scroll itself. The rabbi had learned to form letters with the penmanship of the ancient scribes, and he used this script for writing amulets. A little bag containing one of these amulets hung from the neck of each of his followers. It was known that the rabbi warred constantly with the evil ones. His grandfather, the old Rabbi of Tzivkev, had exorcised a dybbuk from a young girl and the evil spirits had revenged themselves upon the grandson. They had not been able to bring harm to the old man because he had been blessed by the Saint of Kozhenitz. His son, Rabbi Hirsch, Rabbi Aaron Naphtali's father, died young. The grandson, Rabbi Aaron Naphtali, had to contend with the vengeful devils all his life. He lit a candle, they extinguished it. He placed a volume on the bookshelf, they knocked it off. When he undressed in the ritual bath, they hid his silk coat and his fringed garment.

Often, sounds of laughter and wailing seemed to come from the rabbi's chimney. There was a rustling behind the stove. Steps were heard on the roof. Doors opened by themselves. The stairs would screech although nobody had stepped on them. Once the rabbi laid his pen on the table and it sailed out through the open window as if carried by an unseen hand. The rabbi's hair turned white at forty. His back was bent, his hands and feet trembled like those of an ancient man. Hindele often suffered attacks of yawning; red flushes spread over her face, her throat ached, there was a buzzing in her ears. At such times incantations had to be made to drive away the evil eye.

The rabbi used to say, "They will not leave me in peace, not even for a moment." And he stamped his foot and asked the beadle to give him his grandfather's cane. He rapped it against each corner of the room and cried out, "You will not work your evil tricks on me!"

But the black hosts gained ascendency just the same. One autumn day the rabbi became ill with erysipelas and it was soon apparent that he would not recover from his sickness. A doctor was sent for from a nearby town, but on the way the axle of his coach broke and he could not complete the journey. A second physician was called for, but a wheel of his carriage came loose and rolled into a ditch, and the horse sprained his leg. The rabbi's wife went to the memorial chapel of her husband's deceased grandfather to pray, but the vindictive demons tore her bonnet from her head. The rabbi lay in bed with a swollen face and a shrunken beard, and for two days he did not speak a word. Quite suddenly he opened an eye and cried out, "They have won!"

Hindele, who would not leave her father's bed, wrung her hands and began to wail in despair, "Father, what's to become of me?"

The rabbi's beard trembled. "You must keep silent if you are to be spared."

There was a great funeral. Rabbis had come from half of Poland. The women predicted that the rabbi's widow would not last much longer. She was white as a corpse. She hadn't enough strength in her feet to follow the hearse and two women had to support her. At the burial she tried to throw herself into the grave and they could barely restrain her. All through the Seven Days of Mourning, she ate nothing. They tried to force a spoon of chicken broth into her mouth, but she was unable to swallow it. When the Thirty Days of Mourning had passed, the rabbi's wife still had not left her bed. Physicians were brought to her but to no avail. She herself foresaw the day of her death and she foretold it to the minute. After her funeral, the rabbi's disciples began to look around for a young man for Hindele. They had tried to find a match for her even before her father's death, but her father had been difficult to please. The son-in-law would eventually have to take the rabbi's place and who was worthy to sit in the Tzivkev rabbinical chair? Whenever the rabbi finally gave his approval, his wife found fault with the young man. Besides, Hindele was known to be sick, to keep too many fast days and to fall into a swoon when things did not go her way. Nor was she attractive. She was short, frail, had a large head, a skinny neck, and flat breasts. Her hair was bushy. There was an insane look in her black eyes. However, since Hindele's dowry was a following of thousands of Chassidim, a candidate was found, Reb Simon, son of the Yampol Rabbi. His older brother having died, Reb Simon would become Rabbi of Yampol after his father's death. Yampol and Tzivkev had much in common. If they were to unite, the glory of former times would return. True, Reb Simon was a divorced man with five children. But as Hindele was an orphan, who would protest? The Tzivkev Chassidim had one stipulation—that after his father's death, Reb Simon should reside in Tzivkev.

Both Tzivkev and Yampol were anxious to bring the union about. Immediately after the marriage contract was written, wedding preparations were begun, because the Tzivkev rabbinical chair had to be filled. Hindele had not yet seen her husband-to-be. She was told that he was a widower, and nothing was said about the five children. The wedding was a noisy one. Chassidim came from all parts of Poland. The followers of the Yampol court and those of the Tzivkev court began to address one another by the familiar "thou." The inns were full. The innkeeper brought straw mattresses down from the attic and put them out in corridors, granaries, and tool sheds, to accommodate the large crowd. Those who opposed the match foretold that Yampol would engulf Tzivkev. The Chassidim of Yampol were known for their crudeness. When they played, they became boisterous. They drank long draughts of brandy from tin mugs and became drunk. When they danced, the floors heaved under them. When an adversary of Yampol spoke harshly of their rabbi, he was beaten. There was a custom in Yampol that when the wife of a young man gave birth to a girl, the father was placed on a table and lashed thirty-nine times with a strap.

Old women came to Hindele to warn her that it would not be easy to be a daughter-in-law in the Yampol court. Her future mother-in-law, an old woman, was known for her wickedness. Reb Simon and his younger brothers had wild ways. The mother had chosen large women for her sons and the frail Hindele would not please her. Reb Simon's mother had consented to the match only because of Yampol's ambitions regarding Tzivkev.

From the time that the marriage negotiations started until the wedding, Hindele did not stop crying. She cried at the celebration of the writing of the marriage contract, she cried when the tailors fitted her trousseau, she cried when she was led to the ritual bath. There she was ashamed to undress for the immersion before the attendants and the other women, and they had to tear off her stays and her underpants. She would not let them remove from her neck the little bag which contained an amber charm and the tooth of a wolf. She was afraid to immerse herself in the water. The two attendants who led her into the bath, held her tightly by her wrists and she trembled like the sacrificial chicken the day before Yom Kippur. When Reb Simon lifted the veil from Hindele's face after the wedding, she saw him for the first time. He was a tall man with a broad fur hat, a pitch-black disheveled beard, wild eyes, a broad nose, thick lips, and a long moustache. He gazed at her like an animal. He breathed noisily and smelled of perspiration. Clusters of hair grew out of his nostrils and ears. His hands, too, had a growth of hair as thick as fur. The moment Hindele saw him she knew what she had suspected long before —that her bridegroom was a demon and that the wedding was nothing but black magic, a satanic hoax. She wanted to call out "Hear, O Israel" but she remembered her father's deathbed admonition to keep silent. How strange that the moment Hindele understood that her husband was an evil spirit, she could immediately discern what was true and what was false. Although she saw herself sitting in her mother's living room, she knew she was really in a forest. It appeared to be light, but she knew it was dark. She was surrounded by Chassidim with fur hats and satin gabardines, as well as by women who wore silk bonnets and velvet capes, but she knew it was all imaginary and that the fancy garments hid heads grown with elf-locks, goose-feet, unhuman navels, long snouts. The sashes of the young men were snakes in reality, their sable hats were actually hedgehogs, their beards clusters of worms. The men spoke Yiddish and sang familiar songs, but the noise they made was really the bellowing of oxen, the hissing of vipers, the howling of wolves. The musicians had tails, and horns grew from their heads. The maids who attended Hindele had canine paws, hoofs of calves, snouts of pigs. The wedding jester was all beard and tongue. The so-called relatives on the groom's side were lions, bears, boars. It was raining in the forest and a wind was blowing. It thundered and flashed lightning. Alas, this was not a human wedding, but a Black Wedding. Hindele knew, from reading holy books, that demons sometimes married human virgins whom they later carried away behind the black mountains to cohabit with them and sire their children. There was only one thing to do in such a case—not to comply with them, never willingly submit to them, to let them get everything by force as one kind word spoken to Satan is equivalent to sacrificing to the idols. Hindele remembered the story of Joseph De La Rinah and the misfortune that befell him when he felt sorry for the evil one and gave him a pinch of tobacco.

2

Hindele did not want to march to the wedding canopy, and she planted her feet stubbornly on the floor, but the bridesmaids dragged her. They half-pulled her, half-carried her. Imps in the images of girls held the candles and formed an aisle for her. The canopy was a braid of reptiles. The rabbi who performed the ceremony was under contract to Samael. Hindele submitted to nothing. She refused to hold out her finger for the ring and had to be forced to do so. She would not drink from the goblet and they poured some wine into her mouth. Hobgoblins performed all the wedding rites. The evil spirit who appeared in the likeness of Reb Simon was wearing a white robe. He stepped on the bride's foot with his hoof so that he might rule over her. Then he smashed the wine glass. After the ceremony, a witch danced toward the bride carrying a braided bread. Presently the bride and groom were served the so-called soup, but Hindele spat everything into her handkerchief. The musicians played a Kossack, an Angry Dance, a Scissors Dance and a Water Dance. But their webbed roosters' feet peeped out from under their robes. The wedding hall was nothing but a forest swamp, full of frogs, mooncalves, monsters, each with his ticks and grimaces. The Chassidim presented the couple with assorted gifts, but these were devices to ensnare Hindele in the net of evil. The wedding jester recited sad poems and funny poems, but his voice was that of a parrot.

They called Hindele to dance the Good-Luck dance, but she did not want to get up, knowing it was actually a Bad-Luck dance. They urged her, pushed her, pinched her. Little imps stuck pins into her thighs. In the middle of the dance, two she-demons grabbed her by the arms and carried her away into a bedroom which was actually a dark cave full of thistles, scavengers, and rubbish. While these females whispered to her the duties of a bride, they spat in her ear. Then she was thrown upon a heap of mud which was supposed to be linen. For a long while, Hindele lay in that cave, surrounded by darkness, poison weeds and lice. So great was her anxiety that she couldn't even pray. Then the devil to whom she was espoused entered. He assailed her with cruelty, tore off her clothes, martyred her, abused her, shamed her. She wanted to scream for help but she restrained herself knowing that if she uttered a sound she would be lost forever.

All night long Hindele felt herself lying in blood and pus. The one who had raped her snored, coughed, hissed like an adder. Before dawn a group of hags ran into the room, pulled the sheet from under her, inspected it, sniffed it, began to dance. That night never ended. True, the sun rose. It was not really the sun, though, but a bloody sphere which somebody hung in the sky. Women came to coax the bride with smooth talk and cunning but Hindele did not pay any attention to their babble. They spat at her, flattered her, said incantations, but she did not answer them. Later a doctor was brought to her, but Hindele saw that he was a horned buck. No, the black powers could not rule her, and Hindele kept on spiting them. Whatever they bade her do, she did the opposite. She threw the soup and marchpane into the slop can. She dumped the chickens and squab which they baked for her into the outhouse. She found a page of a psalter in the mossy forest and she recited psalms furtively. She also remembered a few passages of the Torah and of the prophets. She acquired more and more courage to pray to God-Almighty to save her. She mentioned the names of holy angels as well those of her illustrious ancestors like the Baal Shem, Rabbi Leib Sarah's, Rabbi Pinchos Korzer and the like.

Strange, that although she was only one and the others were multitudes, they could not overcome her. The one who was disguised as her husband tried to bribe her with sweet-talk and gifts, but she did not satisfy him. He came to her but she turned away from him. He kissed her with his wet lips and petted her with clammy fingers, but she did not let him have her. He forced himself on her, but she tore at his beard, pulled at his sidelocks, scratched his forehead. He ran away from her bloody. It became clear to Hindele that her power was not of this world. Her father was interceding for her. He came to her in his shroud and comforted her. Her mother revealed herself to her and gave her advice. True, the earth was full of evil spirits, but up above angels were hovering. Sometimes Hindele heard the angel Gabriel fighting and fencing with

Satan. Bevies of black dogs and crows came to help him, but the saints drove them away with their palm leaves and hosannahs. The barking and the crowing were drowned out by the song which Hindele's grandfather used to sing Saturday evenings and which was called "The Sons of the Mansion."

But horror of horrors, Hindele became pregnant. A devil grew inside her. She could see him through her own belly as through a cobweb: half-frog, half-ape, with eyes of a calf and scales of a fish. He ate her flesh, sucked her blood, scratched her with his claws, bit her with his pointed teeth. He was already chattering, calling her mother, cursing with vile language. She had to get rid of him, stop his gnawing at her liver. Nor was she able to bear his blasphemy and mockery. Besides, he urinated in her and defiled her with his excrement. Miscarriage was the only way out, but how bring it on? Hindele struck her stomach with her fist. She jumped, threw herself down, crawled, all to get rid of that devil's bastard, but to no avail. He grew quickly and showed inhuman strength, pushed and tore at her insides. His skull was of copper, his mouth of iron. He had capricious urges. He told her to eat lime from the wall, the shell of an egg, all kinds of garbage. And if she refused, he squeezed her gall bladder. He stank like a skunk and Hindele fainted from the stench. In her swoon, a giant appeared to her with one eye in his forehead. He talked to her from a hollowed tree saying, "Give yourself up, Hindele, you are one of us."

"No, never."

"We will take revenge."

He flogged her with a fiery rod and yelled abuses. Her head became as heavy as a millstone from fear. The fingers of her hands became big and hard like rolling pins. Her mouth puckered as from eating unripe fruit. Her ears felt as if they were full of water. Hindele was not free any more. The hosts rolled

ıer in muck, mire, slime. They immersed her in baths of pitch.
They flayed her skin. They pulled the nipples of her breasts
with pliers. They tortured her ceaselessly but she remained
mute. Since the males could not persuade her, the female
devils attacked her. They laughed with abandon, they braided
their hair around her, choked her, tickled her, and pinched
her. One giggled, another cried, another wiggled like a whore.
Hindele's belly was big and hard as a drum and Belial sat in
her womb. He pushed with elbows and pressed with his skull.
Hindele lay in labor. One she-devil was a mid-wife and the
other an aide. They had hung all kinds of charms over her
canopied bed and they put a knife and a Book of Creation
under her pillow, the way the evil ones imitate the humans in
all manners. Hindele was in her birth throes, but she remembered that she was not allowed to groan. One sigh and she
would be lost. She must restrain herself in the name of her
holy forbears.

Suddenly the black one inside her pushed with all his might.
A piercing scream tore itself from Hindele's throat and she
was swallowed in darkness. Bells were ringing as on a gentile
holiday. A hellish fire flared up. It was as red as blood, as
scarlet as leprosy. The earth opened like in the time of Korah,
and Hindele's canopied bed began to sink into the abyss. Hindele had lost everything, this world and the world to come. In
the distance she heard the crying of women, the clapping of
hands, blessings and good wishes, while she flew straight into
the castle of Asmodeus where Lilith, Namah, Machlath, Hur-
mizah rule.

In Tzivkev and in the neighborhood the tidings spread that
Hindele had given birth to a male child by Reb Simon of
Yampol. The mother had died in childbirth.

Translated by Martha Glicklich

The
Man
Who
Came
Back

You may not believe it but there are people in the world who were called back. I myself knew such a one, in our town of Turbin, a rich man. He was taken with a mortal illness, the doctors said a lump of fat had formed under his heart, God forbid it should happen to any of us. He made a journey to the hot springs, to draw off the fat, but it didn't help. His name was Alter, and his wife's name was Shifra Leah; I can see them both, as if they were standing right before my eyes.

She was lean as a stick, all skin and bones, and black as a spade; he was short and fair, with a round paunch and a small round beard. A rich man's wife, but she wore a pair of broken-down clodhoppers and a shawl thrown over her head, and was forever looking out for bargains. When she heard of a village where one could pick up cheap a measure of corn or a pot of buckwheat, she would go all the way on foot and haggle there with the peasant until he let her have it for next to nothing. I beg her pardon—but the family she came from was scum. He was a lumber merchant, a partner in the sawmill; half the town bought their lumber from him. Unlike his wife, he was fond of good living, dressing like a count, always in a shortcoat and fine leather boots. You could count each hair in his beard, it was so carefully combed and brushed.

He liked a good meal too. His old woman stinted on everything for herself—but for him no delicacy was too dear. Because he favored rich broths, with circlets of fat floating on top, she bullied the butcher, demanding fat meat, with a marrow bone thrown in, for her husband's broth with the gold coins in it, as she explained. In my time, when people got married they loved each other; who ever thought of divorce? But this Shifra Leah was so wrapped up in her Alter that people laughed in their fists. My husband this, and my husband that; heaven and earth and Alter. They had no children, and it's well known that when a woman is childless she turns all her love on her husband. The doctor said he was to blame, but who can be sure about such things?

Well, to make the story short. The man took sick and it looked bad. The biggest doctors came to see him—it didn't help; he lay in bed and sank from day to day. He still ate well, she feeding him roast pigeons and marzipans and all sorts of other delicacies, but his strength was ebbing away. One day I came to bring him a prayer book that my father—rest in peace—had sent over to him. There he lay on the sofa in a green dressing gown and white socks, a handsome figure.

He looked healthy, except that his paunch was blown up like a drum, and when he spoke he puffed and he panted. He took the prayer book from me, and gave me a cookie together with a pinch on the cheek.

A day or two later the news was that Alter was dying. The menfolk gathered; the burial society waited at the door. Well, listen to what happened. When she saw that Alter was at his final gasp, Shifra Leah ran for the doctor. But by the time she got back with the doctor in tow, there was Leizer Godl, the elder of the burial society, holding a feather to her Alter's nostrils. It was all over, they were ready to lift him off the bed, as the custom is. The instant Shifra Leah took it in, she flew into a frenzy; God help us, her screaming and wailing could be heard at the edge of town. "Beasts, murderers, thugs! Out of my house! He'll live! He'll live!" She seized a broom and began to lay about her—everybody thought she had gone out of her mind. She knelt by the corpse: "Don't leave me! Take me with you!" and ranting and raving, she shook and jostled him with lamentations louder than those you'd hear on Yom Kippur.

You know you are not allowed to shake a corpse, and they tried to restrain her, but she threw herself prone on the dead man and screeched into his ear: "Alter, wake up! Alter! Alter!" A living man couldn't have stood it—his eardrums would have burst. They were just making a move to pull her away when suddenly the corpse stirred and let out a deep sigh. She had called him back. You should know that when a person dies his soul does not go up to heaven at once. It flutters at the nostrils and longs to enter the body again, it's so used to being there. If someone screams and carries on, it may take fright and fly back in, but it seldom remains long, because it cannot stay inside a body ruined by disease. But once in a great while it does, and when that happens, you have a person who was called back.

Oh, it's forbidden. When the time comes for a man to die, he should die. Besides, one who has been called back is not like other men. He wanders about, as the saying goes, between worlds; he is here, and yet he isn't here; he would be better off in the grave. Still, the man breathes and eats. He can even live with his wife. Only one thing, he casts no shadow. They say there was a man once in Lublin who had been called back. He sat all day in the prayer house and never said a word, for twelve years; he did not even recite the Psalms. When he died at last, all that was left of him was a sack of bones. He had been rotting all those years and his flesh had turned to dust. Not much was left to bury.

Alter's case was different. He immediately began to recover, talking and wisecracking as if nothing had happened. His belly shrank, and the doctor said that the fat was gone from his heart. All Turbin was agog, people even coming from other towns to get a look at him. There was muttering that the burial society put living men into the ground; for if it was possible to call Alter back, then why not others? Perhaps others were also merely cataleptic?

Shifra Leah soon drove everyone away, she allowed no one to enter her house, not even the doctor. She kept the door locked and the curtains drawn, while she tended and watched over her Alter. A neighbor reported he was already sitting up, taking food and drink, and even looking into his account books.

Well, my dear people, it wasn't a month before he showed up at the market place, with his cane and his pampered beard and his shiny boots. Folks greeted him, gathering round and wishing him health, and he answered, "So you thought you were rid of me, eh? Not so soon! Plenty of water will yet run under the bridge before I go." People asked. "What happened after you stopped breathing?" And he said: "I ate of the Leviathan and dipped it in mustard." He was always ready with the usual wisecrack. It was said that the Rabbi summoned him and they were locked up together in the judgment chamber. But no one ever knew what talk passed between them.

Anyhow, it was Alter, only now he had a nickname: the One Who Was Called Back. He was soon back at his trading in boards and logs. The gravediggers' brethren went about with long faces; they had hoped to pick up a juicy bone at the funeral. At first people were a bit afraid of him. But what was there to be afraid of? He was the same merchant. His illness had cost quite a sum, but he had enough left over. On Saturdays he came to prayer, he was called to the reading, offered thanksgiving. He was also expected to contribute to the poorhouse and to give a feast for the townsfolk, but Alter played dumb. As for his wife, Shifra Leah, she strutted like a peacock, looking down her nose at everyone. A small matter?—she had brought a dead man back to life! Ours was quite a big town. Other men fell ill and other wives tried to call them back, but no one had a mouth like hers. If everybody could be recalled, the Angel of Death would have to put aside his sword.

Well, things took a turn. Alter had a partner in his mill, Falik Weingarten; in those days people were not called by their family names, but Falik was a real aristocrat. One day Falik came to the rabbi with a queer story: Alter, his partner, had become a swindler. He stole money from the partnership, he pulled all sorts of tricks and was trying to push him, Falik, out of the business. The rabbi couldn't believe it: when a man had gone through such an ordeal, would he suddenly become a crook? It didn't stand to reason. But Falik was not one to make up tales, and they sent for Alter. He went into a song and dance—black was white, and white was black. He dug up ancient bills and accounts all the way back from King Sobieski's time. He showed bundles of claims. To hear him tell it, his partner still owed *him* a small fortune, and what's more, he threatened to start court action.

The townspeople tried arguing with Alter: "You've done business together for so many years, what's gone wrong all of a sudden?" But Alter was a changed man—he seemed to be looking for quarrels. He started litigation, and the case dragged on and cost a fortune. Falik took it so to heart that he died. Who won, I don't remember, I only remember that the sawmill went over to creditors, and Falik's widow was left penniless. The rabbi rebuked Alter: "Is this how you thank the Lord for putting you back on your feet and raising you from the dead?" Alter's answer was no better than the barking of a dog: "It was not God who did it. It was Shifra Leah." And he said further: "There is no other world. I was good and dead, and I can tell you there is nothing—no hell and no paradise." The rabbi decided he had lost his mind—perhaps so. But wait, hear the rest.

His wife, Shifra Leah, was the worst kind of draggletail—people said that a pile of dirt sprang up wherever she stood. Suddenly Alter began to demand that she should dress up, deck herself out. "A wife's place," he said, "is not only under the quilt. I want you to go promenading with me on Lublin Street." The whole town buzzed. Shifra Leah ordered a new cotton dress made, and on Sabbath afternoon, after the *cholent* meal, there were Alter and his wife Shifra Leah on the promenade, along with the tailors' helpers and shoemakers' apprentices. It was a sight—whoever had the use of his limbs ran out to look.

Alter even trimmed his beard. He became—what's it called? an atheist. Nowadays, they're all over the place; every fool puts on a short jacket and shaves his chin. But in my time we had only one atheist—the apothecary. People began to say that when Shifra Leah called Alter back with her screams, the soul of a stranger had entered his body. Souls come flying when someone dies, souls of kinsfolk and others, and, who knows, evil souls too, ready to take possession. Reb Arieh Vishnitzer, a pupil of the old rabbi, declared that Alter was no longer Alter. True, it was not the same Alter. He talked differently, he laughed differently, he looked at you differently. His eyes were like a hawk's, and when he stared at a woman, it was enough to make a shudder pass through you. He hung out with the musicians and all sorts of riffraff. At first his wife said amen to everything, whatever Alter said or did was all right with her. I beg her pardon, but she was a cow. But then a certain female arrived in our town, from Warsaw. She came to visit her sister, who wasn't much to boast of and whose husband was a barber; on market days he shaved the peasants, and he also bled them. You can expect anything from such people: he had a cage full of birds, twittering all day long, and he also had a dog. His own wife had never shaved off her hair, and the sister from Warsaw was a divorcee—no one knew who her husband was. She came among us bedecked and bejeweled, but who ever looked at her twice? A broomstick can be dressed up too. She showed the women the long stockings she was wearing, hooked, if you'll pardon the word, to her drawers. It was not hard to guess that she had come to trap some man. And who do you think fell into her clutches? Alter. When the townsfolk heard that Alter was running around with the barber's sister-in-law, they couldn't believe it; even coopers and skinners, in those days, had some regard for decency. But Alter was a changed man. God forbid, he had lost all shame. He strolled with the divorcee in the market place, and people looked from all the windows, shaking their heads and spitting in disgust. He went with her to the tavern, for all the world like a peasant with his woman. There they sat, in the middle of the week, guzzling wine.

When Shifra Leah heard it, she knew she was in trouble. She came running to the tavern, but her husband turned on her with the vilest abuse. The newcomer, the slut, also jeered at her and taunted her. Shifra Leah tried to appeal to him: "Have you no shame before the world?" "The world can kiss what we sit on," says he. Shifra Leah cried to the other one: "He is my husband!" "Mine, also," answers she. The tavern keeper tried to put a word in, but Alter and the slut belabored him too; a woman depraved is worse than the worst man. She opened such a mouth that she shocked even the tavern keeper. People said she grabbed a pitcher and threw it at him. Turbin is not Warsaw. The town was in an uproar. The rabbi sent the sexton to summon Alter to him, but Alter refused to come. Then the community threatened him with the three letters of excommunicaion. It didn't help, he had connections with the authorities and defied one and all.

After a couple of weeks, the divorced slut left town, and people thought things would quiet down. Before the week was out, the man who was called back from the dead came to his wife with a tale. He had an opportunity, he said, to buy a wood in Wolhynia, an unusual bargain, and he must leave at once. He collected all his money, and told Shifra Leah that he had to pawn her jewelry too. He bought a barouche and two horses. People suspected he was up to something crooked and warned his wife, but the faith she had in him, he could have been a wonder rabbi. She packed his suits and underwear; roasted chickens and prepared jams for him for the journey. Just before he set off he handed her a small box: "In here," he said, "are three promissory notes. On Thursday, eight days from today, take the notes to the rabbi. The money was left with him." He spun her a story, and she swallowed it. Then he was off.

Thursday, eight days later, she opened the box and discovered a writ of divorce. She let out a scream and fell into a faint. When she came to, she ran to the Rabbi, but he took one look at the paper and said: "There is nothing to be done. A writ of divorce can be hung on your doorknob, or it can be slipped under your door." You can imagine what went on in Turbin that day. Shifra Leah pulled at her cheeks, screaming: "Why didn't I let him croak? May he drop dead wherever he is!" He had cleaned her out—even her holiday kerchief was gone. The house was there still, but it was mortgaged to the barber. In olden times, runners would have been sent after such a shameless betrayer. The Jews once had power and authority, and there was a pillory in the synagogue court, to which a wretch would have been bound. But among our Gentile officials a Jew was of small consequence—they couldn't care less. Besides, Alter had taken care to bribe his way.

Well, Shifra Leah took sick, climbed into her bed and refused to get up. She would take nothing to eat, and kept cursing him with the deadliest curses. Then suddenly she started beating her breast and lamenting: "It's all my fault. I did not do enough to please him." She wept and she laughed —she was like one possessed by an evil spirit. The barber, who claimed now to be the legal owner of the house, wanted to throw her out of her home, but the community wouldn't let him, and she remained, in a room in the attic.

In time, after a few weeks, she recovered, and she went out with a peddler's pack, like a man, to trade among the peasants. She turned out to be a good hand at buying and selling; soon the matchmakers were approaching her with proposals of marriage. She wouldn't hear of it; all she talked about, she bent your ear if you would listen, was her Alter. "You wait," she said, "he'll come back to me. The other one didn't want him, she was after his money. She'll clean him out and leave him flat." "And you'd take such riffraff back again?" folks asked her, to which she answered: "Only let him come. I'll wash his feet and drink the water." She still had a trunk left and she collected linens and woolens, like a bride. "This will be my dowry for when he returns," she boasted. "I'll marry him again." Nowadays you call it infatuation; we called it plumb crazy.

Whenever people came from the big cities, she ran to them: "Have you run into my Alter?" But no one had seen him: it was rumored that he had become an apostate. Some said he had married a she-demon. Such things happen. The years went by, and people began to think that Alter would never be heard of again.

One Sabbath afternoon, when Shifra Leah was dozing on her bench-bed (she had never learned to read the Holy Book, as the women do), the door opened and in stepped a soldier. He took out a sheet of paper. "Are you Shifra Leah, the wife of the scoundrel Alter?" She turned white as chalk; she could not understand Russian, and an interpreter was brought in. Well, Alter was in prison, a serious crime, because he was sentenced to life. He was being kept in the Lublin jail, and he had managed to bribe the soldier, who was going home on leave, to bring a letter to Shifra Leah. Who knows where Alter got the money to bribe in prison? He must have hidden it somewhere in his cot when he was first brought in. Those who read the letter said that it would have melted a stone; he wrote to his former wife: "Shifra Leah, I have sinned against you. Save me! Save me! I am going under. Death is better than such a life." The other one, the slut, the barber's sister-in-law, had stripped him of everything and left him only his shirt. She probably informed on him too.

The town buzzed with excitement. But what could anyone do to help him?—you may be sure he was not put away for reading the Holy Book. But Shifra Leah ran to all the important people in town. "It is not his fault," she cried, "it comes from his sickness." She was not yet sobered up, the old cow. People asked her: "What do you need that lecher for?" She would not allow a speck to fall on his name. She sold everything, even her Passover dishes; she borrowed money, she got what she could from high and low. Then she took herself off to Lublin, and there she must have turned heaven and earth, for she finally got him freed from jail.

Back she came to Turbin with him, and young and old ran out to meet them. When he stepped out from the covered wagon, you couldn't recognize him: without a beard, only a thick mustache, and he had on a short caftan and high boots. It was a *goy*, not Alter. On looking closer, you saw that it was Alter after all: the same walk, the same swagger. He called each man by his name and asked about all kinds of detail. He wisecracked and said things to make the women blush. They asked him: "Where's your beard?" He answers: "I pawned it with a moneylender." They asked him: "How does a Jew take up such ways?" He replies: "Are you any better? Everybody is a thief." On the spot he gave a recital of everybody's secret sins. It was plain to see that he was in the hands of the Evil One.

Shifra Leah tried to make excuses for him and to restrain him; she fluttered over him like a mother hen. She forgot that they were divorced and wanted to take him home, but the rabbi sent word that they must not live under the same roof; it was even wrong for her, he said, to have traveled with him in the same wagon. Alter might scoff at Jewishness, but the law still remained. The women took a hand. The pair were separated for twelve days, while she took the prescribed ablutions, and then they were led under the wedding canopy. A bride must go to the ritual bath even if she is taking back her own husband.

Well, a week after the wedding he started thieving. On market days he was among the carts, picking pockets. He went off to the villages to steal horses. He was no longer plump, but lean as a hound. He clambered over roofs, forced locks, broke open stable doors. He was strong as iron and nimble as a devil. The peasants got together and posted a watch with dogs and lanterns. Shifra Leah was ashamed to show her face and kept her window shuttered; you can imagine what must have gone on between man and wife. Soon Alter became the leader of a band of roughnecks. He guzzled at the tavern with them, and they sang a Polish song in his honor; I remember the words to this day: "Our Alter is a decent sort, he hands out beer by the quart."

There is a saying: a thief will end up on the gallows.

One day, as Alter was drinking with his toughs, a squadron of Cossacks came riding up to the tavern with drawn swords. Orders had come from the governor to throw him into irons and bring him to the jail. Alter saw at once that this was the end, and he grabbed a knife; his drinking pals ran off—they left him to fight it out alone. The tavern keeper said afterwards that he fought with the strength of a demon, chopping away at the Cossacks as though they were a field of cabbages. He turned over tables and threw barrels at them; he was no longer a young man, but for a while it almost looked as though he might get the better of them all. Still, as the saying goes, one is none. The Cossacks slashed and hacked at him till there was no more blood left in his veins. Someone brought the bad news to Shifra Leah, and she came running like crazy to his side. There he lay, and she wanted to call him back again, but he said one word to her: "Enough!" Shifra Leah fell silent. The Jews ransomed his body from the officials.

I didn't see him dead. But those who did swore that he looked like an old corpse that had been dug up from the grave. Pieces were dropping from his body. The face could not be recognized, it was a shapeless pulp. It was said that when he was being cleansed for burial, an arm came off, and then a foot; I wasn't there, but why should people lie? Men who are called back rot while they are alive. He was buried in a sack outside the graveyard fence, at midnight. After his death, an epidemic struck our town, and many innocent children died. Shifra Leah, that deluded woman, put up a stone for him and went to visit his grave. What I mean to say is—it is not proper to recall the dying. If she had let him go at his appointed hour, he would have left behind a good name. And who knows how many men who were called back are out in the world today? All our misfortunes come from them.

Translated by Mirra Ginsburg

Short
Friday

In the village of Lapschitz lived a tailor named Shmul-Leibele with his wife, Shoshe. Shmul-Leibele was half tailor, half furrier, and a complete pauper. He had never mastered his trade. When filling an order for a jacket or a gaberdine, he inevitably made the garment either too short or too tight. The belt in the back would hang either too high or too low, the lapels never matched, the vent was off-center. It was said that he had once sewn a pair of trousers with the fly off to one side. Shmul-Leibele could not count the wealthy citizens among his customers. Common people brought him their shabby garments to have patched and turned, and the peasants gave him their old pelts to reverse. As is usual with bunglers, he was also slow. He would dawdle over a garment for weeks at a time. Yet despite his shortcomings, it must be said that Shmul-Leibele was an honorable man. He used only strong thread and none of his seams ever gave. If one ordered a lining from Shmul-Leibele, even one of common sack-cloth or cotton, he bought only the very best material, and thus lost most of his profit. Unlike other tailors who hoarded every last bit of remaining cloth, he returned all scraps to his customers.

Had it not been for his competent wife, Shmul-Leibele would certainly have starved to death. Shoshe helped him in whatever way she could. On Thursdays she hired herself out to wealthy families to knead dough, and on summer days went off to the forest to gather berries and mushrooms, as well as pine cones and twigs for the stove. In winter she plucked down for brides' featherbeds. She was also a better tailor than her husband, and when he began to sigh, or dally and mumble to himself, an indication that he could no longer muddle through, she would take the chalk from his hand and show him how to continue. Shoshe had no children, but it was common knowledge that it wasn't she who was barren, but rather her husband who was sterile, since all of her sisters had borne children, while his only brother was likewise childless. The townswomen repeatedly urged Shoshe to divorce him, but she turned a deaf ear, for the couple loved one another with a great love.

Shmul-Leibele was small and clumsy. His hands and feet were too large for his body, and his forehead bulged on either side as is common in simpletons. His cheeks, red as apples, were bare of whiskers, and but a few hairs sprouted from his chin. He had scarcely any neck at all; his head sat upon his shoulders like a snowman's. When he walked, he scraped his shoes along the ground so that every step could be heard far away. He hummed continuously and there was always an amiable smile on his face. Both winter and summer he wore the same caftan and sheepskin cap with earlaps. Whenever there was any need for a messenger, it was always Shmul-Leibele who was pressed into service, and however far away he was sent, he always went willingly. The wags saddled him with a variety of nicknames and made him the butt of all sorts of pranks, but he never took offense. When others scolded his tormentors, he would merely observe: "What do I care? Let them have their fun. They're only children, after all. . . ."

Sometimes he would present one or another of the mischief-makers with a piece of candy or a nut. This he did without any ulterior motive, but simply out of good-heartedness.

Shoshe towered over him by a head. In her younger days she had been considered a beauty, and in the households where she worked as a servant they spoke highly of her honesty and diligence. Many young men had vied for her hand, but she had selected Shmul-Leibele because he was quiet and because he never joined the other town boys who gathered on the Lublin road at noon Saturdays to flirt with the girls. His piety and retiring nature pleased her. Even as a girl Shoshe had taken pleasure in studying the Pentateuch, in nursing the infirm at the almshouse, in listening to the tales of the old women who sat before their houses darning stockings. She would fast on the last day of each month, the Minor Day of Atonement, and often attended the services at the women's synagogue. The other servant girls mocked her and thought her old-fashioned. Immediately following her wedding she shaved her head and fastened a kerchief firmly over her ears, never permitting a stray strand of hair from her matron's wig to show as did some of the other young women. The bath attendant praised her because she never frolicked at the ritual bath, but performed her ablutions according to the laws. She purchased only indisputably kosher meat, though it was a half-cent more per pound, and when she was in doubt about the dietary laws she sought out the rabbi's advice. More than once she had not hesitated to throw out all the food and even to smash the earthen crockery. In short, she was a capable, God-fearing woman, and more than one man envied Shmul-Leibele his jewel of a wife.

Above all of life's blessings the couple revered the Sabbath. Every Friday noon Shmul-Leibele would lay aside his tools and cease all work. He was always among the first at the ritual bath, and he immersed himself in the water four times for the four letters of the Holy Name. He also helped the beadle set the candles in the chandeliers and the candelabra. Shoshe scrimped throughout the week, but on the Sabbath she was lavish. Into the heated oven went cakes, cookies and the Sabbath loaf. In winter, she prepared puddings made of chicken's neck stuffed with dough and rendered fat. In summer she made puddings with rice or noodles, greased with chicken fat and sprinkled with sugar or cinnamon. The main dish consisted of potatoes and buckwheat, or pearl barley with beans, in the midst of which she never failed to set a marrowbone. To insure that the dish would be well cooked, she sealed the oven with loose dough. Shmul-Leibele treasured every mouthful, and at every Sabbath meal he would remark: "Ah, Shoshe love, it's food fit for a king! Nothing less than a taste of Paradise!" to which Shoshe replied, "Eat hearty. May it bring you good health."

Although Shmul-Leibele was a poor scholar, unable to memorize a chapter of the Mishnah, he was well versed in all the laws. He and his wife frequently studied *The Good Heart* in Yiddish. On half-holidays, holidays, and on each free day, he studied the Bible in Yiddish. He never missed a sermon, and though a pauper, he bought from peddlers all sorts of books of moral instructions and religious tales, which he then read together with his wife. He never wearied of reciting sacred phrases. As soon as he arose in the morning he washed his hands and began to mouth the preamble to the prayers. Then he would walk over to the study house and worship as one of the quorum. Every day he recited a few chapters of the Psalms, as well as those prayers which the less serious tended to skip over. From his father he had inherited a thick prayer book with wooden covers, which contained the rites and laws pertaining to each day of the year. Shmul-Leibele and his wife heeded each and every one of these. Often he would observe to his wife: "I shall surely end up in Gehenna, since there'll be no one on earth to say Kaddish over me." "Bite your tongue, Shmul-Leibele," she would counter, "For one, everything is possible under God. Secondly, you'll live until the Messiah comes. Thirdly, it's just possible that I will die before you and you will marry a young woman who'll bear you a dozen children." When Shoshe said this, Shmul-Leibele would shout: "God forbid! You must remain in good health. I'd rather rot in Gehenna!"

Although Shmul-Leibele and Shoshe relished every Sabbath, their greatest satisfaction came from the Sabbaths in wintertime. Since the day before the Sabbath evening was a short one, and since Shoshe was busy until late Thursday at her work, the couple usually stayed up all of Thursday night. Shoshe kneaded dough in the trough, covering it with cloth and a pillow so that it might ferment. She heated the oven with kindling-wood and dry twigs. The shutters in the room were kept closed, the door shut. The bed and bench-bed remained unmade, for at daybreak the couple would take a nap. As long as it was dark Shoshe prepared the Sabbath meal by the light of a candle. She plucked a chicken or a goose (if she had managed to come by one cheaply), soaked it, salted it and scraped the fat from it. She roasted a liver for Shmul-Leibele over the glowing coals and baked a small Sabbath loaf for him. Occasionally she would inscribe her name upon the loaf with letters of dough, and then Shmul-Leibele would tease her: "Shoshe, I am eating you up. Shoshe, I have already swallowed you." Shmul-Leibele loved warmth, and he would climb up on the oven and from there look down as his spouse cooked, baked, washed, rinsed, pounded and carved. The Sabbath loaf would turn out round and brown. Shoshe braided the loaf so swiftly that it seemed to dance before Shmul-Leibele's eyes. She bustled about efficiently with spatulas, pokers, ladles and goosewing dusters, and at times even snatched up a live coal with her bare fingers. The pots perked and bubbled. Occasionally a drop of soup would spill and the hot tin would hiss and squeal. And all the while the cricket continued its chirping. Although Shmul-Leibele had finished his supper by this time, his appetite would be whetted afresh, and Shoshe would throw him a knish, a chicken gizzard, a cookie, a plum from the plum stew or a chunk of the pot roast. At the same time she would chide him, saying that he was a glutton. When he attempted to defend himself she would cry: "Oh, the sin is upon me, I have allowed you to starve . . ."

At dawn they would both lie down in utter exhaustion. But because of their efforts Shoshe would not have to run herself ragged the following day, and she could make the benediction over the candles a quarter of an hour before sunset.

The Friday on which this story took place was the shortest Friday of the year. Outside, the snow had been falling all night and had blanketed the house up to the windows and barricaded the door. As usual, the couple had stayed up until morning, then had lain down to sleep. They had arisen later than usual, for they hadn't heard the rooster's crow, and since the windows were covered with snow and frost, the day seemed as dark as night. After whispering, "I thank Thee," Shmul-Leibele went outside with a broom and shovel to clear a path, after which he took a bucket and fetched water from the well. Then, as he had no pressing work, he decided to lay off for the whole day. He went to the study house for the morning prayers, and after breakfast wended his way to the bathhouse. Because of the cold outside, the patrons kept up an eternal plaint: "A bucket! A bucket!" and the bath attendant poured more and more water over the glowing stones so that the steam grew constantly denser. Shmul-Leibele located a scraggly willow-broom, mounted to the highest bench and whipped himself until his skin glowed red. From the bathhouse, he hurried over to the study house where the beadle had already swept and sprinkled the floor with sand. Shmul-Leibele set the candles and helped spread the tablecloths over the tables. Then he went home again and changed into his Sabbath clothes. His boots, resoled but a few days before, no longer let the wet through. Shoshe had done her washing for the week, and had given him a fresh shirt, underdrawers, a fringed garment, even a clean pair of stockings. She had already performed the benediction over the candles, and the spirit of the Sabbath emanated from every corner of the room. She was wearing her silk kerchief with the silver spangles, a yellow and gray dress, and shoes with gleaming, pointed tips. On her throat hung the chain that Shmul-Leibele's mother, peace be with her, had given her to celebrate the signing of the wedding contract. The marriage band sparkled on her index finger. The candlelight reflected in the windowpanes, and Shmul-Leibele fancied that there was a duplicate of this room outside and that another Shoshe was out there lighting the Sabbath candles. He yearned to tell his wife how full of grace she was, but there was no time for it, since it is specifically stated in the prayer book that it is fitting and proper to be among the first ten worshipers at the synagogue; as it so happened, going off to prayers he was the tenth man to arrive. After the congregation had intoned the Song of Songs, the cantor sang, "Give thanks," and "O come, let us exult." Shmul-Leibele prayed with fervor. The words were sweet upon his tongue, they seemed to fall from his lips with a life of their own, and he felt that they soared to the eastern wall, rose above the embroidered curtain of the Holy Ark, the gilded lions, and the tablets, and floated up to the ceiling with its painting of the twelve constellations. From there, the prayers surely ascended to the Throne of Glory.

2

The cantor chanted, "Come, my beloved," and Shmul-Leibele trumpeted along in accompaniment. Then came the prayers, and the men recited, "It is our duty to praise . . ." to which Shmul-Leibele added a "Lord of the Universe." Afterwards, he wished everyone a good Sabbath: the rabbi, the ritual slaughterer, the head of the community, the assistant rabbi, everyone present. The *cheder* lads shouted, "Good Sabbath, Shmul-Leibele," while they mocked him with gestures and grimaces, but Shmul-Leibele answered them all with a smile, even occasionally pinched a boy's cheek affectionately. Then he was off for home. The snow was piled high so that one could barely make out the contours of the roofs, as if the entire settlement had been immersed in white. The sky, which had hung low and overcast all day, now grew clear. From among white clouds a full moon peered down, casting a daylike brilliance over the snow. In the west, the edge of a cloud still held the glint of sunset. The stars on this Friday seemed larger and sharper, and through some miracle Lapschitz seemed to have blended with the sky. Shmul-Leibele's hut, which was situated not far from the synagogue, now hung suspended in space, as it is written: "He suspendeth the earth on nothingness." Shmul-Leibele walked slowly since, according to law, one must not hurry when coming from a holy place. Yet he longed to be home. "Who knows?" he thought. "Perhaps Shoshe has become ill? Maybe she's gone to fetch water and, God forbid, has fallen into the well? Heaven save us, what a lot of troubles can befall a man."

On the threshold he stamped his feet to shake off the snow, then opened the door and saw Shoshe. The room made him think of Paradise. The oven had been freshly whitewashed, the candles in the brass candelabras cast a Sabbath glow. The aromas coming from the sealed oven blended with the scents of the Sabbath supper. Shoshe sat on the bench-bed apparently awaiting him, her cheeks shining with the freshness of a young girl's. Shmul-Leibele wished her a happy Sabbath and she in turn wished him a good year. He began to hum, "Peace upon ye ministering angels . . ." and after he had said his farewells to the invisible angels that accompany each Jew leaving the synagogue, he recited: "The worthy woman." How well he understood the meaning of these words, for he had read them often in Yiddish, and each time reflected anew on how aptly they seemed to fit Shoshe.

Shoshe was aware that these holy sentences were being said in her honor, and thought to herself, "Here am I, a simple woman, an orphan, and yet God has chosen to bless me with a devoted husband who praises me in the holy tongue."

Both of them had eaten sparingly during the day so that they would have an appetite for the Sabbath meal. Shmul-Leibele said the benediction over the raisin wine and gave Shoshe the cup so that she might drink. Afterwards, he rinsed his fingers from a tin dipper, then she washed hers, and they both dried their hands with a single towel, each at either end. Shmul-Leibele lifted the Sabbath loaf and cut it with the bread knife, a slice for himself and one for his wife.

He immediately informed her that the loaf was just right, and she countered: "Go on, you say that every Sabbath."

"But it happens to be the truth," he replied.

Although it was hard to obtain fish during the cold weather, Shoshe had purchased three-fourths of a pound of pike from the fishmonger. She had chopped it with onions, added an egg, salt and pepper, and cooked it with carrots and parsley. It took Shmul-Leibele's breath away, and after it he had to drink a tumbler of whiskey.

When he began the table chants, Shoshe accompanied him quietly. Then came the chicken soup with noodles and tiny circlets of fat which glowed on the surface like golden ducats. Between the soup and the main course, Shmul-Leibele again sang Sabbath hymns. Since goose was cheap at this time of year, Shoshe gave Shmul-Leibele an extra leg for good measure. After the dessert, Shmul-Leibele washed for the last time and made a benediction. When he came to the words: "Let us not be in need either of the gifts of flesh and blood nor of their loans," he rolled his eyes upward and brandished his fists. He never stopped praying that he be allowed to continue to earn his own livelihood and not, God forbid, become an object of charity.

After grace, he said yet another chapter of the Mishnah, and all sorts of other prayers which were found in his large prayer book. Then he sat down to read the weekly portion of the Pentateuch twice in Hebrew and once in Aramaic. He enunciated every word and took care to make no mistake in the difficult Aramaic paragraphs of the Onkelos. When he reached the last section, he began to yawn and tears gathered in his eyes. Utter exhaustion overcame him. He could barely keep his eyes open and between one passage and the next he dozed off for a second or two. When Shoshe noticed this, she made up the bench-bed for him and prepared her own featherbed with clean sheets. Shmul-Leibele barely managed to say the retiring prayers and began to undress. When he was already lying on his bench-bed he said: "A good Sabbath, my pious wife. I am very tired . . ." and turning to the wall, he promptly began to snore.

Shoshe sat a while longer gazing at the Sabbath candles which had already begun to smoke and flicker. Before getting into bed, she placed a pitcher of water and a basin at Shmul-Leibele's bedstead so that he would not rise the following morning without water to wash with. Then she, too, lay down and fell asleep.

They had slept an hour or two or possibly three— what does it matter, actually?—when suddenly Shoshe heard Shmul-Leibele's voice. He waked her and whispered her name. She opened one eye and asked, "What is it?"

"Are you clean?" he mumbled.

She thought for a moment and replied, "Yes."

He rose and came to her. Presently he was in bed with her. A desire for her flesh had roused him. His heart pounded rapidly, the blood coursed in his veins. He felt a pressure in his loins. His urge was to mate with her immediately, but he remembered the law which admonished a man not to copulate with a woman until he had first spoken affectionately to her, and he now began to speak of his love for her and how this mating could possibly result in a male child.

"And a girl you wouldn't accept?" Shoshe chided him, and he replied, "Whatever God deigns to bestow would be welcome."

"I fear this privilege isn't mine anymore," she said with a sigh.

"Why not?" he demanded. "Our mother Sarah was far older than you."

"How can one compare oneself to Sarah? Far better you divorce me and marry another."

He interrupted her, stopping her mouth with his hand. "Were I sure that I could sire the twelve tribes of Israel with another, I still would not leave you. I cannot even imagine myself with another woman. You are the jewel of my crown."

"And what if I were to die?" she asked.

"God forbid! I would simply perish from sorrow. They would bury us both on the same day."

"Don't speak blasphemy. May you outlive my bones. You are a man. You would find somebody else. But what would I do without you?"

He wanted to answer her, but she sealed his lips with a kiss. He went to her then. He loved her body. Each time she gave herself to him, the wonder of it astonished him anew. How was it possible, he would think, that he, Shmul-Leibele, should have such a treasure all to himself? He knew the law, one dared not surrender to lust for pleasure. But somewhere in a sacred book he had read that it was permissible to kiss and embrace a wife to whom one had been wed according to the laws of Moses and Israel, and he now caressed her face, her throat and her breasts. She warned him that this was frivolity. He replied, "So I'll lie on the torture rack. The great saints also loved their wives." Nevertheless, he promised himself to attend the ritual bath the following morning, to intone Psalms and to pledge a sum to charity. Since she loved him also and enjoyed his caresses, she let him do his will.

After he had satiated his desire, he wanted to return to his own bed, but a heavy sleepiness came over him. He felt a pain in his temples. Shoshe's head ached as well. She suddenly said, "I'm afraid something is burning in the oven. Maybe I should open the flue?"

"Go on, you're imagining it," he replied. "It'll become too cold in here."

And so complete was his weariness that he fell asleep, as did she.

That night Shmul-Leibele suffered an eerie dream. He imagined that he had passed away. The burial-society brethren came by, picked him up, lit candles by his head, opened the windows, intoned the prayer to justify God's ordainment. Afterwards, they washed him on the ablution board, carried him on a stretcher to the cemetery. There they buried him as the gravedigger said Kaddish over his body.

"That's odd," he thought, "I hear nothing of Shoshe lamenting or begging forgiveness. Is it possible that she would so quickly grow unfaithful? Or has she, God forbid, been overcome by grief?"

He wanted to call her name, but he was unable to. He tried to tear free of the grave, but his limbs were powerless. All of a sudden he awoke.

"What a horrible nightmare!" he thought. "I hope I come out of it all right."

At that moment Shoshe also awoke. When he related his dream to her, she did not speak for a while. Then she said, "Woe is me. I had the very same dream."

"Really? You too?" asked Shmul-Leibele, now frightened. "This I don't like."

He tried to sit up, but he could not. It was as if he had been shorn of all his strength. He looked towards the window to see if it were day already, but there was no window visible, nor any windowpane. Darkness loomed everywhere. He cocked his ears. Usually he would be able to hear the chirping of a cricket, the scurrying of a mouse, but this time only a dead silence prevailed. He wanted to reach out to Shoshe, but his hand seemed lifeless.

"Shoshe," he said quietly, "I've grown paralyzed."

"Woe is me, so have I," she said. "I cannot move a limb."

They lay there for a long while, silently, feeling their

numbness. Then Shoshe spoke: "I fear that we are already in our graves for good."

"I'm afraid you're right," Shmul-Leibele replied in a voice that was not of the living.

"Pity me, when did it happen? How?" Shoshe asked. "After all, we went to sleep hale and hearty."

"We must have been asphyxiated by the fumes from the stove," Shmul-Leibele said.

"But I said I wanted to open the flue."

"Well, it's too late for that now."

"God have mercy upon us, what do we do now? We were still young people . . ."

"It's no use. Apparently it was fated."

"Why? We arranged a proper Sabbath. I prepared such a tasty meal. An entire chicken neck and tripe."

"We have no further need of food."

Shoshe did not immediately reply. She was trying to sense her own entrails. No, she felt no appetite. Not even for a chicken neck and tripe. She wanted to weep, but she could not.

"Shmul-Leibele, they've buried us already. It's all over."

"Yes, Shoshe, praised be the true Judge! We are in God's hands."

"Will you be able to recite the passage attributed to your name before the Angel Dumah?"

"Yes."

"It's good that we are lying side by side," she muttered.

"Yes, Shoshe," he said, recalling a verse: *Lovely and pleasant in their lives, and in their death they were not divided.*

"And what will become of our hut? You did not even leave a will."

"It will undoubtedly go to your sister."

Shoshe wished to ask something else, but she was ashamed. She was curious about the Sabbath meal. Had it been removed from the oven? Who had eaten it? But she felt that such a query would not be fitting of a corpse. She was no longer Shoshe the dough-kneader, but a pure, shrouded corpse with shards covering her eyes, a cowl over her head, and myrtle twigs between her fingers. The Angel Dumah would appear at any moment with his fiery staff, and she would have to be ready to give an account of herself.

Yes, the brief years of turmoil and temptation had come to an end. Shmul-Leibele and Shoshe had reached the true world. Man and wife grew silent. In the stillness they heard the flapping of wings, a quiet singing. An angel of God had come to guide Shmul-Leibele the tailor and his wife, Shoshe, into Paradise.

Translated by Joseph Singer
and Roger Klein

Yentl
the
Yeshiva
Boy

After her father's death, Yentl had no reason to remain in Yanev. She was all alone in the house. To be sure, lodgers were willing to move in and pay rent; and the marriage brokers flocked to her door with offers from Lublin, Tomashev, Zamosc. But Yentl didn't want to get married. Inside her, a voice repeated over and over: "No!" What becomes of a girl when the wedding's over? Right away she starts bearing and rearing. And her mother-in-law lords it over her. Yentl knew she wasn't cut out for a woman's life. She couldn't sew, she couldn't knit. She let the food burn and the milk boil over; her Sabbath pudding never turned out right, and her *challah* dough didn't rise. Yentl much preferred men's activities to women's. Her father Reb Todros, may he rest in peace, during many bedridden years had studied Torah with his daughter as if she were a son. He told Yentl to lock the doors and drape the windows, then together they pored over the Pentateuch, the Mishnah, the Gemara, and the Commentaries. She had proved so apt a pupil that her father used to say:

"Yentl—you have the soul of a man."

"So why was I born a woman?"

"Even heaven makes mistakes."

There was no doubt about it, Yentl was unlike any of the girls in Yanev—tall, thin, bony, with small breasts and narrow hips. On Sabbath afternoons, when her father slept, she would dress up in his trousers, his fringed garment, his silk coat, his skullcap, his velvet hat, and study her reflection in the mirror. She looked like a dark, handsome young man. There was even a slight down on her upper lip. Only her thick braids showed her womanhood—and if it came to that, hair could always be shorn. Yentl conceived a plan and day and night she could think of nothing else. No, she had not been created for the noodle board and the pudding dish, for chattering with silly women and pushing for a place at the butcher's block. Her father had told her so many tales of yeshivas, rabbis, men of letters! Her head was full of Talmudic disputations, questions and answers, learned phrases. Secretly, she had even smoked her father's long pipe.

Yentl told the dealers she wanted to sell the house and go to live in Kalish with an aunt. The neighborhood women tried to talk her out of it, and the marriage brokers said she was crazy, that she was more likely to make a good match right here in Yanev. But Yentl was obstinate. She was in such a rush that she sold the house to the first bidder, and let the furniture go for a song. All she realized from her inheritance was one hundred

and forty rubles. Then late one night in the month of
Av, while Yanev slept, Yentl cut off her braids, arranged sidelocks at her temples, and dressed herself in
her father's clothes. Packing underclothes, phylacteries,
and a few books into a straw suitcase, she started off on
foot for Lublin.

On the main road, Yentl got a ride in a carriage that
took her as far as Zamosc. From there, she again set out
on foot. She stopped at an inn along the way, and gave
her name there as Anshel, after an uncle who had died.
The inn was crowded with young men journeying to
study with famous rabbis. An argument was in progress
over the merits of various yeshivas, some praising those
of Lithuania, others claiming that study was more inten-
sive in Poland and the board better. It was the first time
Yentl had ever found herself alone in the company of
young men. How different their talk was from the
jabbering of women, she thought, but she was too shy
to join in. One young man discussed a prospective match
and the size of the dowry, while another, parodying the
manner of a Purim rabbi, declaimed a passage from the
Torah, adding all sorts of lewd interpretations. After a
while, the company proceeded to contests of strength.
One pried open another's fist; a second tried to bend a
companion's arm. One student, dining on bread and tea,
had no spoon and stirred his cup with his penknife.
Presently, one of the group came over to Yentl and
poked her in the shoulder:

"Why so quiet? Don't you have a tongue?"

"I have nothing to say."

"What's your name?"

"Anshel."

"You *are* bashful. A violet by the wayside."

And the young man tweaked Yentl's nose. She would

have given him a smack in return, but her arm refused to budge. She turned white. Another student, slightly older than the rest, tall and pale, with burning eyes and a black beard, came to her rescue.

"Hey, you, why are you picking on him?"

"If you don't like it, you don't have to look."

"Want me to pull your sidelocks off?"

The bearded young man beckoned to Yentl, then asked where she came from and where she was going. Yentl told him she was looking for a yeshiva, but wanted a quiet one. The young man pulled at his beard.

"Then come with me to Bechev."

He explained that he was returning to Bechev for his fourth year. The yeshiva there was small, with only thirty students, and the people in the town provided board for them all. The food was plentiful and the housewives darned the students' socks and took care of their laundry. The Bechev rabbi, who headed the yeshiva, was a genius. He could pose ten questions and answer all ten with one proof. Most of the students eventually found wives in the town.

"Why did you leave in the middle of the term?" Yentl asked.

"My mother died. Now I'm on my way back."

"What's your name?"

"Avigdor."

"How is it you're not married?"

The young man scratched his beard.

"It's a long story."

"Tell me."

Avigdor covered his eyes and thought a moment.

"Are you coming to Bechev?"

"Yes."

"Then you'll find out soon enough anyway. I was en-

gaged to the only daughter of Alter Vishkower, the
richest man in town. Even the wedding date was set when
suddenly they sent back the engagement contract."

"What happened?"

"I don't know. Gossips, I guess, were busy spreading
tales. I had the right to ask for half the dowry, but it
was against my nature. Now they're trying to talk me
into another match, but the girl doesn't appeal to me."

"In Bechev, yeshiva boys look at women?"

"At Alter's house, where I ate once a week, Hadass,
his daughter, always brought in the food. . . ."

"Is she good-looking?"

"She's blond."

"Brunettes can be good-looking too."

"No."

Yentl gazed at Avigdor. He was lean and bony with
sunken cheeks. He had curly sidelocks so black they appeared blue, and his eyebrows met across the bridge of
his nose. He looked at her sharply with the regretful
shyness of one who has just divulged a secret. His lapel
was rent, according to the custom for mourners, and the
lining of his gaberdine showed through. He drummed
restlessly on the table and hummed a tune. Behind the
high furrowed brow his thoughts seemed to race. Suddenly he spoke:

"Well, what of it. I'll become a recluse, that's all."

2

It was strange, but as soon as Yentl—or Anshel—
arrived in Bechev, she was allotted one day's board a
week at the house of that same rich man, Alter Vishkower, whose daughter had broken off her betrothal to
Avigdor.

The students at the yeshiva studied in pairs, and Avigdor chose Anshel for a partner. He helped her with the lessons. He was also an expert swimmer and offered to teach Anshel the breast stroke and how to tread water, but she always found excuses for not going down to the river. Avigdor suggested that they share lodgings, but Anshel found a place to sleep at the house of an elderly widow who was half blind. Tuesdays, Anshel ate at Alter Vishkower's and Hadass waited on her. Avigdor always asked many questions: "How does Hadass look? Is she sad? Is she gay? Are they trying to marry her off? Does she ever mention my name?" Anshel reported that Hadass upset dishes on the tablecloth, forgot to bring the salt, and dipped her fingers into the plate of grits while carrying it. She ordered the servant girl around, was forever engrossed in storybooks, and changed her hairdo every week. Moreover, she must consider herself a beauty, for she was always in front of the mirror, but, in fact, she was not that good-looking.

"Two years after she's married," said Anshel, "she'll be an old bag."

"So she doesn't appeal to you?"

"Not particularly."

"Yet if she wanted you, you wouldn't turn her down."

"I can do without her."

"Don't you have evil impulses?"

The two friends, sharing a lectern in a corner of the study house, spent more time talking than learning. Occasionally Avigdor smoked, and Anshel, taking the cigarette from his lips, would have a puff. Avigdor liked baked flatcakes made with buckwheat, so Anshel stopped at the bakery every morning to buy one, and wouldn't let him pay his share. Often Anshel did things that greatly surprised Avigdor. If a button came off Avigdor's coat, for example, Anshel would arrive at the yeshiva the next day with needle and thread and sew it back on. Anshel bought Avigdor all kinds of presents: a silk handkerchief, a pair of socks, a muffler. Avigdor grew more and more attached to this boy, five years younger than himself, whose beard hadn't even begun to sprout. Once Avigdor said to Anshel:

"I want you to marry Hadass."

"What good would that do *you?*"

"Better you than a total stranger."

"You'd become my enemy."

"Never."

Avigdor liked to go for long walks through the town and Anshel frequently joined him. Engrossed in conversation, they would go off to the water mill, or to the pine forest, or to the crossroads where the Christian shrine stood. Sometimes they stretched out on the grass.

"Why can't a woman be like a man?" Avigdor asked once, looking up at the sky.

"How do you mean?"

"Why couldn't Hadass be just like you?"

"How like me?"

"Oh—a good fellow."

Anshel grew playful. She plucked a flower and tore off the petals one by one. She picked up a chestnut and threw it at Avigdor. Avigdor watched a ladybug crawl across the palm of his hand. After a while he spoke up:

"They're trying to marry me off."

Anshel sat up instantly.

"To whom?"

"To Feitl's daughter, Peshe."

"The widow?"

"That's the one."

"Why should you marry a widow?"

"No one else will have me."

"That's not true. Someone will turn up for you."

"Never."

Anshel told Avigdor such a match was bad. Peshe was neither good-looking nor clever, only a cow with a pair of eyes. Besides, she was bad luck, for her husband died in the first year of their marriage. Such women were husband-killers. But Avigdor did not answer. He lit a cigarette, took a deep puff, and blew out smoke rings. His face had turned green.

"I need a woman. I can't sleep at night."

Anshel was startled.

"Why can't you wait until the right one comes along?"

"Hadass was my destined one."

And Avigdor's eyes grew moist. Abruptly he got to his feet.

"Enough lying around. Let's go."

After that, everything happened quickly. One day Avigdor was confiding his problem to Anshel, two days later he became engaged to Peshe, and brought honey cake and brandy to the yeshiva. An early wedding date was set. When the bride-to-be is a widow, there's no need to wait for a trousseau. Everything is ready. The groom, moreover, was an orphan and no one's advice had to be asked. The yeshiva students drank the brandy and offered their congratulations. Anshel also took a sip, but promptly choked on it.

"Oy, it burns!"

"You're not much of a man," Avigdor teased.

After the celebration, Avigdor and Anshel sat down with a volume of the Gemara, but they made little progress, and their conversation was equally slow.

Avigdor rocked back and forth, pulled at his beard, muttered under his breath.

"I'm lost," he said abruptly.

"If you don't like her, why are you getting married?"

"I'd marry a she-goat."

The following day Avigdor did not appear at the study house. Feitl the Leatherdealer belonged to the Hasidim and he wanted his prospective son-in-law to continue his studies at the Hasidic prayer house. The yeshiva students said privately that though there was no denying the widow was short and round as a barrel, her mother the daughter of a dairyman, her father half an ignoramus, still the whole family was filthy with money. Feitl was part-owner of a tannery; Peshe had invested her dowry in a shop that sold herring, tar, pots and pans, and was always crowded with peasants. Father and daughter were outfitting Avigdor and had placed orders for a fur coat, a cloth coat, a silk capote, and two pair of boots. In addition, he had received many gifts immediately, things that had belonged to Peshe's first husband: the Vilna edition of the Talmud, a gold watch, a Chanukah candelabra, a spice box. Anshel sat alone at the lectern. On Tuesday when Anshel arrived for dinner at Alter Vishkower's house, Hadass remarked:

"What do you say about your partner—back in clover, isn't he?"

"What did you expect—that no one else would want him?"

Hadass reddened.

"It wasn't my fault. My father was against it."

"Why?"

"Because they found out a brother of his had hanged himself."

Anshel looked at her as she stood there—tall, blond,

with a long neck, hollow cheeks, and blue eyes, wearing a cotton dress and a calico apron. Her hair, fixed in two braids, was flung back over her shoulders. A pity I'm not a man, Anshel thought.

"Do you regret it now?" Anshel asked.

"Oh, yes!"

Hadass fled from the room. The rest of the food, meat dumplings and tea, was brought in by the servant girl. Not until Anshel had finished eating and was washing her hands for the Final Blessings did Hadass reappear. She came up to the table and said in a smothered voice:

"Swear to me you won't tell him anything. Why should he know what goes on in my heart! . . ."

Then she fled once more, nearly falling over the threshold.

3

The head of the yeshiva asked Anshel to choose another study partner, but weeks went by and still Anshel studied alone. There was no one in the yeshiva who could take Avigdor's place. All the others were small, in body and in spirit. They talked nonsense, bragged about trifles, grinned oafishly, behaved like shnorrers. Without Avigdor the study house seemed empty. At night Anshel lay on her bench at the widow's, unable to sleep. Stripped of gaberdine and trousers, she was once more Yentl, a girl of marriageable age, in love with a young man who was betrothed to another. Perhaps I should have told him the truth, Anshel thought. But it was too late for that. Anshel could not go back to being a girl, could never again do without books and a study house. She lay there thinking outlandish thoughts that brought her close to madness. She fell asleep, then awoke with a start. In her dream she had been at the same time a man and a woman, wearing both a woman's bodice and a man's fringed garment. Yentl's period was late and she was suddenly afraid . . . who knew? In *Medrash Talpioth* she had read of a woman who had conceived merely through desiring a man. Only now did Yentl grasp the meaning of the Torah's prohibition against wearing the clothes of the other sex. By doing so one deceived not only others but also oneself. Even the soul was perplexed, finding itself incarnate in a strange body.

At night Anshel lay awake; by day she could scarcely keep her eyes open. At the houses where she had her meals, the women complained that the youth left everything on his plate. The rabbi noticed that Anshel no longer paid attention to the lectures but stared out the window lost in private thoughts. When Tuesday came, Anshel appeared at the Vishkower house for dinner. Hadass set a bowl of soup before her and waited, but Anshel was so disturbed she did not even say thank you. She reached for a spoon but let it fall. Hadass ventured a comment:

"I hear Avigdor has deserted you."

Anshel awoke from her trance.

"What do you mean?"

"He's no longer your partner."

"He's left the yeshiva."

"Do you see him at all?"

"He seems to be hiding."

"Are you at least going to the wedding?"

For a moment Anshel was silent as though missing the meaning of the words. Then she spoke:

"He's a big fool."

"Why do you say that?"

"You're beautiful, and the other one looks like a monkey."

Hadass blushed to the roots of her hair.

"It's all my father's fault."

"Don't worry. You'll find someone who's worthy of you."

"There's no one I want."

"But everyone wants you. . . ."

There was a long silence. Hadass' eyes grew larger, filling with the sadness of one who knows there is no consolation.

"Your soup is getting cold."

"I, too, want you."

Anshel was astonished at what she had said. Hadass stared at her over her shoulder.

"What are you saying!"

"It's the truth."

"Someone might be listening."

"I'm not afraid."

"Eat the soup. I'll bring the meat dumplings in a moment."

Hadass turned to go, her high heels clattering. Anshel began hunting for beans in the soup, fished one up, then let it fall. Her appetite was gone; her throat had closed up. She knew very well she was getting entangled in evil, but some force kept urging her on. Hadass reappeared, carrying a platter with two meat dumplings on it.

"Why aren't you eating?"

"I'm thinking about you."

"What are you thinking?"

"I want to marry you."

Hadass made a face as though she had swallowed something.

"On such matters, you must speak to my father."

"I know."

"The custom is to send a matchmaker."

She ran from the room, letting the door slam behind her. Laughing inwardly, Anshel thought: "With girls I can play as I please!" She sprinkled salt on the soup and then pepper. She sat there lightheaded. What have I done? I must be going mad. There's no other explanation. . . . She forced herself to eat, but could taste nothing. Only then did Anshel remember that it was Avigdor who had wanted her to marry Hadass. From her confusion, a plan emerged: she would exact vengeance for Avigdor, and at the same time, through Hadass, draw him closer to herself. Hadass was a virgin: what did she know about men? A girl like that could be deceived for a long time. To be sure, Anshel too was a virgin but she knew a lot about such matters from the Gemara and from hearing men talk. Anshel was seized by both fear and glee, as a person is who is planning to deceive the whole community. She remembered the saying: "The public are fools." She stood up and said aloud: "Now I'll really start something."

That night Anshel didn't sleep a wink. Every few minutes she got up for a drink of water. Her throat was parched, her forehead burned. Her brain worked away feverishly of its own volition. A quarrel seemed to be going on inside her. Her stomach throbbed and her knees ached. It was as if she had sealed a pact with Satan, the Evil One who plays tricks on human beings, who sets stumbling blocks and traps in their paths. By the time Anshel fell asleep, it was morning. She awoke more exhausted than before. But she could not go on sleeping on the bench at the widow's. With an effort she rose and, taking the bag that held her phylacteries, set out for the study house. On the way, whom should she meet but Hadass's father. Anshel bade him a respectful good morning and received a friendly greeting in return. Reb Alter stroked his beard and engaged her in conversation:

"My daughter Hadass must be serving you leftovers. You look starved."

"Your daughter is a fine girl, and very generous."

"So why are you so pale?"

Anshel was silent for a minute.

"Reb Alter, there's something I must say to you."

"Well, go ahead, say it."

"Reb Alter, your daughter pleases me."

Alter Vishkower came to a halt.

"Oh, does she? I thought yeshiva students didn't talk about such things."

His eyes were full of laughter.

"But it's the truth."

"One doesn't discuss these matters with the young man himself."

"But I'm an orphan."

"Well . . . in that case the custom is to send a marriage broker."

"Yes. . . ."

"What do you see in her?"

"She's beautiful . . . fine . . . intelligent. . . ."

"Well, well, well. . . . Come along, tell me something about your family."

Alter Vishkower put his arm around Anshel and in this fashion the two continued walking until they reached the courtyard of the synagogue.

4

Once you say "A," you must say "B." Thoughts lead to words, words lead to deeds. Reb Alter Vishkower gave his consent to the match. Hadass's mother Freyda Leah held back for a while. She said she wanted no more Bechev yeshiva students for her daughter and would rather have someone from Lublin or Zamosc; but Hadass gave warning that if she were shamed publicly once more (the way she had been with Avigdor) she would throw herself into the well. As often happens with such ill-advised matches, everyone was strongly in favor of it—the rabbi, the relatives, Hadass's girl friends. For some time the girls of Bechev had been eyeing Anshel longingly, watching from their windows when the youth passed by on the street. Anshel kept his boots well polished and did not drop his eyes in the presence of women. Stopping in at Beila the Baker's to buy a *pletzl*, he joked with them in such a worldly fashion that they marveled. The women agreed there was something special about Anshel: his sidelocks curled like nobody else's and he tied his neck scarf differently; his eyes, smiling yet distant, seemed always fixed on some faraway point. And the fact that Avigdor had become betrothed to Feitl's daughter Peshe, forsaking Anshel, had endeared him all the more to the people of the town. Alter Vishkower had a provisional contract drawn up for the betrothal, promising Anshel a bigger dowry, more presents, and an even longer period of maintenance than he had promised Avigdor. The girls of Bechev threw their arms around Hadass and congratulated her. Hadass immediately began crocheting a sack for Anshel's phylacteries, a *challah* cloth, a matzoh bag. When Avigdor heard the news of Anshel's betrothal, he came to the study house to offer his congratulations. The past few weeks had aged him. His beard was disheveled, his eyes were red. He said to Anshel:

"I knew it would happen this way. Right from the beginning. As soon as I met you at the inn."

"But it was you who suggested it."

"I know that."

"Why did you desert me? You went away without even saying goodbye."

"I wanted to burn my bridges behind me."

Avigdor asked Anshel to go for a walk. Though it was already past Succoth, the day was bright with sunshine. Avigdor, friendlier than ever, opened his heart to Anshel. Yes, it was true, a brother of his had succumbed to melancholy and hanged himself. Now he too felt himself near the edge of the abyss. Peshe had a lot of money and her father was a rich man, yet he couldn't sleep nights. He didn't want to be a storekeeper. He couldn't forget Hadass. She appeared in his dreams. Sabbath night when her name occurred in the Havdala prayer, he turned dizzy. Still it was good that Anshel and no one else was to marry her. . . . At least she would fall into decent hands. Avigdor stooped and tore aimlessly at the shriveled grass. His speech was incoherent, like that of a man possessed. Suddenly he said:

"I have thought of doing what my brother did."

"Do you love her *that* much?"

"She's engraved in my heart."

The two pledged their friendship and promised never again to part. Anshel proposed that, after they were both married, they should live next door or even share the same house. They would study together every day, perhaps even become partners in a shop.

"Do you want to know the truth?" asked Avigdor.

"It's like the story of Jacob and Benjamin: my life is bound up in your life."

"Then why did you leave me?"

"Perhaps for that very reason."

Though the day had turned cold and windy, they continued to walk until they reached the pine forest, not turning back until dusk when it was time for the evening prayer. The girls of Bechev, from their posts at the windows, watched them going by with their arms round each other's shoulders and so engrossed in conversation that they walked through puddles and piles of trash without noticing. Avigdor looked pale, disheveled, and the wind whipped one sidelock about; Anshel chewed his fingernails. Hadass, too, ran to the window, took one look, and her eyes filled with tears. . . .

Events followed quickly. Avigdor was the first to marry. Because the bride was a widow, the wedding was a quiet one, with no musicians, no wedding jester, no ceremonial veiling of the bride. One day Peshe stood beneath the marriage canopy, the next she was back at the shop, dispensing tar with greasy hands. Avigdor prayed at the Hasidic assembly house in his new prayer shawl. Afternoons, Anshel went to visit him and the two whispered and talked until evening. The date of Anshel's wedding to Hadass was set for the Sabbath in Chanukah week, though the prospective father-in-law wanted it sooner. Hadass had already been betrothed once. Besides, the groom was an orphan. Why should he toss about on a makeshift bed at the widow's when he could have a wife and home of his own?

Many times each day Anshel warned herself that what she was about to do was sinful, mad, an act of utter depravity. She was entangling both Hadass and herself in a chain of deception and committing so many transgressions that she would never be able to do penance. One lie followed another. Repeatedly Anshel made up her mind to flee Bechev in time, to put an end to this weird comedy that was more the work of an imp than a human being. But she was in the grip of a power she could not resist. She grew more and more attached to Avigdor, and could not bring herself to destroy Hadass's illusory happiness. Now that he was married, Avigdor's desire to study was greater than ever, and the friends met twice each day: in the mornings they studied the Gemara and the Commentaries, in the afternoons the Legal Codes with their glosses. Alter Vishkower and Feitl the Leatherdealer were pleased and compared Avigdor and Anshel to David and Jonathan. With all the complications, Anshel went about as though drunk. The tailors took her measurements for a new wardrobe and she was forced into all kinds of subterfuge to keep them from discovering she was not a man. Though the imposture had lasted many weeks, Anshel still could not believe it: How was it possible? Fooling the community had become a game, but how long could it go on? And in what way would the truth come to the surface? Inside, Anshel laughed and wept. She had turned into a sprite brought into the world to mock people and trick them. I'm wicked, a transgressor, a Jeroboam ben Nabat, she told herself. Her only justification was that she had taken all these burdens upon herself because her soul thirsted to study Torah. . . .

Avigdor soon began to complain that Peshe treated him badly. She called him an idler, a schlemiel, just another mouth to feed. She tried to tie him to the store, assigned him tasks for which he hadn't the slightest inclination, begrudged him pocket money. Instead of consoling Avigdor, Anshel goaded him on against Peshe.

She called his wife an eyesore, a shrew, a miser, and said that Peshe had no doubt nagged her first husband to death and would Avigdor also. At the same time, Anshel enumerated Avigdor's virtues: his height and manliness, his wit, his erudition.

"If I were a woman and married to you," said Anshel, "I'd know how to appreciate you."

"Well, but you aren't. . . ."

Avigdor sighed.

Meanwhile Anshel's wedding date drew near.

On the Sabbath before Chanukah Anshel was called to the pulpit to read from the Torah. The women showered her with raisins and almonds. On the day of the wedding Alter Vishkower gave a feast for the young men. Avigdor sat at Anshel's right hand. The bridegroom delivered a Talmudic discourse, and the rest of the company argued the points, while smoking cigarettes and drinking wine, liqueurs, tea with lemon or raspberry jam. Then followed the ceremony of veiling the bride, after which the bridegroom was led to the wedding canopy that had been set up at the side of the synagogue. The night was frosty and clear, the sky full of stars. The musicians struck up a tune. Two rows of girls held lighted tapers and braided wax candles. After the wedding ceremony the bride and groom broke their fast with golden chicken broth. Then the dancing began and the announcement of the wedding gifts, all according to custom. The gifts were many and costly. The wedding jester depicted the joys and sorrows that were in store for the bride. Avigdor's wife, Peshe, was one of the guests but, though she was bedecked with jewels, she still looked ugly in a wig that sat low on her forehead, wearing an enormous fur cape, and with traces of tar on her hands that no amount of washing could ever remove. After the Virtue Dance the bride and groom were led separately to the marriage chamber. The wedding attendants instructed the couple in the proper conduct and enjoined them to "be fruitful and multiply."

At daybreak Anshel's mother-in-law and her band descended upon the marriage chamber and tore the bedsheets from beneath Hadass to make sure the marriage had been consummated. When traces of blood were discovered, the company grew merry and began kissing and congratulating the bride. Then, brandishing the sheet, they flocked outside and danced a Kosher Dance in the newly fallen snow. Anshel had found a way to deflower the bride. Hadass in her innocence was unaware that things weren't quite as they should have been. She was already deeply in love with Anshel. It is commanded that the bride and groom remain apart for seven days after the first intercourse. The next day Anshel and Avigdor took up the study of the Tractate on Menstruous Women. When the other men had departed and the two were left to themselves in the synagogue, Avigdor shyly questioned Anshel about his night with Hadass. Anshel gratified his curiosity and they whispered together until nightfall.

5

Anshel had fallen into good hands. Hadass was a devoted wife and her parents indulged their son-in-law's every wish and boasted of his accomplishments. To be sure, several months went by and Hadass was still not with child, but no one took it to heart. On the other hand, Avigdor's lot grew steadily worse. Peshe tormented him and finally would not give him enough to eat and even refused him a clean shirt. Since he was always penniless, Anshel again brought him a daily buck-wheat cake. Because Peshe was too busy to cook and too stingy to hire a servant, Anshel asked Avigdor to dine at his house. Reb Alter Vishkower and his wife disap-proved, arguing that it was wrong for the rejected suitor to visit the house of his former fiancée. The town had plenty to talk about. But Anshel cited precedents to show that it was not prohibited by the law. Most of the townspeople sided with Avigdor and blamed Peshe for everything. Avigdor soon began pressing Peshe for a divorce, and, because he did not want to have a child by such a fury, he acted like Onan, or, as the Gemara translates it: he threshed on the inside and cast his seed without. He confided in Anshel, told him how Peshe came to bed unwashed and snored like a buzz saw, of how she was so occupied with the cash taken in at the store that she babbled about it even in her sleep.

"Oh, Anshel, how I envy you," he said.

"There's no reason for envying me."

"You have everything. I wish your good fortune were mine—with no loss to you, of course."

"Everyone has troubles of his own."

"What sort of troubles do *you* have? Don't tempt Providence."

How could Avigdor have guessed that Anshel could not sleep at night and thought constantly of running away? Lying with Hadass and deceiving her had be-come more and more painful. Hadass's love and tender-ness shamed her. The devotion of her mother- and father-in-law and their hopes for a grandchild were a burden. On Friday afternoons all of the townspeople went to the baths and every week Anshel had to find a new excuse. But this was beginning to awake suspicions. There was talk that Anshel must have an unsightly birthmark, or a rupture, or perhaps was not properly circumcised. Judging by the youth's years, his beard should certainly have begun to sprout, yet his cheeks remained smooth. It was already Purim and Passover was approaching. Soon it would be summer. Not far from Bechev there was a river where all the yeshiva students and young men went swimming as soon as it was warm enough. The lie was swelling like an abscess and one of these days it must surely burst. Anshel knew she had to find a way to free herself.

It was customary for the young men boarding with their in-laws to travel to nearby cities during the half-holidays in the middle of Passover week. They enjoyed the change, refreshed themselves, looked around for business opportunities, bought books or other things a young man might need. Bechev was not far from Lublin and Anshel persuaded Avigdor to make the journey with her at her expense. Avigdor was delighted at the prospect of being rid for a few days of the shrew he had at home. The trip by carriage was a merry one. The fields were turning green; storks, back from the warm countries, swooped across the sky in great arcs. Streams rushed toward the valleys. The birds chirped. The windmills turned. Spring flowers were beginning to bloom in the fields. Here and there a cow was already grazing. The companions, chatting, ate the fruit and little cakes that Hadass had packed, told each other jokes, and exchanged confidences until they reached Lublin. There they went to an inn and took a room for two. On the journey, Anshel had promised to reveal an astonishing secret to Avigdor in Lublin. Avigdor had joked: what sort of secret could it be? Had Anshel discovered a hidden treasure? Had he written an essay? By studying the cabala, had he created a dove? . . . Now they entered the room and while Anshel carefully locked the door, Avigdor said teasingly:

"Well, let's hear your great secret."

"Prepare yourself for the most incredible thing that ever was."

"I'm prepared for anything."

"I'm not a man but a woman," said Anshel. "My name isn't Anshel, it's Yentl."

Avigdor burst out laughing.

"I knew it was a hoax."

"But it's true."

"Even if I'm a fool, I won't swallow this."

"Do you want me to show you?"

"Yes."

"Then I'll get undressed."

Avigdor's eyes widened. It occurred to him that Anshel might want to practice pederasty. Anshel took off the gaberdine and the fringed garment, and threw off her underclothes. Avigdor took one look and turned first white, then fiery red. Anshel covered herself hastily.

"I've done this only so that you can testify at the courthouse. Otherwise Hadass will have to stay a grass widow."

Avigdor had lost his tongue. He was seized by a fit of trembling. He wanted to speak, but his lips moved and nothing came out. He sat down quickly, for his legs would not support him. Finally he murmured:

"How is it possible? I don't believe it!"

"Should I get undressed again?"

"No!"

Yentl proceeded to tell the whole story: how her father, bedridden, had studied Torah with her; how she had never had the patience for women and their silly

chatter; how she had sold the house and all the furnish-
ings, left the town, made her way disguised as a man to
Lublin, and on the road met Avigdor. Avigdor sat
speechless, gazing at the storyteller. Yentl was by now
wearing men's clothes once more. Avigdor spoke:

"It must be a dream."

He pinched himself on the cheek.

"It isn't a dream."

"That such a thing should happen to me . . . !"

"It's all true."

"Why did you do it? *Nu*, I'd better keep still."

"I didn't want to waste my life on a baking shovel and
a kneading trough."

'And what about Hadass—why did you do that?"

"I did it for your sake. I knew that Peshe would torment you and at our house you would have some
peace. . . ."

Avigdor was silent for a long time. He bowed his
head, pressed his hands to his temples, shook his head.

"What will you do now?"

"I'll go away to a different yeshiva."

"What? If you had only told me earlier, we could
have . . ."

Avigdor broke off in the middle.

"No—it wouldn't have been good."

"Why not?"

"I'm neither one nor the other."

"What a dilemma I'm in!"

"Get a divorce from that horror. Marry Hadass."

"She'll never divorce me and Hadass won't have me."

"Hadass loves you. She won't listen to her father
again."

Avigdor stood up suddenly but then sat down.

"I won't be able to forget you. Ever. . . ."

6

According to the law Avigdor was now forbidden to spend another moment alone with Yentl; yet dressed in the gaberdine and trousers, she was again the familiar Anshel. They resumed their conversation on the old footing:

"How could you bring yourself to violate the commandment every day: 'A woman shall not wear that which pertaineth to a man'?"

"I wasn't created for plucking feathers and chattering with females."

"Would you rather lose your share in the world to come?"

"Perhaps. . . ."

Avigdor raised his eyes. Only now did he realize that Anshel's cheeks were too smooth for a man's, the hair too abundant, the hands too small. Even so he could not believe that such a thing could have happpened. At any moment he expected to wake up. He bit his lips, pinched his thigh. He was seized by shyness and could not speak without stammering. His friendship with Anshel, their intimate talk, their confidences, had been turned into a sham and delusion. The thought even occurred to him that Anshel might be a demon. He shook himself as if to cast off a nightmare; yet that power which knows the difference between dream and reality told him it was all true. He summoned up his courage. He and Anshel could never be strangers to one another, even though Anshel was in fact Yentl. . . . He ventured a comment:

"It seems to me that the witness who testifies for a deserted woman may not marry her, for the law calls him 'a party to the affair.' "

"What? That didn't occur to me!"

"We must look it up in Eben Ezer."

"I'm not even sure that the rules pertaining to a deserted woman apply in this case," said Anshel in the manner of a scholar.

"If you don't want Hadass to be a grass widow, you must reveal the secret to her directly."

"That I can't do."

"In any event, you must get another witness."

Gradually the two went back to their Talmudic conversation. It seemed strange at first to Avigdor to be disputing holy writ with a woman, yet before long the Torah had reunited them. Though their bodies were different, their souls were of one kind. Anshel spoke in a singsong, gesticulated with her thumb, clutched her sidelocks, plucked at her beardless chin, made all the customary gestures of a yeshiva student. In the heat of argument she even seized Avigdor by the lapel and called him stupid. A great love for Anshel took hold of Avigdor, mixed with shame, remorse, anxiety. If I had only known this before, he said to himself. In his thoughts he likened Anshel (or Yentl) to Bruria, the wife of Reb Meir, and to Yalta, the wife of Reb Nachman. For the first time he saw clearly that this was what he had always wanted: a wife whose mind was not taken up with material things. . . . His desire for Hadass was gone now, and he knew he would long for Yentl, but he dared not say so. He felt hot and knew that his face was burning. He could no longer meet Anshel's eyes. He began to enumerate Anshel's sins and saw that he too was implicated, for he had sat next to Yentl and had touched her during her unclean days. *Nu*, and what could be said about her marriage to Hadass? What a multitude of transgressions there! Wilful deception, false vows, misrepresentation!—Heaven knows what else. He asked suddenly:

"Tell the truth, are you a heretic?"

"God forbid!"

"Then how could you bring yourself to do such a thing?"

The longer Anshel talked, the less Avigdor understood. All Anshel's explanations seemed to point to one thing: she had the soul of a man and the body of a woman. Anshel said she had married Hadass only in order to be near Avigdor.

"You could have married me," Avigdor said.

"I wanted to study the Gemara and Commentaries with you, not darn your socks!"

For a long time neither spoke. Then Avigdor broke the silence:

"I'm afraid Hadass will get sick from all this, God forbid!"

"I'm afraid of that too."

"What's going to happen now?"

Dusk fell and the two began to recite the evening prayer. In his confusion Avigdor mixed up the blessings, omitted some and repeated others. He glanced sideways at Anshel who was rocking back and forth, beating her breast, bowing her head. He saw her, eyes closed, lift her face to heaven as though beseeching: You, Father in Heaven, know the truth. . . . When their prayers were finished, they sat down on opposite chairs, facing one another yet a good distance apart. The room filled with shadows. Reflections of the sunset, like purple embroidery, shook on the wall opposite the window. Avigdor again wanted to speak but at first the words, trembling on the tip of his tongue, would not come. Suddenly they burst forth:

"Maybe it's still not too late? I can't go on living with that accursed woman. . . . You. . . ."

"No, Avigdor, it's impossible."

"Why?"

"I'll live out my time as I am. . . ."

"I'll miss you. Terribly."

"And I'll miss you."

"What's the sense of all this?"

Anshel did not answer. Night fell and the light faded. In the darkness they seemed to be listening to each other's thoughts. The law forbade Avigdor to stay in the room alone with Anshel, but he could not think of her just as a woman. What a strange power there is in clothing, he thought. But he spoke of something else:

"I would advise you simply to send Hadass a divorce."

"How can I do that?"

"Since the marriage sacraments weren't valid, what difference does it make?"

"I suppose you're right."

"There'll be time enough later for her to find out the truth."

The maidservant came in with a lamp but as soon as she had gone, Avigdor put it out. Their predicament and the words which they must speak to one another could not endure light. In the blackness Anshel related all the particulars. She answered all Avigdor's questions. The clock struck two, and still they talked. Anshel told Avigdor that Hadass had never forgotten him. She talked of him frequently, worried about his health, was sorry—though not without a certain satisfaction—about the way things had turned out with Peshe.

"She'll be a good wife," said Anshel. "I don't even know how to bake a pudding."

"Nevertheless, if you're willing. . . ."
"No, Avigdor. It wasn't destined to be. . . ."

7

It was all a great riddle to the town: the messenger who arrived bringing Hadass the divorce papers; Avigdor's remaining in Lublin until after the holidays; his return to Bechev with slumping shoulders and lifeless eyes as if he had been ill. Hadass took to her bed and was visited by the doctor three times a day. Avigdor went into seclusion. If someone ran across him by chance and addressed him, he did not answer. Peshe complained to her parents that Avigdor paced back and forth smoking all night long. When he finally collapsed from sheer fatigue, in his sleep he called out the name of an unknown female—Yentl. Peshe began talking of a divorce. The town thought Avigdor wouldn't grant her one or would demand money at the very least, but he agreed to everything.

In Bechev the people were not used to having mysteries stay mysteries for long. How can you keep secrets in a little town where everyone knows what's cooking in everyone else's pots? Yet, though there were plenty of persons who made a practice of looking through keyholes and laying an ear to shutters, what happened remained an enigma. Hadass lay in her bed and wept. Chanina the herb doctor reported that she was wasting away. Anshel had disappeared without a trace. Reb Alter Vishkower sent for Avigdor and he arrived, but those who stood straining beneath the window couldn't catch a word of what passed between them. Those individuals who habitually pry into other people's affairs came up with all sorts of theories, but not one of them was consistent.

One party came to the conclusion that Anshel had fallen into the hands of Catholic priests, and had been converted. That might have made sense. But where could Anshel have found time for the priests, since he was always studying in the yeshiva? And apart from that, since when does an apostate send his wife a divorce?

Another group whispered that Anshel had cast an eye on another woman. But who could it be? There were no love affairs conducted in Bechev. And none of the young women had recently left town—neither a Jewish woman nor a Gentile one.

Somebody else offered the suggestion that Anshel had been carried away by evil spirits, or was even one of them himself. As proof he cited the fact that Anshel had never come either to the bathhouse or to the river. It is well known that demons have the feet of geese. Well, but had Hadass never seen him barefoot? And who ever heard of a demon sending his wife a divorce? When a demon marries a daughter of mortals, he usually lets her remain a grass widow.

It occurred to someone else that Anshel had committed a major transgression and gone into exile in order to do penance. But what sort of transgression could it have been? And why had he not entrusted it to the rabbi? And why did Avigdor wander about like a ghost?

The hypothesis of Tevel the Musician was closest to the truth. Tevel maintained that Avigdor had been unable to forget Hadass and that Anshel had divorced her so that his friend would be able to marry her. But was such friendship possible in this world? And in that case, why had Anshel divorced Hadass even before Avigdor divorced Peshe? Furthermore, such a thing can be accomplished only if the wife has been informed of the arrangement and is willing, yet all signs pointed to Hadass's great love for Anshel, and in fact she was ill from sorrow.

One thing was clear to all: Avigdor knew the truth. But it was impossible to get anything out of him. He remained in seclusion and kept silent with an obstinancy that was a reproof to the whole town.

Close friends urged Peshe not to divorce Avigdor, though they had severed all relations and no longer lived as man and wife. He did not even, on Friday night, perform the kiddush blessing for her. He spent his nights either at the study house or at the widow's where Anshel had found lodgings. When Peshe spoke to him he didn't answer, but stood with bowed head. The tradeswoman Peshe had no patience for such goings-on. She needed a young man to help her out in the store, not a yeshiva student who had fallen into melancholy. Someone of that sort might even take it into his head to depart and leave her deserted. Peshe agreed to a divorce.

In the meantime Hadass had recovered, and Reb Alter Vishkower let it be known that a marriage contract was being drawn up. Hadass was to marry Avigdor. The town was agog. A marriage between a man and a woman who had once been engaged and their betrothal broken off was unheard of. The wedding was held on the first Sabbath after Tishe b'Ov, and included all that is customary at the marriage of a virgin: the banquet for the poor, the canopy before the synagogue, the musicians, the wedding jester, the Virtue Dance. Only one thing was lacking: joy. The bridegroom stood beneath the marriage canopy, a figure of desolation. The bride had recovered from her sickness, but had remained pale and thin. Her tears fell into the golden chicken broth. From all eyes the same question looked out: why had Anshel done it?

After Avigdor's marriage to Hadass, Peshe spread the rumor that Anshel had sold his wife to Avigdor for a price, and that the money had been supplied by Alter Vishkower. One young man pondered the riddle at great length until he finally arrived at the conclusion that Anshel had lost his beloved wife to Avigdor at cards, or even on a spin of the Chanukah *dreidl*. It is a general rule that when the grain of truth cannot be found, men will swallow great helpings of falsehood. Truth itself is often concealed in such a way that the harder you look for it, the harder it is to find.

Not long after the wedding, Hadass became pregnant. The child was a boy and those assembled at the circumcision could scarcely believe their ears when they heard the father name his son Anshel.

Translated by Marion Magid
and Elizabeth Pollet

Blood

The cabalists know that the passion for blood and the passion for flesh have the same origin, and this is the reason "Thou shalt not kill" is followed by "Thou shalt not commit adultery."

Reb Falik Ehrlichman was the owner of a large estate not far from the town of Laskev. He was born Reb Falik but because of his honesty in business his neighbors had called him *ehrlichman* for so long that it had become a part of his name. By his first wife Reb Falik had had two children, a son and a daughter, who had both died young and without issue. His wife had died too. In later years he had married again, according to the Book of Ecclesiastes: "In the morning sow thy seed, and in the evening withhold not thy hand." Reb Falik's second wife was thirty years younger than he and his friends had tried to dissuade him from the match. For one thing Risha had been widowed twice and was considered a man-killer. For another, she came of a coarse family and had a bad name. It was said of her that she had beaten her first husband with a stick, and that during the two years her second husband had lain paralyzed she had never called in a doctor. There was other gossip as well. But Reb Falik was not frightened by warnings or whisperings. His first wife, peace be with her, had been ill for a long time before she died of consumption. Risha, corpulent and strong as a man, was a good housekeeper and knew how to manage a farm. Under her kerchief she had a full head of red hair and eyes as green as gooseberries. Her bosom was high and she had the broad hips of a childbearer. Though she had not had children by either of her first two husbands, she contended it was their fault. She had a loud voice and when she laughed one could hear her from far off. Soon after marrying Reb Falik, she began to take charge: she sent away the old bailiff who drank and hired in his place a young and diligent one; she supervised the sowing, the reaping, the cattle breeding; she kept an eye on the peasants to make sure they did not steal eggs, chickens, honey from the hives. Reb Falik hoped Risha would bear him a son to recite Kaddish after his death, but the years passed without her becoming pregnant. She said he was too old. One day she took him with her to Laskev to the notary public where he signed all his property over to her.

Reb Falik gradually ceased to attend to the affairs of the estate at all. He was a man of moderate height with a snowy white beard and rosy cheeks flushed with that half-faded redness of winter apples characteristic of affluent and meek old men. He was friendly to rich and poor alike and never shouted at his servants or peasants.

Every spring before Passover he sent a load of wheat to Laskev for the poor, and in the fall after the Feast of Tabernacles he supplied the poorhouse with firewood for the winter as well as sacks of potatoes, cabbages, and beets. On the estate was a small study house which Reb Falik had built and furnished with a bookcase and Holy Scroll. When there were ten Jews on the estate to provide a quorum, they could pray there. After he had signed over all his possessions to Risha, Reb Falik sat almost all day long in this study house, reciting Psalms, or sometimes dozing on the sofa in a side room. His strength began to leave him; his hands trembled; and when he spoke his head shook sidewise. Nearly seventy, completely dependent on Risha, he was, so to speak, already eating the bread of mercy. Formerly, the peasants could come to him for relief when one of their cows or horses wandered into his fields and the bailiff demanded payment for damages. But now that Risha had the upper hand, the peasant had to pay to the last penny.

On the estate there lived for many years a ritual slaughterer named Reb Dan, an old man who acted as beadle in the study house, and who, together with Reb Falik, studied a chapter of the Mishnah every morning. When Reb Dan died, Risha began to look about for a new slaughterer. Reb Falik ate a piece of chicken every evening for supper; Risha herself liked meat. Laskev was too far to visit every time she wanted an animal killed. Moreover, in both fall and spring, the Laskev road was flooded. Asking around, Risha heard that among the Jews in the nearby village of Krowica there was a ritual slaughterer named Reuben whose wife had died giving birth to their first child and who, in addition to being a butcher, owned a small tavern where the peasants drank in the evenings.

One morning Risha ordered one of the peasants to harness the britska in order to take her to Krowica to talk to Reuben. She wanted him to come to the estate from time to time to do their slaughtering. She took along several chickens and a gander in a sack so tight it was a wonder the fowl did not choke.

When she reached the village, they pointed out Reuben's hut near the smithy. The britska stopped and Risha, followed by the driver carrying the bag of poultry, opened the front door and went in. Reuben was not there but looking out a window into the courtyard behind she saw him standing by a flat ditch. A barefooted woman handed him a chicken which he slaughtered. Unaware he was being watched from his own house, Reuben was being playful with the woman. Jokingly, he swung the slaughtered chicken as if about to toss it into her face. When she handed him the penny fee, he clasped her wrist and held it. Meanwhile the chicken, its throat slit, fell to the ground where it fluttered about, flapping its wings in its attempt to fly and spattering Reuben's boots with blood. Finally the little rooster gave a last start and then lay still, one glassy eye and its slit neck facing up to God's heaven. The creature seemed to say: "See, Father in Heaven, what they have done to me. And still they make merry."

2

Reuben, like most butchers, was fat with a big stomach and a red neck. His throat was short and fleshy. On his cheeks grew bunches of pitchblack hair. His dark eyes held the cold look of those born under the sign of Mars. When he caught sight of Risha, mistress of the large neighboring estate, he became confused and his face turned even redder than it was. Hurriedly, the woman with him picked up the slaughtered bird and scurried away. Risha went into the courtyard, directing the peasant to set the sack with the fowl near Reuben's feet. She could see that he did not stand on his dignity, and she spoke to him lightly, half jokingly, and he answered her in kind. When she asked if he would slaughter the birds in the sack for her, he answered: "What else should I do? Revive dead ones?" And when she remarked how important it was to her husband that his food be strictly kosher, he said: "Tell him he shouldn't worry. My knife is as smooth as a fiddle!"—and to show her he drew the bluish edge of the blade across the nail of his index finger. The peasant untied the sack and handed Reuben a yellow chicken. He promptly turned back its head, pulled a tuft of down from the center of its throat and slit it. Soon he was ready for the white gander.

"He's a tough one," said Risha. "All the geese were afraid of him."

"He won't be tough much longer," Reuben answered.

"Don't you have any pity?" Risha teased. She had never seen a slaughterer who was so deft. His hands were thick, with short fingers matted with dense black hair.

"With pity, one doesn't become a slaughterer," answered Reuben. A moment later, he added, "When you scale a fish on the Sabbath, do you think the fish enjoys it?"

Holding the fowl, Reuben looked at Risha intently, his gaze traveling up and down her and finally coming to rest on her bosom. Still staring at her, he slaughtered the gander. Its white feathers grew red with blood. It shook its neck menacingly and suddenly went up in the air and flew a few yards. Risha bit her lip.

"They say slaughterers are destined to be born murderers but become slaughterers instead," Risha said.

"If you're so softhearted, why did you bring me the birds?" Reuben asked.

"Why? One has to eat meat."

"If someone has to eat meat, someone has to do the slaughtering."

Risha told the peasant to take away the fowl. When she paid Reuben, he took her hand and held it for a moment in his. His hand was warm and her body shivered pleasurably. When she asked him if he would be willing to come to the estate to slaughter, he said yes if in addition to paying him she would send a cart for him.

"I won't have any herd of cattle for you," Risha joked.

"Why not?" Reuben countered. "I have slaughtered cattle before. In Lublin I slaughtered more in one day than I do here in a month," he boasted.

Since Risha did not seem to be in any hurry, Reuben asked her to sit down on a box and he himself sat on a log. He told her of his studies in Lublin and explained how he had happened to come to this God-forsaken village where his wife, peace be with her, had died in childbirth due to the lack of an experienced midwife.

"Why haven't you remarried?" Risha questioned. "There's no shortage of women—widows, divorcees, or young girls."

Reuben told her the matchmakers were trying to find him a wife but the destined one had not yet appeared.

"How will you know the one who is destined for you?" Risha asked.

"My stomach will know. She will grab me right here" —and Reuben snapped his fingers and pointed at his navel. Risha would have stayed longer, except that a girl came in with a duck. Reuben arose. Risha returned to the britska.

On the way back Risha thought about the slaughterer Reuben, his levity and his jocular talk. Though she came to the conclusion that he was thick-skinned and his future wife would not lick honey all her life, still she could not get him out of her mind. That night, retiring to her canopied bed across the room from her husband's, she tossed and turned sleeplessly. When she finally dozed off, her dreams both frightened and excited her. She got up in the morning full of desire, wanting to see Reuben as quickly as possible, wondering how she might arrange it, and worried that he might find some woman and leave the village.

Three days later Risha went to Krowica again even though the larder was still full. This time she caught the birds herself, bound their legs, and shoved them into the sack. On the estate was a black rooster with a voice clear as a bell, a bird famous for its size, its red comb, and its crowing. There was also a hen that laid an egg every day and always at the same spot. Risha now caught both of these creatures, murmuring, "Come, children, you will soon taste Reuben's knife," and as she said these words a tremor ran down her spine. She did not order a peasant to drive the britska but, harnessing the horse herself, went off alone. She found Reuben standing at the threshold of his house as if he were waiting impatiently for her, as in fact he was. When a male and a female lust after each other, their thoughts meet and each can foresee what the other will do.

Reuben ushered Risha in with all the formality due a

guest. He brought her a pitcher of water, offered her liqueur and a slice of honey cake. He did not go into the courtyard but untrussed the fowl indoors. When he took out the black rooster, he exclaimed, "What a fine cavalier!"

"Don't worry. You will soon take care of him," said Risha.

"No one can escape my knife," Reuben assured her. He slaughtered the rooster on the spot. The bird did not exhale its spirit immediately but finally, like an eagle caught by a bullet, it slumped to the floor. Then Reuben set the knife down on the whetstone, turned, and came over to Risha. His face was pale with passion and the fire in his dark eyes frightened her. She felt as if he were about to slaughter her. He put his arms around her without a word and pressed her against his body.

"What are you doing? Have you lost your mind?" she asked.

"I like you," Reuben said hoarsely.

"Let me go. Somebody might come in," she warned.

"Nobody will come," Reuben assured her. He put up the chain on the door and pulled Risha into a windowless alcove.

Risha wrangled, pretending to defend herself, and exclaimed, "Woe is me. I'm a married woman. And you—a pious man, a scholar. We'll roast in Gehenna for this . . ." But Reuben paid no attention. He forced Risha down on his bench-bed and she, thrice married, had never before felt desire as great as on that day. Though she called him murderer, robber, highwayman, and reproached him for bringing shame to an honest woman, yet at the same time she kissed him, fondled him, and responded to his masculine whims. In their amorous play, she asked him to slaughter her. Taking her head, he bent it back and fiddled with his finger across her throat. When Risha finally arose, she said to Reuben: "You certainly murdered me that time."

"And you, me," he answered.

3

Because Risha wanted Reuben all to herself and was afraid he might leave Krowica or marry some younger woman, she determined to find a way to have him live on the estate. She could not simply hire him to replace Reb Dan, for Reb Dan had been a relative whom Reb Falik would have had to provide for in any case. To keep a man just to slaughter a few chickens every week did not make sense and to propose it would arouse her husband's suspicions. After puzzling for a while, Risha found a solution.

She began to complain to her husband about how little profit the crops were bringing; how meager the harvests were; if things went on this way, in a few years they would be ruined. Reb Falik tried to comfort his wife saying that God had not forsaken him hitherto and that one must have faith, to which Risha retorted that faith could not be eaten. She proposed that they stock the pastures with cattle and open a butcher shop in Laskev—that way there would be a double profit both from the dairy and from the meat sold at retail. Reb Falik opposed the plan as impractical and beneath his dignity. He argued that the butchers in Laskev would raise a commotion and that the community would never agree to him, Reb Falik, becoming a butcher. But Risha insisted. She went to Laskev, called a meeting of the community elders, and told them that she intended to open a butcher shop. Her meat would be sold at two cents a pound less than the meat in the other shops. The town was in an uproar. The rabbi warned her he would prohibit the meat from the estate. The butchers threatened to stab anyone who interfered with their livelihood. But Risha was not daunted. In the first place she had influence with the government, for the *starosta* of the neighborhood had received many fine gifts from her, often visited her estate and went hunting in her woods. Moreover, she soon found allies among the Laskev poor who could not afford to buy much meat at the usual high prices. Many took her side, coachmen, shoemakers, tailors, furriers, potters, and they announced that if the butchers did her any violence, they would retaliate by burning the butcher shops. Risha invited a mob of them to the estate, gave them bottles of homemade beer from her brewery, and got them to promise her their support. Soon afterwards she rented a store in Laskev and employed Wolf Bonder, a fearless man known as a horse-thief and brawler. Every other day, Wolf Bonder drove to the estate with his horse and buggy to cart meat to the city. Risha hired Reuben to do the slaughtering.

For many months the new business lost money, the rabbi having proscribed Risha's meat. Reb Falik was ashamed to look the townspeople in the face, but Risha had the means and strength to wait for victory. Since her meat was cheap, the number of her customers increased steadily, and soon because of competition several butchers were forced to close their shops and of the two Laskev slaughterers, one lost his job. Risha was cursed by many.

The new business proved the cover Risha needed to conceal the sins she was committing on Reb Falik's estate. From the beginning it was her custom to be pres-

ent when Reuben slaughtered. Often she helped him
bind an ox or a cow. And her thirst to watch the cutting
of throats and the shedding of blood soon became so
mixed with carnal desire that she hardly knew where
one began and the other ended. As soon as the business
became profitable, Risha built a slaughtering shed and
gave Reuben an apartment in the main house. She
bought him fine clothes and he ate his meals at Reb
Falik's table. Reuben grew sleeker and fatter. During
the day he seldom slaughtered but wandered about in a
silken robe, soft slippers on his feet, a skullcap on his
head, watching the peasants working in the fields, the
shepherds caring for the cattle. He enjoyed all the pleasures of the outdoors and, in the afternoons, often went
swimming in the river. The aging Reb Falik retired
early. Late in the evening Reuben, accompanied by
Risha, went to the shed where she stood next to him as
he slaughtered and while the animal was throwing itself about in the anguish of its death throes she would
discuss with him their next act of lust. Sometimes she
gave herself to him immediately after the slaughtering.
By then all the peasants were in their huts asleep except
for one old man, half deaf and nearly blind, who aided
them at the shed. Sometimes Reuben lay with her on a
pile of straw in the shed, sometimes on the grass just
outside, and the thought of the dead and dying creatures
near them whetted their enjoyment. Reb Falik disliked
Reuben. The new business was repulsive to him but he
seldom said a word in opposition. He accepted the
annoyance with humility, thinking that he would soon
be dead anyway and what was the point of starting a
quarrel? Occasionally it occurred to him that his wife
was overly familiar with Reuben, but he pushed the suspicion out of his mind since he was by nature honest and

righteous, a man who gave everyone the benefit of the doubt.

One transgression begets another. One day Satan, the father of all lust and cunning, tempted Risha to take a hand in the slaughtering. Reuben was alarmed when she first suggested this. True, he was an adulterer, but nevertheless he was also a believer as many sinners are. He argued that for their sins they would be whipped, but why should they lead other people into iniquity, causing them to eat non-kosher carcasses? No, God forbid he and Risha should do anything like that. To become a slaughterer it was necessary to study the *Shulchan Aruch* and the Commentaries. A slaughterer was responsible for any blemish on the knife, no matter how small, and for any sin one of his customers incurred by eating impure meat. But Risha was adamant. What difference did it make? she asked. They would both toss on the bed of needles anyhow. If one committed sins, one should get as much enjoyment as possible out of them. Risha kept after Reuben constantly, alternating threats and bribes. She promised him new excitements, presents, money. She swore that if he would let her slaughter, immediately upon Reb Falik's death she would marry him and sign over all her property so that he could redeem some part of his iniquity through acts of charity. Finally Reuben gave in. Risha took such pleasure in killing that before long she was doing all the slaughtering herself, with Reuben acting merely as her assistant. She began to cheat, to sell tallow for kosher fat, and she stopped extracting the forbidden sinews in the thighs of the cows. She began a price war with the other Laskev butchers until those who remained became her hired employees. She got the contract to supply meat to the Polish army barracks, and since the officers took bribes, and the soldiers received only the worst meat, she earned vast sums. Risha became so rich that even she did not know how large her fortune was. Her malice grew. Once she slaughtered a horse and sold it as kosher beef. She killed some pigs too, scalding them in boiling water like the pork butchers. She managed never to be caught. She got so much satisfaction from deceiving the community that this soon became as powerful a passion with her as lechery and cruelty.

Like all those who devote themselves entirely to the pleasures of the flesh, Risha and Reuben grew prematurely old. Their bodies became so swollen they could barely meet. Their hearts floated in fat. Reuben took to drink. He lay all day long on his bed, and when he woke drank liquor from a carafe with a straw. Risha brought him refreshments and they passed their time in idle talk, chattering as do those who have sold their souls for the vanities of this world. They quarreled and kissed, teased and mocked, bemoaned the fact that time was passing and the grave coming nearer. Reb Falik was now sick most of the time but, though it often seemed his end was near, somehow his soul did not forsake his body. Risha toyed with ideas of death and even thought of poisoning Reb Falik. Another time, she said to Reuben: "Do you know, already I am satiated with life! If you want, slaughter me and marry a young woman."

After saying this, she transferred the straw from Reuben's lips to hers and sucked until the carafe was empty.

4

There is a proverb: Heaven and earth have sworn together that no secret can remain undivulged. The sins of Reuben and Risha could not stay hidden forever. People began to murmur that the two lived too well together. They remarked how old and feeble Reb Falik had become, how much oftener he stayed in bed than on his feet, and they concluded that Reuben and Risha were having an affair. The butchers Risha had forced to close their businesses had been spreading all kinds of calumny about her ever since. Some of the more scholarly housewives found sinews in Risha's meat which, according to the law, should have been removed. The Gentile butcher to whom Risha had been accustomed to sell the forbidden flanken complained that she had not sold him anything for months. With this evidence, the former butchers went in a body to the rabbi and community leaders and demanded an investigation of Risha's meat. But the council of elders was hesitant to start a quarrel with her. The rabbi quoted the Talmud to the effect that one who suspects the righteous deserves to be lashed, and added that, as long as there were no witnesses to any of Risha's transgression, it was wrong to shame her, for the one who shames his fellow man loses his portion in the world to come.

The butchers, thus rebuffed by the rabbi, decided to hire a spy and they chose a tough youth named Jechiel. This young man, a ruffian, set out from Laskev one night after dark, stole into the estate, managing to avoid the fierce dogs Risha kept, and took up his position behind the slaughtering shed. Putting his eye to a large crack, he saw Reuben and Risha inside and watched with astonishment as the old servant led in the hobbled animals and Risha, using a rope, threw them one by one to the ground. When the old man left, Jechiel was amazed in the torchlight to see Risha catch up a long knife and begin to cut the throats of the cattle one after the other. The steaming blood gurgled and flowed.

While the beasts were bleeding, Risha threw off all her clothes and stretched out naked on a pile of straw. Reuben came to her and they were so fat their bodies could barely join. They puffed and panted. Their wheezing mixed with the death-rattles of the animals made an unearthly noise; contorted shadows fell on the walls; the shed was saturated with the heat of blood. Jechiel was a hoodlum, but even he was terrified because only devils could behave like this. Afraid that fiends would seize him, he fled.

At dawn, Jechiel knocked on the rabbi's shutter. Stammering, he blurted out what he had witnessed. The rabbi roused the beadle and sent him with his wooden hammer to knock at the windows of the elders and summon them at once. At first no one believed Jechiel could be telling the truth. They suspected he had been hired by the butchers to bear false witness and they threatened him with beating and excommunication. Jechiel, to prove he was not lying, ran to the Ark of the Holy Scroll which stood in the Judgment Chamber, opened the door, and before those present could stop him swore by the Scroll that his words were true.

His story threw the town into a turmoil. Women ran out into the streets, striking their heads with their fists, crying and wailing. According to the evidence, the townspeople had been eating non-kosher meat for years. The wealthy housewives carried their pottery into the marketplace and broke it into shards. Some of the sick and several pregnant women fainted. Many of the pious tore their lapels, strewed their heads with ashes, and sat down to mourn. A crowd formed and ran to the butcher shops to punish the men who sold Risha's meat. Refusing to listen to what the butchers said in their own defense, they beat up several of them, threw whatever carcasses were on hand outdoors, and overturned the butcher blocks. Soon voices arose suggesting they go to Reb Falik's estate and the mob began to arm itself with bludgeons, rope, and knives. The rabbi, fearing bloodshed, came out into the street to stop them, warning that punishment must wait until the sin had been proved intentional and a verdict had been passed. But the mob wouldn't listen. The rabbi decided to go with them, hoping to calm them down on the way. The elders followed. Women trailed after them, pinching their cheeks and weeping as if at a funeral. Schoolboys dashed alongside.

Wolf Bonder, to whom Risha had given gifts and whom she had always paid well to cart the meat from the estate to Laskev, remained loyal to her. Seeing how ugly the temper of the crowd was becoming, he went to his stable, saddled a fast horse, and galloped out toward the estate to warn Risha. As it happened, Reuben and Risha had stayed overnight in the shed and were still there. Hearing hoofbeats, they got up and came out and watched with surprise as Wolf Bonder rode up. He explained what had happened and warned them of the mob on its way. He advised them to flee, unless they could prove their innocence; otherwise the angry men would surely tear them to pieces. He himself was afraid to stay any longer lest before he could get back the mob turn against him. Mounting his horse, he rode away at a gallop.

Reuben and Risha stood frozen with shock. Reuben's face turned a fiery red, then a deadly white. His hands trembled and he had to clutch at the door behind him to remain on his feet. Risha smiled anxiously and her face turned yellow as if she had jaundice, but it was Risha who moved first. Approaching her lover, she stared into his eyes. "So, my love," she said, "the end of a thief is the gallows."

"Let's run away." Reuben was shaking so violently that he could hardly get the words out.

But Risha answered that it was not possible. The estate had only six horses and all of them had been taken early that morning by peasants going to the forest for wood. A yoke of oxen would move so slowly that the rabble could overtake them. Besides, she, Risha, had no intention of abandoning her property and wandering like a beggar. Reuben implored her to flee with him, since life is more precious than all possessions, but Risha remained stubborn. She would not go. Finally they went into the main house where Risha rolled some linen up into a bundle for Reuben, gave him a roast chicken, a loaf of bread, and a pouch with some money. Standing outdoors, she watched as he set out, swaying and wobbling across the wooden bridge that led into the pine woods. Once in the forest he would strike the path to the Lublin road. Several times Reuben turned about-face, muttered and waved his hand as if calling her, but Risha stood impassively. She had already learned he was a coward. He was only a hero against a weak chicken and a tethered ox.

5

As soon as Reuben was out of sight, Risha moved towards the fields to call in the peasants. She told them to pick up axes, scythes, shovels, explained to them that a mob was on its way from Laskev, and promised each man a gulden and a pitcher of beer if he would help defend her. Risha herself seized a long knife in one hand and brandished a meat cleaver in the other. Soon the noise of the crowd could be heard in the distance and before long the mob was visible. Surrounded by her peasant guard, Risha mounted a hill at the entrance to the estate. When those who were coming saw peasants with axes and scythes, they slowed down. A few even tried to retreat. Risha's fierce dogs ran among them snarling, barking, growling.

The rabbi, seeing that the situation could lead only to bloodshed, demanded of his flock that they return home, but the tougher of the men refused to obey him. Risha called out taunting them: "Come on, let's see what you can do! I'll cut your heads off with this knife—the same knife I used on the horses and pigs I made you eat." When a man shouted that no one in Laskev would buy her meat anymore and that she would be excommunicated, Risha shouted back: "I don't need your money. I don't need your God either. I'll convert. Immediately!" And she began to scream in Polish, calling the Jews cursed Christ-killers and crossing herself as if she were already a Gentile. Turning to one of the peasants beside her, she said: "What are you waiting for, Maciek? Run and summon the priest. I don't want to belong to this filthy sect anymore." The peasant went and the mob became silent. Everyone knew that converts soon became enemies of Israel and invented all kinds of accusations against their former brethren. They turned away and went home. The Jews were afraid to instigate the anger of the Christians.

Meanwhile Reb Falik sat in his study house and recited the Mishnah. Deaf and half blind, he saw nothing and heard nothing. Suddenly Risha entered, knife in hand, screaming: "Go to your Jews. What do I need a synagogue here for?" When Reb Falik saw her with her head uncovered, a knife in her hand, her face contorted by abuse, he was seized by such anguish that he lost his tongue. In his prayer shawl and phylacteries, he rose to ask her what had happened, but his feet gave way and he collapsed to the floor dead. Risha ordered his body placed in an oxcart and she sent his corpse to the Jews in Laskev without even linen for a shroud. During the time the Laskev Burial Society cleansed and laid out Reb Falik's body, and while the burial was taking place and the rabbi speaking the eulogy, Risha prepared for her conversion. She sent men out to look for Reuben, for she wanted to persuade him to follow her example, but her lover had vanished.

Risha was now free to do as she pleased. After her conversion she reopened her shops and sold non-kosher meats to the Gentiles of Laskev and to the peasants who came in on market days. She no longer had to hide anything. She could slaughter openly and in whatever manner she pleased pigs, oxen, calves, sheep. She hired a Gentile slaughterer to replace Reuben and went hunting with him in the forest and shot deer, hares, rabbits. But she no longer took the same pleasure in torturing creatures; slaughtering no longer incited her lust; and she got little satisfaction from lying with the pig butcher. Fishing in the river, sometimes when a fish dangled on her hook or danced in her net, a moment of joy came to her heart imbedded in fat and she would mutter: "Well, fish, you are worse off than I am . . . !"

The truth was that she yearned for Reuben. She missed their lascivious talk, his scholarship, his dread of reincarnation, his terror of Gehenna. Now that Reb Falik was in his grave, she had no one to betray, to pity, to mock. She had bought a pew in the Christian church immediately upon conversion and for some months went every Sunday to listen to the priest's sermon.

Going and coming, she had her driver take her past the synagogue. Teasing the Jews gave her some satisfaction for a while, but soon this too palled.

With time Risha became so lazy that she no longer went to the slaughtering shed. She left everything in the hands of the pork butcher and did not even care that he was stealing from her. Immediately upon getting up in the morning, she poured herself a glass of liqueur and crept on her heavy feet from room to room talking to herself. She would stop at a mirror and mutter: "Woe, woe, Risha. What has happened to you? If your saintly mother should rise from her grave and see you—she would lie down again!" Some mornings she tried to improve her appearance but her clothes would not hang straight, her hair could not be untangled. Frequently she sang for hours in Yiddish and in Polish. Her voice was harsh and cracked and she invented the songs as she went along, repeating meaningless phrases, uttering sounds that resembled the cackling of fowl, the grunting of pigs, the death-rattles of oxen. Falling onto her bed she hiccuped, belched, laughed, cried. At night in her dreams, phantoms tormented her: bulls gored her with their horns; pigs shoved their snouts into her face and bit her; roosters cut her flesh to ribbons with their spurs. Reb Falik appeared dressed in his shroud, covered with wounds, waving a bunch of palm leaves, screaming: "I cannot rest in my grave. You have defiled my house."

Then Risha, or Maria Pawlowska as she was now called, would start up in bed, her limbs numb, her body covered with a cold sweat. Reb Falik's ghost would vanish but she could still hear the rustle of the palm leaves, the echo of his outcry. Simultaneously she would cross herself and repeat a Hebrew incantation learned in childhood from her mother. She would force her bare feet down to the floor and would begin to stumble through the dark from one room to another. She had thrown out all Reb Falik's books, had burned his Holy Scroll. The study house was now a shed for drying hides. But in the dining room there still remained the table on which Reb Falik had eaten his Sabbath meals, and from the ceiling hung the candelabra where his Sabbath candles had once burned. Sometimes Risha remembered her first two husbands whom she had tortured with her wrath, her greed, her curses and shrewish tongue. She was far from repenting, but something inside her was mourning and filling her with bitterness. Opening a window, she would look out into the midnight sky full of stars and cry out: "God, come and punish me! Come Satan! Come Asmodeus! Show your might. Carry me to the burning desert behind the dark mountains!"

6

One winter Laskev was terrified by a carnivorous animal lurking about at night and attacking people. Some who had seen the creature said it was a bear, others a wolf, others a demon. One woman, going outdoors to urinate, had her neck bitten. A yeshiva boy was chased through the streets. An elderly night-watchman had his face clawed. The women and children of Laskev were afraid to leave their houses after nightfall. Everywhere shutters were bolted tight. Many strange things were recounted about the beast: someone had heard it rave with a human voice; another had seen it rise on its hind legs and run. It had overturned a barrel of cabbage in a courtyard, had opened chicken coops, thrown out the dough set to rise in the wooden trough in the bakery, and it had defiled the butcher blocks in the kosher shops with excrement.

One dark night the butchers of Laskev gathered with axes and knives determined either to kill or capture the monster. Splitting up into small groups they waited, their eyes growing accustomed to the darkness. In the middle of the night there was a scream and running toward it they caught sight of the animal making for the outskirts of town. A man shouted that he had been bitten in the shoulder. Frightened, some of the men dropped back, but others continued to give chase. One of the hunters saw it and threw his axe. Apparently the animal was hit, for with a ghastly scream it wobbled and fell. A horrible howling filled the air. Then the beast began to curse in Polish and Yiddish and to wail in a high-pitched voice like a woman in labor. Convinced that they had wounded a she-devil, the men ran home.

All that night the animal groaned and babbled. It even dragged itself to a house and knocked at the shutters. Then it became silent and the dogs began to bark. When day dawned, the bolder people came out of their houses. They discovered to their amazement that the animal was Risha. She lay dead dressed in a skunk fur coat wet with blood. One felt boot was missing. The hatchet had buried itself in her back. The dogs had already partaken of her entrails. Nearby was the knife she had used to stab one of her pursuers. It was now clear that Risha had become a werewolf. Since the Jews refused to bury her in their cemetery and the Christians were unwilling to give her a plot in theirs, she was taken to the hill on the estate where she had fought off the mob, and a ditch was dug for her there. Her wealth was confiscated by the city.

Some years later a wandering stranger lodged in the poorhouse of Laskev became sick. Before his death, he summoned the rabbi and the seven elders of the town and divulged to them that he was Reuben the slaughterer, with whom Risha had sinned. For years he had wandered from town to town, eating no meat, fasting Mondays and Thursdays, wearing a shirt of sack cloth, and repenting his abominations. He had come to Laskev to die because it was here his parents were buried. The rabbi recited the confession with him and Reuben revealed many details of the past which the townspeople had not known.

Risha's grave on the hill soon became covered with refuse. Yet long afterwards it remained customary for the Laskev schoolboys on the thirty-third day of Omer, when they went out carrying bows and arrows and a provision of hard-boiled eggs, to stop there. They danced on the hill and sang:

> *Risha slaughtered*
> *Black horses*
> *Now she's fallen*
> *To evil forces.*
>
> *A pig for an ox*
> *Sold Risha the witch*
> *Now she's roasting*
> *In sulphur and pitch.*

Before the children left, they spat on the grave and recited:

Thou shalt not suffer a witch to live
A witch to live thou shalt not suffer
Suffer a witch to live thou shalt not.

Translated by the author
and Elizabeth Pollet

The
Fast

Itche Nokhum was always a small eater, but after Roise
Genendel had left him and his father, may he live long,
had ordered him to send her a writ of divorce, Itche
Nokhum had given himself over to fasting. It was easy
to fast in the house of the Bechever rebbe. The rebbetzin, his wife, was dead. Aunt Peshe, who kept house,
never paid attention to whether one ate or didn't. The
servant, Elke Dobe, often forgot to bring Itche Nokhum
his meals. Under his window there was a pit where refuse was dumped. Itche Nokhum threw the food out of
the window. Dogs, cats and birds ate the scraps. It was
only now, at the age of forty, that Itche Nokhum understood why the sages of old had fasted from Sabbath
to Sabbath. An empty stomach, a pure bowel, is an
exquisite pleasure. The body is light as though freed of

gravity; the mind is clear. At first there is a slight gnawing at the stomach and the mouth waters, but after the
first two days all hunger ceases. Itche Nokhum had long
felt a repugnance to eating meat or anything that came
from living creatures. Ever since he had seen Leizer the
shokhet slaughter an ox at the slaughterhouse, meat
made him nauseous. Even milk, drawn from udders, and
eggs, laid by hens, were repellent. All of these had to do
with blood, veins, gut. True, the Holy Books permitted the eating of meat, but only to saints, who have
the power to deliver the sinful souls incarnated in kine
and fowl. Itche Nokhum would have none of it.

Even bread, potatoes and greens were too much. It
was enough to eat just to sustain life. And for that, a
bite or two sufficed for several days. Anything more
was self-indulgence. Why yield to gluttony? Since Roise
Genendel, daughter of the Bialer rebbe, had left Itche
Nokhum, he had discovered that a man can curb every
desire. There is something in the heart that lusts, but one
can thumb his nose at it. It wants to think carnal
thoughts, but one compels it to pore over the Holy
Book. It tempts one into longings and imaginings, but
just to thwart it one recites the Psalms. In the morning
it wants to sleep till nine, but one awakens it at daybreak. What this enemy within hates most of all is a cold
ritual bath. But there is a little spot in the brain that has
the final word, and when it commands the feet to go,
they go, be the water cold as ice. In time, opposing this
lusting creature becomes a habit. One bends it, gags it,
or else one lets it babble on without answering—as it is
written: "Answer not a fool according to his folly."

Itche Nokhum paced his room, back and forth—
small, lean, with a wispy straw-colored beard, a face
white as chalk, with a reddish, pointed nose and watery-

blue eyes under shaggy yellow eyebrows. Over his forehead sat a crumpled skullcap with bits of straw and feathers clinging to it. Since Itche Nokhum had lost weight, everything hung loosely on his body: his trousers, held up by a sash, his gaberdine, down to his ankles, his creased, unbuttoned shirt. Even his slippers and white socks were now too big. He did not walk, but shuffled. When the tempter became too strong, Itche Nokhum fooled him with a pinch of snuff or a pipe. Tobacco dulls the appetite. Itche Nokhum grappled with the enemy without respite. One moment he was seized with lust for Roise Genendel, the next with anger at his father, may he live long, for urging him to divorce her; now he wanted to sleep under a quilt, and now he was consumed with thirst for a cup of coffee. When he tired of pacing, he lay down on a bench, with his handkerchief under his head in place of a pillow. The boards pressed against his ribs, made it impossible to remain long in one position. If Itche Nokhum managed to doze off, he was immediately attacked by dreams—not one after another, as in the past, but in a swarm, like locusts, as though the visions and delusions had hovered over him, just waiting till he closed his eyes. Roise Genendel appeared to him, as naked as mother Eve, spoke perverse words, laughed shamelessly. Itche Nokhum ate pastries, marzipans, drank wine, swooped through the air like a bat. Musicians played, drums pounded. It was both Purim and Simkhas Torah. "How can this be?" Itche Nokhum wondered. "The Messiah must have come—Sabbati Zevi himself . . ."

He woke with a start, drenched with perspiration. For a while he still remembered all the apparitions, absurdities and delusions, but soon they vanished from his mind, leaving only the image of Roise Genendel. Her body dazzled. He heard the echo of her laughter. "I shouldn't have divorced her!" Itche Nokhum muttered to himself. "I should have left her and disappeared, so that she wouldn't know where my bones were resting. Too late now . . ." People were saying in Bechev that she was about to become the daughter-in-law of a Galician, the wife of the Komarner rebbe. A Hasid who knew the Komarner rebbe said that he was tall up to the ceiling, black as a gypsy and three times a widower . . .

Itche Nokhum caught himself in a sin. Why did he want to leave her a deserted wife? Out of revenge. He had mentally broken the Mosaic precept: Thou shalt not avenge nor bear any grudge. Itche Nokhum took *The Beginning of Wisdom* from the bookshelf. What were the penances for vengefulness? He turned the yellowed pages, scanning them. There was a long list of sins, but revenge was not among them. Itche Nokhum grimaced. This was not the first time that he cursed Roise Genendel in his mind, wishing her ill. He had imagined her sick, dying, dead. He knew that he was consumed with rancor, hatred, evil thoughts. The stiff-necked body refused to yield. It was full of spite.

Itche Nokhum opened a drawer where he had put a handful of pebbles collected in the courtyard, some nettles he had gathered by the fence, and burrs, such as the urchins throw on Tishe b'Ov. Itche Nokhum latched the door, removed his slippers and put in the pebbles: let them cut his soles. He held the nettles against his arms and neck, and rubbed his chest with them. They stung, but not too badly. The blisters would come later. "And now I'll treat you to a cold immersion!" he said to himself. "Come along! . . ." He unlocked the door and started down the stairs. Itche

Nokhum was no longer one man, but two. One meted out punishment, and the other resisted. One Itche Nokhum dragged the other to the ritual bath, and the other babbled obscenities, cursed, blasphemed. Itche Nokhum raised his hand and gave himself a slap on the face:

"Wanton!"

2

It was the fifth day of Itche Nokhum's fast. He had begun the fast on Sabbath evening, and now it was Thursday night. At first, Itche Nokhum had wanted to prove to himself that what the men of old could do, could also be done today. If Rabbi Zadock of Jerusalem had been able to nourish himself for forty years by sucking at a fig, he, Itche Nokhum, could surely abstain from glutting for a week. Secondly, the other one, the adversary, had become altogether too obstreperous. He sat in Itche Nokhum like a dybbuk, forever doing spite. One Itche Nokhum prayed, and the other gabbled rhymes like a clown. One applied the phylacteries, and the other belched, hiccuped, spat. One recited the Eighteen Benedictions, and the other conjured pictures of the Komarner disporting himself with Roise Genendel. Itche Nokhum no longer knew what he was doing. He repeated the same prayer three times. He was no longer in a wrestling bout, but in a fight for life or death. Itche Nokhum stopped sleeping. If a man cannot overcome the enemy by fasting, by lying on thorns, by cold immersions, then how is he to drive him out? By destroying himself? But that is forbidden! A man is expected to break the casket without spilling the wine. Yet how could this be done? Itche Nokhum lay on the bench in his trousers and socks, with a stone for a pillow, like the patriarch Jacob. His skin tingled, but he refused to scratch. Beads of sweat trickled down his neck, but he would not wipe it. The evil one thought of a different trick every minute. Itche Nokhum's hair pricked his skull. His ear buzzed as if a gnat had gotten into it. His nostrils itched to sneeze, his mouth tried to yawn. His knees ached. His belly swelled as though overstuffed with food. Itche Nokhum felt ants running up and down his back. He muttered in the dark:

"Go on, torment me, tear at my flesh! . . ."

For a while the other relented and Itche Nokhum dozed off. A huge frog opened its maw, ready to swallow him. The church bell rang out. Itche Nokhum started up, trembling. Was there a fire or some other disaster? He waited for the bell to ring again. But there was only a distant, hollow echo. Itche Nokhum felt a need to urinate. He stood by the pail, but nothing came. He washed his hands, preparing to say the prayer proper for the occasion, but the urge returned. He felt a burning and a throbbing. His entrails contracted with cramps. A bitterness flooded his mouth, as on the verge of vomiting. "Shall I take a drink of water?" Itche Nokhum asked himself. He went to the stool, where a pitcher stood, half filled with water for ritual hand-washing, and turned it over reluctantly. One of his socks became wet. "I'll not give in to him!" Itche Nokhum whispered. "Show a dog a finger and he'll snap up the whole hand . . ."

Itche Nokhum stretched out again on his bench, his limbs numb. The pains and aches, the gnawing hunger, the dryness of thirst had suddenly vanished. He was neither asleep nor awake. The brain was thinking, but Itche Nokhum did not know what it thought. The other, the spiteful one, was gone, and there was once again only one Itche Nokhum. He was no longer divided. "Am I dying?" he asked himself. All fear of death had disappeared. He was ready to go. When a funeral is held on Friday afternoon, he thought, the newly dead is spared interrogation and torture by the Black Angel. Itche Nokhum watched his strength ebbing away. His mind slipped over a stretch of time, leaving a blank. It was as if Purah, the Angel of Forgetfulness, had plucked out a piece of Itche Nokhum's memory. He marveled at it in the dark. The lapse may have lasted a minute, an hour, or a day and a night. Itche Nokhum had once read a story about a bewitched young man who bent over a barrel to dip some water, and when he straightened up it was seventy years later.

Suddenly Itche Nokhum was petrified. Something began to stir in the dark by the door—a coiling wisp of vapor, airy and misty. Itche Nokhum was so astonished that he forgot to be frightened. A figure loomed up, an apparition with head and shoulders, neck and hair—a woman. Her face seemed to glow with its own light. Itche Nokhum recognized her: Roise Genendel! The upper part of her body was now quite distinct; the face swayed as if trying to speak. The eyesockets grinned. Below, the phantasm trailed off in ragged wisps and shreds. Itche Nokhum heard his own voice:

"What do you want?"

He tried to rise, but his legs were numb and heavy. The specter flowed toward him, dragging its tail of slime like a chick prematurely breaking out of the shell. "The Primeval Substance!" something cried in Itche Nokhum. He recalled the Psalm: "Thine eyes did see my substance, yet being unperfect." He wanted to speak to the night-creature, but he was robbed of the power of speech. For a time he watched dumbly as she approached, half woman, half shapeless ooze, a monstrous fungus straining to break away from its root, a creature put together in haste. After a while she began to melt away. Pieces dropped from her. The face dissolved, the hair scattered, the nose stretched out and became a snout, as in the manikins that people put on their window sills in winter to mock the frost. She spat out her tongue. Roise Genendel vanished, and the sun flashed in the east sharp as a knife. Bloody stains spattered the walls, the ceilings, the floor. The morning had slaughtered Roise Genendel and splashed her blood. A last bubble of life had burst, and everything returned to the void. Itche Nokhum sat up and rocked as men do over a corpse.

"Roise Genendel! . . . Woe is me! . . ."

3

They were blowing the ram's horn in Bechev. Elul breezes blew in from the willows in the cemetery. Bright gossamer floated high in the air over the courtyard. Ripe fruit dropped from the trees in the rebbe's orchard. Desolation rustled in the prayer house. Sparrows skipped over the tables. The community goat wandered into the antechamber, leaned against the box with torn, discarded prayer books and tried to chew at the corner of a psalm book. It was Thursday again, and Itche Nokhum had not tasted food since the Sabbath evening meal, but no one paid any attention. When a man fasts all year, he does not begin to eat in Elul, the month of repentance. Itche Nokhum sat in his room, turning the pages of *The Covenant of Rest*. He mumbled for a while. Then he leaned his head on the back of the chair and dozed off.

Suddenly Itche Nokhum heard steps and loud voices. Someone was coming rapidly upstairs to him. The door was flung open and Itche Nokhum saw Roise Genendel and behind her, Yente, her maidservant. It was not the Roise Genendel who revealed herself to him in the nights and through whom he could see as through the weave of his sash, but Roise Genendel in the living flesh: tall, narrow, with a crooked nose, fiery black eyes, thick lips and a long neck. She was dressed in a black shawl, a silk cloak and high-heeled shoes. She was scolding her servant and made her a sign to follow her no further. Roise Genendel entered Itche Nokhum's room, leaving the door open—evidently in order not to remain alone with him. Yente remained standing halfway up the stairs. Itche Nokhum was astounded. "Have I already attained such power?" the thought flashed through his brain. For a long while she stood upon the threshold, holding up her skirt, appraising him with a sidelong stare, in which anger mingled with silent pity. Then she said:

"White as a corpse!"

"What do you want?" asked Itche Nokhum in a faint voice that he could scarcely hear himself.

"What are you doing? Fasting, eh?" Roise Genendel asked mockingly.

Itche Nokhum did not answer.

"Itche Nokhum, I must speak to you!"

Roise Genendel slammed the door to.

"What is it?"

"Itche Nokhum, leave me in peace!" Roise Genendel almost shouted. "We were divorced, we are strangers now. I want to marry, and you can also marry. Everything must have an end!"

"I don't know what you mean."

"You know, you know. You're sitting here and casting spells. I was already on the eve of marriage, and I had to postpone it. Why don't you let me be? You'll drive me from this world. I'll throw myself into the well!"

Roise Genendel stamped her foot. She truculently placed her hand on the doorpost. A diamond ring flashed on her finger. She breathed both fear and strength. Itche Nokhum raised his eyebrows. His heart knocked once and seemed to stop.

"I swear, I don't know . . ."

"You wake me up! You scream into my ear! What do you want of me? It wasn't right between us. From the very first. Forgive me, but you're not a man. Why do you torment me, then? Will you tell me?"

"What am I doing?"

"You come to me, you pinch me, you flay me. I hear your steps. I don't eat and I don't sleep because of you. I am losing weight. People see you in our courtyard, they see you, I'm not mad! . . . Yente almost died of fright. I'll call her in, she will tell you herself. She was going, if you will pardon me, to the outhouse, and you floated toward her. She raised such screams that everybody in the yard came running . . . Just before sunrise you came and sat on my bed, and I could not move my feet. What are you, a devil?"

Itche Nokhum was silent.

"We've kept it secret," Roise Genendel went on. "But I can't suffer forever. I'll tell the whole world who you are and what you're doing. You will be excommunicated. I'm only sorry for your old father . . ."

Itche Nokhum wanted to answer, but he could not utter a single word. Everything in him shrank and dried up. He began to gasp and croak like a grandfather clock before striking. Something inside him leaped like a snake. Itche Nokhum was filled with a strange fluttering. An icy feather brushed down his spine. He shook his head from side to side, as if to say, "No."

"I've come to warn you! Swear that you will release me. If not, I'll raise such a commotion that all Bechev will come running. I'll put aside all shame. Come down to the prayer house and swear upon the Holy Scrolls. It's either my death or yours! . . ."

Itche Nokhum made another effort and began to mumble in a choked voice, as if he were being strangled.

"I swear to you, I am not to blame."

"Who is then? You're using Sacred Names. You've plunged yourself into the cabala. You've lost this world —you'll lose the next one too. My father, may he live long, has sent me to you. He also has intercessors in heaven. You're dealing with the evil ones, woe is me. You'll be driven behind the Black Mountains! You'll be thrown into the Hollow of the Sling! Mooncalf! . . ."

"Roise Genendel!"

"Fiend! Satan! Asmodeus!"

Roise Genendel was suddenly stricken mute. She stared at Itche Nokhum with her enormous black eyes, recoiling from him. The room became so still that one could hear the buzzing of a single fly. Itche Nokhum strained to speak. His throat contracted as if he had swallowed something.

"Roise Genendel, I cannot . . . I cannot forget you!"

"Miserable leech! I'm in your power . . ."

Roise Genendel's mouth twisted. She covered her face with both hands and broke into a hoarse wail.

Translated by Mirra Ginsburg

The
Séance

It was during the summer of 1946, in the living room of Mrs. Kopitzky on Central Park West. A single red bulb burned behind a shade adorned with one of Mrs. Kopitzky's automatic drawings—circles with eyes, flowers with mouths, goblets with fingers. The walls were all hung with Lotte Kopitzky's paintings, which she did in a state of trance and at the direction of her control—Bhaghavar Krishna, a Hindu sage supposed to have lived in the fourth century. It was he, Bhaghavar Krishna, who had painted the peacock with the golden tail, in the middle of which appeared the image of Buddha; the otherworldly trees hung with elflocks and fantastic fruits; the young women of the planet Venus with their branch-like arms and their ears from which stretched silver nets—organs of telepathy. Over the pic-

tures, the old furniture, the shelves with books, there
hovered reddish shadows. The windows were covered
with heavy drapes.

At the round table on which lay a Ouija board, a
trumpet, and a withered rose, sat Dr. Zorach Kalisher,
small, broad-shouldered, bald in front and with sparse
tufts of hair in the back, half yellow, half gray. From
behind his yellow bushy brows peered a pair of small,
piercing eyes. Dr. Kalisher had almost no neck—his
head sat directly on his broad shoulders, making him
look like a primitive African statue. His nose was
crooked, flat at the top, the tip split in two. On his chin
sprouted a tiny growth. It was hard to tell whether this
was a remnant of a beard or just a hairy wart. The face
was wrinkled, badly shaven, and grimy. He wore a
black corduroy jacket, a white shirt covered with ash
and coffee stains, and a crooked bow tie.

When conversing with Mrs. Kopitzky, he spoke an
odd mixture of Yiddish and German. "What's keeping
our friend Bhaghavar Krishna? Did he lose his way in
the spheres of heaven?"

"Dr. Kalisher, don't rush me," Mrs. Kopitzky answered. "We cannot give them orders . . . they have
their motives and their moods. Have a little patience."

"Well, if one must, one must."

Dr. Kalisher drummed his fingers on the table. From
each finger sprouted a little red beard. Mrs. Kopitzky
leaned her head on the back of the upholstered chair
and prepared to fall into a trance. Against the dark glow
of the red bulb, one could discern her freshly dyed hair,
black without luster, waved into tiny ringlets; her
rouged face, the broad nose, high cheekbones, and eyes
spread far apart and heavily lined with mascara. Dr.
Kalisher often joked that she looked like a painted bull-

dog. Her husband, Leon Kopitzky, a dentist, had died eighteen years before, leaving no children. The widow supported herself on an annuity from an insurance company. In 1929 she had lost her fortune in the Wall Street crash, but had recently begun to buy securities again on the advice of her Ouija board, planchette, and crystal ball. Mrs. Kopitzky even asked Bhaghavar Krishna for tips on the races. In a few cases, he had divulged in dreams the names of winning horses.

Dr. Kalisher bowed his head and covered his eyes with his hands, muttering to himself as solitary people often do. "Well, I've played the fool enough. This is the last night. Even from kreplach one has enough."

"Did you say something, Doctor?"

"What? Nothing."

"When you rush me, I can't fall into the trance."

"Trance-shmance," Dr. Kalisher grumbled to himself. "The ghost is late, that's all. Who does she think she's fooling? Just crazy—meshugga."

Aloud, he said: "I'm not rushing you, I've plenty of time. If what the Americans say about time is right, I'm a second Rockefeller."

As Mrs. Kopitzky opened her mouth to answer, her double chin, with all its warts, trembled, revealing a set of huge false teeth. Suddenly she threw back her head and sighed. She closed her eyes, and snorted once. Dr. Kalisher gaped at her questioningly, sadly. He had not yet heard the sound of the outside door opening, but Mrs. Kopitzky, who probably had the acute hearing of an animal, might have. Dr. Kalisher began to rub his temples and his nose, and then clutched at his tiny beard.

There was a time when he had tried to understand all things through his reason, but that period of rationalism had long passed. Since then, he had constructed an anti-rationalistic philosophy, a kind of extreme hedonism which saw in eroticism the *Ding an sich*, and in reason the very lowest stage of being, the entropy which led to absolute death. His position had been a curious compound of Hartmann's idea of the Unconscious with the cabala of Rabbi Isaac Luria, according to which all things, from the smallest grain of sand to the very Godhead itself, are Copulation and Union. It was because of this system that Dr. Kalisher had come from Paris to New York in 1939, leaving behind in Poland his father, a rabbi, a wife who refused to divorce him, and a lover, Nella, with whom he had lived for years in Berlin and later in Paris. It so happened that when Dr. Kalisher left for America, Nella went to visit her parents in Warsaw. He had planned to bring her over to the United States as soon as he found a translator, a publisher, and a chair at one of the American universities.

In those days Dr. Kalisher had still been hopeful. He had been offered a cathedra in the Hebrew University in Jerusalem; a publisher in Palestine was about to issue one of his books; his essays had been printed in Zurich and Paris. But with the outbreak of the Second World War, his life began to deteriorate. His literary agent suddenly died, his translator was inept and, to make matters worse, absconded with a good part of the manuscript, of which there was no copy. In the Yiddish press, for some strange reason, the reviewers turned hostile and hinted that he was a charlatan. The Jewish organizations which arranged lectures for him cancelled his tour. According to his own philosophy, he had believed that all suffering was nothing more than negative expressions of universal eroticism: Hitler, Stalin, the Nazis who sang the Horst Wessel song and made the Jews wear yellow armbands, were actually searching for new forms and variations of sexual salvation. But Dr. Kalisher began to doubt his own system and fell into despair. He had to leave his hotel and move into a cheap furnished room. He wandered about in shabby clothes, sat all day in cafeterias, drank endless cups of coffee, smoked bad cigars, and barely managed to survive on the few dollars that a relief organization gave him each month. The refugees whom he met spread all sorts of rumors about visas for those left behind in Europe, packages of food and medicines that could be sent them through various agencies, ways of bringing over relatives from Poland through Honduras, Cuba, Brazil. But he, Zorach Kalisher, could save no one from the Nazis. He had received only a single letter from Nella.

Only in New York had Dr. Kalisher realized how attached he was to his mistress. Without her, he became impotent.

2

Everything was exactly as it had been yesterday and the day before. Bhaghavar Krishna began to speak in English with his foreign voice that was half male and half female, duplicating Mrs. Kopitzky's errors in pronunciation and grammar. Lotte Kopitzky came from a village in the Carpathian Mountains. Dr. Kalisher could never discover her nationality—Hungarian, Rumanian, Galician? She knew no Polish or German, and little English; even her Yiddish had been corrupted through her long years in America. Actually she had been left languageless and Bhaghavar Krishna spoke her various jargons. At first Dr. Kalisher had asked Bhaghavar Krishna the details of his earthly existence but had been told by Bhaghavar Krishna that he had forgotten everything in the heavenly mansions in which he dwelt. All he could recall was that he had lived in the suburbs of Madras. Bhaghavar Krishna did not even know that in that part of India Tamil was spoken. When Dr. Kalisher tried to converse with him about Sanskrit, the Mahabharata, the Ramayana, the Sakuntala, Bhaghavar Krishna replied that he was no longer interested in terrestrial literature. Bhaghavar Krishna knew nothing but a few theosophic and spiritualistic brochures and magazines which Mrs. Kopitzky subscribed to.

For Dr. Kalisher it was all one big joke; but if one lived in a bug-ridden room and had a stomach spoiled by cafeteria food, if one was in one's sixties and completely without family, one became tolerant of all kinds of crackpots. He had been introduced to Mrs. Kopitzky in 1942, took part in scores of her séances, read her automatic writings, admired her automatic paintings, listened to her automatic symphonies. A few times he had borrowed money from her which he had been unable to return. He ate at her house—vegetarian suppers, since Mrs. Kopitzky touched neither meat, fish, milk, nor eggs, but only fruit and vegetables which mother earth produces. She specialized in preparing salads with nuts, almonds, pomegranates, avocados.

In the beginning, Lotte Kopitzky had wanted to draw him into a romance. The spirits were all of the opinion that Lotte Kopitzky and Zorach Kalisher derived from the same spiritual origin: *The Great White Lodge.* Even Bhaghavar Krishna had a taste for matchmaking. Lotte Kopitzky constantly conveyed to Dr. Kalisher regards from the Masters, who had connections with Tibet, Atlantis, the Heavenly Hierarchy, the Shambala, the Fourth Kingdom of Nature and the Council of Sanat

Kumara. In heaven as on the earth, in the early forties, all kinds of crises were brewing. The Powers having realigned themselves, the members of the Ashrams were preparing a war on Cosmic Evil. The Hierarchy sent out projectors to light up the planet Earth, and to find esoteric men and women to serve special purposes. Mrs. Kopitzky assured Dr. Kalisher that he was ordained to play a huge part in the Universal Rebirth. But he had neglected his mission, disappointed the Masters. He had promised to telephone, but didn't. He spent months in Philadelphia without dropping her a postcard. He returned without informing her. Mrs. Kopitzky ran into him in an automat on Sixth Avenue and found him in a torn coat, a dirty shirt, and shoes worn so thin they no longer had heels. He had not even applied for United States citizenship, though refugees were entitled to citizenship without going abroad to get a visa.

Now, in 1946, everything that Lotte Kopitzky had prophesied had come true. All had passed over to the other side—his father, his brothers, his sisters, Nella. Bhaghavar Krishna brought messages from them. The Masters still remembered Dr. Kalisher, and still had plans for him in connection with the Centennial Conference of the Hierarchy. Even the fact that his family had perished in Treblinka, Maidanek, Stutthof was closely connected with the Powers of Light, the Development of Karma, the New Cycle after Lemuria, and with the aim of leading humanity to a new ascent in Love and a new Aquatic Epoch.

During the last few weeks, Mrs. Kopitzky had become dissatisfied with summoning Nella's spirit in the usual way. Dr. Kalisher was given the rare opportunity of coming into contact with Nella's materialized form. It happened in this way: Bhaghavar Krishna would give a sign to Dr. Kalisher that he should walk down the dark corridor to Mrs. Kopitzky's bedroom. There in the darkness, near Mrs. Kopitzky's bureau, an apparition hovered which was supposed to be Nella. She murmured to Dr. Kalisher in Polish, spoke caressing words into his ear, brought him messages from friends and relatives. Bhaghavar Krishna had admonished Dr. Kalisher time and again not to try to touch the phantom, because contact could cause severe injury to both, to him and Mrs. Kopitzky. The few times that he sought to approach her, she deftly eluded him. But confused though Dr. Kalisher was by these episodes, he was aware that they were contrived. This was not Nella, neither her voice nor her manner. The messages he received proved nothing. He had mentioned all these names to Mrs. Kopitzky and had been questioned by her. But Dr. Kalisher remained curious: Who was the apparition? Why did she act the part? Probably for money. But the fact that Lotte Kopitzky was capable of hiring a ghost proved that she was not only a self-deceiver but a swindler of others as well. Every time Dr. Kalisher walked down the dark corridor, he murmured, "Crazy, meshugga, a ridiculous woman."

Tonight Dr. Kalisher could hardly wait for Bhaghavar Krishna's signal. He was tired of these absurdities. For years he had suffered from a prostate condition and now had to urinate every half hour. A Warsaw doctor who was not allowed to practice in America, but did so clandestinely nonetheless, had warned Dr. Kalisher not to postpone an operation, because complications might arise. But Kalisher had neither the money for the hospital nor the will to go there. He sought to cure himself with baths, hot-water bottles, and with pills he had brought with him from France. He even tried to massage his prostate gland himself. As a rule, he went to the bathroom the moment he arrived at Mrs. Kopitzky's, but this evening he had neglected to do so. He felt a pressure on his bladder. The raw vegetables which Mrs. Kopitzky had given him to eat made his intestines twist. "Well, I'm too old for such pleasures," he murmured. As Bhaghavar Krishna spoke, Dr. Kalisher could scarcely listen. "What is she babbling, the idiot? She's not even a decent ventriloquist."

The instant Bhaghavar Krishna gave his usual sign, Dr. Kalisher got up. His legs had been troubling him greatly but had never been as shaky as tonight. "Well, I'll go to the bathroom first," he decided. To reach the bathroom in the dark was not easy. Dr. Kalisher walked hesitantly, his hands outstretched, trying to feel his way. When he had reached the bathroom and opened the door, someone inside pulled the knob back. It is she, the girl, Dr. Kalisher realized. So shaken was he that he forgot why he was there. "She most probably came here to undress." He was embarrassed both for himself and for Mrs. Kopitzky. "What does she need it for, for whom is she playing this comedy?" His eyes had become accustomed to the dark. He had seen the girl's silhouette. The bathroom had a window giving on to the street, and the shimmer of the street lamp had fallen on to it. She was small, broadish, with a high bosom. She appeared to have been in her underwear. Dr. Kalisher stood there hypnotized. He wanted to cry out, "Enough, it's all so obvious," but his tongue was numb. His heart pounded and he could hear his own breathing.

After a while he began to retrace his steps, but he was dazed with blindness. He bumped into a clothes tree and hit a wall, striking his head. He stepped backwards. Something fell and broke. Perhaps one of Mrs.

Kopitzky's otherworldly sculptures! At the moment the telephone began to ring, the sound unusually loud and menacing. Dr. Kalisher shivered. He suddenly felt a warmth in his underwear. He had wet himself like a child.

3

"Well, I've reached the bottom," Dr. Kalisher muttered to himself. "I'm ready for the junkyard." He walked toward the bedroom. Not only his underwear, his pants also had become wet. He expected Mrs. Kopitzky to answer the telephone; it happened more than once that she awakened from her trance to discuss stocks, bonds, and dividends. But the telephone kept on ringing. Only now he realized what he had done—he had closed the living-room door, shutting out the red glow which helped him find his way. "I'm going home," he resolved. He turned toward the street door but found he had lost all sense of direction in that labyrinth of an apartment. He touched a knob and turned it. He heard a muffled scream. He had wandered into the bathroom again. There seemed to be no hook or chain inside. Again he saw the woman in a corset, but this time her face half in the light. In that split second he knew she was middle-aged.

"Forgive, please." And he moved back.

The telephone stopped ringing, then began anew. Suddenly Dr. Kalisher glimpsed a shaft of red light and heard Mrs. Kopitzky walking toward the telephone. He stopped and said, half statement, half question: "Mrs. Kopitzky!"

Mrs. Kopitzky started. "Already finished?"

"I'm not well, I must go home."

"Not well? Where do you want to go? What's the matter? Your heart?"

"Everything."

"Wait a second."

Mrs. Kopitzky, having approached him, took his arm and led him back to the living room. The telephone continued to ring and then finally fell silent. "Did you get a pressure in your heart, huh?" Mrs. Kopitzky asked. "Lie down on the sofa, I'll get a doctor."

"No, no, not necessary."

"I'll massage you."

"My bladder is not in order, my prostate gland."

"What? I'll put on the light."

He wanted to ask her not to do so, but she had already turned on a number of lamps. The light glared in his eyes. She stood looking at him and at his wet pants. Her head shook from side to side. Then she said, "This is what comes from living alone."

"Really, I'm ashamed of myself."

"What's the shame? We all get older. Nobody gets younger. Were you in the bathroom?"

Dr. Kalisher didn't answer.

"Wait a moment, I still have *his* clothes. I had a premonition I would need them someday."

Mrs. Kopitzky left the room. Dr. Kalisher sat down on the edge of a chair, placing his handkerchief beneath him. He sat there stiff, wet, childishly guilty and helpless, and yet with that inner quiet that comes from illness. For years he had been afraid of doctors, hospitals, and especially nurses, who deny their feminine shyness and treat grownup men like babies. Now he was prepared for the last degradations of the body. "Well, I'm finished, *kaput*." . . . He made a swift summation of his existence. "Philosophy? what philosophy? Eroticism? whose eroticism?" He had played with phrases for years, had come to no conclusions. What had happened to him, in him, all that had taken place in Poland, in Russia, on the planets, on the far-away galaxies, could not be reduced either to Schopenhauer's blind will or to his, Kalisher's, eroticism. It was explained neither by Spinoza's substance, Leibnitz's monads, Hegel's dialectic, or Heckel's monism. "They all just juggle words like Mrs. Kopitzky. It's better that I didn't publish all that scribbling of mine. What's the good of all these preposterous hypotheses? They don't help at all. . . ." He looked up at Mrs. Kopitzky's pictures on the wall, and in the blazing light they resembled the smearings of school children. From the street came the honking of cars, the screams of boys, the thundering echo of the subway as a train passed. The door opened and Mrs. Kopitzky entered with a bundle of clothes: a jacket, pants and shirt, and underwear. The clothes smelled of mothballs and dust. She said to him, "Have you been in the bedroom?"

"What? No."

"Nella didn't materialize?"

"No, she didn't materialize."

"Well, change your clothes. Don't let me embarrass you."

She put the bundle on the sofa and bent over Dr. Kalisher with the devotion of a relative. She said, "You'll stay here. Tomorrow I'll send for your things."

"No, that's senseless."

"I knew that this would happen the moment we were introduced on Second Avenue."

"How so? Well, it's all the same."

"*They* tell me things in advance. I look at someone, and I know what will happen to him."

"So? When am I going to go?"

"You still have to live many years. You're needed here. You have to finish your work."

"My work has the same value as your ghosts."

"There *are* ghosts, there are! Don't be so cynical. They watch over us from above, they lead us by the hand, they measure our steps. We are much more important to the Cyclic Revival of the Universe than you imagine."

He wanted to ask her: "Why then, did you have to hire a woman to deceive me?" but he remained silent. Mrs. Kopitzky went out again. Dr. Kalisher took off his pants and his underwear and dried himself with his handkerchief. For a while he stood with his upper part fully dressed and his pants off like some mad jester. Then he stepped into a pair of loose drawers that were as cool as shrouds. He pulled on a pair of striped pants that were too wide and too long for him. He had to draw the pants up until the hem reached his knees. He gasped and snorted, had to stop every few seconds to rest. Suddenly he remembered! This was exactly how as a boy he had dressed himself in his father's clothes when his father napped after the Sabbath pudding: the old man's white trousers, his satin robe, his fringed garment, his fur hat. Now his father had become a pile of ashes somewhere in Poland, and he, Zorach, put on the musty clothes of a dentist. He walked to the mirror and looked at himself, even stuck out his tongue like a child. Then he lay down on the sofa. The telephone rang again, and Mrs. Kopitzky apparently answered it, because this time the ringing stopped immediately. Dr. Kalisher closed his eyes and lay quietly. He had nothing to hope for. There was not even anything to think about.

4

He dozed off and found himself in the cafeteria on Forty-second Street, near the Public Library. He was breaking off pieces of an egg cookie. A refugee was telling him how to save relatives in Poland by dressing them up in Nazi uniforms. Later they would be led by ship to the North Pole, the South Pole, and across the Pacific. Agents were prepared to take charge of them in Tierra del Fuego, in Honolulu and Yokohama. . . . How strange, but that smuggling had something to do with his, Zorach Kalisher's, philosophic system, not with his former version but with a new one, which blended eroticism with memory. While he was combining all these images, he asked himself in astonishment: "What kind of relationship can there be between sex, memory, and the redemption of the ego? And how will it work in infinite time? It's nothing but casuistry, casuistry. It's a way of explaining my own impotence. And how can I bring over Nella when she has already perished? Unless death itself is nothing but a sexual amnesia." He awoke and saw Mrs. Kopitzky bending over him with a pillow which she was about to put behind his head.

"How do you feel?"

"Has Nella left?" he asked, amazed at his own words. He must still be half asleep.

Mrs. Kopitzky winced. Her double chin shook and trembled. Her dark eyes were filled with motherly reproach.

"You're laughing, huh? There is no death, there isn't any. We live forever, and we love forever. This is the pure truth."

Translated by Roger H. Klein
and Cecil Hemley

The
Slaughterer

Yoineh Meir should have become the Kolomir rabbi. His father and his grandfather had both sat in the rabbinical chair in Kolomir. However, the followers of the Kuzmir court had set up a stubborn opposition: this time they would not allow a Hasid from Trisk to become the town's rabbi. They bribed the district official and sent a petition to the governor. After long wrangling, the Kuzmir Hasidim finally had their way and installed a rabbi of their own. In order not to leave Yoineh Meir without a source of earnings, they appointed him the town's ritual slaughterer.

When Yoineh Meir heard of this, he turned even paler than usual. He protested that slaughtering was not for him. He was softhearted; he could not bear the sight of blood. But everybody banded together to persuade him

—the leaders of the community; the members of the Trisk synagogue; his father-in-law, Reb Getz Frampoler; and Reitze Doshe, his wife. The new rabbi, Reb Sholem Levi Halberstam, also pressed him to accept. Reb Sholem Levi, a grandson of the Sondz rabbi, was troubled about the sin of taking away another's livelihood; he did not want the younger man to be without bread. The Trisk rabbi, Reb Yakov Leibele, wrote a letter to Yoineh Meir saying that man may not be more compassionate than the Almighty, the Source of all compassion. When you slaughter an animal with a pure knife and with piety, you liberate the soul that resides in it. For it is well known that the souls of saints often transmigrate into the bodies of cows, fowl, and fish to do penance for some offense.

After the rabbi's letter, Yoineh Meir gave in. He had been ordained a long time ago. Now he set himself to studying the laws of slaughter as expounded in the *Grain of the Ox*, the *Shulchan Aruch*, and the Commentaries. The first paragraph of the *Grain of the Ox* says that the ritual slaughterer must be a God-fearing man, and Yoineh Meir devoted himself to the law with more zeal than ever.

Yoineh Meir—small, thin, with a pale face, a tiny yellow beard on the tip of his chin, a crooked nose, a sunken mouth, and yellow frightened eyes set too close together—was renowned for his piety. When he prayed, he put on three pairs of phylacteries: those of Rashi, those of Rabbi Tam, and those of Rabbi Sherira Gaon. Soon after he had completed his term of board at the home of his father-in-law, he began to keep all fast days and to get up for mdnight service.

His wife, Reitze Doshe, already lamented that Yoineh

Meir was not of this world. She complained to her mother that he never spoke a word to her and paid her no attention, even on her clean days. He came to her only on the nights after she had visited the ritual bath, once a month. She said that he did not remember the names of his own daughters.

After he agreed to become the ritual slaughterer, Yoineh Meir imposed new rigors upon himself. He ate less and less. He almost stopped speaking. When a beggar came to the door, Yoineh Meir ran to welcome him and gave him his last groschen. The truth is that becoming a slaughterer plunged Yoineh Meir into melancholy, but he did not dare to oppose the rabbi's will. It was meant to be, Yoineh Meir said to himself; it was his destiny to cause torment and to suffer torment. And only heaven knew how much Yoineh Meir suffered.

Yoineh Meir was afraid that he might faint as he slaughtered his first fowl, or that his hand might not be steady. At the same time, somewhere in his heart, he hoped that he would commit an error. This would release him from the rabbi's command. However, everything went according to rule.

Many times a day, Yoineh Meir repeated to himself the rabbi's words: "A man may not be more compassionate than the Source of all compassion." The Torah says, "Thou shalt kill of thy herd and thy flock as I have commanded thee." Moses was instructed on Mount Sinai in the ways of slaughtering and of opening the animal in search of impurities. It is all a mystery of mysteries—life, death, man, beast. Those that are not slaughtered die anyway of various diseases, often ailing for weeks or months. In the forest, the beasts devour one another. In the seas, fish swallow fish. The Kolomir poorhouse is full of cripples and paralytics who lie there for years, befouling themselves. No man can escape the sorrows of this world.

And yet Yoineh Meir could find no consolation. Every tremor of the slaughtered fowl was answered by a tremor in Yoineh Meir's own bowels. The killing of every beast, great or small, caused him as much pain as though he were cutting his own throat. Of all the punishments that could have been visited upon him, slaughtering was the worst.

Barely three months had passed since Yoineh Meir had become a slaughterer, but the time seemed to stretch endlessly. He felt as though he were immersed in blood and lymph. His ears were beset by the squawking of hens, the crowing of roosters, the gobbling of geese, the lowing of oxen, the mooing and bleating of calves and goats; wings fluttered, claws tapped on the floor. The bodies refused to know any justification or excuse— every body resisted in its own fashion, tried to escape, and seemed to argue with the Creator to its last breath.

And Yoineh Meir's own mind raged with questions. Verily, in order to create the world, the Infinite One had had to shrink His light; there could be no free choice without pain. But since the beasts were not endowed with free choice, why should they have to suffer? Yoineh Meir watched, trembling, as the butchers chopped the cows with their axes and skinned them before they had heaved their last breath. The women plucked the feathers from the chickens while they were still alive.

It is the custom that the slaughterer receives the spleen and tripe of every cow. Yoineh Meir's house overflowed with meat. Reitze Doshe boiled soups in pots as huge as cauldrons. In the large kitchen there was a constant frenzy of cooking, roasting, frying, baking, stirring, and skimming. Reitze Doshe was pregnant again, and her stomach protruded into a point. Big and stout, she had five sisters, all as bulky as herself. Her sisters came with their children. Every day, his mother-in-law, Reitze Doshe's mother, brought new pastries and delicacies of her own baking. A woman must not let her voice be heard, but Reitze Doshe's maidservant, the daughter of a water carrier, sang songs, pattered around barefoot, with her hair down, and laughed so loudly that the noise resounded in every room.

Yoineh Meir wanted to escape from the material world, but the material world pursued him. The smell of the slaughterhouse would not leave his nostrils. He tried to forget himself in the Torah, but he found that the Torah itself was full of earthly matters. He took to the cabala, though he knew that no man may delve into the mysteries until he reaches the age of forty. Nevertheless, he continued to leaf through the *Treatise of the Hasidim*, *The Orchard*, the *Book of Creation*, and *The Tree of Life*. There, in the higher spheres, there was no death, no slaughtering, no pain, no stomachs and intestines, no hearts or lungs or livers, no membranes, and no impurities.

This particular night, Yoineh Meir went to the window and looked up into the sky. The moon spread a radiance around it. The stars flashed and twinkled, each with its own heavenly secret. Somewhere above the World of Deeds, above the constellations, Angels were flying, and Seraphim, and Holy Wheels, and Holy Beasts. In Paradise, the mysteries of the Torah were revealed to souls. Every holy zaddik inherited three hundred and ten worlds and wove crowns for the Divine

Presence. The nearer to the Throne of Glory, the brighter the light, the purer the radiance, the fewer the unholy host.

Yoineh Meir knew that man may not ask for death, but deep within himself he longed for the end. He had developed a repugnance for everything that had to do with the body. He could not even bring himself to go to the ritual bath with the other men. Under every skin he saw blood. Every neck reminded Yoineh Meir of the knife. Human beings, like beasts, had loins, veins, guts, buttocks. One slash of the knife and those solid house-holders would drop like oxen. As the Talmud says, all that is meant to be burned is already as good as burned. If the end of man was corruption, worms, and stench, then he was nothing but a piece of putrid flesh to start with.

Yoineh Meir understood now why the sages of old had likened the body to a cage—a prison where the soul sits captive, longing for the day of its release. It was only now that he truly grasped the meaning of the words of the Talmud: "Very good, this is death." Yet man was forbidden to break out of his prison. He must wait for the jailer to remove the chains, to open the gate.

Yoineh Meir returned to his bed. All his life he had slept on a featherbed, under a feather quilt, resting his head on a pillow; now he was suddenly aware that he was lying on feathers and down plucked from fowl. In the other bed, next to Yoineh Meir's, Reitze Doshe was snoring. From time to time a whistle came from her nostrils and a bubble formed on her lips. Yoineh Meir's daughters kept going to the slop pail, their bare feet pattering on the floor. They slept together, and some-times they whispered and giggled half the night.

Yoineh Meir had longed for sons who would study the Torah, but Reitze Doshe bore girl after girl. While they were small, Yoineh Meir occasionally gave them a pinch on the cheek. Whenever he attended a circumcision, he would bring them a piece of cake. Sometimes he would even kiss one of the little ones on the head. But now they were grown. They seemed to have taken after their mother. They had spread out in width. Reitze Doshe complained that they ate too much and were getting too fat. They stole tidbits from the pots. The eldest, Bashe, was already sought in marriage. At one moment, the girls quarreled and insulted each other, at the next they combed each other's hair and plaited it into braids. They were forever babbling about dresses, shoes, stockings, jackets, panties. They cried and they laughed. They looked for lice, they fought, they washed, they kissed.

When Yoineh Meir tried to chide them, Reitze Doshe cried, "Don't butt in! Let the children alone!" Or she would scold, "You had better see to it that your daughters shouldn't have to go around barefoot and naked!"

Why did they need so many things? Why was it necessary to clothe and adorn the body so much, Yoineh Meir would wonder to himself.

Before he had become a slaughterer, he was seldom at home and hardly knew what went on there. But now he began to stay at home, and he saw what they were doing. The girls would run off to pick berries and mushrooms; they associated with the daughters of common homes. They brought home baskets of dry twigs. Reitze Doshe made jam. Tailors came for fittings. Shoemakers measured the women's feet. Reitze Doshe and her mother argued about Bashe's dowry. Yoineh Meir heard talk about a silk dress, a velvet dress, all sorts of skirts, cloaks, fur coats.

Now that he lay awake, all those words reechoed in his ears. They were rolling in luxury because he, Yoineh Meir, had begun to earn money. Somewhere in Reitze Doshe's womb a new child was growing, but Yoineh Meir sensed clearly that it would be another girl. "Well, one must welcome whatever heaven sends," he warned himself.

He had covered himself, but now he felt too hot. The pillow under his head became strangely hard, as though there were a stone among the feathers. He, Yoineh Meir, was himself a body: feet, a belly, a chest, elbows. There was a stabbing in his entrails. His palate felt dry.

Yoineh Meir sat up. "Father in Heaven, I cannot breathe!"

2

Elul is a month of repentance. In former years, Elul would bring with it a sense of exalted serenity. Yoineh Meir loved the cool breezes that came from the woods and the harvested fields. He could gaze for a long time at the pale-blue sky with its scattered clouds that reminded him of the flax in which the citrons for the Feast of Tabernacles were wrapped. Gossamer floated in the air. On the trees the leaves turned saffron yellow. In the twittering of the birds he heard the melancholy of the Solemn Days, when man takes an accounting of his soul.

But to a slaughterer Elul is quite another matter. A great many beasts are slaughtered for the New Year. Before the Day of Atonement, everybody offers a sacrificial fowl. In every courtyard, cocks crowed and hens cackled, and all of them had to be put to death. Then comes the Feast of Booths, the Day of the Willow Twigs, the Feast of Azereth, the Day of Rejoicing in the Law, the Sabbath of Genesis. Each holiday brings its own slaughter. Millions of fowl and cattle now alive were doomed to be killed.

Yoineh Meir no longer slept at night. If he dozed off, he was immediately beset by nightmares. Cows assumed human shape, with beards and sidelocks, and skullcaps over their horns. Yoineh Meir would be slaughtering a calf, but it would turn into a girl. Her neck throbbed, and she pleaded to be saved. She ran to the study house and spattered the courtyard with her blood. He even dreamed that he had slaughtered Reitze Doshe instead of a sheep.

In one of his nightmares, he heard a human voice come from a slaughtered goat. The goat, with his throat slit, jumped on Yoineh Meir and tried to butt him, cursing in Hebrew and Aramaic, spitting and foaming at him. Yoineh Meir awakened in a sweat. A cock crowed like a bell. Others answered, like a congregation answering the cantor. It seemed to Yoineh Meir that the fowl were crying out questions, protesting, lamenting in chorus the misfortune that loomed over them.

Yoineh Meir could not rest. He sat up, grasped his sidelocks with both hands, and rocked.

Reitze Doshe woke up. "What's the matter?"

"Nothing, nothing."

"What are you rocking for?"

"Let me be."

"You frighten me!"

After a while Reitze Doshe began to snore again. Yoineh Meir got out of bed, washed his hands, and dressed. He wanted to put ash on his forehead and recite

the midnight prayer, but his lips refused to utter the
holy words. How could he mourn the destruction of
the Temple when a carnage was being readied here in
Kolomir, and he, Yoineh Meir, was the Titus, the
Nebuchadnezzar!

The air in the house was stifling. It smelled of sweat,
fat, dirty underwear, urine. One of his daughters muttered something in her sleep, another one moaned. The
beds creaked. A rustling came from the closets. In the
coop under the stove were the sacrificial fowls that
Reitze Doshe had locked up for the Day of Atonement.
Yoineh Meir heard the scratching of a mouse, the
chirping of a cricket. It seemed to him that he could hear
the worms burrowing through the ceiling and the floor.
Innumerable creatures surrounded man, each with its
own nature, its own claims on the Creator.

Yoineh Meir went out into the yard. Here everything
was cool and fresh. The dew had formed. In the sky,
the midnight stars were glittering. Yoineh Meir inhaled
deeply. He walked on the wet grass, among the leaves
and shrubs. His socks grew damp above his slippers. He
came to a tree and stopped. In the branches there seemed
to be some nests. He heard the twittering of awakened
fledglings. Frogs croaked in the swamp beyond the hill.
"Don't they sleep at all, those frogs?" Yoineh Meir
asked himself. "They have the voices of men."

Since Yoineh Meir had begun to slaughter, his
thoughts were obsessed with living creatures. He
grappled with all sorts of questions. Where did flies
come from? Were they born out of their mother's
womb, or did they hatch from eggs? If all the flies died
out in winter, where did the new ones come from in
summer? And the owl that nested under the synagogue
roof—what did it do when the frosts came? Did it re-

main there? Did it fly away to warm countries? And how could anything live in the burning frost, when it was scarcely possible to keep warm under the quilt?

An unfamilar love welled up in Yoineh Meir for all that crawls and flies, breeds and swarms. Even the mice —was it their fault that they were mice? What wrong does a mouse do? All it wants is a crumb of bread or a bit of cheese. Then why is the cat such an enemy to it?

Yoineh Meir rocked back and forth in the dark. The rabbi may be right. Man cannot and must not have more compassion than the Master of the Universe. Yet he, Yoineh Meir, was sick with pity. How could one pray for life for the coming year, or for a favorable writ in heaven, when one was robbing others of the breath of life?

Yoineh Meir thought that the Messiah Himself could not redeem the world as long as injustice was done to beasts. By rights, everything should rise from the dead: every calf, fish, gnat, butterfly. Even in the worm that crawls in the earth there glows a divine spark. When you slaughter a creature, you slaughter God. . . .

"Woe is me, I am losing my mind!" Yoineh Meir muttered.

A week before the New Year, there was a rush of slaughtering. All day long, Yoineh Meir stood near a pit, slaughtering hens, roosters, geese, ducks. Women pushed, argued, tried to get to the slaughterer first. Others joked, laughed, bantered. Feathers flew, the yard was full of quacking, gabbling, the screaming of roosters. Now and then a fowl cried out like a human being.

Yoineh Meir was filled with a gripping pain. Until this day he had still hoped that he would get accustomed to slaughtering. But now he knew that if he continued for a hundred years his suffering would not cease. His knees shook. His belly felt distended. His mouth was flooded with bitter fluids. Reitze Doshe and her sisters were also in the yard, talking with the women, wishing each a blessed New Year, and voicing the pious hope that they would meet again next year.

Yoineh Meir feared that he was no longer slaughtering according to the law. At one moment, a blackness swam before his eyes; at the next, everything turned golden green. He constantly tested the knife blade on the nail of his forefinger to make sure it was not nicked. Every fifteen minutes he had to go to urinate. Mosquitoes bit him. Crows cawed at him from among the branches.

He stood there until sundown, and the pit became filled with blood.

After the evening prayers, Reitze Doshe served Yoineh Meir buckwheat soup with pot roast. But though he had not tasted any food since morning, he could not eat. His throat felt constricted, there was a lump in his gullet, and he could scarcely swallow the first bite. He recited the Shema of Rabbi Isaac Luria, made his confession, and beat his breast like a man who was mortally sick.

Yoineh Meir thought that he would be unable to sleep that night, but his eyes closed as soon as his head was on the pillow and he had recited the last benediction before sleep. It seemed to him that he was examining a slaughtered cow for impurities, slitting open its belly, tearing out the lungs and blowing them up. What did it mean? For this was usually the butcher's task. The lungs grew larger and larger; they covered the whole table and swelled upward toward the ceiling. Yoineh Meir ceased blowing, but the lobes continued to expand by themselves. The smaller lobe, the one that is called "the thief," shook and fluttered, as if trying to break away. Suddenly a whistling, a coughing, a growling lamentation broke from the windpipe. A dybbuk began to speak, shout, sing, pour out a stream of verses, quotations from the Talmud, passages from the Zohar. The lungs rose up and flew, flapping like wings. Yoineh Meir wanted to escape, but the door was barred by a black bull with red eyes and pointed horns. The bull wheezed and opened a maw full of long teeth.

Yoineh Meir shuddered and woke up. His body was bathed in sweat. His skull felt swollen and filled with sand. His feet lay on the straw pallet, inert as logs. He made an effort and sat up. He put on his robe and went out. The night hung heavy and impenetrable, thick with the darkness of the hour before sunrise. From time to time a gust of air came from somewhere, like a sigh of someone unseen.

A tingling ran down Yoineh Meir's spine, as though someone brushed it with a feather. Something in him wept and mocked. "Well, and what if the rabbi said so?" he spoke to himself. "And even if God Almighty had commanded, what of that? I'll do without rewards in the world to come! I want no Paradise, no Leviathan, no Wild Ox! Let them stretch me on a bed of nails. Let them throw me into the Hollow of the Sling. I'll have none of your favors, God! I am no longer afraid of your Judgment! I am a betrayer of Israel, a willful transgressor!" Yoineh Meir cried. "I have more compassion that God Almighty—more, more! He is a cruel God, a Man of War, a God of Vengeance. I will not serve Him. It is an abandoned world!" Yoineh Meir laughed, but tears ran down his cheeks in scalding drops.

Yoineh Meir went to the pantry where he kept his knives, his whetstone, the circumcision knife. He gathered them all and dropped them into the pit of the out-house. He knew that he was blaspheming, that he was desecrating the holy instruments, that he was mad, but he no longer wished to be sane.

He went outside and began to walk toward the river, the bridge, the wood. His prayer shawl and phylacteries? He needed none! The parchment was taken from the hide of a cow. The cases of the phylacteries were made of calf's leather. The Torah itself was made of animal skin. "Father in Heaven, Thou art a slaughterer!" a voice cried in Yoineh Meir. "Thou art a slaughterer and the Angel of Death! The whole world is a slaughterhouse!"

A slipper fell off Yoineh Meir's foot, but he let it lie, striding on in one slipper and one sock. He began to call, shout, sing. I am driving myself out of my mind, he thought. But this is itself a mark of madness. . . .

He had opened a door to his brain, and madness flowed in, flooding everything. From moment to moment, Yoineh Meir grew more rebellious. He threw away his skullcap, grasped his prayer fringes and ripped them off, tore off pieces of his vest. A strength possessed him, the recklessness of one who had cast away all burdens.

Dogs chased him, barking, but he drove them off. Doors were flung open. Men ran out barefoot, with feathers clinging to their skullcaps. Women came out in their petticoats and nightcaps. All of them shouted, tried to bar his way, but Yoineh Meir evaded them.

The sky turned red as blood, and a round skull pushed up out of the bloody sea out of the womb of a woman in childbirth.

Someone had gone to tell the butchers that Yoineh Meir had lost his mind. They came running with sticks and rope, but Yoineh Meir was already over the bridge and was hurrying across the harvested fields. He ran and vomited. He fell and rose, bruised by the stubble. Shepherds who take the horses out to graze at night mocked him and threw horse dung at him. The cows at pasture ran after him. Bells tolled as for a fire.

Yoineh Meir heard shouts, screams, the stamping of running feet. The earth began to slope and Yoineh Meir rolled downhill. He reached the wood, leaped over tufts of moss, rocks, running brooks. Yoineh Meir knew the truth: this was not the river before him; it was a bloody swamp. Blood ran from the sun, staining the tree trunks. From the branches hung intestines, livers, kidneys. The forequarters of beasts rose to their feet and sprayed him with gall and slime. Yoineh Meir could not escape. Myriads of cows and fowls encircled him, ready to take revenge for every cut, every wound, every slit gullet, every plucked feather. With bleeding throats, they all chanted, "Everyone may kill, and every killing is permitted."

Yoineh Meir broke into a wail that echoed through the wood in many voices. He raised his fist to heaven: "Fiend! Murderer! Devouring beast!"

For two days the butchers searched for him, but they did not find him. Then Zeinvel, who owned the watermill, arrived in town with the news that Yoineh Meir's body had turned up in the river by the dam. He had drowned.

The members of the burial society immediately went to bring the corpse. There were many witnesses to testify that Yoineh Meir had behaved like a madman, and the rabbi ruled that the deceased was not a suicide. The body of the dead man was cleansed and given burial near the graves of his father and his grandfather. The rabbi himself delivered the eulogy.

Because it was the holiday season and there was danger that Kolomir might remain without meat, the community hastily dispatched two messengers to bring a new slaughterer.

Translated by Mirra Ginsburg

The
Lecture

I was on my way to Montreal to deliver a lecture. It was midwinter and I had been warned that the temperature there was ten degrees lower than in New York. Newspapers reported that trains had been stalled by the snow and fishing villages cut off, so that food and medical supplies had to be dropped to them by plane.

I prepared for the journey as though it were an expedition to the North Pole. I put on a heavy coat over two sweaters and packed warm underwear and a bottle of cognac in case the train should be halted somewhere in the fields. In my breast pocket I had the manuscript that I intended to read—an optimistic report on the future of the Yiddish language.

In the beginning, everything went smoothly. As usual, I arrived at the station an hour before train departure and therefore could find no porter. The station teemed with travelers and I watched them, trying to guess who they were, where they were going, and why.

None of the men was dressed as heavily as I. Some even wore spring coats. The ladies looked bright and elegant in their minks and beavers, nylon stockings and stylish hats. They carried colorful bags and illustrated magazines, smoked cigarettes and chattered and laughed with a carefree air that has never ceased to amaze me. It was as though they knew nothing of the existence of world problems or eternal questions, as though they had never heard of death, sickness, war, poverty, betrayal, or even of such troubles as missing a train, losing a ticket, or being robbed. They flirted like young girls, exhibiting their blood-red nails. The station was chilly that morning, but no one except myself seemed to feel it. I wondered whether these people knew there had been a Hitler. Had they heard of Stalin's murder machine? They probably had, but what does one body care when another is tortured?

I was itchy from the woolen underwear. Now I began to feel hot. But from time to time a shiver ran through my body. The lecture, in which I predicted a brilliant future for Yiddish, troubled me. What had made me so optimistic all of a sudden? Wasn't Yiddish going under before my very eyes?

The prompt arrival of American trains and the ease in boarding them have always seemed like miracles to me. I remember journeys in Poland when Jewish passengers were not allowed into the cars and I had to hang on to the handrails. I remember railway strikes when trains were halted midway for many hours and it was impossible in the dense crowd to push through to the washroom.

But here I was, sitting on a soft seat, right by the window. The car was heated. There were no bundles, no high fur hats, no sheepskin coats, no boxes, and no gendarmes. Nobody was eating bread and lard. Nobody drank vodka from a bottle. Nobody was berating Jews for state treason. In fact, nobody discussed politics at all. As soon as the train started, a huge Negro in a white apron came in and announced lunch. The train was not rattling, it glided smoothly on its rails along the frozen Hudson. Outside, the landscape gleamed with snow and light. Birds that remained here for the winter flew busily over the icy river.

The farther we went, the wintrier the landscape. The weather seemed to change every few miles. Now we went through dense fog, and now the air cleared and the sun was shining again over silvery distances.

A heavy snowfall began. It suddenly turned dark. The day was flickering out. The express no longer ran but crept slowly and cautiously, as though feeling its way. The heating system in the train seemed to have broken down. It became chilly and I had to put on my coat. The other passengers pretended for a while that they did not notice anything, as though reluctant to admit too quickly that they were cold. But soon they began to tap their feet, grumble, grin sheepishly, and rummage in their valises for sweaters, scarves, boots, or whatever else they had brought along. Collars were turned up, hands stuffed into sleeves. The makeup on women's faces dried up and began to peel like plaster.

The American dream gradually dissolves and harsh Polish reality returns. Someone is drinking whiskey from a bottle. Someone is eating bread and sausage to warm his stomach. There is also a rush to the toilets. It is difficult to understand how it happened, but the floor of the car becomes wet and muddy. The windowpanes become crusted with ice and bloom with frost patterns.

Suddenly the train stops. I look out and see a sparse wood. The trees are thin and bent, and though they are covered with snow, they look bare and charred, as after a fire. The sun has already set, but purple stains still glow in the west. The snow on the ground is no longer white, but violet. Crows walk on it, flap their wings, and I can hear their cawing. The snow falls in gray, heavy lumps, as though the guardians of the Treasury of Snow up above had been too lazy to flake it more finely. Passengers walk from car to car, leaving the doors open. Conductors and other train employees run past; when they are asked questions, they do not stop, but mumble something rudely.

We are not far from the Canadian border, and Uncle Sam's domain is virtually at an end. Some passengers begin to take down their luggage; they may have to show it soon to the customs officials. A naturalized American citizen gets out his citizenship papers and studies his own photograph, as if trying to convince himself that the document is not a false one.

One or two passengers venture to step out of the train, but they sink up to their knees into the snow. It is not long before they clamber back into the car. The twilight lingers for a while, then night falls.

I see people using the weather as a pretext for striking up acquaintance. Women begin to talk among themselves and there is sudden intimacy. The men have also formed a group. Everyone picks up bits of information. People offer each other advice. But nobody pays any attention to me. I sit alone, a victim of my own isolation, shyness, and alienation from the world. I begin to read a book, and this provokes hostility, for reading a book at such a time seems like a challenge and an insult to the other passengers. I exclude myself from society, and all the faces say to me silently: You don't need us and we don't need you. Never mind, you will still have to turn to us, but we won't have to turn to you. . . .

I open my large, heavy valise, take out the bottle of cognac, and take a stealthy sip now and then. After that, I lean my face against the cold windowpane and try to look out. But all I see is the reflection of the interior of the car. The world outside seems to have disappeared. The solipsistic philosophy of Bishop Berkeley has won over all the other systems. Nothing remains but to wait patiently until God's idea of a train halted in its tracks by snowdrifts will give way to God's ideas of movement and arrival.

Alas for my lecture! If I arrive in the middle of the night, there will not even be anyone waiting for me. I shall have to look for a hotel. If only I had a return ticket. However, was Captain Scott, lost in the polar ice fields, in a better position after Amundsen had discovered the South Pole? How much would Captain Scott have given to be able to sit in a brightly lit railway car? No, one must not sin by complaining.

The cognac had made me warm. Drunken fumes rise from an empty stomach to the brain. I am awake and dozing at the same time. Whole minutes drift away, leaving only a blur. I hear talk, but I don't quite know what it means. I sink into blissful indifference. For my part, the train can stand here for three days and three nights. I have a box of crackers in my valise. I will not die of hunger. Various themes float through my mind. Something within me mutters dreamlike words and phrases.

The diesel engine must be straining forward. I am

aware of dragging, knocking, growling sounds, as of a monstrous ox, a legendary steel bull. Most of the passengers have gone to the bar or the restaurant car, but I am too lazy to get up. I seem to have grown into the seat. A childish obstinacy takes possession of me: I'll show them all that I am not affected by any of this commotion; I am above the trivial happenings of the day.

Everyone who passes by—from the rear cars to the front, or the other way—glances at me; and it seems to me that each one forms some judgment of his own about the sort of person I am. But does anyone guess that I am a Yiddish writer late for his lecture? This, I am sure, occurs to no one. This is known only to the higher powers.

I take another sip, and another. I have never understood the passion for drinking, but now I see what power there is in alcohol. This liquid holds within itself the secrets of nirvana. I no longer look at my wristwatch. I no longer worry about a place to sleep. I mock in my mind the lecture I had prepared. What if it is not delivered? People will hear fewer lies! If I could open the window, I would throw the manuscript out into the woods. Let the paper and ink return to the cosmos, where there can be no errors and no lies. Atoms and molecules are guiltless; they are a part of the divine truth. . . .

2

The train arrived exactly at half past two. No one was waiting for me. I left the station and was caught in a blast of icy night wind that no coat or sweaters could keep out. All taxis were immediately taken. I returned to the station, prepared to spend the night sitting on a bench.

Suddenly I noticed a lame woman and a young girl looking at me and pointing with their fingers. I stopped and looked back. The lame woman leaned on two thick, short canes. She was wrinkled, disheveled, like an old woman in Poland, but her black eyes suggested that she was more sick and broken than old. Her clothes also reminded me of Poland. She wore a sort of sleeveless fur jacket. Her shoes had toes and heels I had not seen in years. On her shoulders she wore a fringed woolen shawl, like one of my mother's. The young woman, on the other hand, was stylishly dressed, but also rather slovenly.

After a moment's hesitation, I approached them.

The girl said: "Are you Mr. N.?"

I answered, "Yes, I am."

The lame woman made a sudden movement, as though to drop her canes and clap her hands. She immediately broke into a wailing cry so familiar to me.

"Dear Father in Heaven!" she sang out. "I was telling my daughter, it's he, and she said no. I recognized you! Where were you going with the valise? It's a wonder you came back. I'd never have forgiven myself! Well, Binele, what do you say now? Your mother still has some sense. I am only a woman, but I am a rabbi's daughter, and a scholar has an eye for people. I took one look and I thought to myself—it's he! But nowadays the eggs are cleverer than the chickens. She says to me: 'No, it can't be.' And in the meantime you disappear. I was already beginning to think, myself: Who knows, one's no more than human, anybody can make a mistake. But when I saw you come back, I knew it was you. My dear man, we've been waiting here since half past seven in the evening. We weren't alone; there was a whole group of teachers, educators, a few writers too. But then it grew later and later and people went home. They have wives, children. Some have to get up in the morning to go to work. But I said to my daughter, 'I won't go. I won't allow my favorite writer, whose every word I treasure as a pearl, to come here and find no one waiting for him. If you want, my child,' I said to her, 'you can go home and go to bed.' What's a night's sleep? When I was young, I used to think that if you missed a night's sleep the world would go under. But Hitler taught us a lesson. He taught us a lesson I won't forget until I lie with shards over my eyes. You look at me and you see an old, sick woman, a cripple, but I did hard labor in Hitler's camps. I dug ditches and loaded railway cars. Was there anything I didn't do? It was there that I caught my rheumatism. At night we slept on plank shelves not fit for dogs, and we were so hungry that—"

"You'll have enough time to talk later, Momma. It's the middle of the night," her daughter interrupted.

It was only then that I took a closer look at the daughter. Her figure and general appearance were those of a young girl, but she was obviously in her late twenties, or even early thirties. She was small, narrow, with yellowish hair combed back and tied into a bun. Her face was of a sickly pallor, covered with freckles. She had yellow eyes, a round forehead, a crooked nose, thin lips, and a long chin. Around her neck she wore a mannish scarf. She reminded me of a Hasidic boy.

The few words she spoke were marked by a provincial Polish accent I had forgotten during my years in America. She made me think of rye bread, caraway seeds, cottage cheese, and the water brought by water carriers from the well in pails slung on a wooden yoke over their shoulders.

"Thank you, but I have patience to listen," I said.

"When my mother begins to talk about those years, she can talk for a week and a day—"

"Hush, hush, your mother isn't as crazy as you think. It's true, our nerves were shattered out there. It is a wonder we are not running around stark mad in the streets. But what about her? As you see her, she too was in Auschwitz waiting for the ovens. I did not even know she was alive. I was sure she was lost, and you can imagine a mother's feelings! I thought she had gone the way of her three brothers; but after the liberation we found each other. What did they want from us, the beasts? My husband was a holy man, a scribe. My sons worked hard to earn a piece of bread, because inscribing mezuzahs doesn't bring much of an income. My husband, himself, fasted more often than he ate. The glory of God rested on his face. My sons were killed by the murderers—"

"Momma, will you please stop?"

"I'll stop, I'll stop. How much longer will I last, anyway? But she is right. First of all, my dear man, we must take care of you. The president gave me the name of a hotel—they made all the reservations for you—but my daughter didn't hear what he said, and I forgot it. This forgetting is my misfortune. I put something down and I don't know where. I keep looking for things, and that's how my whole days go by. So maybe, my dear writer, you'll spend the night with us? We don't have such a fine apartment. It's cold, it's shabby. Still, it's better than no place at all. I'd telephone the president, but I'm afraid to wake him up at night. He has such a temper, may he forgive me; he keeps shouting that we aren't civilized. So I say to him: 'The Germans are civilized, go to them. . . .' "

"Come with us, the night is three-quarters gone, anyway," the daughter said to me. "He should have written it down instead of just saying it; and if he said it, he should have said it to me, not to my mother. She forgets everything. She puts on her glasses and cries, 'Where are my glasses?' Sometimes I have to laugh. Let me have your valise."

"What are you saying? I can carry it myself, it isn't heavy."

"You are not used to carrying things, but I have learned out there to carry heavy loads. If you would see the rocks I used to lift, you wouldn't believe your eyes. I don't even believe it myself anymore. Sometimes it seems to me it was all an evil dream. . . ."

"Heaven forbid, you will not carry my valise. That's all I need. . . ."

"He is a gentleman, he is a fine and gentle man. I knew it at once as soon as I read him for the first time," the mother said. "You wouldn't believe me, but we read your stories even in the camps. After the war, they began to send us books, and I came across one of your stories. I don't remember what it was called, but I read it and a darkness lifted off my heart. 'Binele,' I said—she was already with me then—'I've found a treasure.' Those were my words. . . ."

"Thank you, thank you very much."

"Don't thank me, don't thank me. It's we who have to thank you. All the troubles come from people being deaf and blind. They don't see the next man and so they torture him. We are wandering among blind evildoers. . . . Binele, don't let this dear man carry the valise. . . ."

"Yes, please give it to me!"

I had to plead with Binele to let me carry it. She almost tried to pull it out of my hands.

We went outside and a taxi drove up. It was not easy to get the mother into it. I still cannot understand how she had managed to come to the station. I had to lift her up and put her in. In the process, she dropped one of her canes, and Binele and I had to look for it in the snow. The driver had already begun to grumble and scold in his Canadian French. Afterward, the car began to pitch and roll over dimly lit streets covered with snow and overgrown with mountains of ice. The tires had chains on them, but the taxi skidded backward several times.

We finally drove into a street that was reminiscent of a small town in Poland: murky, narrow, with wooden houses. The sick woman hastily opened her purse, but I paid before she had time to take out her money. Both women chided me, and the driver demanded that we get out as quickly as possible. I virtually had to carry the crippled woman out of the taxi. Again, we had to look for her cane in the deep snow. Afterward, her daughter and I half led, half dragged her up a flight of steps. They opened the door and I was suddenly enveloped in odors I had long forgotten: moldy potatoes, rotting onions, chicory, and something else I could not even name. In some mysterious way the mother and daughter had managed to bring with them the whole atmosphere of wretched poverty from their old home in Poland.

They lit a kerosene lamp and I saw an apartment with tattered wallpaper, a rough wooden floor, and spider webs in every corner. The kerosene stove was out and the rooms were drafty. On a bench stood cracked pots, chipped plates, cups without handles. I even caught sight of a besom on a pile of sweepings. No stage director, I thought, could have done a better job of reproducing such a scene of old-country misery.

Binele began to apologize. "What a mess, no? We were in such a hurry to get to the station, we didn't even have time to wash the dishes. And what's the good of washing or cleaning here, anyway? It's an old, run-down shanty. The landlady knows only one thing: to come for the rent every month. If you're late one day, she's ready to cut your throat. Still, after everything we went through over there, this is a palace. . . ."

And Binele laughed, exposing a mouthful of widely spaced teeth with gold fillings that must have been made when she was still across the ocean.

3

They made my bed on a folding cot in a tiny room with barred windows. Binele covered me with two blankets and spread my coat on top of them. But it was still as cold as outside. I lay under all the coverings and could not warm up.

Suddenly I remembered my manuscript. Where was the manuscript of my lecture? I had had it in the breast pocket of my coat. Afraid to sit up, lest the cot should collapse, I tried to find it. But the manuscript was not there. I looked in my jacket, which hung on a chair nearby, but it was not there either. I was certain that I had not put it into the valise, for I had opened the valise only to get the cognac. I had intended to open it for the customs officers, but they had only waved me on, to indicate it was not necessary.

It was clear to me that I had lost the manuscript. But how? The mother and daughter had told me that the lecture was postponed to the next day, but what would I read? There was only one hope: perhaps it had dropped on the floor when Binele was covering me with the coat. I felt the floor, trying not to make a sound, but the cot creaked at the slightest movement. It even seemed to me that it began to creak in advance, when I only thought of moving. Inanimate things are not really inanimate. . . .

The mother and daughter were evidently not asleep. I heard a whispering, a mumbling from the next room. They were arguing about something quietly, but about what?

The loss of the manuscript, I thought, was a Freudian accident. I was not pleased with the essay from the very first. The tone I took in it was too grandiloquent. Still, what was I to talk about that evening? I might get confused from the very first sentences, like that speaker who had started his lecture with, "Peretz was a peculiar man," and could not utter another word.

If only I could sleep! I had not slept the previous night either. When I have to make a public appearance, I don't sleep for nights. The loss of the manuscript was a real catastrophe! I tried to close my eyes, but they kept opening by themselves. Something bit me; but as soon as I wanted to scratch, the cot shook and screamed like a sick man in pain.

I lay there, silent, stiff, wide-awake. A mouse scratched somewhere in a hole, and then I heard a sound, as of some beast with saw and fangs trying to saw through the floorboards. A mouse could not have raised such noise. It was some monster trying to cut down the foundations of the building. . . .

"Well, this adventure will be the end of me!" I said to myself. "I won't come out of here alive."

I lay benumbed, without stirring a limb. My nose was stuffed and I was breathing the icy air of the room through my mouth. My throat felt constricted. I had to cough, but I did not want to disturb the mother and daughter. A cough might also bring down the ramshackle cot. . . . Well, let me imagine that I had remained under Hitler in wartime. Let me get some taste of that, too. . . .

I imagined myself somewhere in Treblinka or Maidanek. I had done hard labor all day long. Now I was lying on a plank shelf. Tomorrow there would probably be a "selection," and since I was no longer well, I would be sent to the ovens. . . . I mentally began to say goodbye to the few people close to me. I must have dozed off, for I was awakened by loud cries. Binele was shouting: "Momma! Momma! Momma! . . ." The door flew open and Binele called me: "Help me! Mother is dead!"

I wanted to jump off the cot but it collapsed under me, and instead of jumping, I had to raise myself. I cried: "What happened?"

Binele screamed: "She is cold! Where are the matches? Call a doctor! Call a doctor! Put on the light! Oh, Momma! . . . Momma! Momma!"

I never carry matches with me, since I do not smoke. I went in my pajamas to the bedroom. In the dark I collided with Binele. I asked her: "How can I call a doctor?"

She did not answer, but opened the door into the hallway and shouted, "Help, people, help! My mother is dead!" She cried with all her strength, as women cry in the Jewish small towns in Poland, but nobody responded. I tried to look for matches, knowing in advance that I would not find them in this strange house.

Binele returned and we collided again in the dark. She clung to me with unexpected force and wailed: "Help! Help! I have nobody else in the world! She was all I had!"

And she broke into a wild lament, leaving me stunned and speechless.

"Find a match! Light the lamp!" I finally cried out, although I knew that my words were wasted.

"Call a doctor! Call a doctor!" she screamed, undoubtedly realizing herself the senselessness of her demand.

She half led, half pulled me to the bed where her mother lay. I put out my hand and touched her body. I began to look for her hand, found it, and tried to feel her pulse, but there was no pulse. The hand hung heavy and limp. It was cold as only a dead thing is cold. Binele seemed to understand what I was doing and kept silent for a while.

"Well, well? She's dead? . . . She's dead! . . . She had a sick heart! . . . Help me! Help me!"

"What can I do? I can't see anything!" I said to her, and my words seemed to have double meaning.

"Help me! . . . Help me! . . . Momma!"

"Are there no neighbors in the house?" I asked.

"There is a drunkard over us. . . ."

"Perhaps we can get matches from him?"

Binele did not answer. I suddenly became aware of how cold I felt. I had to put something on or I would catch pneumonia. I shivered and my teeth chattered. I started out for the room where I had slept but found myself in the kitchen. I returned and nearly threw Binele over. She was, herself, half naked. Unwittingly I touched her breast.

"Put something on!" I told her. "You'll catch a cold!"

"I do not want to live! I do not want to live! . . . She had no right to go to the station! . . . I begged her, but she is so stubborn. . . . She had nothing to eat. She would not even take a glass of tea. . . . What shall I do now? Where shall I go? Oh, Momma, Momma!"

Then, suddenly, it was quiet. Binele must have gone upstairs to knock on the drunkard's door. I remained alone with a corpse in the dark. A long-forgotten terror possessed me. I had the eerie feeling that the dead woman was trying to approach me, to seize me with her cold hands, to clutch at me and drag me off to where she was now. After all, I was responsible for her death. The strain of coming out to meet me had killed her. I started toward the outside door, as though ready to run out into the street. I stumbled on a chair and struck my knee. Bony fingers stretched after me. Strange beings screamed at me silently. There was a ringing in my ears and saliva filled my mouth as though I were about to faint.

Strangely, instead of coming to the outside door, I found myself back in my room. My feet stumbled on the flattened cot. I bent down to pick up my overcoat and put it on. It was only then that I realized how cold I was and how cold it was in that house. The coat was like an ice bag against my body. I trembled as with ague. My teeth clicked, my legs shook. I was ready to fight off the dead woman, to wrestle with her in mortal combat. I felt my heart hammering frighteningly loud and fast. No heart could long endure such violent knocking. I thought that Binele would find two corpses when she returned, instead of one.

I heard talk and steps and saw a light. Binele had brought down the upstairs neighbor. She had a man's coat over her shoulders. The neighbor carried a burning candle. He was a huge man, dark, with thick black hair and a long nose. He was barefoot and wore a bathrobe over his pajamas. What struck me most in my panic was the enormous size of his feet. He went to the bed with his candle and shadows danced after him and wavered across the dim ceiling.

One glance at the woman told me that she was dead. Her face had altered completely. Her mouth had become strangely thin and sunken; it was no longer a mouth, but a hole. The face was yellow, rigid, and clay-like. Only the gray hair looked alive. The neighbor muttered something in French. He bent over the woman and felt her forehead. He uttered a single word and Binele began to scream and wail again. He tried to speak to her, to tell her something else, but she evidently did not understand his language. He shrugged his shoulders, gave me the candle, and started back. My hand trembled so uncontrollably that the small flame tossed in all directions and almost went out. I let some tallow drip on the wardrobe and set the candle in it.

Binele began to tear her hair and let out such a wild lament that I cried angrily at her: "Stop screaming!"

She gave me a sidelong glance, full of hate and astonishment, and answered quietly and sensibly: "She was all I had in the world. . . ."

"I know, I understand. . . . But screaming won't help."

My words appeared to have restored her to her senses. She stood silently by the bed, looking down at her mother. I stood on the opposite side. I clearly remembered that the woman had had a short nose; now it had grown long and hooked, as though death had made manifest a hereditary trait that had been hidden during her lifetime. Her forehead and eyebrows had acquired a new and masculine quality. Binele's sorrow seemed for a while to have given way to stupor. She stared, wide-eyed, as if she did not recognize her own mother.

I glanced at the window. How long could a night last, even a winter night? Would the sun never rise? Could this be the moment of that cosmic catastrophe that David Hume had envisaged as a theoretical possibility? But the panes were just beginning to turn gray.

I went to the window and wiped the misty pane. The night outside was already intermingled with blurs of daylight. The contours of the street were becoming faintly visible; piles of snow, small houses, roofs. A street lamp glimmered in the distance, but it cast no light. I raised my eyes to the sky. One half was still full of stars; the other was already flushed with morning. For a few seconds I seemed to have forgotten all that had happened and gave myself up entirely to the birth of the new day. I saw the stars go out one by one. Streaks of red and rose and yellow stretched across the sky, as in a child's painting.

"What shall I do now? What shall I do now?" Binele began to cry again. "Whom shall I call? Where shall I go? Call a doctor! Call a doctor!" And she broke into sobs.

I turned to her. "What can a doctor do now?"

"But someone should be called."

"You have no relatives?"

"None, I've no one in the world."

"What about the members of your lecture club?"

"They don't live in this neighborhood. . . ."

I went to my room and began to dress. My clothes were icy. My suit, which had been pressed before my journey, was crumpled. My shoes looked like misshapen clodhoppers. I caught sight of my face in a mirror, and it shocked me. It was hollow, dirty, paper-gray, covered with stubble. Outside, the snow began to fall again.

"What can I do for you?" I asked Binele. "I'm a stranger here. I don't know where to go."

"Woe is me! What am I doing to you? You are the victim of our misfortune. I shall go out and telephone the police, but I cannot leave my mother alone."

"I'll stay here."

"You will? She loved you. She never stopped talking about you. . . . All day yesterday. . . ."

I sat down on a chair and kept my eyes away from the dead woman. Binele dressed herself. Ordinarily I would be afraid to remain alone with a corpse. But I was half frozen, half asleep. I was exhausted after the miserable night. A deep despair came over me. It was a long, long time since I had seen such wretchedness and so much tragedy. My years in America seemed to have been swept away by that one night and I was taken back, as though by magic, to my worst days in Poland, to the bitterest crisis of my life. I heard the outside door close. Binele was gone. I could no longer remain sitting in the room with the dead woman. I ran out to the kitchen. I opened the door leading to the stairs. I stood by the open door as though ready to escape as soon as the corpse began to do those tricks that I had dreaded since childhood. . . . I said to myself that it was foolish to be afraid of this gentle woman, this cripple who had loved me while alive and who surely did not hate me now, if the dead felt anything. But all the boyhood fears were back upon me. My ribs felt chilled, as if some icy fingers moved over them. My heart thumped and fluttered like the spring in a broken clock. . . . Everything within me was strained. The slightest rustle and I would have dashed down the stairs in terror. The door to the street downstairs had glass panes, but they were half frosted over, half misty. A pale glow filtered through them as at dusk. An icy cold came from below. Suddenly I heard steps. The corpse? I wanted to run, but I realized that the steps came from the upper floor. I saw someone coming down. It was the upstairs neighbor on his way to work, a huge man in rubber boots and a coat with a kind of cowl, a metal lunch box in his hands. He glanced at me curiously and began to speak to me in Canadian French. It was good to be with another human being for a moment. I nodded, gestured with my hands, and answered him in English. He tried again and again to say something in his unfamiliar language, as though he believed that if I listened more carefully I would finally understand him. In the end he mumbled something and threw up his arms. He went out and slammed the door. Now I was all alone in the whole house.

What if Binele should not return? I began to toy with the fantasy that she might run away. Perhaps I'd be suspected of murder? Everything was possible in this world. I stood with my eyes fixed on the outside door. I wanted only one thing now—to return as quickly as possible to New York. My home, my job seemed totally remote and insubstantial, like memories of a previous incarnation. Who knows? Perhaps my whole life in New York had been no more than a hallucination? I began to search in my breast pocket. . . . Did I lose my citizenship papers, together with the text of my lecture? I felt a stiff paper. Thank God, the citizenship papers are here. I could have lost them, too. This document was now testimony that my years in America had not been an invention.

Here is my photograph. And my signature. Here is the government stamp. True, these were also inanimate,

without life, but they symbolized order, a sense of be-
longing, law. I stood in the doorway and for the first
time really read the paper that made me a citizen of the
United States. I became so absorbed that I had almost
forgotten the dead woman. Then the outside door
opened and I saw Binele, covered with snow. She wore
the same shawl that her mother had worn yesterday.

"I cannot find a telephone!"

She broke out crying. I went down to meet her,
slipping the citizenship papers back into my pocket. Life
had returned. The long nightmare was over. I put my
arms around Binele and she did not try to break away. I
became wet from the melting snow. We stood there
midway up the stairs and rocked back and forth—a lost
Yiddish writer, and a victim of Hitler and of my ill-
starred lecture. I saw a number tattooed above her
wrist and heard myself saying: "Binele, I won't abandon
you. I swear by the soul of your mother. . . ."

Binele's body became limp in my arms. She raised her
eyes and whispered: "Why did she do it? She just waited
for your coming. . . ."

Translated by Mirra Ginsburg

Getzel
the
Monkey

My dear friends, we all know what a mimic is. Once we had such a man living in our town, and he was given a fitting name. In that day they gave nicknames to everybody but the rich people. Still, Getzel was even richer than the one he tried to imitate, Todrus Broder. Todrus himself lived up to his fancy name. He was tall, broad-shouldered like a giant, with a black beard as straight as a squire's and a pair of dark eyes that burned through you when they looked at you. Now, I know what I'm talking about. I was still a girl then, and a good-looking one, too. When he stared at me with those fiery eyes, the marrow in my bones trembled. If an envious man were to have a look like that, he could, God preserve us, easily give you the evil eye. Todrus had no cause for envy, though. He was as healthy as an ox, and he had a beautiful wife and two graceful daughters, real princesses. He lived like a nobleman. He had a carriage with a coachman, and a hansom as well. He went driving to the villages and played around with the peasant women. When he threw coins to them, they cheered. Sometimes he would go horseback riding through the town, and he sat up in the saddle as straight as a Cossack.

His surname was Broder, but Todrus came from Great Poland, not from Brody. He was a great friend of all the nobles. Count Zamoysky used to come to his table on Friday nights to taste his gefilte fish. On Purim the count sent him a gift, and what do you imagine the gift turned out to be? Two peacocks, a male and a female!

Todrus spoke Polish like a Pole and Russian like a Russian. He knew German, too, and French as well. What didn't he know? He could even play the piano. He went hunting with Zamoysky and he shot a wolf. When the Tsar visited Zamosc and the finest people went to greet him, who do you think spoke to him? Todrus Broder. No sooner were the first three words out of his mouth than the Tsar burst out laughing. They say that later the two of them played a game of chess and Todrus won. I wasn't there, but it probably happened. Later Todrus received a gold medal from Petersburg.

His father-in-law, Falk Posner, was rich, and Falk's daughter Fogel was a real beauty. She had a dowry of twenty thousand rubles, and after her father's death she inherited his entire fortune. But don't think that Todrus married her for her money. It is said that she was traveling with her mother to the spas when suddenly Todrus entered the train. He was still a bachelor then, or perhaps a widower. He took one look at Fogel and

then he told her mother that he wanted her daughter to
be his wife. Imagine, this happened some fifty years ago.
. . . Everyone said that it was love at first sight for
Todrus, but later it turned out that love didn't mean a
thing to him. I should have as many blessed years as the
nights Fogel didn't sleep because of him! They joked,
saying that if you were to dress a shovel in a woman's
skirts, he would chase after it. In those days, Jewish
daughters didn't know about love affairs, so he had to
run after Gentile girls and women.

Not far from Zamosc, Todrus had an estate where
the greatest nobles came to admire his horses. But he
was a terrible spendthrift, and over the years his debts
grew. He devoured his father-in-law's fortune, and that
is the plain truth.

Now, Getzel the Monkey, whose name was really
Getzel Bailes, decided to imitate everything about
Todrus Broder. He was a rich man, and stingy to boot.
His father had also been known as a miser. It was said
that he had built up his fortune by starving himself.
The son had a mill that poured out not flour but gold.
Getzel had an old miller who was as devoted as a dog to
him. In the fall, when there was a lot of grain to mill,
this miller stayed awake nights. He didn't even have a
room for himself; he slept with the mice in the hayloft.
Getzel grew rich because of him. In those times people
were used to serving. If they didn't serve God, they
served the boss.

Getzel was a moneylender, too. Half the town's
houses were mortgaged to him. He had one precious
little daughter, Dishke, and a wife, Risha Leah, who was
as sick as she was ugly. Getzel could as soon become
Todrus as I the rabbi of Turisk. But a rumor spread
through the town that Getzel was trying to become

another Todrus. At the beginning it was only the talk of the peddlers and the seamstresses, and who pays attention to such gossip? But then Getzel went to Selig the tailor and he ordered a coat just like Todrus's, with a broad fox collar and a row of tails. Later he had the shoemaker fit him with a pair of boots exactly the same as Todrus's, with low uppers and shiny toes. Zamosc isn't Warsaw. Sooner or later everyone knows what everyone else is doing. So why mimic anyone? Still, when the rumors reached Todrus's ears he merely said, "I don't care. It shows that he has a high opinion of my taste." Todrus never spoke a bad word about anyone. If he was going down Lublin Street and a girl of twelve walked by, he would lift his hat to her just as though she were a lady. Had a fool done this, they would have made fun of him. But a clever person can afford to be foolish sometimes. At weddings Todrus got drunk and cracked such jokes that they thought he, not Berish Venngrover, was the jester. When he danced a kozotsky, the floor trembled.

Well, Getzel Bailes was determined to become a second Todrus. He was small and thick as a barrel, and a stammerer to boot. To hear him try to get a word out was enough to make you faint. The town had something to mock. He bought himself a carriage, but it was a tiny carriage and the horses were two old nags. Getzel rode from the marketplace to the mill and from the mill to the marketplace. He wanted to be gallant, and he tried to take his hat off to the druggist's wife. Before he could raise his hand, she had already disappeared. People were barely able to keep from laughing in his face, and the town rascals immediately gave him his nickname.

Getzel's wife, Risha Leah, was a shrew, but she had

sense enough to see what was happening. They began to quarrel. There was no lack in Zamosc of curious people who listened at the cracks in the shutters and looked through the keyhole. Risha Leah said to him, "You can as much become Todrus as I can become a man! You are making a fool of yourself. Todrus is Todrus; you stay Getzel."

But who knows what goes on in another person's head? It seemed to be an obsession. Getzel began to pronounce his words like a person from Great Poland and to use German expressions: *mädchen, schmädchen, grädchen*. He found out what Todrus ate, what he drank, and, forgive me for the expression, what drawers he wore. He began to chase women, too. And, my dear friends, just as Todrus had succeeded in everything, so Getzel failed. He would crack a joke and get a box on the ear in return. Once, in the middle of a wedding celebration, he tried to seduce a woman, and her husband poured chicken soup down the front of his gaberdine. Dishke cried and implored him, "Daddy, they are making fun of you!" But it is written somewhere that any fancy can become a madness.

Getzel met Todrus in the street and said, "I want to see your furniture."

"With the greatest pleasure," said Todrus and took him into his living room. What harm would it do Todrus, after all, if Getzel copied him?

So Getzel kept on mimicking. He tried to imitate Todrus's voice. He tried to make friends with the squires and their wives. He had studied everything in detail. Getzel had never smoked, but suddenly he came out with cigars and the cigars were bigger than he was. He also started a subscription to a newspaper in Petersburg. Todrus's daughters went to a Gentile boarding school, and Getzel wanted to send Dishke there, even though she was already too old for that. Risha Leah raised an uproar and she was barely able to prevent him from doing it. If he had been a pauper, Getzel would have been excommunicated. But he was loaded with money. For a long time Todrus didn't pay any attention to all of this, but at last in the marketplace he walked over to Getzel and asked: "Do you want to see how I make water?" He used plain language, and the town had something to laugh about.

2

Now, listen to this. One day Risha Leah died. Of what did she die? Really, I couldn't say. Nowadays people run to the doctor; in those times a person got sick and it was soon finished. Perhaps it was Getzel's carryings on that killed her. Anyway, she died and they buried her. Getzel didn't waste any tears over it. He sat on the stool during the seven days of mourning and cracked jokes like Todrus. His daughter Dishke was already engaged. After the thirty days of bereavement the matchmakers showered him with offers, but he wasn't in a hurry.

Two months hadn't passed when there was bedlam in the town. Todrus Broder had gone bankrupt. He had borrowed money from widows and orphans. Brides had invested their dowries with him, and he owed money to nobles. One of the squires came over and tried to shoot him. Todrus's wife wept and fainted, and the girls hid in the attic. It came out that Todrus owed Getzel a large sum of money. A mortgage, or God knows what. Getzel came to Todrus. He was carrying a cane with a silver tip and an amber handle, just like Todrus's, and he

pounded on the floor with it. Todrus tried to laugh off
the whole business, but you could tell that he didn't feel
very good about it. They wanted to auction off all his
possessions, tear him to pieces. The women called him a
murderer, a robber, and a swindler. The brides howled:
"What did you do with our dowries?" and wailed as if
it were Yom Kippur. Todrus had a dog as big as a lion,
and Getzel had gotten one the image of it. He brought
the dog with him, and both animals tried to devour each
other. Finally Getzel whispered something to Todrus;
they locked themselves in a room and stayed there for
three hours. During that time the creditors almost tore
the house down. When Todrus came out, he was as pale
as death; Getzel was perspiring. He called out to the
men: "Don't make such a racket! I'll pay all the debts.
I have taken over the business from Todrus." They
didn't believe their own ears. Who puts a healthy head
into a sickbed? But Getzel took out his purse, long and
deep, just like Todrus's. However, Todrus's was empty,
and this one was full of bank notes. Getzel began to pay
on the spot. To some he paid off the whole debt and to
others an advance, but they all knew that he was sol-
vent. Todrus looked on silently. Fogel, his wife, came
to herself and smiled. The girls came out of their hiding
places. Even the dogs made peace; they began to sniff
each other and wag their tails. Where had Getzel put
together so much cash? As a rule, a merchant has all his
money in his business. But Getzel kept on paying. He
had stopped stammering and he spoke now as if he
really were Todrus. Todrus had a bookkeeper whom
they called the secretary, and he brought out the
ledgers. Meanwhile, Todrus had become his old self
again. He told jokes, drank brandy, and offered a drink
to Getzel. They toasted *l'chayim.*

To make a long story short, Getzel took over everything. Todrus Broder left for Lublin with his wife and daughters, and it seemed that he had moved out altogether. Even the maids went with him. But then why hadn't he taken his featherbeds with him? By law, no creditor is allowed to take these. For three months there was no word of them. Getzel had already become the boss. He went here, he went there, he rode in Todrus's carriage with Todrus's coachman. After three months Fogel came back with her daughters. It was hard to recognize her. They asked her about her husband and she answered simply, "I have no more husband." "Some misfortune, God forbid?" they asked, and she answered no, that they had been divorced.

There is a saying that the truth will come out like oil on water. And so it happened here. In the three hours that Getzel and Todrus had been locked up in the office, Todrus had transferred everything to Getzel—his house, his estate, all his possessions, and on top of it all, his wife. Yes, Fogel married Getzel. Getzel gave her a marriage contract for ten thousand rubles and wrote up a house—it was actually Todrus's—as estate. For the daughters he put away large dowries.

The turmoil in the town was something awful. If you weren't in Zamosc then, you have no idea how excited a town can become. A book could be written about it. Not one book, ten books! Even the Gentiles don't do such things. But that was Todrus. As long as he could, he acted like a king. He gambled, he lost, and then it was all over; he disappeared. It seems he had been about to go to jail. The squires might have murdered him. And in such a situation, what won't a man do to save his life? Some people thought that Getzel had known everything in advance and that he had plotted it all. He

had managed a big loan for Todrus and had lured him
into his snare. No one would have thought that Getzel
was so clever. But how does the saying go? If God wills,
a broom will shoot.

Todrus's girls soon got married. Dishke went to live
with her in-laws in Lemberg. Fogel almost never
showed her face outside. Todrus's grounds had a garden
with a pavilion, and she sat there all summer. In the winter she hid inside the house. Todrus Broder had vanished
like a stone in the water. Some held that he was in
Krakow; others, that he had gone to Warsaw. Still
others said that he had converted and had married a rich
squiress. Who can understand such a man? If a Jew is
capable of selling his wife in such a way, he is no longer
a Jew. Fogel had loved him with a great love, and it was
clear that she had consented to everything just to save
him. In the years that followed, nobody could say a
word against Todrus to her. On Rosh Hashanah and
Yom Kippur she stood in her pew in the women's section at the grating and she didn't utter a single word to
anybody. She remained proud.

Getzel took over Todrus's language and his manners.
He even became taller, or perhaps he put lifts in his
boots. He became a bosom friend of the squires. It was
rumored that he drank forbidden wine with them. After
he had stopped stammering, he had begun to speak
Polish like one of them.

Dishke never wrote a word to her father. About
Todrus's daughters I heard that they didn't have a good
end. One died in childbirth. Another was supposed to
have hanged herself. But Getzel became Todrus and I
saw it happen with my own eyes, from beginning to
end. Yes, mimicking is forbidden. If you imitate a person, his fate is passed on to you. Even with a shadow

one is not allowed to play tricks. In Zamosc there was a young man who used to play with his shadow. He would put his hands together so that the shadow on the wall would look like a buck with horns, eating and butting. One night the shadow jumped from the wall and gored the young man as if with real horns. He got such a butt that he had two holes in his forehead afterwards. And so it happened here.

Getzel did not need other people's money. He had enough. But suddenly he began to borrow from widows and orphans. Anywhere he could find credit he did, and he paid high interest. He didn't have to renovate his mill either. The flour was as white as snow. But he built a new mill and put in new millstones. His old and devoted miller had died, and Getzel hired a new miller who had long mustaches, a former bailiff. This one swindled him right and left. Getzel also bought an estate from a nobleman even though he already had an estate with a stable and horses. Before this he had kept to his Jewishness, but now he began to dress like a fop. He stopped coming to the synagogue except on High Holy Days. As if this wasn't enough, Getzel started a brewery and he sowed hops for beer. He didn't need any of this. Above all, it cost him a fortune. He imported machines, God knows from where, and they made such a noise at night that the neighbors couldn't sleep. Every few weeks he made a trip to Warsaw. Who can guess what really happened to him? Ten enemies don't do as much harm to a man as he does to himself. One day the news spread that Getzel was bankrupt. My dear friends, he didn't have to go bankrupt; it was all an imitation of Todrus. He had taken over the other's bad luck. People streamed from every street and broke up his window-panes. Getzel had no imitator. No one wanted his wife;

Fogel was older than Getzel by a good many years. He assured everyone that he wouldn't take anything away from them. But they beat him up. A squire came and put his pistol to Getzel's forehead in just the same way as the other had to Todrus.

To make a long story short, Getzel ran away in the middle of the night. When he left, the creditors took over and it turned out that there was more than enough for everybody. Getzel's fortune was worth God knows how much. So why had he run away? And where had he gone? Some said that the whole bankruptcy was nothing but a sham. There was supposed to have been a woman involved, but what does an old man want with a woman? It was all to be like Todrus. Had Todrus buried himself alive, Getzel would have dug his own grave. The whole thing was the work of demons. What are demons if not imitators? And what does a mirror do? This is why they cover a mirror when there is a corpse in the house. It is dangerous to see the reflection of the body.

Every piece of property Getzel had owned was taken away. The creditors didn't leave as much as a scrap of bread for Fogel. She went to live in the poorhouse. When this happened I was no longer in Zamosc. But may my enemies have such an old age as they say Fogel had. She lay down on a straw mattress and she never got up again. It was said that before her death she asked to be inscribed on the tombstone not as the wife of Getzel but as the wife of Todrus. Nobody even bothered to put up a stone. Over the years the grave become overgrown and was finally lost.

What happened to Getzel? And what happened to Todrus? No one knew. Somebody thought they might have met somewhere, but for what purpose? Todrus must have died. Dishke tried to get a part of her father's estate, but nothing was left. A man should stay what he is. The troubles of the world come from mimicking. Today they call it fashion. A charlatan in Paris invents a dress with a train in front and everybody wears it. They are all apes, the whole lot of them.

I could also tell you a story about twins, but I wouldn't dare to talk about it at night. They had no choice. They were two bodies with one soul. Both sisters died within a single day, one in Zamosc and the other in Kovle. Who knows? Perhaps one sister was real and the other was her shadow?

I am afraid of a shadow. A shadow is an enemy. When it has the chance, it takes revenge.

Translated by the author
and Ellen Kantarov

A
Friend
of
Kafka

I had heard about Franz Kafka years before I read any of his books from his friend Jacques Kohn, a former actor in the Yiddish theater. I say "former" because by the time I knew him he was no longer on the stage. It was the early thirties, and the Yiddish theater in Warsaw had already begun to lose its audience. Jacques Kohn himself was a sick and broken man. Although he still dressed in the style of a dandy, his clothes were shabby. He wore a monocle in his left eye, a high old-fashioned collar (known as "father-murderer"), patent-leather shoes, and a derby. He had been nicknamed "the lord" by the cynics in the Warsaw Yiddish writers' club that we both frequented. Although he stooped more and more, he worked stubbornly at keeping his shoulders back. What was left of his once yellow hair he combed to form a bridge over his bare skull. In the tradition of the old-time theater, every now and then he would lapse into Germanized Yiddish—particularly when he spoke of his relationship with Kafka. Of late, he had begun writing newspaper articles, but the editors were unanimous in rejecting his manuscripts. He lived in an attic room somewhere on Leszno Street and was constantly ailing. A joke about him made the rounds of the club members: "All day long he lies in an oxygen tent, and at night he emerges a Don Juan."

We always met at the club in the evening. The door would open slowly to admit Jacques Kohn. He had the air of an important European celebrity who was deigning to visit the ghetto. He would look around and grimace, as if to indicate that the smells of herring, garlic, and cheap tobacco were not to his taste. He would glance disdainfully over the tables covered with tattered newspapers, broken chess pieces, and ashtrays filled with cigarette stubs, around which the club members sat endlessly discussing literature in their shrill voices. He would shake his head as if to say, "What can you expect from such schlemiels?" The moment I saw him entering, I would put my hand in my pocket and prepare the zloty that he would inevitably borrow from me.

This particular evening, Jacques seemed to be in a better mood than usual. He smiled, displaying his porcelain teeth, which did not fit and moved slightly when he spoke, and swaggered over to me as if he were on-stage. He offered me his bony, long-fingered hand and said, "How's the rising star doing tonight?"

"At it already?"

"I'm serious. Serious. I know talent when I see it, even though I lack it myself. When we played Prague in 1911, no one had ever heard of Kafka. He came backstage, and the moment I saw him I knew that I was in the presence of genius. I could smell it the way a cat smells a mouse. That was how our great friendship began."

I had heard this story many times and in as many variations, but I knew that I would have to listen to it again. He sat down at my table, and Manya, the waitress, brought us glasses of tea and cookies. Jacques Kohn raised his eyebrows over his yellowish eyes, the whites of which were threaded with bloody little veins. His expression seemed to say, "This is what the barbarians call tea?" He put five lumps of sugar into his glass and stirred, rotating the tin spoon outward. With his thumb and index finger, the nail of which was unusually long, he broke off a small piece of cookie, put it into his mouth, and said, "*Nu ja,*" which meant, One cannot fill one's stomach on the past.

It was all play-acting. He himself came from a Hasidic family in one of the small Polish towns. His name was not Jacques but Jankel. However, he had lived for many years in Prague, Vienna, Berlin, Paris. He had not always been an actor in the Yiddish theater but had played on the stage in both France and Germany. He had been friends with many celebrities. He had helped Chagall find a studio in Belleville. He had been a frequent guest at Israel Zangwill's. He had appeared in a Reinhardt production, and had eaten cold cuts with Piscator. He had shown me letters he had received not only from Kafka but from Jakob Wassermann, Stefan Zweig, Romain Rolland, Ilya Ehrenburg, and Martin Buber. They all addressed him by his first name. As we got to know each other better, he had even let me see photographs and letters from famous actresses with whom he had had affairs.

For me, "lending" Jacques Kohn a zloty meant coming into contact with Western Europe. The very way he carried his silver-handled cane seemed exotic to me. He even smoked his cigarettes differently from the way we did in Warsaw. His manners were courtly. On the rare occasion when he reproached me, he always managed to save my feelings with some elegant compliment. More than anything else, I admired Jacques Kohn's way with women. I was shy with girls—blushed, became embarrassed in their presence—but Jacques Kohn had the assurance of a count. He had something nice to say to the most unattractive woman. He flattered them all, but always in a tone of good-natured irony, affecting the blasé attitude of a hedonist who has already tasted everything.

He spoke frankly to me. "My young friend, I'm as good as impotent. It always starts with the development of an overrefined taste—when one is hungry, one does not need marzipan and caviar. I've reached the point where I consider no woman really attractive. No defect can be hidden from me. That is impotence. Dresses, corsets are transparent for me. I can no longer be fooled by paint and perfume. I have lost my own teeth, but a woman has only to open her mouth and I spot her fillings. That, by the way, was Kafka's problem when it came to writing: he saw all the defects—his own and everyone else's. Most of literature is produced by such plebeians and bunglers as Zola and D'Annunzio. In the theater, I saw the same defects that Kafka found in literature, and that brought us together. But, oddly enough, when it came to judging the theater Kafka was completely blind. He praised our cheap Yiddish plays to heaven. He fell madly in love with a ham actress—Madam Tschissik. When I think that Kafka loved this creature, dreamed about her, I am ashamed for man and his illusions. Well, immortality is not choosy. Anyone who happens to come in contact with a great man marches with him into immortality, often in clumsy boots.

"Didn't you once ask what makes me go on, or do I imagine that you did? What gives me the strength to bear poverty, sickness, and, worst of all, hopelessness? That's a good question, my young friend. I asked the same question when I first read the Book of Job. Why did Job continue to live and suffer? So that in the end he would have more daughters, more donkeys, more camels? No. The answer is that it was for the game itself. We all play chess with Fate as partner. He makes a move; we make a move. He tries to checkmate us in three moves; we try to prevent it. We know we can't win, but we're driven to give him a good fight. My opponent is a tough angel. He fights Jacques Kohn with every trick in his bag. It's winter now; it's cold even with the stove on, but my stove hasn't worked for months and the landlord refuses to fix it. Besides, I wouldn't have the money to buy coal. It's as cold inside my room as it is outdoors. If you haven't lived in an attic, you don't know the strength of the wind. My window-panes rattle even in the summertime. Sometimes a tom-cat climbs up on the roof near my window and wails all night like a woman in labor. I lie there freezing under my blankets and he yowls for a cat, though it may be he's merely hungry. I might give him a morsel of food to quiet him, or chase him away, but in order not to freeze to death I wrap myself in all the rags I possess, even old newspapers—the slightest move and the whole works comes apart.

"Still, if you play chess, my dear friend, it's better to

play with a worthy adversary than with a botcher. I admire my opponent. Sometimes I'm enchanted with his ingenuity. He sits up there in an office in the third or seventh heaven, in that department of Providence that rules our little planet, and has just one job—to trap Jacques Kohn. His orders are 'Break the keg, but don't let the wine run out.' He's done exactly that. How he manages to keep me alive is a miracle. I'm ashamed to tell you how much medicine I take, how many pills I swallow. I have a friend who is a druggist, or I could never afford it. Before I go to bed, I gulp down one after another—dry. If I drink, I have to urinate. I have prostate trouble, and as it is I must get up several times during the night. In the dark, Kant's categories no longer apply. Time ceases to be time and space is not space. You hold something in your hand and suddenly it isn't there. To light my gas lamp is not a simple matter. My matches are always vanishing. My attic teems with demons. Occasionally, I address one of them: 'Hey, you, Vinegar, son of Wine, how about stopping your nasty tricks!'

"Some time ago, in the middle of the night, I heard a pounding on my door and the sound of a woman's voice. I couldn't tell whether she was laughing or crying. 'Who can it be?' I said to myself. 'Lilith? Namah? Machlath, the daughter of Ketev M'riri?' Out loud, I called, 'Madam, you are making a mistake.' But she continued to bang on the door. Then I heard a groan and someone falling. I did not dare to open the door. I began to look for my matches, only to discover that I was holding them in my hand. Finally, I got out of bed, lit the gas lamp, and put on my dressing gown and slippers. I caught a glimpse of myself in the mirror, and my reflection scared me. My face was green and unshaven. I finally opened the door, and there stood a young woman in bare feet, wearing a sable coat over her nightgown. She was pale and her long blond hair was disheveled. 'Madam, what's the matter?' I said.

" 'Someone just tried to kill me. I beg you, please let me in. I only want to stay in your room until daylight.'

"I wanted to ask who had tried to kill her, but I saw that she was half frozen. Most probably drunk, too. I let her in and noticed a bracelet with huge diamonds on her wrist. 'My room is not heated,' I told her.

" 'It's better than to die in the street.'

"So there we were both of us. But what was I to do with her? I only have one bed. I don't drink—I'm not allowed to—but a friend had given me a bottle of cognac as a gift, and I had some stale cookies. I gave her a drink and one of the cookies. The liquor seemed to revive her. 'Madam, do you live in this building?' I asked.

" 'No,' she said. 'I live on Ujazdowskie Boulevard.'

"I could tell that she was an aristocrat. One word led to another, and I discovered that she was a countess and a widow, and that her lover lived in the building—a wild man, who kept a lion cub as a pet. He, too, was a member of the nobility, but an outcast. He had already served a year in the Citadel, for attempted murder. He could not visit her, because she lived in her mother-in-law's house, so she came to see him. That night, in a jealous fit, he had beaten her and placed his revolver at her temple. To make a long story short, she had managed to grab her coat and run out of his apartment. She had knocked on the doors of the neighbors, but none of them would let her in, and so she had made her way to the attic.

" 'Madam,' I said to her, 'your lover is probably still looking for you. Supposing he finds you? I am no longer what one might call a knight.'

" 'He won't dare make a disturbance,' she said. 'He's on parole. I'm through with him for good. Have pity—please don't put me out in the middle of the night.'

" 'How will you get home tomorrow?' I asked.

" 'I don't know,' she said. 'I'm tired of life anyhow, but I don't want to be killed by him.'

" 'Well, I won't be able to sleep in any case,' I said. 'Take my bed and I will rest here in this chair.'

" 'No. I wouldn't do that. You are not young and you don't look very well. Please, go back to bed and I will sit here.'

"We haggled so long we finally decided to lie down together. 'You have nothing to fear from me,' I assured her. 'I am old and helpless with women.' She seemed completely convinced.

"What was I saying? Yes, suddenly I find myself in bed with a countess whose lover might break down the door at any moment. I covered us both with the two blankets I have and didn't bother to build the usual cocoon of odds and ends. I was so wrought up I forgot about the cold. Besides, I felt her closeness. A strange warmth emanated from her body, different from any I had known—or perhaps I had forgotten it. Was my opponent trying a new gambit? In the past few years he had stopped playing with me in earnest. You know, there is such a thing as humorous chess. I have been told that Nimzowitsch often played jokes on his partners. In the old days, Murphy was known as a chess prankster. 'A fine move,' I said to my adversary. 'A masterpiece.' With that I realized that I knew who her lover was. I had met him on the stairs—a giant of a man, with the face of a murderer. What a funny end for Jacques Kohn —to be finished off by a Polish Othello.

"I began to laugh and she joined in. I embraced her and held her close. She did not resist. Suddenly a miracle happened. I was a man again! Once, on a Thursday evening, I stood near a slaughterhouse in a small village and saw a bull and a cow copulate before they were going to be slaughtered for the Sabbath. Why she consented I will never know. Perhaps it was a way of taking revenge on her lover. She kissed me and whispered endearments. Then we heard heavy footsteps. Someone pounded on the door with his fist. My girl rolled off the bed and lay on the floor. I wanted to recite the prayer for the dying, but I was ashamed before God—and not so much before God as before my mocking opponent. Why grant him this additional pleasure? Even melodrama has its limits.

"The brute behind the door continued beating it, and I was astounded that it did not give way. He kicked it with his foot. The door creaked but held. I was terrified, yet something in me could not help laughing. Then the racket stopped. Othello had left.

"Next morning, I took the countess's bracelet to a pawnshop. With the money I received, I bought my heroine a dress, underwear, and shoes. The dress didn't fit, neither did the shoes, but all she needed to do was get to a taxi—provided, of course, that her lover did not waylay her on the steps. Curious, but the man vanished that night and never reappeared.

"Before she left, she kissed me and urged me to call her, but I'm not that much of a fool. As the Talmud says, 'A miracle doesn't happen every day.'

"And you know, Kafka, young as he was, was possessed by the same inhibitions that plague me in my old age. They impeded him in everything he did—in sex as well as in his writing. He craved love and fled from it. He wrote a sentence and immediately crossed it out. Otto Weininger was like that, too—mad and a genius. I met him in Vienna—he spouted aphorisms and paradoxes. One of his sayings I will never forget: 'God did not create the bedbug'. You have to know Vienna to really understand these words. Yet who did create the bedbug?

"Ah, there's Bamberg! Look at the way he waddles along on his short legs, a corpse refusing to rest in its grave. It might be a good idea to start a club for insomniac corpses. Why does he prowl around all night? What good are the cabarets to him? The doctors gave him up years ago when we were still in Berlin. Not that it prevented him from sitting in the Romanisches Café until four o'clock in the morning, chatting with the prostitutes. Once, Granat, the actor announced that he was giving a party—a real orgy—at his house, and among others he invited Bamberg. Granat instructed each man to bring a lady—either his wife or a friend. But Bamberg had neither wife nor mistress, and so he paid a harlot to accompany him. He had to buy her an evening dress for the occasion. The company consisted exclusively of writers, professors, philosophers, and the usual intellectual hangers-on. They all had the same idea as Bamberg—they hired prostitutes. I was there, too. I escorted an actress from Prague, whom I had known a long time. Do you know Granat? A savage. He drinks cognac like soda water, and can eat an omelette of ten eggs. As soon as the guests arrived, he stripped and began dancing madly around with the whores, just to impress his highbrow visitors. At first, the intellectuals sat on chairs and stared. After a while, they began to discuss sex. Schopenhauer said this. . . . Nietzsche said that. Anyone who hadn't witnessed it would find it difficult to imagine how ridiculous such geniuses can be. In the midst of it all, Bamberg was taken ill. He turned as green as grass and broke out in a sweat. 'Jacques,' he said, 'I'm finished. A good place to die.' He was having a kidney or a gall-bladder attack. I half carried him out and got him to a hospital. By the way, can you lend me a zloty?"

"Two."

"What! Have you robbed Bank Polski?"

"I sold a story."

"Congratuations. Let's have supper together. You will be my guest."

2

While we were eating, Bamberg came over to our table. He was a little man, emaciated as a consumptive, bent over and bowlegged. He was wearing patent-leather shoes, and spats. On his pointed skull lay a few gray hairs. One eye was larger than the other—red, bulging, frightened by its own vision. He leaned against our table on his bony little hands and said in his cackling voice, "Jacques, yesterday I read your Kafka's *Castle*. Interesting, very interesting, but what is he driving at? It's too long for a dream. Allegories should be short."

Jacques Kohn quickly swallowed the food he was chewing. "Sit down," he said. "A master does not have to follow the rules."

"There are some rules even a master must follow. No novel should be longer than *War and Peace*. Even *War and Peace* is too long. If the Bible consisted of eighteen volumes, it would long since have been forgotten."

"The Talmud has thirty-six volumes, and the Jews have not forgotten it."

"Jews remember too much. That is our misfortune. It is two thousand years since we were driven out of the Holy Land, and now we are trying to get back in. Insane, isn't it? If our literature would only reflect this insanity, it would be great. But our literature is uncannily sane. Well, enough of that."

Bamberg straightened himself, scowling with the effort. With his tiny steps, he shuffled away from the table. He went over to the gramophone and put on a dance record. It was known in the writers' club that he had not written a word in years. In his old age, he was learning to dance, influenced by the philosophy of his friend Dr. Mitzkin, the author of *The Entropy of Reason*. In this book Dr. Mitzkin attempted to prove that the human intellect is bankrupt and that true wisdom can only be reached through passion.

Jacques Kohn shook his head. "Half-pint Hamlet. Kafka was afraid of becoming a Bamberg—that is why he destroyed himself."

"Did the countess ever call you?" I asked.

Jacques Kohn took his monocle out of his pocket and put it in place. "And what if she did? In my life, everything turns into words. All talk, talk. This is actually Dr. Mitzkin's philosophy—man will end up as a word machine. He will eat words, drink words, marry words, poison himself with words. Come to think of it, Dr. Mitzkin was also present at Granat's orgy. He came to practice what he preached, but he could just as well have written *The Entropy of Passion*. Yes, the countess does call me from time to time. She, too, is an intellectual, but without intellect. As a matter of fact, although women do their best to reveal the charms of their bodies, they know just as little about the meaning of sex as they do about the intellect.

"Take Madam Tschissik. What did she ever have, except a body? But just try asking her what a body really is. Now she's ugly. When she was an actress in the Prague days, she still had something. I was her leading man. She was a tiny little talent. We came to Prague to make some money and found a genius waiting for us— *Homo sapiens* in his highest degree of self-torture. Kafka wanted to be a Jew, but he didn't know how. He wanted to live, but he didn't know this, either. 'Franz,' I said to him once, 'you are a young man. Do what we all do.' There was a brothel I knew in Prague, and I persuaded him to go there with me. He was still a virgin. I'd rather not speak about the girl he was engaged to. He was sunk to the neck in the bourgeois swamp. The Jews of his circle had one ideal—to become Gentiles, and not Czech Gentiles but German Gentiles. To make it short, I talked him into the adventure. I took him to a dark alley in the former ghetto and there was the brothel. We went up the crooked steps. I opened the door and it looked like a stage set: the whores, the pimps, the guests, the madam. I will never forget that moment. Kafka began to shake, and pulled at my sleeve. Then he turned and ran down the steps so quickly I was afraid he would break a leg. Once on the street, he stopped and vomited like a schoolboy. On the way back, we passed an old synagogue, and Kafka began to speak about the golem. Kafka believed in the golem, and even that the future might well bring another one. There must be magic words that can turn a piece of clay into a living being. Did not God, according to the cabala, create the world by uttering holy words? In the beginning was the Logos.

"Yes, it's all one big chess game. All my life I have been afraid of death, but now that I'm on the threshold of the grave I've stopped being afraid. It's clear, my partner wants to play a slow game. He'll go on taking my pieces one by one. First he removed my appeal as an actor and turned me into a so-called writer. He'd no sooner done that than he provided me with writer's cramp. His next move was to deprive me of my potency. Yet I know he's far from checkmate, and this gives me strength. It's cold in my room—let it be cold. I have no supper—I won't die without it. He sabotages me and I sabotage him. Some time ago, I was returning home late at night. The frost burned outside, and suddenly I realized that I had lost my key. I woke up the janitor, but he had no spare key. He stank of vodka, and his dog bit my foot. In former years I would have been desperate, but this time I said to my opponent, "If you want me to catch pneumonia, it's all right with me.' I left the house and decided to go to the Vienna station. The wind almost carried me away. I would have had to wait at least three-quarters of an hour for the streetcar at that time of night. I passed by the actors' union and saw a light in a window. I decided to go in. Perhaps I could spend the night there. On the steps I hit something with my shoe and heard a ringing sound. I bent down and picked up a key. It was mine! The chance of finding a key on the dark stairs of this building is one in a billion, but it seems that my opponent was afraid I might give up the ghost before he was ready. Fatalism? Call it fatalism if you like."

Jacques Kohn rose and excused himself to make a phone call. I sat there and watched Bamberg dancing on his shaky legs with a literary lady. His eyes were closed, and he leaned his head on her bosom as if it were a pillow. He seemed to be dancing and sleeping simultaneously. Jacques Kohn took a long time—much longer than it normally takes to make a phone call. When he returned, the monocle in his eye shone. "Guess who is in the other room?" he said. "Madam Tschissik! Kafka's great love."

"Really."

"I told her about you. Come, I'd like to introduce you to her."

"No."

"Why not? A woman that was loved by Kafka is worth meeting."

"I'm not interested."

"You are shy, that's the truth. Kafka, too, was shy—as shy as a yeshiva student. I was never shy, and that may be the reason I have never amounted to anything. My dear friend, I need another twenty groschen for the janitors—ten for the one in this building, and ten for the one in mine. Without the money I can't go home."

I took some change out of my pocket and gave it to him.

"So much? You certainly must have robbed a bank today. Forty-six groschen! Piff-paff! Well, if there is a God, He will reward you. And if there isn't, who is playing all these games with Jacques Kohn?"

*Tranlsated by the author
and Elizabeth Shub*

IN
MY
FATHER'S
COURT

My
Father's
Friend

Often I hear Yiddish writers speak of publishing a book. Terms like matrices, composition, plates, and stock are used. But to me these words have been familiar from childhood. Since my father was the author of numerous religious books, I learned early how a book is set in type, how galleys are proofread, matrices struck, plates made, and all about printing and binding. No matter how little my father earned, he saved money to publish his books. He used to say, "A religious book is a permanent testament."

I remember him also preparing for publication a manuscript of the famous Joseph Shor. It was discovered somewhere in a library: a notebook with yellow-gray paper and faded characters, but the writing, although 150 years old, was still legible. Its title was

Nutrikun and, like all Shor's works, it was written in a difficult literary style. My father and his good friend, Reb Nachman, known for his own rabbinical books, copied the old manuscript for the printer.

I loved to be present when Father and Reb Nachman conversed. They both had red beards and blue eyes, but Reb Nachman was a kind of Hasidic dandy, with a dazzling alpaca capote, gold-rimmed glasses dangling from a black ribbon, and polished boots. A fine, intelligent person, of good heritage, Reb Nachman was a disciple of Rabbi Zadock Lubliner, whose numerous religious books he kept editing and publishing. Father enjoyed the wit of Reb Nachman, who, in turn, was pleased with Father's gentle speech. On the other hand, Reb Nachman also resented the Radzymin rabbi, for whom he worked some years before.

Reb Nachman conducted himself like a scholar and aristocrat. Unfortunately, his writing and editing brought him nothing, and if his son did not make and sell cigarettes, Reb Nachman and his family would have starved. It was illegal to sell cigarettes without a stamp signifying that they had been taxed, but they had no other source of livelihood. The boy sold the cigarettes to stores who resold them.

One day, for some reason or other, my father sent me to Reb Nachman. The apartment, different from ours, was somehow similar. There were more children and more furniture. Reb Nachman, who had a talent for drawing, not only would print and draw beautifully but would embellish a title page with all kinds of flowers, circles, and flourishes. He sat at a table in a skullcap and satin vest, with colored slate pencils and bottles of ink before him.

Since Reb Nachman visited Father more often than

Father visited him, I was welcomed warmly and addressed as a grown-up. Having heard that my brother Israel Joshua had become "corrupted," he discussed heresy with me. Then he showed me a piece of paper covered with flowers, lions, small birds, and eagles. "Look," he said, "if someone told you this had drawn itself, you'd say he was crazy—but the heretics say the world created itself, and is that sane?"

"Certainly not."

"Man, they say, comes from the ape. But did the ape come from itself?"

"No."

"They say the earth tore itself from the sun. Well, where did the sun come from? They say all kinds of nonsensical things to keep from admitting that there is a Creator."

I blushed. Such things were never discussed directly with me, a mere boy, at home. Reb Nachman was treating me like an equal. I was offered a glass of tea and a cookie. A girl my age with dark braids came in, and then another girl. I smelled cutlets frying in the kitchen. This apartment didn't seem as bare as ours; everything harmonized—the Torah, wise words, girls, tasty dishes, a table full of pencils, inks, brushes, and seals. And what Reb Nachman had to say about heretics was revealing to me, since I had wondered for a long time what their views were.

Suddenly there was a loud knocking on the front door, then noise and harsh voices. Reb Nachman leaped from his chair and I arose, frightened by a strange sight —the kitchen was full of policemen, officers in brass buttons with "crowns" on their caps. Cap in hand, the janitor followed them, and there was even a civilian official, a secret agent. From the way the Russians, whom I did not understand, yelled and stamped and gripped their swords, I realized it was a raid. Reb Nachman grew white and his frightened daughters huddled in a corner. His wife was arguing and pleading, but the police shouted at her to be quiet. A tremor ran down my spine.

Terrified, I asked Reb Nachman if I could go home.

"If they let you," he said in a confused way.

I was stopped at the door by a guard.

I had no knowledge of Reb Nachman's illegal business and I stood there trembling. Just a while ago, my friend Baruch David and I had seen the Pawiak prison: the yellow walls, the barred windows with wire mesh across the bars, the sallow-faced prisoners peering out, and the black entrance gates. I felt as if my time had come now; I as well as Reb Nachman and his family would be sent to jail to rot behind the thick walls. But why should this happen to me, and what did they have against Reb Nachman? Had he been falsely accused? I remembered the story of Rabbi Akiba, whose body had been raked with metal combs until he expired. Was that to be my fate? Had the era of Chmielnitzky returned or the time when the Temple was destroyed? I wished I could suddenly sprout a couple of wings and soar off through the window, or grow as strong as Samson and smite these Philistines with the jawbone of an ass, or wear a hat that would make me invisible.

I hadn't been arrested yet, but my desire for freedom became so potent that I wondered what I had been missing until then. What had I worried about when it was possible to walk the streets unmolested? Everything became inexpressibly dear to me: the Warsaw streets, our home, the summer day. I felt as if I were suffocating as

I looked fearfully at the swords, epaulets, whistles, and medals. If there is a God, I thought, why is he silent?

The police stopped talking and began to search the apartment. At first they found nothing, then suddenly they began to drag out cartons of cigarettes, cigarette paper, tobacco, and other things wrapped in paper.

As if this wasn't enough, the agent brought in a crowbar and wrenched a board from the floor. It happened to be the right board, because all kinds of boxes wrapped in paper were revealed. "Someone informed!" Reb Nachman called out. "Be quiet!" a policeman ordered.

During the search, which took about three hours, I almost passed out from sweating. My shirt was drenched and rivulets ran over my entire body. The policemen laughed, seeing me so soaked, and one of them seized my sidelock, to find his hand wet. I was melting from anxiety; it seemed to me that I would soon dissolve completely. Reb Nachman's daughters, despite the trouble in the family, looked at me and smiled. I kept trembling with fear and shame, even when the sweating stopped. These Russians with their swords, revolvers, mean speech, and coarse jokes aroused hostility in me that I had never before felt toward anyone.

Eventually Reb Nachman's son came home, took the Russians into the bedroom, and came to some agreement with them. No one was taken to jail and I had been afraid for no reason at all. After the police left, Reb Nachman clutched his beard and said, "You see where they've got us. It's high time the Messiah came."

They insisted that I eat something else, but all I wanted to do was get away. I felt sickened by the experience. I had already heard my brother say that Polish Jews were storekeepers, brokers, idlers, and parasites, and that there were more stores than customers. The fathers-in-law starved in order to board their sons-in-law. My brother referred to Palestine, where Jews led normal lives as farmers. He also had socialistic leanings and complained that those who worked hard had nothing, while the idle never lacked money. He had told Mother about the Bilgoray sieve-makers who toiled in their shops all week and had to beg on Fridays. "If only they'd strike," my brother said, "the bosses would have to give in."

Even my mother, after her return from my sister's wedding in Berlin, spoke in a manner that was strange for her. "In Germany," she said, "people are polite. The police say 'please' and 'excuse me' to everyone. And the border officials did not tear up our things, but addressed Father as 'Herr Rabiner.'"

My brain was whirling with such information. I walked, seething, through the streets, my brother's words mixing with my own thoughts. No, life in Poland was shameful!

With new insight I observed Warsaw's Jews: tiny shops, ragged men, grimy children, slatternly women. The voice of the Torah arose from houses of prayer and study houses, but they were surrounded by Poles, Russians, innumerable Gentiles who hated Jews and considered them a burden. The Jews had one protector: God. But what if the heretics were right?

Dreamers

"How does a livelihood start? With a family, a wife and children. Why doesn't a bachelor earn enough? He doesn't have a family. Even if he works, he scarcely earns enough to support himself. Rich men have wives and children. Without a wife, a man is half a person. I don't know how many times I've wanted to go into business, but when I get up and look around the house, it's as if my hands were paralyzed. . . ."

Reb Ezekiel, a short, stocky man with a partly gray beard, was speaking. Behind gold-rimmed glasses, his eyes were soft and moist. He wore a gaberdine with tails, a silk hat, and polished boots.

It wasn't that Reb Ezekiel was a bachelor. He was married for the third time, but she was a bad wife, and having such a wife is like having none at all.

"It's like this," he said. "When I come home from evening prayers and want to sit down with a book, she wants to go to bed. I can't go to sleep at nine; I toss and turn all night. At four in the morning she's up to tend her fish, with a lot of noise, waking me when she lights the gas. While she and her daughter fumble with the tanks where the fish are, she curses continually. Then they go off without even leaving me a warm drink. At night they're frozen and grouchy and go right to bed. Is this a home? What am I there for except to make a benediction over the wine on the Sabbath? She'd like me to care for the fish too. No! This is no home!"

"Well, why not divorce her?" people would say.

"She doesn't want a divorce. Besides, how would I support myself? I'd have to be able to earn a living."

"Then what can be done?"

"Now you know why I'm so miserable."

He used to visit our house, drink tea, and have a bit of food. He taught me to play chess, and liked to invent things. His pockets were filled with strings, springs, little disks, spindles, wire fragments, and other items used for his inventions. Having studied books on the subject, he already knew how to make ink and salves. Everything fascinated him—why summer was hot and winter cold, why ice formed from water and later dissolved, why the ancient Egyptians were conversant with a magic unknown to moderns, and what countries lay beyond America, China, and the Mountains of Darkness. How could such a man, who was always looking into books, fool around with fish? How could he be expected to stand in Yanash's bazaar among the boors and simpletons, selling carp or pike to housewives?

If he had a household to call his own, it might have been different.

Others in similar situations visited us also, with their real or fancied tragedies. One who came often was Mattes, whom I remembered from Leoncin. The son-in-law of Hirshl the Dairyman, he used to visit the court of the Radzymin rabbi. Short and thickset, with large hands and feet and an amiable naïve face, he, like my father, had devoted his life to being a good Jew. He was always talking about rabbis and saints; it took him three hours to say the morning prayer. He had no time to work. His father-in-law, Hirshl, had tried vainly to make a merchant of him. After the morning prayer, Mattes would eat a piece of bread with onion and sit down to study. There was so much to study that he could not understand how anyone could devote himself to anything else. So many prayers, Hasidic books, so many degrees of piety to be reached. . . . And one had to be constantly on guard against all the devils and goblins that tried to drag one down. How was it possible to take the time to work in a store or care for cattle or worry about the dairy and such matters?

Hirshl wanted his daughter to divorce Mattes, but Leah, who had a couple of children, wouldn't hear of it. She had remained in Leoncin with her father, while Mattes wandered about Warsaw.

Suddenly he announced that he had become a Uman Hasid. For years he had searched for a true saint, and now he had found Uman Hasidism, and Rabbi Nachman from Uman was the greatest. No Hasidic book, he said, could match Rabbi Nachman's collected wisdom, his tales and prayers, so full of the mysteries of the cabala. Mattes threw himself entirely into Uman Hasidism. Coming to see us, without any introduction he would begin to dance, snapping his fingers and quoting his saint: "There is no gloom! Until the coming of the Messiah, my flame will smolder. . . ."

All Mattes longed for was to go to Uman in the Ukraine and spend his time studying in the house of worship that stood over the rabbi's grave. As a Kohen (of priestly descent), Mattes was not permitted to enter a cemetery, but the graves of saints, he knew, did not defile. Nevertheless, Mattes needed train fare. He also wanted to take Leah and the children, but his father-in-law would not permit it. What would they live on, out there in Russia—Mattes's dance steps on the rabbi's grave?

Both Ezekiel and Mattes were dreamers, but they didn't understand each other. Mattes, looking heavenwards, would dance, clapping his hands and crying that the world was full of joy, while Ezekiel, scratching his beard, would ask, "Where does the hail come from? And if it's warm in summer, how does the rain freeze?"

"It's cold up there."

"If it's so cold, why doesn't it snow? And what's wrong with hail in winter? There must be some answer to this!"

"Everything comes from above!" Mattes said bluntly. "For everything there is a guardian angel. Each blade of grass is told when to grow."

"Yes. But there must be a law governing all this."

Mattes managed to get the train fare and went to Uman—not to stay, merely to look it over. Many months later he came back, with his clothes in tatters, his cheeks sunken, and his boots cracked. But his eyes were radiant and he came dancing into our house. When Father asked how things went in Uman, Mattes talked and sang and rejoiced. "It's Paradise!" he said, growing more excited as he spoke. The saint's house of worship overlooked his grave, Mattes said; his spirit hovered everywhere, blazing from every candle. The days, weeks, and months went by as one studied from the rabbi's books, sang and rejoiced. Stepping into the house of worship, one was immediately overcome with feeling of love for every man and child. When there was food, one ate; when there was nothing, one fasted, and one slept in the house of worship, above the rabbi's grave.

"Aren't people afraid?"

"Afraid of the rabbi? Ridiculous! Only villains remain dead; a saint really comes to life when he dies. The rabbi walks through the house of worship, speaks to us, recites the Torah. All the pleasures in the world are nothing compared to one day in Uman. Even if they offered me Rothschild's millions I wouldn't stay away from the rabbi!"

Mattes had come for his family, but Hirshl consulted Father about a divorce. Leah accompanied him, crying, and bringing along with her the smell of the village and dairy. "Why can't we live like other people?" she asked, weeping copiously.

I don't recall exactly, but I think that Mattes, although he finally divorced Leah, remained in Poland. He returned to Uman only after the Bolshevik Revolution, smuggling himself across borders, past armies, hostile bands, and pogroms. I do not know what happened to him there. He may have ended up in a slave camp or Bolshevik prison. The Bolsheviks, who had not molested the house of worship at first, eventually destroyed it.

Ezekiel and Mattes weren't the only dreamers to visit us. Father seemed to attract these men as a candle does moths.

A short, stout young man with a blond beard came to

see us from some Polish village, after deserting his wife
and perhaps even child. He carried a prayer shawl and
phylacteries, and in his prayer-shawl sack there was a
book called *The Sayings of the Holy Jew*. He had come
to Warsaw to study the cabala, he said, having been forbidden to do so in his home town. After asking everywhere in Warsaw about a rabbi who could help him, he
was directed to my father. The young man would not
listen to my father's pleas that he abandon his plan, saying that he himself knew nothing of the cabala. The
young man thought Father was merely being modest.
Father gave him several books—*The Pillar of Service,
The Treasure of Dew, The Gates of Light*—and the
young man settled down in our house to study. Sleeping
in Father's study, he ate breakfast and supper with us.
To Mother's complaints that she didn't have enough for
her own children, Father replied, "I won't turn away a
fellow Jew."

To earn his keep, the young man was asked to teach
me the Torah. He locked himself in the bedroom with
me, and we studied. In the midst of studying, he said,
"What's to become of us?"

"What do you mean?"

"How long do you think we'll sit here like this?"

"What else should we do?"

"Go away."

"Where?"

"Wherever our legs take us."

"How will we live?"

"He who gives life will sustain us."

He longed for the days when a young man could
settle in a rabbi's house and immerse himself in Judaism,
renouncing the world. He suggested that we both become saints; there must still be saintly Jews in the

world, if not in Poland, then at least in the Holy Land. In Jerusalem or Safad there had to be Jews studying the cabala. "Somewhere, in a cave, we'll settle down and live an eternal Day of Atonement, fasting by day and eating at night. No one needs money there; when you're hungry you eat the St.-John's-bread that grows everywhere. There are yeshivas where one can devote oneself to study."

I asked how we would travel, and he said, "On foot."

"To Palestine?"

"Why not?"

"Do you know the way?"

"Yes. One goes to Istanbul."

Even though I knew I wouldn't leave my home to hike to Istanbul with this fellow, I was enchanted with the idea. I would become a second Rabbi Isaac Luria or Haim Vittal. At night, the Prophet Elijah and I would study the Torah together. My soul would ascend to heaven every night. I would visit all the mansions, the Bird's Nest, the Mansion of the Messiah, would speak to angels, and learn how to perform miracles. Like King Solomon, I would understand the speech of devils, woodcocks, and elephants. Maybe I myself might even become the Messiah! At the gates of Rome, binding my wounds, I would hear a voice call out, "Isaac, you are the Messiah!"

Then, mounting an ass, I would ride to Jerusalem.

One day a telegram came for the young man. It said, "Come at once. Your wife is dead."

Wringing her hands, Mother said, "He's to blame for her death. People like him are murderers."

When the young man learned the news, he asked, "When do I tear a rent in my clothes?"

Father gave him train fare, and he went away, saying he would return. But he never did, and I was left with a longing for distant places, mysterious saints, and caves where cabalists in white silk gaberdines ponder the secrets of the Torah.

A
Wedding

Krochmalna Street had many houses of ill repute. That is, they were *houses* only in a manner of speaking. Actually, the prostitutes occupied basements whose small windows were often lower than the entrance. The men who patronized them had to climb through dark, cave-like corridors. Outside on the square that served as the thieves' hangout, the pimps also used to congregate. Even then I already knew that there were whores and that it is forbidden to look at them, for the mere sight of them is defiling. But just *what* they did I had not yet figured out.

Often I saw them standing by the gates or on the square, their cheeks smeared with rouge, their eyes underlined with black shadows, wearing flower-printed shawls and red or blue shoes. Occasionally one would be smoking a cigarette. When I passed by, they would call after me: "Hey there, pious little ninny! Hey you, thief of a Hasid! Mooncalf!"

Once one gave me a piece of chocolate. I started to run and threw it into the gutter. I knew that whatever they had touched was impure. Yet sometimes they would come to ask my father ritual questions. Whenever one of them entered our door, Mother became embarrassed and tongue-tied. But my father knew no distinction. He averted his eyes from all females. Their "questions" inevitably concerned the observance of a *yortzeit*—the anniversary of a parent's death. This was the only religious practice they observed, but they could never calculate the proper day for lighting the memorial candle.

One day a young man who had the appearance of an artisan came to our house. He wore the traditional cap, but a modern short jacket and buttoned shoes. He wore no collar, only a paper shirt-front fastened with a tin collar-pin. He was unshaven. His cheeks were hollow, his crooked nose pale as though he had recently been ill. He had dark eyes whose mildness made me think of fast-days and funerals. Their expression was like that of mourners who came to ask questions concerning the observance of the periods of mourning.

Mother happened to be in the study and I too was sitting there over a volume of the Gemara, pretending to study.

"What good news do you bring?" asked my father.

The young man began to mumble and alternately blushed and grew pale.

"Rabbi, is one permitted to marry a prostitute?"

My mother was dumfounded. Father quietly asked

the young man some questions and threw a stern glance at me.

"Leave the room."

I went out to the kitchen and the young man remained in the study for some time. After a while Mother came into the kitchen and said, "There are all sorts of lunatics in this world."

Father's decision was that such a marriage was permissible. Indeed, it was a deed of piety to rescue a Jewish girl from a sinful life. The young man waited to hear no more. He immediately made arrangements for Father to perform the marriage. Then he rushed out, letting the door slam shut behind him.

Father came into the kitchen.

"What kind of madness is that?" my mother asked.

"He is—as they say—in love."

"With a prostitute?"

"*Nu. . . .*" And Father returned to his books.

I do not remember how much time elapsed before the wedding. The girl had to prepare herself, to go to the ritual bath. The women of the neighborhood began to busy themselves about her. The entire street knew of the affair and it was discussed at the grocer's, in the butcher shop, even in the synagogues.

The weddings in our house were usually quiet affairs, attended by a few people. Most of the time my father had to ask some people in the prayer house to make up the mandatory quorum of ten men. But this time our house took on the appearance of the "Viennese Ballroom." Every minute the door opened and another thief or pimp entered. Most of the guests were prostitutes, adorned in silk and velvet and wearing hats bedecked with ostrich feathers. That a respectable young man had

fallen in love with a whore was a victory for the underworld, especially for its women. It was an omen that
there was hope even for them, the outcasts. The madams
wore the matrons' wigs and shawls that they reserved
for the synagogue on the High Holy Days. The streetwalkers wore high-necked dresses with long sleeves. All
kissed the mezuzah as they entered, and greeted my
mother with a "Good day" or "God help." Mother stood
by, pale and distraught. Some of the respectable women
of the neighborhood had come in and surrounded her
like a bodyguard, so that none of the impurity should
touch her. But on my father's face I could discern no
change of expression. It was as though the tumult did
not in any way concern him. He stood at his lectern,
poring over a volume and writing notes on a scrap of
paper. Everyone else awaited the bride and groom.

I stepped out on the balcony and saw a crowd standing on the sidewalks and the courtyard gate. Some of
the madams and whores had also come out on the
balcony. Suddenly there was a commotion. The couple
emerged from one of the courtyards. The groom wore
a new overcoat and patent-leather shoes. The bride was
frail and dark. She looked like a quiet, respectable girl.

The women on the balcony quickly pulled out their
handkerchiefs and wiped their eyes.

"Just see how pale she is."

"Is she fasting?"

"Isn't she lovely?"

"May my good fortune shine like her face!"

"May we meet again at your wedding."

"Go on now, go on . . ."

"One must never lose hope."

In our study one of the pimps—a giant of a man with
one blind eye and a crooked scar across his forehead—

began to put things in order. A bewigged madam scolded the women, telling them to stay near the walls. One girl with a pimply face laughed and cried at the same time. This was not simply a wedding but a performance like those in Kaminsky's Theater. We usually managed without a sexton, but the pimps had brought one of their own, a tiny manikin who belonged to their crowd.

The bride entered the room and the women pounced upon her. They kissed and embraced her, danced with her, refused to let her go. A stream of blessings was poured upon her. She answered each one with the same phrase: "May God grant you the same good fortune."

This wish called for a stifled sob from each of the women. My father sat down to write out the marriage contract. This, however, presented an awkward problem. Father conferred in a whisper with the sexton. He referred to one of his rabbinic tomes. It was senseless to write that the bride was a virgin, but then neither was she a widow or a divorcee. What the solution was, and whether the bride's portion was put down as two hundred *zuzim* (the traditional portion of a virgin) or less— this I do not remember. Four men took hold of the poles of the wedding canopy. Both bride and groom were orphans, and so their escorts to the canopy were "uncles" and "aunts." All was done in accordance with the prescriptions of the law. The groom was wrapped in the traditional white linen robe. The bride's face was covered with a kerchief. My father pronounced the blessings and let the bride and groom take a sip of wine. When the bride put forth her index finger and the groom placed the ring on it, pronouncing the verse, "Behold, thou art sanctified unto me . . . ," all the women began to sob. Already then, as a youngster, I marveled at how quickly women can alternate between tears and laughter. After the ceremony there was a general exchange of kisses and good wishes. The table was laden with wines, cognac, liqueurs, and other beverages. There were giant loaves of sponge cake. The "ladies" gingerly took pieces of the cake between their thumbs and index fingers, delicately curling their little fingers, bit off small, dainty bites and sipped their drinks slowly. This was their day. Today they were not outcasts skulking in dark cellars but honored relations invited to a celebration. The men drank whiskey in tea glasses and soon began to stammer and fumble in their speech.

One of them ran over to my father and exclaimed, "Rabbi, you are a wonderful Jew!"

"It suffices that one be simply a decent Jew," my father replied.

"Rabbi, I'd give my life for you!"

"God forbid. . . . One must not say such things."

"Rabbi, I'm not worth the mud on the soles of your boots."

Father gazed longingly at his books. If only these people would leave so that he could return to his studies. But they did not hurry. They drank more and more. One of the "uncles" urged my father to take a drink.

Father refused. "I am not allowed to drink. I suffer—may no such evil befall you—from a catarrh of the stomach."

"But, Rabbi, this whiskey is only forty proof."

"I am not allowed. The doctor has forbidden it."

"Ha, what do doctors know? Fiddlesticks!"

After much urging, my father tasted a drop. The women tried to pull Mother into their circle dance, but she quickly left the room. She did not wish to associate

with the riffraff. I was given wine, whiskey, and enough
cake and cookies to stuff all my pockets.

After a while the room began to empty. I went out
on the balcony and saw how the bride and groom were
led back to the same courtyard from which they had
come.

Only when the last guest had left the room did my
mother return. It was cold outside, but she opened
every window to let in fresh air. She threw out whatever remained of the cakes and drinks. For several days
thereafter she walked about in a daze. Again and again I
heard her say:

"That I may live to see the day we get away from
this accursed street . . ."

For a long time thereafter I heard people talking
about the newlyweds. Marvelous things were told of
them. The one-time prostitute was conducting herself
like a proper young matron. Regularly every month she
went to the ritual bath. She bought kosher meat in the
butcher shop. Every Sabbath and holiday she attended
services in the women's section of the synagogue. Later
I heard that she was pregnant. Then—that she had had
a child. The women all swore that she never so much
as looked at a strange man. From time to time I saw the
husband. He had lost the glow of the wedding day.
Again he wore a paper shirt-front without a collar.

Once in a shop where I had been sent to buy something for my mother, I heard a young woman ask: "But
how can he live with her, knowing the kind of life she
led?"

"It is never too late for repentance," answered an
older woman wearing a matron's bonnet.

"But still, one cannot help feeling disgust . . ."

"He's probably in love with her," another young matron chimed in.

"What's there to love? She's as thin as a rail."

"Every man to his taste."

"May God not punish me for this kind of talk," said the shopkeeper. "Tongue, be still!" And she smote her lips with two fingers.

From that time on I looked with greater interest at the girls who stood near the gates and the street lamps. Some looked coarse, heavy, common. An insolent arrogance shone out of their made-up eyes. Others looked quiet, sad, and shriveled. There was one who spoke with a Lithuanian accent, a constant source of amusement for me. She would enter Esther's sweets shop and say: "What thmells so good here today? Give me a thmall piethe of cheesecake—I jutht have a craving for it . . ."

Sometimes I heard the servant girls in our courtyard talking about how procurers drove about by night in caleches and picked up innocent young women—orphans or girls from the villages. They were forced into a life of sin, and then they were put aboard ship and taken to Buenos Aires. There for a while they lived with unclean men, and then a dangerous worm would get into their blood and their flesh would begin to decay . . .

These tales were fascinating and horrible at the same time. Strange things were happening in the world. There were secrets, not only in heaven above but also here on earth. I was consumed by the desire to grow up quickly and to learn all the secrets of heaven and earth from which young boys were barred . . .

Had
He
Been
a
Kohen

The door opened and a bareheaded woman entered. It was rare that a woman with uncovered hair came to our house. Even those who did not wear the traditional matron's wig would put a kerchief over their head before entering our home. But this woman, apparently, was too upset to think about anything except her own shame and disgrace. She was of medium height, stout, with a ruddy complexion. Her yellowish hair was combed back in a bun on her nape and held together by hairpins. She had obviously once been an attractive, even statuesque person, but now she looked disheveled, embittered, angry. She was still in the kitchen when she began to shout: "He's a murderer! A gangster! . . . I cannot take it any more! . . . I want a divorce! A divorce! . . ."

Mother, it seemed, knew her. She lived across the street, at No. 15 Krochmalna Street. With shouts and curses she began to relate what her husband—that wretch—had done to her. He did not earn a living; he paid no attention to the children; he spent his days in the saloon at No. 17 Krochmalna Street drinking beer with his good-for-nothing cronies and women of easy virtue. But what he had done now was the last straw. This she could not forgive. She would never forget it, not even when she was laid out, with her feet toward the door and shards over her eyes.

"What did he do?"

"Rebbetzin, he gambled away the stove!"

"The stove? How can anyone gamble away a stove?"

It appeared that the stove in their house was not a built-in stove like ours but one made of iron—and this he had lost in a card game. Men had come in and carried the stove out of the house.

The woman was shouting in a shrill, fierce voice. Mother, who usually tried to reconcile quarreling couples, was herself angered by this story. She seemed almost to feel ashamed for the utter degradation of mankind. She remained silent. The woman began to recount a list of her husband's sins, one worse than the other. Mother was so preoccupied that she did not even notice me. At any other time she would have chased me from the kitchen. I already knew that people did all sorts of terrible things, but I had never before heard of such dishonorable deeds. Who would have thought so great an evildoer lived so close by?

Father sent me to summon the husband, and I ran, agog with curiosity. I had to climb to one of the upper landings, where I found the door half-open. Inside, several children were playing and screaming. On a broken-down sofa lolled a man—stout, clean-shaven, with a full blondish mustache, wearing a shirt fastened with a pin and boots with high, tight-fitting uppers such as are worn only by common people. He wore no hat and his light hair was close-cropped. He looked sleepy, drunk, and annoyed.

"What do you want?"

"Your wife sent for you to come to the rabbi."

"To the rabbi, ha?"

"Yes."

"She wants a divorce, ha?"

"Yes."

"Well, I won't stop her."

The man stood up. He told the eldest girl to watch the little ones. A few minutes later he was in my father's study. His wife greeted him with curses, shouts, clenched fists. Then he outshouted her, "Quiet! If you want a divorce, you'll get a divorce! Stop screaming!"

Father called Mother aside to confer with her. She told him that he could not divorce this couple—they had children. Father agreed. He came back and repeated what he always said in such cases: getting a divorce is no light matter—such things cannot be done helter-skelter. One has to act with deliberation. The children must be considered.

The woman became enraged. "If that is your answer, I will go to a different rabbi!"

"No rabbi will grant you a divorce on the spot."

As father said this, there was a suspicion of a smile on his lips. Actually, what he had said was not true, but a lie told for the sake of preserving family peace. There were in Warsaw some rabbis who did not bother with long-drawn-out formalities. When a couple asked for a divorce, they granted it. Particularly famous for this was a certain rabbi in a nearby street, who shall remain nameless. Who can tell? Perhaps he was driven to it by dire need. At any rate, he operated a regular divorce mill. It frequently happened that several scribes sat in his house, all writing out divorces at the same time. The other Warsaw rabbis had already discussed the possibility of issuing a ban against these divorces.

For some time longer, husband and wife continued to insult and curse each other in our house. They created such an uproar that the din could be heard in the street. She reminded him of all the wrongs, all the pain and shame she had borne since the day when her accursed fate had driven her to marry him. One minute she wept and the next she shouted with an extraordinarily strong voice; now she spoke softly, almost pleadingly, and then again she became wild. Her hands seemed to be seeking something. Had there been anything in the room that could be used to smash or hurl, she would surely have done something savage in her rage. But there were only the sacred tomes. The man was silent most of this time. But when he did open his mouth, the words he spewed forth were those of a ruffian who is both frightened and ready to wage war.

After much talk and argument, the couple left. Warsaw was a big city, and even Krochmalna Street was like a good-size town. Days or even weeks passed and we heard nothing of what had happened between those two. A quarrel between husband and wife? That happened every day, even ten times a day. There were, on Krochmalna Street, certain couples who, when they felt like quarreling, would go out into the street and wait for a crowd to collect. What pleasure is there in fighting quietly within one's own four walls?

One day our door opened and the man who had gambled away the stove entered. He looked thinner, rumpled, unkempt. His cheeks were sunken, the color of his reddish face had paled. His mustache was no longer stiffly curled as though wound on springs, but drooped like that of a poor janitor. Even his boots had lost their one-time gloss.

"Is the rabbi in?"

"Yes, in the other room."

For a while the man remained silent, and my mother was silent too. But I could sense that both wanted to speak. At last Mother said, "What came of it all?"

"Oh, Rebbetzin, things are bad . . ."

"What happened?"

"We were divorced . . ."

"Where?"

The man named the street.

Mother smote her hands together. "It is a shame and a disgrace! . . . For a few rubles some people are ready to ruin the lives of others!"

Again there was silence in the room. Then Mother asked, "What are you—a Kohen? a Levite? an Israelite?"

"I? . . . I don't know."

"Did your father ever pronounce the Priestly Blessing in the synagogue?"

"My father? The Priestly Blessing? No. But why do you ask?"

"Go in to see my husband."

My mother, the daughter of a rabbi, knew well what she was asking. A Levite or an Israelite may remarry the wife whom he has divorced, but a Kohen may not marry a divorced woman, not even his own former wife.

Yes, the man repented what he had done. He poured out all the bitterness of his heart before my father. He himself had been angry, his wife had been overcome by rage, and the other rabbi had been hungry for the few rubles he stood to earn. But now the wrath had passed. The children cried because they missed their father. The wife was at her wits' end. He himself was sick with yearning for his wife and the little ones. Indeed, he had done wrong, but he wanted to mend his ways. He had vowed never again to hold a card in his hand, nor would he touch another drop of alcohol. He loved his wife; he was a devoted father. For his children's sake he would gladly give his life. Now he wanted to remarry his faithful wife.

"You are not a Kohen, are you?" Father asked quickly.

The man said no, but Father sent me to the divorced wife. She was to bring her writ of divorcement, or her marriage contract. Father looked at these to ascertain that the man was indeed not a Kohen. Now he was relieved. Mother also looked gay. Only now, when he was sure that the rift could be healed, did Father begin to chide the man. Was he not ashamed of himself? How could one become so engrossed in vulgar pleasures? The soul emanates directly from the Throne of Glory. It is sent to this world to be purified, not to be sullied. No one lives forever. There comes a time when each man must render an account . . .

The man nodded assent to everything. The woman stood wringing her hands—not in father's study but in the kitchen, near the open door. She too had in this short time became pale, somber-looking. She showed my mother how loose her dress had become because of the weight she had lost. At night she could not sleep. There was always a lump in her throat and yet she could not cry . . .

And suddenly the woman began to wail in a terrifying voice, a voice that seemed hardly to issue from a human throat. Then I understood that this man and woman loved each other with a passionate love and were tied to each other by forces so strong that no divorce could sunder them.

Yes, the other rabbi had taken the few rubles for the divorce, but the wedding was held in our house. Bride and groom laughed and cried simultaneously while standing under the canopy. The next Sabbath husband and wife walked arm-in-arm down Krochmalna Street, their children at their side.

Dread overcomes me when I think of what would have happened had this man, God forbid, been a Kohen . . .

THE
MAGICIAN
OF
LUBLIN

1

That morning Yasha Mazur, or the Magician of Lublin as he was known everywhere but in his home town, awoke early. He always spent a day or two in bed after returning from a trip; his weariness required the indulgence of continual sleep. His wife, Esther, would bring him cookies, milk, a dish of groats. He would eat and doze off again. The parrot shrieked; Yoktan, the monkey, chattered; the canaries whistled and trilled, but Yasha, disregarding them, merely reminded Esther to water the horses. He need not have bothered with such instructions; she always remembered to draw water from the well for Kara and Shiva, their brace of gray mares, or, as Yasha had nicknamed them, Dust and Ashes.

Yasha, although a magician, was considered rich; he

owned a house and, with it, barns, silos, stables, a hay loft, a courtyard having two apple trees, even a garden where Esther grew her own vegetables. He lacked only children. Esther could not conceive. In every other way she was a good wife; she knew how to knit, sew a wedding gown, bake gingerbread and tarts, tear out the pip of a chicken, apply a cupping-glass or leeches, even bleed a patient. In her younger days she had tried all sorts of remedies for barrenness, but now it was too late —she was nearly forty.

Like every other magician, Yasha was held in small esteem by the community. He wore no beard and went to synagogue only on Rosh Hashonah and Yom Kippur; that is, if he happened to be in Lublin at the time. Esther, on the other hand, wore the customary kerchief and kept a Kosher kitchen; she observed the Sabbath and all the laws. Yasha spent his Sabbath talking and smoking cigarettes among musicians. To the earnest moralists who attempted to get him to mend his ways, he would always answer: "When were you in heaven, and what did God look like?"

It was risky to debate with him since he was no fool, knew how to read Russian and Polish, and was even well-informed on Jewish matters. A reckless man! To win a bet, he had once spent a whole night in the cemetery. He could walk a tightrope, skate on a wire, climb walls, open any lock. Abraham Leibush, the locksmith, had wagered five rubles he could make a lock that Yasha could not open. He had worked over it for months, and Yasha had picked it with a shoemaker's awl. In Lublin they said that if Yasha had chosen crime, no one's house would be safe.

His two days of lounging in bed were over, and that morning Yasha rose with the sun. He was a short man, broad-shouldered and lean-hipped; he had unruly flaxen hair and watery blue eyes, thin lips, a narrow chin and a short Slavic nose. His right eye was somewhat larger than his left, and because of this he always seemed to be blinking with insolent mockery. He was now forty but looked ten years younger. His toes were almost as long and tensile as his fingers, and with a pen in them he could sign his name with a flourish. He could also shell peas with them. He could flex his body in any direction—it was said that he had malleable bones and fluid joints. He rarely performed in Lublin but the few who had seen his act acclaimed his talents. He could walk on his hands, eat fire, swallow swords, turn somersaults like a monkey. No one could duplicate his skill. He would be imprisoned in a room at night with the lock clamped on the outside of the door, and the next morning he would be seen nonchalantly strolling through the market place, while on the outside of the door the lock remained unopened. He could manage this even with his hands and feet chained. Some maintained that he practiced black magic and owned a cap which made him invisible, capable of squeezing through cracks in the wall; others said that he was merely a master of illusion.

Now he got out of bed without pouring water over his hands as he should have done, nor did he say his morning prayers. He put on green trousers, red house slippers, and a black velvet vest decorated with silver sequins. While dressing, he capered and clowned like a schoolboy, whistled at the the canaries, addressed Yoktan, the monkey; spoke to Haman, the dog, and to Meztotze, the cat. This was only part of the menagerie he kept. In the courtyard were a peacock and peahen, a pair of turkeys, a flock of rabbits, even a snake which had to be fed a live mouse every other day.

It was a warm morning, just before Pentecost. Green shoots had already appeared in Esther's garden. Yasha opened the stable door and entered. He inhaled deeply the odor of horse-droppings and petted the mares. Then he curry-combed them and fed the other animals. Sometimes he returned from a trip to find one of his pets gone, but this time there had been no deaths.

He was in good spirits and he strolled about his property aimlessly. The grass in the courtyard was green, and a host of flowers grew there: yellow, white, speckled buds, and tufted blossoms that dispersed with every breeze. Brush and thistle reached almost to the roof of the outhouse. Butterflies fluttered this way and that, and bees buzzed from flower to flower. Every leaf and stalk had its inhabitant: a worm, a bug, a gnat, creatures barely discernible to the naked eye. As always, Yasha marveled at them. Where did they come from? How did they exist? What did they do in the night? They died in winter but, with summer, the swarms came again. How did that happen? When he was in the tavern, Yasha played the atheist but, actually, he believed in God. God's hand was evident everywhere. Each fruit blossom, pebble, and grain of sand proclaimed Him. The leaves of the apple trees were wet with dew and sparkled like little candles in the morning light. His house was near the edge of the city and he could see great fields of wheat which were green now but in six weeks would be golden-yellow, ready for the harvest. Who created all this? Yasha would ask himself. Was it the sun? If so, then perhaps the sun was God. Yasha had read in some holy book that Abraham had worshiped the sun before accepting the existence of Jehovah.

No, he was not illiterate. His father had been a learned man, and Yasha had even studied the Talmud as a boy.

After his father's death, he had been advised to continue his education, but instead had joined a traveling circus. He was half Jew, half Gentile—neither Jew nor Gentile. He had worked out his own religion. There was a Creator, but He revealed Himself to no one, gave no indications of what was permitted or forbidden. Those who spoke in His name were liars.

2

Yasha amused himself in the courtyard and Esther prepared his breakfast: a hard roll with butter and cottage cheese, scallions, radishes, a cucumber, and coffee which she had ground herself and which she brewed with milk. Esther was small and dark, had a youthful face, a straight nose, black eyes in which both joy and sorrow were reflected. There were even times when those eyes would sparkle mischievously. When she smiled her upper lip turned up playfully, revealing small teeth, and her cheeks dimpled. Since she was childless, she associated with the girls rather than with other married women. She employed two seamstresses with whom she was always joking, but it was said that when alone she wept. God had sealed her womb, as it is written in the Pentateuch, and it was rumored that she spent much of what she earned on quacks and miracle workers. Once she had cried out that she even envied those mothers whose children lay in the cemetery.

Now she served Yasha his breakfast. She sat opposite him on the bench and studied him—wryly, appraisingly, curiously. She never bothered him until he had had time to recover from his trip, but this morning she saw from his face that his period of recuperation was over. His being away so much had had its effect upon their relationship; they did not have the intimacy of long-married couples. Esther's small talk might have been exchanged with a casual acquaintance.

"Well, what's new out in the great big world?"

"It's the same old world."

"And how about your magic?"

"It's the same old magic."

"What about the girls? Have there been any changes there?"

"What girls? There aren't any."

"No, no. Of course not. I just wish I had twenty silver pieces for every girl you've had."

"What would you do with such a vast amount of money?" he asked, winking at her. Then he returned to his food, chewing as he stared off into the distance beyond her. Her suspicions never left her, but he admitted to nothing, reassuring her after each trip that he believed in only one God and one wife.

"Those who run around with women don't walk tight ropes. They find it hard enough to creep around on the ground. You know that as well as I do," he argued.

"Just how could I know it?" she asked. "When you're on the road I don't stand at the foot of your bed."

And the smile that she gave him was a mixture of affection and resentment. He could not be watched over like other husbands—he spent more time on the road than at home, met all sorts of women, wandered further than a gypsy. Yes, he was as free as the wind, but, thank God, he always returned to her and always with some gift in his hand. The eagerness with which he kissed and embraced her suggested that he had been living the life of a saint during his absence, but what could a mere woman know of the male appetite? Often Esther regretted that she had married a magician and not some tailor or cobbler who sat at home all day and was constantly in view. But her love for Yasha persisted. He was both son and husband to her. Every day that she spent with him was a holiday.

Esther continued to study him as he ate. Somehow he did things differently from the usual run of people. While he was eating, he would suddenly pause as if in deep thought, and then begin chewing again. Another of his odd habits was to dally with a piece of thread, idly tying knots in it, but so skillfully that an equal space would remain between each knot. Esther would gaze often into his eyes trying to penetrate their artifice, but his impassivity always defeated her. He concealed much, seldom spoke in earnest, always hid his vexations. Even if he were ill, he would walk around burning with fever, and Esther would be none the wiser. Frequently she questioned him about the performances which had made him famous throughout Poland, but he either dismissed her questions with a curt reply or evaded them with a joke. One moment he would be on the most intimate terms with her, and the next he would be equally remote, and she never grew tired of wondering about each move he made, each word, each gesture. Even when he was in one of his exuberant moods and babbled like a schoolboy, everything he said had meaning. Occasionally, it was only after he had left and was once more on the road, that Esther would understand what he had said.

They had been married twenty years, but he was still as playful with her as he had been on the first days after their wedding. He would tug at her kerchief, tweak her nose, call her ridiculous nicknames such as Jerambola, Pussyball, Goose Gizzard—musician's jargon, she knew. Days, he was one thing, and nights another. One moment he crowed elatedly like a rooster, squealed like a pig, whinnied like a horse, and the next was inexplicably melancholy. At home he spent most of his time in his room, occupied with his equipment: locks, chains, ropes, files, tongs, all sorts of odds and ends. Those who had witnessed his stunts spoke of the ease with which they were performed, but Esther had witnessed the days and nights spent perfecting his paraphernalia. She had seen him train a crow to speak like a man; watched him teach Yoktan, the monkey, to smoke a pipe. She dreaded his overworking or being bitten by one of the animals, or falling from the tightrope. To Esther he was all sorcery. Even at night, in bed, she would hear him clicking his tongue or snapping his toes. His eyes were those of a cat; he could see in the dark; he knew how to locate missing articles; he was even able to read her thoughts. Once she had had a quarrel with one of the seamstresses and Yasha, coming in late that night, had scarcely spoken to her before divining that she had had an argument that day. Another time she had lost her wedding ring and searched everywhere for it before she had told him of the loss. He had taken her by the hand and had led her to the water barrel where the ring lay at the bottom. She had long since come to the conclusion that she would never be able to understand all his complexities. He possessed hidden powers; he had more secrets than the blessed Rosh Hashonah pomegranate has seeds.

3

It was midday and Bella's tavern was almost deserted. Bella was dozing in a back room and the bar was tended by her small assistant, Zipporah. Fresh sawdust had been sprinkled on the floor, and roast goose, jellied calf's foot, chopped herring, egg cookies, pretzels, had been laid out on the counter. Yasha sat at a table with Schmul the Musician. Schmul was a large man with bushy black hair, black eyes, sideburns, and a thin mustache. He was dressed in the Russian manner: a satin blouse, tasseled belt, and high boots. For several years Schmul had worked for a Zhitomir nobleman, but having become involved with the wife of his patron's steward, had had to flee. Considered Lublin's most accomplished violinist, he always performed at the more exclusive weddings. This, however, was the period between Passover and Pentecost, a time of no weddings. Schmul had a mug of beer before him; he leaned against the wall, one eye screwed up, the other contemplating the beverage, as if debating whether to drink or not. On the table was a roll and on the roll a large golden-green fly, which also seemed unable to come to a decision: Should it fly off or not?

Yasha had not yet tasted his beer. He seemed entranced by the foam. One by one the bubbles in the brimming glass disintegrated until it was only three-quarters full. Yasha murmured, "Swindle, swindle, bubble, bubble." Schmul had just been bragging about one of his amorous adventures, and now at the end of one story and before the beginning of another, the men sat silently thoughtful. Yasha enjoyed listening to Schmul's stories; he could have replied in kind had he wished, but with the pleasure evoked by Schmul's story, came an inner gnawing, an ominous feeling of doubt. Let's assume he's telling the truth, Yasha thought, then who is deceiving whom? Aloud he said, "It doesn't sound like much of a triumph to me. You captured a soldier who wanted to surrender."

"Well, you've got to catch them at the right moment.

In Lublin it's not as easy as you think. You see some girl. She wants you, you want her—the problem is how can the cat climb the fence? Let's say you're at a wedding; when it's over she goes home with her husband and you don't even know where she lives. And even if you do know, what good is it? There's her mother, her mother-in-law, her sisters, and her sisters-in-law. You don't have such problems, Yasha. Once you're on the other side of the city gate, the world is yours."

"All right, come along with me."

"You'd take me?"

"I'll do more than that. I'll pay your expenses."

"Yes, and what would Yentel say? When a man has children, he's not free any more. You won't believe me, but I'd miss the kids. I leave town for a few days and I'm half crazy. Can you understand that?"

"I? I understand everything."

"Despite yourself, you get involved. It's as if you took a rope and tied yourself with it."

"What would you do if your wife carried on like the one you were telling me about?"

Schmul's face suddenly became serious. "Believe me, I'd strangle her," and he lifted the mug to his lips and drained its contents.

Well, he's no different from anyone else, Yasha thought as he sipped his beer. It's what we're all after. But how do you manage it?

For quite some time now Yasha had been involved in this very dilemma. It disturbed him day and night. Of course he had always been a soul-searcher, prone to fantasy and strange conjecture, but since the advent of Emilia, his mind was never quiet. He had evolved into a regular philosopher. Now instead of swallowing his beer, he rolled the bitterness around on his tongue, gums, and palate. In the past he had sowed every variety of wild oats, had tangled and disentangled himself on numerous occasions, but in some final sense his marriage had remained sacred to him. He had never concealed that he had a wife and he had always made it clear that he would do nothing that would jeopardize this relationship. But Emilia demanded that he sacrifice everything: his home, his religion—nor were these all that were required. Somehow or other he must raise a vast amount of money. But how could he accomplish that honestly?

No, I must end the thing, he told himself, and the sooner the better.

Schmul twirled his mustache and moistened it with saliva to get the ends nicely pointed. "How's Magda?" he asked.

Yasha woke from his reverie. "How should she be? She's just the same."

"Her mother still living?"

"Yes."

"Have you taught the girl anything?"

"Some things."

"What, for instance?"

"She can spin a barrel with her feet and do somersaults."

"Is that all?"

"That's it."

"Someone showed me a newspaper from Warsaw and there was a great to-do about you in it. What a fuss! They say you're as good as Napoleon the Third's magician. What sleight of hand, eh, Yasha? You really are a master of deception."

Schmul's words jarred him; Yasha did not like to discuss his magic, and for a moment he disputed with himself, finally deciding: I won't answer at all. But aloud he said, "I don't deceive anyone."

"No, of course not. You really swallow the sword."

"Of course I do."

"Go tell that to your grandma."

"You big simpleton, how can anyone deceive the eye? You happen to hear the word 'deception' and you keep repeating it like a parrot. Do you have any idea what the word means? Look, the sword does go down the throat and not into the vest pocket."

"The blade goes into your throat?"

"First the throat, and then the stomach."

"And you stay alive?"

"I have so far."

"Oh Yasha, please don't expect me to believe that!"

"Who gives a damn what you believe?" Yasha said, suddenly becoming weary. Schmul was nothing but a loud-mouthed fool who could not think for himself. They see with their own eyes but they don't believe, Yasha thought. As for Schmul's wife, Yentel, he knew something about her that would have driven that big blockhead insane. Well, everyone has something that he keeps to himself. Each person has his secrets. If the world had ever been informed of what went on inside of him, he, Yasha, would have long ago been committed to a madhouse.

4

The dusk descended. Beyond the city there was still some light, but among the narrow streets and high buildings it was already dark. In the shops, oil lamps and candles were lit. Bearded Jews, dressed in long cloaks and wearing wide boots, moved through the streets on their way to evening prayers. A new moon arose, the moon of the month of Sivan. There were still puddles in the streets, vestiges of the spring rains, even though the sun had been blazing down on the city all day. Here and there, sewers had flooded over with rank water; the air smelled of horse and cow dung and milk fresh from the udder. Smoke came from the chimneys; housewives were busy preparing the evening meal: groats with soup, groats with stew, groats with mushrooms. Yasha said goodbye to Schmul and started for home. The world beyond Lublin was in turmoil. Every day the Polish newspapers screamed war, revolution, crisis. Jews everywhere were being driven from their villages. Many were emigrating to America. But here in Lublin one felt only the stability of a long-established community. Some of the town's synagogues had been built as long ago as the time of Chmelnicki. Rabbis were buried in the cemetery, as well as authors of commentaries, legists, and saints, each under his tombstone or chapel. Old customs prevailed here: the women conducted business and the men studied the Torah.

Pentecost was still several days off, but the cheder boys had already decorated the windows with numerous designs and cutouts; there were also birds moulded out of dough and eggshells, and leaves and branches had been brought in from the countryside in honor of the holiday, the day on which the Torah had been given on Mount Sinai.

Yasha paused at one of the prayerhouses and glanced in. The worshipers were chanting the evening services. He heard a tranquil buzz; they were saying the Eighteen Benedictions. Pious Jews who served their Creator the year round beat their breasts, crying: "We have sinned";

"We have transgressed." Some raised their hands, others their eyes—heavenward.

A gabardined old man with a high crowned hat over two skullcaps, one behind the other, tugged at his white beard and moaned softly. Shadows danced on the walls to the flickering of the one memorial candle in the menorah. For a moment, Yasha lingered at the open door inhaling the mixture of wax, tallow, and something musty—something which he remembered from child-hood. Jews—an entire community of them—spoke to a God no one saw. Although plagues, famines, poverty, and pogroms were His gifts to them, they deemed Him merciful and compassionate, and proclaimed them-selves His chosen people. Yasha often envied their un-swerving faith.

He stood there for a moment before continuing. The streetlamps were lit but it made little difference. They scarcely illumined their own darkness. Since there were no customers in sight, it was hard to understand why the shops remained open. Kerchiefs on their shaven skulls, the shopwomen sat darning their men's socks or sewing little aprons and undershirts for their grandchildren. Yasha knew them all. Married at fourteen or fifteen, they had become grandmothers in their thirties. Old age, pre-maturely invited, had puckered their faces, stolen their teeth, and left them benign and affectionate.

Though Yasha, like his father and grandfather, had been born here, he remained a stranger—not simply be-cause he had cast off his Jewishness but because he was always a stranger, here and in Warsaw, amongst Jews as well as Gentiles. They were all settled, domesticated—while he kept moving. They had children and grandchil-dren; there were none for him. They had their God, their saints, their leaders—he had only doubt. Death meant

Paradise to them, but to him only dread. What came after life? Was there such a thing as a soul? And what happened to it after it left the body? Since early childhood he had listened to tales of dybbuks, ghosts, werewolves, and hobgoblins. He, himself, had experienced events unexplained by natural law, but what did it all mean? He became increasingly confused and withdrawn. Within him, forces raged; passions reduced him to terror.

In the darkness as he walked, Emilia's face loomed before him: narrow, olive-skinned, with black Jewish eyes, a Slavic turned-up nose, dimpled cheeks, a high forehead, the hair combed straight back, a dark fuzz shadowing the upper lip. She smiled, shy and lustful at once, and eyed him with an inquisitiveness both worldly and sisterly. He wanted to put out his hand to touch her. Was his imagination so vivid, or was this truly a vision? Her image moved backwards like a holy placard in a religious procession. He saw details of her coiffure, the lace around her neck, the earrings in her ears. He yearned to call her by name. None of his past affairs could compare with this one. Asleep and awake, he hungered for her. Now that fatigue had left him he could scarcely wait for the Pentecost to pass so that he could be with her in Warsaw again. He had not assuaged his passion through Esther, though he had tried.

Someone jostled him. It was Haskell, the water bearer, with two buckets of water on his yoke. He seemed to have sprung out of the earth. The red beard picked up glints of light from somewhere.

"Haskell, is it you?"

"Who else?"

"Isn't it late to carry water?"

"I need money for the holidays."

Yasha rummaged in his pocket, found a twenty-gro-schen piece. "Here, Haskell."

Haskell bristled. "What's this? I don't take alms."

"It's not alms, it's for your boy to buy himself a butter-cookie."

"All right, I'll take it—and thanks."

And Haskell's dirty fingers intertwined for a moment with Yasha's.

Yasha came to his house and looked into the window. The seamstresses were working on a trousseau for a bride. The thimbled fingers sewed swiftly. In the lamp-light, a seamstress' red hair seemed aflame. Esther bustled around the stove, adding pine twigs to the tri-pod on which the supper was cooking. A trough of dough in the center of the room was covered with rags and a cushion; Esther was about to bake a batch of butter-cookies from it for the Pentecost. Can I leave her? Yasha thought. During all these years she's been my only support. Were it not for her devotion, I would have long since drifted like a leaf in a windstorm. . . .

He did not go immediately into his rooms, but walked down the corridor into the courtyard to look in on the mares. The courtyard was like a patch of country in the midst of a city. The grass was dewy, the apples green and raw, but already fragrant. The sky here seemed lower, more dense with stars. As Yasha walked into the courtyard, a star somewhere in space detached itself and plummeted, trailing a fiery wake. The air smelled half-sweet, half-acrid, alive with rustlings, fer-ment, and crickets' chirping—which, every once in a while became a loud ringing. Field mice scurried about. Moles had burrowed humps in the ground, birds' nests were in the branches of trees, in the barn, and the roof-eaves. Chickens dozed in the hayloft. Each night the fowl bickered quietly over the disputed porch-space. Yasha breathed deeply. Strange, that every star was larger than the earth, and millions of miles beyond it. If one were to dig a ditch thousands of miles deep into the earth, one would come up in America. . . . He opened the stable-door. The horses loomed mysteriously, shrouded in the darkness. The pupil-filled eyes were flecked with gold or fire. Yasha recalled what his father—blessed be his memory—had told him: that animals could see the forces of evil. Kara swished her tail and pawed the earth. A gripping animal devotion exuded from the mare to her master.

5

All the temples, prayerhouses and Hasidic assembly rooms were jam-packed for the Pentecost. Even Esther put on the hat she had made for her wedding, took her gold-engraved prayer book and headed for the women's synagogue. But Yasha remained at home. Since God did not answer, why address Him? He began to read a thick Polish book on the Laws of Nature that he had bought in Warsaw. Everything was explained therein: the law of gravity, how each magnet had a north and a south pole, how likes repelled and opposites attracted. It was all here: why a ship floated, how a hydraulic press operated, how a lightning rod drew the lightning, how steam moved a locomotive. This information was as vital to Yasha professionally as it was interesting. He had been walking the tightrope for years without knowing that he had stayed up only because he managed to balance the center of his gravity directly over the rope. But after he had finished this illuminating book, many questions remained unanswered. Why did the ground pull the rock to it? What, actually, was gravity? And why did a magnet attract iron but not copper? What was electricity? And from where had it all come: the sky, the earth, the sun, the moon, the stars? The book mentioned Kant's and Laplace's theory of the solar system, but somehow it did not ring true. Emilia had presented Yasha with a volume on the Christian religion written by a professor of theology, but the story of the immaculate conception and the explanation of the trinity—the Father, the Son, and the Holy Ghost—seemed to Yasha even more unbelievable than the miracles which the Hassidim attributed to their rabbis. How can she believe this? he asked himself. No, she only pretends. They all pretend. The whole world acts out a farce because everyone is ashamed to say: I do not know.

He paced back and forth. His thoughts were always stimulated when he was alone in the house, while others were at temple. How had it come about? His father had been a pious Jew, an impecunious hardware-dealer. His mother had died when Yasha was seven and the father had not remarried; the boy had had to raise himself. He would go to cheder one day, skip the next three days. An abundance of locks and keys were to be found in his father's store and Yasha had been curious about them. He would fumble and fuss with a lock until it opened without a key. When magicians came to Lublin from Warsaw and other big cities, Yasha would follow them from street to street, observing their tricks, and later he would attempt to duplicate them. If he saw someone do a card trick, he would play around with a deck of cards until he mastered it. He watched an acrobat walk the tightrope and went home promptly to try it. After falling, he would mount again. He scampered over rooftops, swam in deep water, leaped from balconies (into straw discarded from mattresses before Passover), but somehow nothing harmed him. He cheated in his prayers and desecrated the Sabbath, but continued to believe that a guardian angel watched and protected him from danger. Despite his reputation as an unbeliever, rascal, and savage, a respectable girl, Esther, had fallen in love with him. He roamed about with a circus, a bear trainer, even with a Polish wandering troupe which performed in firehouses, but Esther waited for him patiently, forgiving all his peccadilloes. It was because of her that he had his home, his estate. The knowledge that Esther awaited him had fired him with the ambition to raise his station, to aspire to the Warsaw circus, and the summer theaters, to become famous throughout Poland. He was no street performer now, who drags about with an accordion and a monkey—he was an artist. The newspapers hailed him, called him a master, a great talent; noblemen and *grand dames* came backstage to greet him. Everyone said that had he lived in Western Europe, he would be world famous by now.

The years had passed but he could not say where. At times he felt as if he were still a boy, at other times he seemed a hundred years old. He had taught himself Polish, Russian, grammar, and arithmetic; he had read textbooks on algebra, physics, geography, chemistry, and history. His mind was crammed with facts, dates, information. He remembered everything, forgot nothing. One glance determined a person's character for him. Someone need only open his mouth and Yasha would know what was about to be said. He could read while blindfolded, was expert at mesmerism, magnetism, and hypnotism. But what was happening between Emilia—a high-born professor's widow—and himself, was something different. It was not he who had magnetized her, but the other way around. Although they were miles apart, she never left him. He felt her gaze, heard her voice, inhaled her aroma. He was tense as though walking the tightrope. As soon as he went to sleep, she would come to him—in spirit, but vibrantly alive, whispering sweet nothings, kissing, embracing, showering him with affection and, strangely enough, her daughter, Halina, would be there too.

The door opened and Esther came in, prayer-book in one hand, the train of her silken gown, with the tucks and stripes, in the other. Her feathered hat reminded Yasha of the first Saturday after the wedding, when Esther, the bride, had been led to the temple. Her eyes sparkled with joy now—the high spirits of one who has shared ceremonies with others.

"Happy holiday!"

"Happy holiday to you, Esther!"

He embraced her and she blushed like a bride. The long periods of separation had preserved in them the eagerness of newlyweds.

"What's new at the temple?"

"The men's or the women's?"

"The women's."

Esther laughed.

"Women are women. A little praying and a little gossip. You should have heard the hymn of Acdamuth. It was glorious. Compare it to your finest opera!"

She immediately began to prepare the holiday meal. No matter what Yasha chose to be, she was determined to have a good Jewish home like the others. She placed a carafe of wine, a benediction winecup, twin jars of salt and honey, a Sabbath loaf, and a pearl-handled breadknife, on the table. Yasha said a benediction over the wine. It was one thing he dared not refuse her. They were alone, and this always reminded Esther of her infecundity. Children would have made all the difference. She smiled sadly and wiped away a tear with the edge of an embroidered apron. She served the fish, the noodles with milk, the kreplach with cheese and cinnamon, the dessert of stewed prunes, butter-cake, and coffee. Yasha was always home for the holidays; it was the only time they were together. Esther looked at her husband as she ate. Who was he? Why did she love him? She knew he led a wicked life. She did not reveal all she knew; only God knew how far he had fallen. But she could hold no grudges against him. Everyone villified him and pitied her, but she preferred him above any man, no matter how exalted—even a rabbi.

After the meal, the couple retired to their bedroom. Man and wife don't usually lie together in the daytime, but when he went outside to close the shutters, she did not protest. As soon as he put his arm around her she was aroused, like an adolescent—since a woman who has not been pregnant, remains virginal forever.

2

The Pentecost was over. Yasha again prepared to go on the road. During his last night home, he said things that frightened Esther.

"How would you feel if I never returned?" he asked her. "What would you do if I died on the road?"

Esther silenced him with her hand over his mouth, and begged him never to speak like that, but he persisted. "Such things do happen, you know. Only recently I climbed the tower of a city hall; I could easily have slipped right there and then." He also mentioned his will and admonished her not to mourn him for too long a period, should he pass away. Then he showed her a hiding place where he had secreted a few hundred rubles in golden ducats. When Esther protested that he was ruining the last few hours they had before their next meeting on the Days of Awe, he countered: "Well, suppose I'd fallen in love with someone else and were going to leave you. What would you say to that?"

"What? Have you fallen in love with someone else?"

"Don't be ridiculous."

"You'd better tell me the truth."

He kissed her and vowed eternal love. These scenes between them were not new. He liked to tease her with all sorts of contingencies and vex her with puzzling questions. How long would she wait for him if he were imprisoned? Or if he went to America? Or if he contracted consumption and were confined to a sanitarium? Esther always offered the same reply: She could love no one else; without him, her life would end. But he often resorted to this kind of interrogation. He now demanded, "What would happen if I became an ascetic and, to repent, had myself bricked into a cell without a door like that saint in Lithuania? Would you remain true to me? Would you give me food through a slit in the wall?"

Esther said, "It's not necessary to seal one's self in a cell to repent."

"It all depends on what sort of passion one is trying to control," he answered.

"Then I would seal myself in with you," she said.

It all ended with fresh caresses, endearments, and protestations of undying love. When Esther later fell asleep, she suffered a terrifying nightmare and on the following day fasted until noon. She quietly uttered a prayer which she'd found in a prayer-book: "God Almighty, I am Yours and my dreams are Yours. . . ." She also dropped six groschen into the alms box of Reb Mayer, The Miracle Worker. She asked Yasha to give his holy promise never again to torment her with such idle talk, since, what could a person know of the future?—Everything was ordained in Heaven.

The holidays were over. Yasha hitched up the wagon and prepared to leave on his journey. He took along the monkey, the crow, and the parrot. Esther cried so much that her eyes swelled. One side of her head ached, a weight seemed to press against her left breast. She was not a drinker, but for the first days after his departure she always sipped cherry-brandy to uplift her spirit. The seamstresses suffered from her grief; she found fault with every stitch. Strangely enough, the girls sulked as well after Yasha left—he was that "lucky."

He went on a Saturday night. Esther accompanied him all the way to the highway with his wagon. She would have gone further, but he playfully drove her back with his whip. He did not want her walking back so far alone in the dark. He kissed her for the last time and left her standing there—tearful and with arms outstretched. For years they had parted this way but the leave-taking seemed more difficult now than ever.

He clicked his tongue and the horses broke into a trot. The night was mild, a three-quarter moon hung in the sky. Yasha's eyes misted; after a while he gave the horses free rein. The moon rode with him. In the gloriously moonlit fields, the tips of the green wheat gleamed bright and silvery. He could distinguish every scarecrow, every path, every cornflower along the road. The dew descended like flour from a heavenly sieve. There was a seething in the fields, as if unseen grains poured into an unseen mill. Even the horses occasionally turned their heads. One could almost hear the roots sucking the earth, the stalks growing, the underground streams trickling. Occasionally a shadow, as of a mythical bird, crossed the fields. At times a droning became audible, neither human nor animal, but as if a monster hovered somewhere in space. Yasha breathed deeply and fingered his pistol, which he carried as protection against highwaymen. He was on the road to Piask. There, outside of town, lived Magda's mother, the widow of a blacksmith. In Piask itself, he numbered among his acquaintances notorious thieves, as well as one Zeftel, a deserted wife, with whom he was having an affair.

Soon the smithy, a sooty structure, its crooked roof torn apart like an abandoned nest, its walls askew, its window a hole, materialized. Once, Adam Zbarski, Magda's father, had forged axes and plough-shares here. The son of a nobleman ruined by the uprising in 1831, he had sent Magda to a school in Lublin and had later perished during an epidemic. For eight years Magda had been Yasha's assistant. Since she was an acrobat, she had short hair and wore a leotard during the performances, where she turned somersaults, spun a barrel on her feet and handed Yasha his juggling paraphernalia. In the Old City of Warsaw they shared the same apartment. She was registered with the municipal authorities as his maid.

The horses must have recognized the smithy for they went faster. Now they moved through buckwheat and potato fields, past a roadside shrine where the Virgin Mary held the Christ child in her arms. In the moonlight the statue appeared strangely alive. On a hill further on, the Catholic cemetery stood, surrounded by a low fence. Yasha focused his eyes. Here lay the ones who rested eternally. In cemeteries, he always sought omens of life after death. He had heard all kinds of stories of little flames which flickered between the graves—as well as of shades and phantoms. It was said of Yasha's own grandfather that he had revealed himself to his children and even to strangers weeks and months after his death. It was even said that he once rapped on his daughter's window. But Yasha could see nothing now. The birch trees, leaning together, looked petrified. Although there was no wind, their leaves rustled as if self-stirred. The tombstones gazed at each other with the silence of beings who had had their final say.

2

The Zbarskis had been expecting Yasha; neither mother nor daughter had retired for the night. Elzbieta Zbarski, the smith's widow, was a stout woman, built like a haystack. Her white hair was pinned up in back and her face was gentle despite her size. She sat playing patience. Although she could neither read nor write, having been orphaned at an early age, her knowledge of cards indicated irrevocably an aristocratic descent. Once, she must have been beautiful since even now her features were regular: her nose well cut and slightly turned up, her mouth thin and shapely, without a tooth missing, her eyes bright. But she had a broad double-chin, underhung with a goiter which extended nearly to the breast; her bosom jutted out like a balcony; her arms were uncommonly thick and weighty; her torso like a sack stuffed with flesh of which little mounds burst out here and there. She had bad feet and had to use a cane, even around the house. The deck of playing cards was soiled and wrinkled. She mumbled to herself, "Again the ace of spades! It's a bad sign. Something is going to happen, children, something is going to happen! . . ."

"What's going to happen, Mother? Don't be so superstitious!" Magda cried out.

Magda had already packed her possessions in a chest with brass hoops—a present from Yasha. She was in her late twenties but appeared younger; audiences thought her no more than eighteen. Slight, swarthy, flat-chested, barely skin-and-bones, it was hard to believe she was Elzbieta's child. Her eyes were grayish-green, her nose snub, her lips full and pouting as if ready to be kissed, or like those of a child about to cry. Her neck was long and thin, her hair ash-colored, the high cheekbones roseola-red. Her skin was pimply; at boarding school she had been nicknamed the Frog. She had been a surly, introspective schoolgirl with a furtive air, given to preposterous antics. Even then she had already proved unusually agile. She could scurry up a tree, master the latest dance, and, after lights-out, leave the dormitory by way of the window and later return the same way. Magda still spoke of the boarding-school as a hell hole. Inept at her studies, she had been taunted by her schoolmates because her father had been a smith; even her teachers had been hostile. Several times she had tried to run away, quarreled frequently with other students, and, once, after punishment, had spat in a nun's face. When her father died, Magda left the school without a diploma. Soon afterwards, Yasha hired her as his assistant.

When Magda was younger it had been said that a man in her life would drive the rash out, since it was obviously due to virginal frustration; but she had been Yasha's mistress for years and her skin was as bad as ever. Magda made no secret of the relationship with her master. Each time that Yasha spent the night at the

Zbarski's, she slept with him in the wide bed in the alcove, and in the morning her mother even brought the
bedded couple tea with milk. Elzbieta called Yasha
"my son." In the past, Bolek, Magda's younger brother,
furious at Yasha, had sworn revenge, but eventually
even Bolek became accustomed to the situation. Yasha
supported the family, gave Bolek money for his carousing and his gambling at cards and dominoes. Each time
the drunken Bolek threatened to avenge himself upon
this damned Jew who had disgraced the name of Zbarski, Elzbieta would beat her head with her fists and
Magda would say, "You touch a hair of his head and
both of us will die! You'll come with me to the grave. I
swear it on Father's memory. . . ."

And she'd rear back and hiss and spit like a cat at a
dog.

The family had sunk low. Magda tramped about with
a magician. Bolek drove for the Piask thieves. They
sent him with their loot to those who received stolen
goods and he often slept among cut-throats. Elzbieta,
on the other hand, had become a glutton. She was so
huge she could barely get through the doorway. From
early dawn to the last "Holy Father" before retiring,
she nibbled at various delicacies: sausages with sauerkraut, cakes baked in lard, eggs fried with onions and
fat drippings, or fritters filled with meat or groats. Her
legs had become so heavy that she no longer went to
church, even on Sundays. She would lament to her
children, "We are forsaken, forsaken! Since your father,
may his soul find peace in Heaven, passed away, we're
nothing but dirt. . . . No one cares about us. . . ."

The neighbors said that Elzbieta had sacrificed
Magda because of Bolek. Elzbieta adored him blindly,
indulged his every whim, justified all his excesses, sur-

rendered to him her last groschen. Although she no longer went to church, she still prayed to Jesus, lit candles to the saints, and genuflected before the holy images, mouthing the prayers from memory. Elzbieta was possessed by one fear—that something would happen to their benefactor, Yasha; that he might, God forbid, lose interest in Magda. The family owed its existence to his generosity. She, Elzbieta, was like a broken shard with her arthritic limbs, pain-wracked spine, the varicose veins in her legs, and the lump in her breast grown hard as a pebble—a constant worry to her lest it spread as had her mother's, may she rest in Paradise. . . .

Bolek had gone to Piask in the morning and no one could say whether he would spend the night with that rabble, as Elzbieta had branded the band of thieves. He also had a sweetheart in town. Thus, Elzbieta was expecting either Yasha or Bolek that night, and the game of Patience served not only to predict the future, but to tell her which of the two would arrive first—and at what time. Each card signified something to her. And, whenever the deck was shuffled, the same king, queen, or jack would take on another expression. The printed portraits were alive to her, knowing and mysterious. When she heard her dog, Burek, bark, and the wagon wheels rasp, she crossed herself gratefully. Blessed be Jesus, he was here, her precious boy from Lublin, her benefactor. She knew that he had a wife in Lublin, and associated with that gang of rogues in Piask, but she would not permit herself to dwell upon this—to what avail? One had to take what one could get. She was an impoverished widow, her children were orphans, and—how could one fathom the ways of a man? It was still better than sending her daughter to toil in the factories where she'd cough out her lungs, or to a brothel. Each time that Yasha's wagon approached, Elzbieta felt the same sensation—the forces of evil had conspired to engulf her but she had vanquished them with her prayers and supplications to the Saviour. She clapped her hands and looked triumphantly at Magda, but her daughter, proud as ever, remained impassive, although her mother well knew that she was inwardly delighted. Yasha was both lover and father to the girl. Who else would bother with such a dried-up snip, thin as a twig, and with a bosom so flat?

Elzbieta began to sigh, pant, and scrape her chair backwards, in an effort to raise herself. Magda hesitated a little while longer, then dashed outside and ran to Yasha with open arms: "Darling! . . ."

He dismounted, kissed and embraced her. Her skin felt almost feverish. Burek had been fawning upon the visitor from the beginning. The parrot scolded from her cage, the monkey screeched, the crow cawed and spoke. Elzbieta waited for Yasha to finish with her daughter before she appeared on the threshold. She stood there—large and ungainly as a snowman, waiting patiently for him to come and kiss her hand like a gentleman. Every time he came, she would embrace him, kiss his forehead, and offer the same greeting: "A guest in the house—God in the house. . . ."

And then she would weep and dab at her eyes with her apron.

3

Elzbieta looked forward to Yasha's visits not only for her daughter's sake, but for her own as well. He always brought her something from Lublin: some delicatessen, liver, halvah, or store-bought pastry. But even more than the delicacies, she longed for someone with whom to converse. Bolek refused to listen despite her sacrifices and servitude. As soon as she began a story he would interrupt brutally, "That's right, Mama, keep lying, keep lying."

And at his impudence the words would choke in Elzbieta's throat. She would begin to cough and turn apoplectically red. Gasping, hiccuping, she had to allow this same foul brute of a Bolek to fetch water and pound her nape and back in order to subdue the lump in her throat.

Magda, on the other hand, scarcely spoke. One could address her for three hours, relating the most unusual events, and she would not even blink an eye. Only Yasha, the Jew, the magician, would draw Elzbieta out, encourage her to express herself, treat her as a mother-in-law should be treated, not as a hated mother-in-law, but as one beloved. He, the poor boy, had himself been orphaned at an early age and Elzbieta was like a mother to him. She secretly felt that Magda owed it to her that Yasha had remained with them these many years. She, Elzbieta, cooked his favorite dishes for him, offered him all sorts of practical advice, warned him to beware of enemies, even interpreted his dreams. She had presented him with a miniature elephant, an heirloom from her grandmother's estate, which he wore under his lapel whenever he walked the tightrope or performed any other of his dangerous stunts.

Although when he arrived he insisted he was not hungry, Elzbieta always had a meal ready for him. Everything had been prepared beforehand: the freshly laundered tablecloth, the kindling wood for the stove, the porcelain cup from which he drank, the blue-patterned platter from which he ate. Nothing was missing, not even the table napkin. Elzbieta was considered an excellent housekeeper. Her husband might have been a blacksmith but her grandfather, the Squire Czapinski, had owned an estate of four hundred peasants, and had hunted with the noble Radziwills.

Elzbieta had already eaten supper but Yasha's arrival rekindled her appetite. After the first warm exchanges, Yasha and Magda retired to the alcove and Elzbieta occupied herself preparing the meal. Her weariness vanished miraculously; her legs, which usually felt leaden at night, seemed to have had their numbness exorcised by an amulet. In no time she had the fire started in the stove, she cooked and fried with an astonishing agility. She sighed pleasurably. Was it any wonder Magda adored him? He even breathed new life into her, Elzbieta.

The events followed their usual pattern. He assured her that he was not hungry, but the food was already before him, its aroma permeating every corner of the room. She had prepared blintzes with cherries and cheese, sprinkled with sugar and cinnamon. A bottle of cherry-brandy stood on the table as well as the sweet liquor Yasha had brought from Warsaw during a previous visit. As soon as Yasha tasted the food, he immediately requested more. Magda, who had a shrunken stomach and also suffered from constipation, suddenly developed a healthy appetite. The dog, tail wagging, hovered at Yasha's knee. After the coffee and the lard-cookies, Elzbieta began to reminisce: of how devoted her late husband had been to her, how he had carried her around in his arms, how once the Czar's carriage had stopped before the smithy to replace a lost horseshoe and the Czar, himself, had gone into their house while waiting, and she, Elzbieta, had given him a drink of vodka. Her greatest adventure had been during the time of the uprising of 1863 when she had given refuge to condemned rebels and had warned the Polish troops of the approaching Cossacks. Eloquently, tearfully, she had saved a noblewoman from being lashed by Russian soldiers. Magda had been only a child then but Elzbieta turned to her for confirmation. "Don't you remember, Magda? You sat on the general's lap, he was wearing the trousers with the red stripes and you sat there and played with his medals. You don't remember? Ah, children . . . they have heads like cabbages. . . . Eat, darling boy, take another blintze. It won't hurt you. My grandma, may she intercede for us in heaven, used to say, 'The intestine is endless.' "

One story led to another. Elzbieta had suffered all sorts of illnesses. She had had a breast cut open and sewn up again with a needle. She lowered her blouse to show the scar. Once she'd been at the point of death—the priest had given her extreme unction and they had measured her for a coffin. She lay as if dead and saw angels, ghosts, and visions. Suddenly her dead father appeared and drove away all the phantoms, shouting, "My daughter has small children. She must not die! . . ." and in that moment she had begun to sweat drops of perspiration large as sugar beans.

The clock with the wooden weights indicated midnight already, but Elzbieta was only warming up. She still had dozens of stories waiting. Yasha listened courteously, asked the proper questions, nodded at re-

quired intervals. The miracles and omens she described
sounded oddly similar to those told by the Jews in
Lublin. Magda began yawning and blushing.

"Last time, Mama, you told the same story entirely
differently."

"What are you saying, child? How dare you? You
disgrace me before my precious boy. Yes, your mother
is a humble widow without money, without honor, but
a liar—never!"

"You forget, Mother."

"I forget nothing. My whole life stands before my
eyes like a tapestry." And she began telling a new tale
of a terrible frost. The winter had begun so early that
year that the Jews had been unable to use the booths
during the Feast of the Tabernacles. The winds had
blown away the thatch. The raging torrents had destroyed the sluice-gates in the mill, pierced the dam,
and inundated half a village. Afterwards, such deep
snowdrifts had formed that people had sunk in them as
if in swamps and their bodies were not recovered until
the following spring. Starving wolves had deserted the
forests to invade the villages and snatch babies out of
cribs. So severe had the frosts been that the oaks had
burst. Just then, Bolek swaggered in, a young man of
medium height, husky, with a red pock-marked face,
pale blue eyes, yellow hair, and a snub nose with nostrils wide as a bulldog's. He wore an embroidered
waistcoat, jodhpurs, high boots, and a hat with a feather
—the picture of a huntsman! A cigaret drooped from
the corner of his mouth. He came whistling, and
stumbled on the threshold like a drunkard. When he
spied Yasha, he laughed—then promptly grew serious,
even grim.

"Well, well—so you are here."

"Kiss each other, brothers-in-law!" Elzbieta trilled. "You are kin, after all . . . As long as Yasha is with Magda, he is like your brother, Bolek—even closer, closer."

"Stop it, Mama!"

"What am I asking, after all? Only for peace. The priest once preached that peace was like the dew that falls from heaven and satiates the fields. It was the time the Bishop from Czestochow came to us. I remember as if it were today—he wore a red skullcap."

And Elzbieta could say no more. Her tears had begun to flow again.

4

Yasha was anxious to start for Warsaw, but he was compelled to linger a day or two. After a while he retired for the night in the wide bed in the alcove. Elzbieta had stuffed fresh straw into the mattress and covered the pillow and comforter with fresh linen. Magda did not come to him immediately. She first washed and combed her hair. Her mother helped soap her down, and afterwards dressed her in a long nightgown with lace at the hem and bosom. Yasha lay quietly, amazed at his own behavior. "It's all because I'm so bored," he said to himself. He listened intently. Mother and daughter were bickering over something. Elzbieta liked to offer Magda advice before she went to bed. She also tried to make her daughter tie a lavender sachet on her person. Bolek snored, stretched out on the bench-bed. Funny, but he, Yasha, lived his whole life as if walking the tightrope, merely inches from disaster. One false move on his part, and Bolek would surely plunge a knife into his heart.

Yasha dozed off and dreamt that he was flying. He rose above the ground and soared, soared. He wondered why he had not tried it before—it was so easy, so easy. He dreamt this almost every night, and each time awoke with the sensation that a distorted kind of reality had been revealed to him. Often he wondered if it had been a dream or simply a train of thought. For years now he had been fascinated by the idea of putting on a pair of wings and flying. If a bird could do it, why not man? The wings would have to be large enough and made of a strong silk like the kind used in balloons. They should be sewn onto ribs and should be able to fold and unfold like an umbrella. And if the wings were not enough, a sort of web, like a bat's, could be attached between the legs to assist buoyancy. Man was heavier than a bird, but eagles and hawks were not exactly light either, and they could even lift a lamb and fly away with it. Whatever time Yasha could spare from thoughts of Emilia, he dedicated to this problem. He had drawers full of plans and diagrams, bales of clippings from newspapers and magazines. Of course, many of those who'd tried to fly had been killed, but it was a fact that they had flown, if only temporarily. Simply let the material be strong enough, the ribs elastic, the man agile, light, and sprightly, and the deed must be accomplished. What a sensation it would cause throughout the world if he, Yasha, flew over the roof-tops of Warsaw or better still—Rome, Paris, or London.

He apparently dozed off again, for when Magda got into bed he woke with a start although he had been lying there with his eyes open. She brought with her the odor of camomile. She was, and always had been, shy.

She came to him like a timid virgin, smiled as if apologizing. She lay down next to him—bony, icy, in a nightgown too spacious, her hair still damp from combing. He ran his hand down her emaciated ribs.

"What's the matter with you? Don't you eat?"

"Yes, I eat."

"It would be easy for you to fly. You weigh about as much as a goose."

Once they were on the road they grew quite familiar, but now after the long absence—the weeks he'd spent away from her with his wife, Esther—they had grown apart and had to reacquaint themselves. It was like a wedding night. She lay with her back to him and he had to court her silently to make her turn to him. She still felt ashamed before her mother and brother. When he made too loud a sound she placed her palm over his mouth to silence him. He embraced her and she fluttered like a pullet in his arms. She whispered to him so quietly he could barely hear her. Why had he stayed away so long? She had certainly feared he would never come again. Mother went around talking a blue streak, complaining . . . worrying about his abandoning her, Magda. Bolek was in with that pack of thieves. It was a disgrace, a disgrace. He might be thrown in jail. And he drank too much. Got drunk and went around looking for trouble. And what had Yasha been doing in Lublin all those weeks? The days had gone slowly like molasses.

It was astonishing that this shy girl could grow so passionate, as if bewitched. She showered Yasha with kisses, surrendered herself to him in all the ways he had taught her—but in silence, afraid that her brother or mother might waken. It was like a secret rite they performed before a night spirit. Although she had been taught a flawless Polish at the school, she now babbled in a rustic gibberish which he could scarcely understand; uttered words—strange, stilted, inherited from generations of peasants.

He said, "If by chance I should leave you, remember that I'll come back. Be true to me."

"Yes, beloved, until death!"

"I'll put wings on you, make you fly."

"Yes, my Lord . . . I'm flying now."

5

It was market day in Piask. Bolek had gone to Lublin right after breakfast. Yasha started out by foot to Piask, claiming that he had to make some purchases in the stores. Elzbieta tried to deter him, desiring his presence at lunchtime, but Magda stopped her with a shake of the head. She never interfered with him. He kissed her and she said, humbly, "Don't forget the way home."

The market had opened at daybreak but late-arriving peasants were still walking down the road. One led a scrawny cow ready for the slaughter, another a hog, or a goat. Women with wooden frames under their headkerchiefs—signifying married status—carried their wares in bowls, pitchers, and baskets covered with linen cloths. They laughed and called out to Yasha. They remembered his touring the villages with his act years ago. A wagon appeared and, in it, a peasant bride and groom and a band of musicians. The team was decorated with green twigs and garlands of flowers. Musicians, sawing small fiddles, chanted a long drawn-out melody. From a wagon of peasant girls jammed together like geese rose a song vowing revenge upon men:

Black am I, oh black.
I'll blacken myself some more
I'll be the blackest thing, dear lad,
That ever made you care.

White am I, oh white.
I'll whiten myself some more
When you look at me, dear boy,
You'll long, but I won't care.

Zeftel, the deserted wife, lived on a hill behind the slaughterhouses. Her husband, Leibush Lekach, had, some time ago, escaped from the Yanov prison and his present whereabouts were unknown. Some said that he had fled to America, others thought he was somewhere deep in the wilds of Russia. For many months there had been no word from him. The thieves, who had their own brotherhood—with elders and by-laws—gave Zeftel two gulden every week as they usually did when the man of the house was in prison; but it was becoming apparent that Leibush had vanished permanently. The couple had been childless. Zeftel, who was not a local girl, came from somewhere on the other side of the Vistula. Usually, the wives of imprisoned thieves conducted themselves honorably, but Zeftel was considered suspect. She wore jewelry even on weekdays, kept her head uncovered, and cooked on the Sabbath. Any day now her allowance would be cut off.

Yasha was aware of all this, but he had involved himself with the woman, nevertheless; he came to her through back-alleys and gave her three-ruble bills. He now carried a present for her from Warsaw—a coral necklace. It was madness. He had a wife, he had Magda, he was wildly infatuated with Emilia,—what was he looking for on top of this dung-heap? He had repeatedly decided to break off, but whenever he came to Piask he was again drawn to her. He now ran towards her house with the fear and anticipation of a schoolboy about to go to bed with his first woman. He approached her house not by Lublin Street but through the back way. Although it was past Pentecost, the ground here was still slimy and soggy, but Zeftel's house was clean inside, with curtains, a lamp with a paper-fringed shade, a cushion on the bed, the floor freshly scrubbed and sprinkled with sand as if on Friday night for the benediction of the candles. Zeftel was standing in the center of the room—a young-looking, curly-haired woman with eyes black as a gypsy's, a beauty patch on her left cheek and a string of glass beads around her neck. She smiled cunningly at him, revealing her white teeth, and spoke in her other-side-of-the-Vistula dialect, "I thought you surely weren't coming!"

"I come when I say I will," Yasha replied sternly.

"An unexpected guest!"

It was all humiliating to him, the kissing, the offering of the present, the waiting while she fetched the coffee with chicory, but just as the thieves had to steal money —he had to steal love. She bolted the door to avoid interruptions, and stuffed paper into the keyhole. She was as much disposed to dawdle as he was to hurry. He kept looking meaningfully at the bed, but she drew the calico curtain, indicating that it was not yet time.

"What's going on in the world?" she asked.

"I don't know myself."

"Who would know if you don't? We're stuck here but you roam about as free as a bird."

She sat down near him, her round knee against his. She arranged her skirt so that he could see the tops of her black stockings and her red garters.

"I see you so seldom," she complained, "that I forget from one time to the next."

"Have you heard anything from your husband?"

"Gone—like a stone in the sea." And she smiled—humbly, arrogantly, deceitfully.

He had to hear her out since a woman who is loquacious is passionately so. Even as she complained, the words shot out—smooth and round, like peas from a peashooter. What did the future hold for her here in Piask? Leibush would never return. The other side of the ocean might as well be the other world. She was practically a widow already. They doled out the two gulden a week to her, but for how long would this continue? Their treasury was bare. Half the brotherhood was behind bars. And what could she buy with this chicken feed? Water for groats. She was in debt to everybody. She didn't have a thing to wear. All the women were her enemies. They gossiped about her constantly and her ears were forever burning. While it was still summer she could bear it, but as soon as the rains came she would go out of her mind. And while Zeftel spoke of doom, she continued to trifle with the loop of her necklace. A dimple suddenly appeared in her right cheek.

"Oh, Yashale, take me with you."

"You know I can't."

"Why not? You have a team and wagon."

"What would Magda say? What would your neighbors say?"

"They say it anyhow. Whatever that Polack of yours can do, I can do as well. Maybe even a little better."

"Can you turn a somersault?"

"If I can't, I'll learn."

It was all idle chatter. She was too stout to become

an acrobat. Her legs were too short, her hips too broad, her bosom too protuberant.

She could never be anything but a servant—and one other thing, Yasha thought. Although he, Yasha, surely did not love her, he grew momentarily jealous. How did she behave all the weeks he was on the road? Well, this is the last time I'll come here, he thought. It's only because I'm so bored and I want to forget for a little while—he justified his conduct to himself. Like a drunkard who drowns his sorrow in alcohol, he thought. He could never understand how other people managed to live in one place and spend their entire lives with one woman without becoming melancholy. He, Yasha, was forever at the point of depression. He suddenly drew three silver rubles and with childish gravity placed them upon her leg beneath the dress—one near the knee, the other a trifle higher, the third upon her thigh. Zeftel watched him with a curious smile.

"This won't help."

"It certainly won't hurt any."

He addressed her crudely—at her own level. It was one of his attributes to adjust to any character. It was a useful factor when applied to the art of magnetism. Deliberately, Zeftel collected the coins and deposited them in a mortar on the dresser.

"Well, thanks anyhow."

"I'm in a hurry."

"What's the rush? I've missed you. For weeks I don't hear a word from you. How have you been, Yashale? We are good friends, too, after all."

"Yes, yes . . ."

"Why the wool-gathering? I know—it must be a new girl! Tell me, Yashale, tell me. I'm not the jealous type. I know what's going on. But to you women are like flowers to a bee. Always a new one. A sniff here, a lick there and 'whist!'—you buzz away. How I envy you! It would be worth surrendering my last pair of drawers to be a man!"

6

"Yes, there is a new one," Yasha said. He needed to talk to someone. With Zeftel, he felt as uninhibited as with himself. He feared neither her jealousy nor her wrath. She yielded to him as a peasant girl to a squire. Her eyes began to sparkle. She smiled the bitter smile of those who are wronged and take pleasure in this.

"Didn't I know it? Who is she?"

"A professor's widow."

"Widow, eh? Well, well."

"Well nothing."

"Are you in love with her?"

"Yes, a little."

"If a man says 'a little,' he means a whole lot. What is she—young? Pretty?"

"Not so young. She has a daughter of fourteen."

"Which one is it you love, the mother or the daughter?"

"Both."

Zeftel's throat moved, as if she had swallowed something. "You can't have both, brother."

"For the present, I'll be satisfied with the mother."

"What's a professor like—a doctor?"

"He used to teach mathematics at the university."

"What's mathematics?"

"Figuring."

She thought it over for a moment. "I knew it, I just knew it. Me, you can't fool. One look at a man and

I can tell everything. What do you want to do, marry her?"

"But I have a wife already."

"What can a wife mean to you? How did you meet her?"

"She was at the theater and someone introduced us. No, I was mind-reading and I told her that she was a widow and the rest of it."

"How did you know that?"

"That's my secret."

"Well, what else?"

"She fell in love with me. She wants to leave everything behind and go abroad with me."

"Just like that?"

"She wants to marry me."

"A Jew?"

"She wants me to convert a little. . . ."

"Just a little, eh?—Why do you have to leave the country?"

Yasha's face grew suddenly grim. "What do I have here? For twenty-five years I've been doing my act and I'm still a pauper. How much longer can I keep walking the tightrope? Ten years at the most. Everyone praises me but nobody wants to pay. In other countries they appreciate somebody like me. There a fellow who knows only a handful of tricks is rich and famous. He performs before royalty, travels about in a fancy carriage. I'd be treated differently even here, in Poland, if my name became famous in Western Europe. Do you understand what I'm saying to you? Here, they imitate everything from abroad. An opera singer can screech like an owl, but if he has sung in Italy, everyone shouts: 'Bravo!' "

"Yes, but you'd have to convert."

"What of it? You cross yourself and they sprinkle you with water. How do I know which God is the right one? No one's been up to Heaven. I don't pray anyhow."

"Once you're a Catholic, you'll pray, all right."

"Abroad, no one pays any attention to it. I'm a magician, not a priest. —You know, there is a new fad now. The lights are put out and you call up the spirits of the dead. You sit around a table with your hands on top of it and the table rises. All the newspapers are full of it."

"Real spirits?"

"Don't be ridiculous. The medium does it all. He sticks out his foot and raises the table. He clicks his big toe and that means the spirits are sending messages. The wealthiest people attend these seances, especially the women. Let's say someone's son dies and they wish to communicate with him. They give the medium money and he produces the son's ghost."

Zeftel's eyes grew big. "Really?"

"Silly."

"Maybe it's black magic?"

"They don't know any black magic."

"I was told there is a man in Lublin who can show the dead in a black mirror. They say I could see Leibush there."

"Then why don't you go? They'll show you a picture and tell you it's Leibush."

"Well, they do show you something."

"Idiotic," Yasha said, amazed that he should be discussing such matters with someone like Zeftel. "I can show you whomever you like in the mirror, even your grandmother."

"There is no God, is that it?"

"Of course there is, but no one has spoken with Him. How could God speak? If He spoke in Yiddish, the Christians wouldn't understand; if He spoke French, the English would complain. The Torah claims that He spoke in Hebrew but I wasn't there to hear it. As for spirits, they also exist, but no magician can conjure them up."

"And what of the soul? Oh, I'm afraid."

"Afraid of what?"

"At night I lie down and I can't close my eyes: All the dead parade before me. I see how they put Mama into the grave. All white she is . . . Why do we live anyhow? I miss you so much, Yashale! I don't want to be offering advice, but that gentile will drag you down to hell."

Yasha bristled. "Why should she? She loves me."

"It's no good. You can do anything you like but you must remain a Jew. What will become of your wife?"

"What would she do if I were to die? The husband dies and four weeks later the woman rushes to stand under the wedding canopy again. Zeftel, I can be frank with you. There are no secrets between us. I want to have another fling."

"What about me?"

"If I become rich, I'll not forget you either."

"No, you'll forget. The minute you step over the threshold, you'll have forgotten already. Don't think that I'm jealous. When I first knew you, I tingled. I would have washed your feet and drunk the bathwater. But when I knew you better, I told myself, 'Zeftel, it's a waste—all this trembling.' I'm not an educated woman and don't know much, but I've got a head on my shoulders. I do a lot of thinking and I get all kinds of ideas. When the wind whistles through the chimney I get very moody. You won't believe me, Yashale, but recently I even thought of suicide."

"Why that of all things?"

"Just because I was tired and there was a rope nearby. I saw a hook on the beam. This very hook by the lamp. I climbed up on the footstool and it fit to a hair. Then I began to laugh."

"Why?"

"For no reason at all. You yank the rope and it's all over . . . Yashale, take me to Warsaw."

"What about the furniture?"

"I'll sell everything. Let somebody get a bargain."

"What will you do in Warsaw?"

"Don't worry, I won't sponge off you. I'll go off like that beggar-woman in the story. I'll stop at some door and say, 'Here I stay.' One can do laundry and carry baskets anywhere."

3

Yasha had planned to be back at Elzbieta's for supper, but Zeftel would not hear of it. She prepared a favorite dish for him: wide noodles with cheese and cinnamon. As soon as Zeftel unbolted the door and drew the curtains, visitors began to arrive. The women came in to show off the bargains which they had found in the market, and the presents that their men had given them. The older amongst them wore battered slippers, shapeless dresses, soiled head-kerchiefs. They grinned at Yasha with their toothless mouths and coquettishly displayed their own ugliness. The young matrons, in honor of the guest, had dressed up and had covered themselves with trinkets. Although Zeftel supposedly kept their relationship secret, she proudly showed each braggart the string of coral that Yasha had given her. Some of the women tried it on, smirked, winked knowingly. Licentiousness was not the fashion on the hill. The wives of thieves serving in prison remained true for years until their husbands were released. But Zeftel was an outsider—lower than a gypsy. Besides, she was a deserted wife. And Yasha, the magician, had the reputation of being a libertine. The women bobbed their heads, whispered, cast sheep's-eyes at Yasha. His magical powers were well known here. The thieves often claimed that if he joined the brotherhood, his path would be strewn with gold. It was the general opinion on the hill that it was even better to be the wife of a thief than of someone like Yasha, who traveled around with a gentile girl, came home only on holidays and gave his wife nothing but shame and disgrace.

After a while, the men, too, began to drift in. Chaim-Leib, short, broad-shouldered, with a yellow beard, face, and eyes, came in to cadge a Warsaw cigaret. Yasha gave him the whole pack. Zeftel put a bottle of spirits and a platter of onion rolls before Chaim-Leib. He was one of the old guard but already worn out, useless. He had served time in every prison. His ribs had been staved in. A brother of his, Baruch Klotz, a horse-thief, had been boiled alive by peasants. Chaim-Leib thoughtfully puffed on the Warsaw cigaret, drank a tumblerful of vodka, and asked, "What's happening in Warsaw? How is the old Pawiak prison?"

Blind Mechl, a tall, heavy-set individual with the shoulders of a giant, a straight nape, a scar on the forehead, and a torn eye-socket, had brought along a paper-wrapped package. Yasha knew already what it contained: a padlock for him to open. Mechl, himself, was an expert at lock-breaking. He always carried a jimmy and before taking up burglary as a trade, he had been a

journeyman locksmith. For years Mechl had been trying to construct a lock that Yasha would not be able to
pry. He now sat shyly at the table, waiting patiently for
the conversation to come around to locks. Until now
he had failed with Yasha for no matter how intricate and
artful the lock, Yasha had always managed to spring it
within minutes, frequently employing nothing more
than a nail or a hairpin. But Mechl would not give up:
he kept betting he would construct a "peter" the like of
which the angel Gabriel couldn't "jimmy." Every time
Mechl visited Lublin he held consultations with the
locksmith, Abraham Leibush, as well as with any number of blacksmiths and mechanics. Mechl's room was set
up like a tool-shop, with hammers, files, metal saws, all
sorts of bars, hooks, drills, pliers, and soldering irons.
His wife, Black Bella, claimed Mechl's interest in tools
had grown into an obsession. Yasha greeted him with
a smile and a wink. Just as Mechl was sure that this
time Yasha would fail, so Yasha was convinced that
through some inexplicable power he would, with a twist
here and a turn there, open the mechanism as if by magic.

Eventually, they were all there: Mendele Katshke,
Yosele Deitch, Lazerel Kratzmich. Their current leader
was one Berish Visoker, a tiny fellow with shifty eyes,
a pointed, bald head, sharp nose and chin, and long
arms like an ape. Berish Visoker, like Zeftel, came from
Greater Poland. He dressed foppishly, with his colored
trousers, yellow shoes, velvet vests, and embroidered
shirts. A hat with a feather in it was always on his head.
Especially high heels on his boots added to his stature.
Berish was so skillful that he could steal a watch from
a pickpocket. He knew Russian, Polish, and German,
and was on good terms with the authorities, was, in
fact, less thief than grafter and intermediary. Years

ago he had served a prison term, not for theft but for having cheated a nobleman at a card game known as "Little Chain." Berish Visoker was as sharp at cards as Blind Mechl was at locks. But he was no match for Yasha. Yasha always showed Berish new tricks that baffled him. Even now he had several packs of cards in his pocket, both marked and unmarked. Berish was notoriously restless. He could not stay in a chair. While everyone else sat around the table, he wriggled like a caged animal, or a wolf trying to bite his own tail. He cocked his head and spoke out of the side of his mouth. "When will you become one of us, eh?" he asked Yasha in his nasal tones. "Clasp my hand and join the brotherhood."

"And rot in jail?"

"Keep your wits about you and you skim the cream right off the top."

"Well, you can't be too smart," called out Blind Mechl. "Anybody can get caught."

"All you have to know is how the wind is blowing," Berish Visoker shot back.

Yasha knew well that he must not linger. Elzbieta would be bursting with impatience for him to return. Magda, also, expected him. Bolek despised him, and only sought an excuse such as this to destroy him. But Yasha couldn't just walk out. He had known these people since childhood. They had seen his progress from a bear-trainer's assistant to a star in the Polish theater. The men clapped him on the back, the women flirted with him. They all admired him as a master. He doled our cigars, cigarets. There were also several former sweethearts of his in the crowd, who, although respectably married now and mothers, looked at him coquettishly, grinning reminiscently. Although he had at first been discreet with Zeftel, she herself had revealed their relationship. For such a trollop, a lover was something to advertise.

At first, they gossiped about current events. What was new in the world? When would war start with Turkey again? And what did those rebels want, who threw bombs, tried to assassinate the Czar, and called strikes against the railroads? What was new in Palestine? Who were these heretics who built colonies in the dried-out swamps? Yasha explained everything. He read all the Warsaw newspapers as well as the *Israelita*. He even glanced at the Hebrew gazette although he did not understand the modern expressions. Here in Piask the citizens squatted like toads on a tree-stump, but out in the world things were happening fast. Prussia had become a powerful nation. The French had annexed parts of Africa—where the black people lived. In England, ships that could cross the ocean in ten days were being built. In America, trains ran right over the rooftops and a building thirty stories high had been erected. Even Warsaw grew larger and more beautiful each year. The wooden sidewalks had been torn up, inside-plumbing installed; Jewish children were permitted to attend the gymnasia and go abroad to study at foreign universities.

The thieves listened, scratching their heads. The women, their faces flushed, traded glances. Yasha told them of the Black Hand Society in America. He related how they sent a note signed with a black hand to a millionaire: Send this many dollars or you'll get a bullet in your head. Even if the millionaire had a thousand bodyguards, if he didn't pay the ransom he was murdered.

Berish Visoker suddenly interrupted, "It can be done here, too."

"And who will get the letter, Treitel the Water-carrier?"

The thieves laughed loudly and relit their burnt-out cigarets.

2

Blind Mechl could not wait. He said, "Yasha, I want to tell you something."

Yasha winked. "I know, I know, show me the bargain."

Mechl unwrapped the paper slowly, revealing a huge lock, complete with clamps and appendages. Yasha instantly grew light-hearted. He began to examine the lock with the crossed eyes and comical mien of bewilderment and mockery which had always brought laughter from a tavern full of peasants as well as from the audience of the Warsaw summer theater, Alhambra. In one second he had become transformed. He hissed, wriggled his nose, even artfully waggled his ears. The women giggled.

"Where did you dig up this contraption?"

"Better show what you can do," Blind Mechl said, half in anger.

"God, Himself, couldn't open such a sealed chamber-pot," Yasha jested. "Once you put a peter like this together, it is finished. But if you blindfold me, I'll jimmy it open with my eyes shut. Maybe you'd like to bet on it, eh? Suppose I put up ten rubles to your one."

"Done."

"Put your money where your mouth is," Chaim-Leib shouted.

"We don't need money. I trust him."

"Children, blindfold me!" Yasha said, "but do it so I can't see a thing."

"I'll blindfold you with my apron," said Small Malka, a woman with red hair tied up in back by a kerchief. Her husband was serving time in the Yanov penitentiary. She undid the apron from her waist and, standing behind Yasha, bound his eyes. Meanwhile, she tickled him between the ears with her forefinger. Yasha remained silent.

"What have they put into the mechanism?" he wondered. Although confident as ever, he conceded the possibility of failure. A locksmith had once made a lock for him that no key or jimmy could open. Everything inside had been welded together. Malka folded the alpaca apron several times and knotted it firmly, powerfully, despite her small hands; but, as usual, between the eye and the bridge of the nose there was a space through which he could see. Yasha, nevertheless, did not need to see. He drew from his pocket a thick piece of wire with a sharp point. This was his skeleton key for all locks. He displayed it to the group before turning to the lock. Now he tapped the lock from outside like a doctor tapping his patient with a stethoscope. Still blindfolded, he located the keyhole and inserted the point of the wire. Once within, he worked the wire so that it kept penetrating deeper, reaching to the lock's entrails. For a while he probed and burrowed. He marveled at his own competence. That piece of wire revealed all the secrets, all the wiles that the Lublin experts had incorporated into the lock. Complex as it seemed, it was as childishly simple as the riddles schoolboys ask each other in cheder. If you guessed one, you guessed them all. Yasha could have opened the lock immediately, but he did not wish to shame Blind Mechl. He decided to act out a little scene.

"Say, this *is* a hard nut to crack!" he grumbled. "What sort of beehive have they braided in there? So many teeth and hooks, a regular machine!" He strained, pushed the wire. He raised his shoulders as if to signify, "I don't have the faintest idea of what's inside this thing!" The crowd grew so quiet that the only sound was Chaim-Leib snorting through his broken, polyp-filled nose. Several of the women began to whisper and giggle, a sign of tension. Now Yasha made the same remark he had made at numerous performances, "A lock is like a woman. Sooner or later it must surrender."

Laughter broke out amongst the women.

"All women aren't the same."

"It's a matter of patience."

"Don't be so sure of yourself," Blind Mechl said in anticipation.

"Stop rushing me, Mechl. You've been fussing with this thing for half a year. You've put everything into it. After all, I'm not Moses."

"It doesn't give, eh?"

"It'll give, it'll give. You only need to squeeze the bellybutton."

And at that moment, the lock sprang open. Laughter, applause, and a general din followed.

"Malka, untie me," Yasha said.

And with trembling fingers Malka untied the apron. The lock lay on the table as if impotent and disgraced. Everyone's eyes were merry, but Blind Mechl's single eye remained grimly earnest.

"You're a warlock or my name isn't Mechl!"

"Sure, I took up black magic in Babylon. I can turn you and Malka here into rabbits."

"Why pick on me? My husband needs a wife, not a rabbit."

"Why not a rabbit? You could jump into his cell through the bars."

Yasha felt ashamed, sitting amongst this unsavory band. If Emilia only knew with whom he associated! She considered him a genius, an exalted artist. They discussed religion, philosophy, the immortality of the soul. He quoted the wise sayings of the Talmud to her. They spoke of Copernicus, Galileo—and here he was with the thieves of Piask. But that's how he was. There was always another role for him to play. He was a maze of personalities—religious and heretical, good and evil, false and sincere. He could love many women at once. Here he was, ready to renounce his religion, yet—when he found a torn page from a holy book he always picked it up and put it to his lips. Everyone was like a lock, each with his own key. Only one such as he, Yasha, could unlock all souls.

"Well, here is your money!"

And Blind Mechl produced a silver ruble from a deep purse. For a moment Yasha considered refusing the ruble, but he realized that this would have been a mortal insult to Mechl, especially now that the band's treasury was so depleted. The brotherhood had a high regard for honor. He could get knifed for refusing. Yasha took the proffered ruble, weighing it in his palm.

"An easy profit."

"Every one of your fingertips should be kissed!" boomed Blind Mechl in the deep voice of a giant. It seemed as if his voice emanated from his thick belly.

"It's a gift from God," Small Malka said. Zeftel's eyes

glistened with triumph, her cheeks grew red. Her lips mutely suggested kisses and endearments. Yasha knew he was idolized by all here, both men and women. He was the shining beacon to the citizens of Piask. Chaim-Leib's face seemed yellow as the brass of the samovar Zeftel had placed upon the table.

"If you became one of us, the world would be yours."

"I still believe in the Eighth Commandment."

"Listen to him! He thinks he's a saint!" Berish Visoker sprayed his words. "Everyone steals. What did the Prussians do some time ago? Tore a hunk out of France, then demanded a billion marks besides. They held France by the windpipe. Isn't that stealing?"

"War is war," Chaim-Leib said.

"Whoever can, grabs. That's the way it's always been. The little *goniff* gets the noose, the big *goniff* the fat goose . . . How about a game of cards?"

"You want to play?" Yasha asked, teasingly.

"Did you bring some new hocus-pocus from Warsaw?" Berish Visoker asked. "Let's see you do your stuff!"

"Is this a theater?"

And Yasha took the deck of cards from Berish Visoker. He began to shuffle them very fast. The cards flew into the air, leaped like fish in a net. Suddenly Yasha did something with his hand and the cards fanned out like an accordion.

4

It was restful to be alone with Magda in the wagon again. The summer was in full bloom. The fields grew golden, fruit ripened in the orchards. Intoxicating earth aromas induced lassitude and an ethereal calm. "Oh, God Almighty, You are the magician, not I!" Yasha whispered. "To bring out plants, flowers and colors from a bit of black soil!"

But how had it all come about? How did the stalks of rye know about bearing grain? And how did the wheat know about reproducing itself? No—they didn't know. They did it instinctively. But someone must know. Yasha sat in the driver's seat with Magda and gave the horses free rein. They knew the road by now. All sorts of creatures crossed their path: a field mouse, a squirrel, even a tortoise. Unseen birds sang and trilled. In a forest clearing Yasha spied a flock of gray birds. They were lined up as if about to hold an assembly.

Magda cuddled next to him, silently. It seemed as if her peasant's eyes saw things a city dweller could not see. Yasha was preoccupied also. Towards evening, when the sun set and the wagon trundled along a forest road, he clearly perceived Emilia's face. Like the moon over the pine trees, it moved backwards. The black eyes smiled, the lips moved continuously. He put his arm around Magda and she laid her head on his shoulder, but he was not with her. He was asleep and awake at the same time. He tried to will a sort of decision, but none would come. His fancy grew vivid, and he dreamed this was not a wagon but a train to Italy, in which he rode with Emilia and Halina. He could almost hear the locomotive whistle. Outside the window, cypress trees, palms, mountains, castles, vineyards, orchards of orange and olive trees passed. Everything seemed different: the peasants, their women, the houses, the haystacks. Where have I seen such things? Yasha wondered. In paintings? In the opera? It's as if I'd already experienced all this in an earlier existence.

Customarily he made two stopovers on his trip but he decided now to ride ahead and arrive in Warsaw in the morning. Highwaymen supposedly lurked along the road, but Yasha kept a pistol in his pocket. Riding, he imagined himself performing at European theaters. Ladies in boxes fixed their lorgnettes upon him. Ambassadors, barons, and generals came backstage to pay respects. Now, with a pair of artificial wings he flew over the capitals of the world. Multitudes of people ran through the streets, pointing, shouting and, as he flew, he received messages by carrier pigeon—invitations from rulers, princes, cardinals. In his estate in the south of Italy, Emilia and Halina waited for him. He, Yasha, was no longer a magician, but a divine hypnotist who could control armies, heal the sick, flush criminals, locate buried treasures, and raise sunken ships from the ocean depths. He, Yasha, had become the emperor of the entire world. He ridiculed his fancies but could not banish them. Like locusts they fell upon him: daydreams of harem girls, slaves; tricks that were beyond nature; magic potions, charms, and incantations that unfolded all secrets and bestowed infinite powers. In his imagination he even led the Jews out of exile, gave them back the land of Israel, rebuilt the temple of Jerusalem. He suddenly began to crack his whip as if to dispel the demons which had invaded his thoughts. He needed a clear head now more than ever. He had prepared a series of new and dangerous stunts for his repertoire. One of these involved performing a somersault on the tightrope, a stunt as yet unattempted by any other performer. The important thing was to make up his mind about Emilia. Was he truly prepared to forsake Esther and go to Italy with Emilia? Could he treat Esther so cruelly after her many years of devotion and loyalty? And was he, Yasha, reconciled to converting, becoming a Christian? He had given Emilia his solemn promise, sworn an oath—but was he ready to honor it? And another thing: he could not carry out his plans with Emilia without a large sum of money, at least fifteen thousand rubles. For months now he had been toying with the possibilities of a robbery, but was he indeed capable of becoming a thief? Just recently he had told Chaim-Leib that the Eighth Commandment was holy to him. He, Yasha, had always prided himself on his honesty. And what would Emilia's reaction be if she knew what he intended? What would Esther say? Yes, and his mother and father in the other world? After all, he believed in immortality. A while back, his mother had even saved his life. He had heard her voice caution him, "Move back, Son, move back!" and minutes later a heavy chandelier fell where he had been standing. It would surely have crushed him had he not heeded his dead mother's warning.

He had put off his decision until now. But he could not delay any longer. Emilia was waiting for him to make up his mind. He also had to decide what to do about Wolsky, his impresario who handled all of his engagements. This same Wolsky had elevated him, Yasha, from poverty, had advanced his career. He, Yasha, could not repay Wolsky with evil. As strong as Yasha's love was for Emilia, just as full was it of temptations.

He had to decide this very night, choose between his religion and the cross, between Esther and Emilia, between honesty and crime (a single crime for which, with God's help, he would later make restitution). But his mind would resolve nothing. Instead of attacking the main problem, it dallied, went off on tangents, became frivolous. He could have been the father of grown children by this time, yet he remained the schoolboy who had played with his father's locks and keys and trailed the magicians through the streets of Lublin. He could not even be sure of the extent of his love for Emilia, decide whether the feeling he had was really what is known as love. Would he be able to remain true to her? Already the devil tempted him with all sorts of speculations about Halina, how she would grow up, become enamored of him, become her mother's rival for his affections.

It's true, I *am* depraved, he thought. What was it

Father called me? A scoundrel. Lately, his father had appeared in his dreams every night. Just as Yasha closed his eyes, he would see his father. The older man would moralize, warn him, counsel him.

"What are you thinking of?" Magda asked.

"Oh, nothing."

"Is it true that Zeftel the Thief is coming to Warsaw?"

Yasha stirred. "Who said that?"

"Bolek."

"Why didn't you say anything about it until now?"

"I keep quiet about a great many things."

"She is coming but what's that have to do with me? Her husband's left her and she's starving. She's looking for work as a maid or cook."

"You go to bed with her."

"No."

"You have a girl in Warsaw too."

"You're babbling."

"A widow by the name of Emilia. That's whom you're in such a hurry to see."

Yasha was dumfounded. How could she have learned about Emilia? Had he said something? Yes, he had. He always had to boast, it was his nature. He had even confessed it to Zeftel.

He hesitated a moment. "It is no concern of yours, Magda. My love for you won't change."

"She wants to go off to Italy with you."

"Never mind what she wants. I could as easily forget you as my mother."

He did not know himself if he were telling the truth or lying. Magda remained silent. Once again she laid her head on his shoulder.

2

In the middle of the night it suddenly grew warm as if a nocturnal sun had begun to shine. The moon was overcast. The sky writhed with clouds. All at once thunder and lightning began. In a flash of light the fields were illumined as far as the horizon. The stalks of wheat bowed and the rain struck like a deluge. Before Yasha could collect his thoughts the sheets of water began to flail the wagon like a hailstorm. The tarpaulin tore loose from the frame. The monkey choked off a terrified scream. In less than a minute the highway was mired. Magda clung to Yasha like a dumb creature. Yasha began to lash the horses. The village of Makov was nearby and they would be able to find shelter there.

It was a miracle that the wheels did not leave the road. The horses waded in water nearly up to their posterns. Somehow or other, the wagon rolled into Makov, but he knew of no inn or public house in town. Yasha drove into a synagogue courtyard. The rain ceased and the sky began to clear. Clouds drifted westward, their edges glowing in the rising sun like cinders after a fire. The puddles and gutters ran red as blood. Yasha left the team and wagon in the courtyard and he and Magda walked into the study-house to dry off. It was not right for him to escort a gentile into a house of worship, but it was a matter of life or death now. She had already begun to cough and sneeze.

Outside, day was breaking, but in the prayer-house it was still night. A memorial candle flickered in the *menorah* at the prayer stand. At a lectern sat an old man reciting from a thick prayer-book. Yasha observed that the old man's head was sprinkled with ash. "What is he doing?" Yasha wondered. "Have I already forgotten so much of my heritage?" Yasha nodded to the old man and he nodded back and placed his finger upon his lips to signify that he must not, at this time, speak. Magda sat down on a bench near the stove and Yasha turned to her. There was nothing with which they could wipe themselves. They would just have to wait until everything dried of its own accord. It was warm here. Magda's face glowed in the murk like a pale stain. A puddle had collected beneath her body. Stealthily, Yasha kissed her on the forehead. He looked at the reading-desk with the four pillars, the Holy Ark, the cantor's lectern, the shelves of sacred books. Standing there soaking wet, dripping water and sweat, he tried, by the light of the memorial candle, to read the tablet on the cornice of the Holy Ark supported by the gilded lions: "I am the Lord . . . Thou shalt have no other gods . . . Honor thy father and mother . . . Thou shalt not commit adultery . . . Thou shalt not kill . . . Thou shalt not steal . . . Thou shalt not covet . . ." Now it was dark and all of a sudden the prayer-house was suffused with a purple glow as if from a heavenly lamp. Suddenly, Yasha recalled what the old man was doing: he was still reciting the midnight service. Lamenting the destruction of the temple!

Soon, other Jews began to arrive, mostly older men, bent, with gray beards and feet that could barely scrape along. God in Heaven, how long was it since he, Yasha, had been in a holy temple? Everything seemed new to him: the way the Jews recited the introductory prayers, how they donned the prayer-shawls, kissed the fringed garment, wound the phylacteries, unrolled the thongs. It was all strangely foreign to him, yet familiar. Magda had gone back to the wagon as if fearful of all this intense Jewishness. He, Yasha, chose to remain a moment longer. He was part of this community. Its roots were his roots. He bore its mark upon his flesh. He understood the prayers. One old man said: "God, my soul." A second slowly told the story of how God had tested Abraham, commanded him to offer his son Isaac as a sacrifice. A third intoned: "What are we? What is our life? What is our piety? All the mighty men are as naught before Thee, the men of renown as though they have not been, for most of their works are void, and the days of their lives are vanity before Thee." He recited it all in a lamenting chant and looking all the while at him, Yasha, as if aware of what went on in his mind. Yasha breathed deeply. He smelled tallow, wax, and something else, a blend of putrefaction and spirits of hartshorn, as during the Days of Atonement, when he had been but a lad. A small man with a red beard came up to Yasha.

"You want to pray?" he asked. "I'll fetch you phylacteries and a prayer shawl."

"Thank you, but my wagon is waiting."

"The wagon won't run away."

Yasha gave the man a kopek. On his way out he kissed the *mezuzah*. In the ante-chamber he saw a barrel filled with pages torn from holy books. He rummaged through the barrel and came up with a torn book. An exalted scent arose from the tattered leaves as if, lying there in the barrel, they had continued being read by themselves.

After a while Yasha located an inn. He and Magda had to put on some dry clothes; he had to repair the wagon, grease the axles, rest the team. They had to eat breakfast and catch a few hours sleep. Since he was traveling with a gentile, Yasha spoke Polish to the innkeeper, posing as a Pole himself. He and Magda sat down at a long, bare table and a Jewess in a head-kerchief, with red eyes and a hairy, pointed chin, served them black bread, cottage cheese, and coffee with chicory. She looked at the prayer-book which Yasha had tucked into his pocket and said, "Where did you get that, Sir?"

Yasha stirred. "Oh, I picked it up near your temple. What is it? A holy book?"

"Let me have it, Sir. You wouldn't understand it anyway. To us, it is sacred."

"I want to look it over."

"How can you? It's in Hebrew."

"I have a friend, a priest. He knows Hebrew."

"The book is torn. Give it to me, Sir!"

"Lay off—," her husband growled from a distance in Yiddish.

"I don't want him walking around with a Jewish book," she replied aggressively.

"What's written here?" Yasha asked. "How to swindle Christians?"

"We swindle nobody, Sir, neither Jews nor Christians. We earn our bread honestly."

A side door opened and a boy walked in, wearing a lint-covered cap and an unbuttoned dressing-gown from under which showed a fringed garment. He had a narrow face and two wide side-locks like skeins of flax. He had apparently just gotten up as his eyes were still heavy with sleep.

"Grandma, give me milk and water," he said.

"Did you make your ablutions?"

"Yes, I did."

"Did you say your 'I thank Thee'?"

"Yes, I did."

And he wiped his nose on his sleeve.

Yasha continued eating and looked at the boy. "Can I forsake all this?" he asked himself. "This is mine after all, mine . . . Once I looked exactly like that boy." A strange urge came over him to examine as quickly as possible the writing in the torn prayer book. A wave of affection drew him to this grandmother who rose each day with the sun and cooked and baked, swept the house, and served the guests. An almsbox hung on the doorpost. Here she deposited any spare groschen she could scrape together, to help the Jews who wished to go to the Holy Land to die. The atmosphere in this house was alive with Sabbath, holidays, the anticipation of the Messiah, and of the world to come. As the old woman hustled about, she whispered through her whitish lips and nodded her head as if aware of a truth known only to those not deceived by the vanity of worldly things.

3

The arrival in Warsaw was always an event for Yasha. This was where his income came from. It was here that his impresario lived, Miechislaw Wolsky. Posters already plastered on the walls read: "On July first, the summer theater, Alhambra, presents the distinguished circus performer and hypnotist, Yasha Mazur, with a new repertoire of tricks that will astound the esteemed public." Yasha had an apartment here on Freta Street near the Avenue Dluga. Even the mares, Kara and Shiva—Dust and Ashes—revived when they approached Warsaw. It was no longer necessary to urge them on. As soon as the wagon crossed the Praga Bridge it lost itself in the congestion of houses, palaces, omnibuses, carriages, droshkies, shops, cafés. The air smelled of fresh baking, coffee, horse manure, smoke from trains and factories. In front of the castle occupied by the Russian governor-general a military band performed. It must have been some sort of holiday, since every balcony flew Russian flags. The women already wore wide-brimmed straw hats decorated with artificial fruits and flowers. Carefree young men in straw hats and light-colored suits strolled about, twirling their canes. Through the tumult the locomotives whistled and hissed; the railroad couplings clanged. Trains for Petersburg, Moscow, Vienna, Berlin, Vladivostok left from here. After the sobering period following the uprising of 1863, Poland had entered an age of industrial reform. Lodz had expanded with American haste. In Warsaw, wooden sidewalks were ripped up, interior plumbing installed, rails for horse trolleys laid, tall buildings erected, as well as entire courtyards and markets. The theaters offered a new season of drama, comedy, operas, and concerts. Prominent actors and actresses arrived from Paris, Petersburg, Rome, and even distant America. The bookstores featured newly published novels, as well as scientific works, encyclopedias, lexicons, and dictionaries. Yasha breathed deeply. The journey had been wearying but the city exhilarated him. If it's this stimulating here, how much more must it be abroad, he mused. He wanted to run immediately to Emilia but checked himself. He could not very well come sleepy, unshaven, disheveled. Also, he had first to see Miechislaw Wolsky. Yasha had sent him a telegram while still in Lublin.

Yasha had not been in Warsaw recently. He had been touring the provinces. While on the road, he always worried that his apartment would be burglarized. He kept his library there, his antiques, and his collection of billboards, newspaper clippings, and reviews. But, God be praised, the door was still securely locked by two heavy locks and everything within was in order. Layers of dust were everywhere and the air smelled musty.

Magda immediately began to tidy up. Wolsky came in a droshky—a Jewish-looking gentile with black eyes, a beaked nose, a high forehead. His artist's cravat perched crookedly on his shirtfront. Yasha received from him numerous offers to perform in Russian and Polish cities. Twirling his black mustache, Wolsky spoke with the fervor of those who depend upon the fame of others for their livelihood. He had even prepared a schedule for Yasha to follow after his summer engagement at the Alhambra had ended. But Yasha realized that Wolsky's bombast was unnecessary. Only the provinces wanted him. No offers had come from Moscow, Kiev, or Petersburg. His earnings in the provinces were negligible. Even in Warsaw, nothing had changed. The proprietor of the Alhambra had consistently refused to increase Yasha's wage. Praise enough they gave him, but the clowns from abroad were paid more. It was somewhat of a mystery—this obstinacy of the theater-owners. Wolsky's arguments and contentions were useless. Yasha was always among the last to be paid. Emilia was right. As long as he remained in Poland they would treat him like a third-rate performer.

After Wolsky had gone, Yasha lay down in the bedroom. The janitor would tend to the horses, Magda would see that the other animals were fed and watered. All three, the parrot, crow, and monkey were quartered in one room. Scrawny though Magda was, she promptly began to scrub the floor. From generations of peasants she had inherited her strength, along with her servility. Yasha dozed off, awoke, dozed off again. The house was an old one. In the unpaved courtyard below, geese cackled, ducks quacked, roosters crowed, just as in the country. Through the open window, breezes from the Vistula and the Praga forest wafted in. Downstairs, a beggar scratched out a tune on a street-organ and sang an old Warsaw melody. Yasha would have thrown him a coin if his limbs had not felt so numb. He was dreaming and thinking at once. Again to drag himself through the boggy hinterlands? Again to perform in fire-stations? No, he'd had enough of it! His thoughts whirled to the rhythm of the street-organ. He must go away, away, abandon everything. At whatever cost, he must tear himself free of this swamp. If not, someday he, Yasha, would also wander about with a street-organ.

It had just been morning and now it was dusk. Magda brought him a dish of new potatoes with sour milk and parsley. He ate in bed and again placed his head on the pillow. When he opened his eyes once more, it was nighttime. The bedroom was dark, but it could not have been too late, since he could still detect the sound of a cobbler driving tacks into a shoe. No one in the neighborhood had installed gas lamps yet. By the light of naphtha lamps, housewives mended, washed dishes, darned, sewed patches. A drunk argued with his wife while his dog barked at him.

Yasha called to Magda but she had apparently gone out. Only the crow, whom Yasha had taught to speak like a human, answered him. Every time that Yasha returned to Warsaw it was with the anticipation of favorable tidings, but the fates, which are so frequently generous to all sorts of dilettantes and amateurs, were severely sparing with him, Yasha. They never permitted him to get the best of any bargain. On the contrary, everyone took advantage of him. Yasha knew that it was all because of his attitude. He felt inferior and, sensing this, others exploited him. Having surrounded himself with a low class of people, his reward was to be treated like one of them. Emilia was the only miracle in his life, his only hope of salvation from the pit he had dug for himself.

Their introduction had been shrouded in mystery. He had not at first caught her name. He had begun to think of her, had been unable to forget her. His thoughts had rushed on of their own accord. He became inexplicably aware that she was thinking of him as much as he was of her; that she also yearned for and desired him. Through the streets of Warsaw he had roamed like a somnambulist, seeking her in coach-windows, shops, cafés, theater lobbies. On the Marshalkowska Boulevard he had looked for her, on the Nowy Swiat, on the paths of the Saxony Gardens. He stationed himself by a pillar in the Theater Square and waited. One evening, convinced of finding her, he had gone out. He walked the length of the Marshalkowska Boulevard. When he approached a shop-window, there she was, waiting, as if they had previously arranged a rendezvous—dressed in a fur collar and muff, her black eyes focused directly upon him. He moved closer and she smiled, knowingly and enigmatically. He bowed to her and she proffered her hand. And while all this was happening, she blurted, "What an odd coincidence!"

But later she admitted actually having been waiting for him there. She had had a premonition that he had heard her summon him.

4

The affluent householders had already installed telephones, but Emilia could not yet afford such a luxury. Emilia and her daughter, Halina, existed on a meager pension. All that remained from the days when the professor had been alive was the apartment and an old maid-servant, Yadwiga, who for years now had drawn no wages.

Yasha awoke early. He shaved. The apartment contained a wooden tub and Magda filled it with kettles of water. She lathered Yasha with scented soap and massaged him. And as she did she observed slyly, "When one visits a noblewoman, one must smell sweet."

"I'm not visiting any noblewoman, Magda."

"Oh, sure, sure, your Magda is a fool but she can put two and two together."

During breakfast, Yasha's mood suddenly brightened. He spoke only of testing his theory of flight, and the sooner the attempt was made the better. He would also fit her, Magda, with a set of wings. They would soar together like a goose and gander and become as world famous as Montgolfier had been over a hundred years ago. He embraced Magda, kissed her, and assured her that no matter what happened to him he would never forsake her. "Perhaps you may have to be alone for a time while I go abroad but, don't worry, I will send for you. I ask only one thing—trust me." And as he spoke, he looked into her eyes. He smoothed her hair and rubbed her temples. He had such power over her that he could put her to sleep in a minute. In the midst of a heat wave, he could tell her that she was cold and immediately she would begin to shiver. During a frost, he could convince her that she was overheated and her body would flush and perspire. He could prick her with a needle and draw no blood. He had performed innumerable experiments upon her. But he had also evolved a system of mesmerism while she was awake. He would tell her something and it would stick in her brain. He would give her commands weeks and months in advance and she would carry them out later with uncanny promptness. He had already begun to prepare her for the time when he would go away with Emilia. Magda heard him out, smiled tacitly with peasant slyness. She understood all his wiles but at the same time acquiesced, neither capable nor desirous of opposition. At times her mien and grimaces reminded him of the parrot, the monkey, or the crow.

After breakfast, he put on a light suit, kid-leather boots, a hard hat, and tied a black silk tie over his collar. Kissing Magda, he left without a word. He flagged a droshky. Emilia lived on Krolevska Street, opposite the Saxony Gardens. On the way, he ordered the coachman to stop at a florist's where he bought a bouquet of roses. At another shop he purchased a bottle of wine, a pound of sturgeon, a tin of sardines. Emilia often observed jocularly that he came as laden down with presents as Santa Claus on Christmas Eve, but it was already a tradition with him. He knew it for a fact—the mother and daughter had barely enough for necessities. And besides, Halina had weak lungs. It was because of this that her mother wanted to go to southern Italy. Halina had left the boarding-school because money for her tuition had run out. Emilia, herself, sewed and reversed all their dresses, since there was no money left for tailors and seamstresses. In the droshky, holding the packages firmly to keep them from sliding, Yasha looked out at the city which was both strange to him, yet familiar. At one time Warsaw had seemed an unattainable dream. More than anything, he had wished to see his name in print in a Warsaw newspaper or on a theatrical poster. But now he was already trying to free himself of this city which, despite its cosmopolitan pretenses, remained provincial. Only now was it beginning to expand. The droshky rolled between piles of bricks, heaps of sand, mounds of lime. The air, on this June day, smelled of lilac, paint, raw earth, and gutter slops. Gangs of laborers tore the entrails from the streets, dug into the foundations.

On Krolevska Street, the air was clearer. The trees in Saxony Gardens were shedding their last blossoms. Through the fence one could see flower beds, hothouses filled with exotic plants, and a café where young couples ate their second breakfast under the open sky. This was also the season of lotteries, the raffling of prizes for worthy causes. Nursemaids and governesses wheeled infants in baby carriages. Boys in sailor suits rolled their hoops along with small sticks. With colored shovels, tiny girls dressed like fashionable ladies burrowed in sandpiles, digging among pebbles. Others danced in circles. There was a summer theater in the park, too, but Yasha had never performed in it. He had been barred for being a Jew. He paid a higher penalty for his Jewishness than those pious individuals with their beards and sidelocks. In other parts of Europe these restrictions were no longer honored, Emilia had told him. There, an artist was judged simply by his talent.

"Well, we'll see, we'll see," he mumbled to himself. "As fate decrees, so shall it be."

No matter how bold Yasha was when walking the tightrope or mind-reading in the theater, he always lost confidence whenever he came to Emilia's. He was unsure of his appearance, whether his conduct was exemplary enough for a cosmopolite, whether he'd erred in his grammar or etiquette. Was he, perhaps, calling too early in the day? What would he do should he not find Emilia at home? Should he leave the bouquet and the presents, or the flowers only? Don't be so frightened, Yashale, he counseled himself. Nobody is going to eat you, after all . . . she's mad about you, that wench. Fever consumes her. She can hardly wait for you. He puckered his lips and whistled. If he wanted to perform at royal courts he must not be intimidated by an impoverished widow. Who could tell? Perhaps even countesses and princesses would seek his attentions? Women were women, whether in Piask or Paris. . . .

He paid off the coachman, passed through the gate, climbed the marble stairs, and rang the doorbell. Yadwiga opened it promptly—a gray little woman in a white apron and bonnet, her face wrinkled as a fig. He asked for Mrs. Chrabotzky. Was she home? Yadwiga nodded affirmatively, smiled knowingly, took the flowers, the packages, his cane and hat. She opened the door into the drawing-room. The last time he was here had been during a cold spell. Emilia had been sick, her neck enveloped. Now the room was summery. Shafts of sunlight filtered through the curtains, highlighted the rug and the parquet, danced off the vases, the picture frames, the keys of the pianoforte. The rubber-plant in the bucket had sprouted new leaves. On the divan lay a length of material which Emilia was apparently in the process of embroidering, a needle stuck in the cloth. Yasha began to pace to and fro. What a far cry this was from Leibush Lekach's Zeftel!—Still, it was really all the same.

The door opened and Emilia came in. Yasha opened his eyes wide and almost whistled. Until now he had seen her only in black. She had been in mourning for the late professor, Stephan Chrabotzky, and also for the abortive uprising of 1863 and the martyrs who had been tortured and had perished in Siberia. Emilia read Schopenhauer, was enamored of the poetry of Byron, Slowacki, and Leopardi, and idolized the Polish mystics,

Norwid and Towianski. She even let Yasha know that she was a Wolowsky on her mother's side and a great-grandchild of the famous Frankist Elisha Shur. Yes, Jewish blood flowed in her veins as it did in most Polish nobility. Now she wore a light, café-au-lait gown. She'd never seemed as beautiful as now: straight, supple, a Polish beauty with high cheekbones, a Slavic nose, but with black Jewish eyes full of wit and passion. Her hair in back was upswept and circled by a wreathlike braid. Her waist was narrow, her bosom high, she seemed a full ten years younger than her actual middle-thirties. Even the down on her upper lip favored her and contributed a sort of female boyishness. Her smile was shy, yet wanton. They had already, in the past, kissed and embraced like lovers. She often confessed that it required all of her self-control to keep herself from complete surrender. But it was her wish to marry in church, to begin their wedded life on a pure basis. He had already promised that, to please her, he would convert to Christianity.

"Thank you for the flowers," she said and extended her hand, not small, but pale and delicate. He lifted it to his lips and kissed it, holding it for a while within his own. Scents of lilac and late spring surrounded them.

"When did you come?" she asked. "I expected you yesterday."

"I was too tired."

"Halina hasn't stopped asking about you. There was something about you yesterday in the *Courier Warshawski.*"

"Yes, Wolsky showed it to me."

"A somersault on the tightrope?"

"Yes."

"God in heaven, what people won't try," she cried

with astonishment and regret. "Well, it's all a gift, I suppose. You're looking well!" She changed her tone. "Lublin seems to agree with you."

"I rest up there."

"With all the women?"

He did not answer. She said, "You haven't even kissed me yet." And she opened her arms to him.

5

They remained locked in their kiss as if it were a contest to see who would take the first breath. Suddenly she tore herself loose. She always had to make him promise to control himself. She had lived four years already without a man, but it was better to suffer than to act promiscuously. She always observed: God sees all. The souls of the dead are ever present and behold the deeds of their near ones. Emilia had her own religious convictions. The Catholic dogma was to her nothing more than a set of rules. She had read the mystic writing of Svedenborg, Jakob Boehme. With Yasha she often discussed clairvoyance, premonitions, mind-reading, and communication with the spirits of the dead. After Stephan Chrabotzky's death, she conducted seances for a time in her salon, supposedly exchanging greetings with Chrabotzky through table-tipping. Later, she realized that the medium, a woman, was a charlatan. The mysticism had through some strange fashion blended within Emilia with skepticism and a quiet sense of humor. She ridiculed Yadwiga and the Egyptian book of dream interpretations which the servant kept under her pillow —yet she, Emilia, believed in dreams herself. After Chrabotzky's death, several of his colleagues proposed marriage to her, but her dead husband had appeared before her in a dream and urged her to reject them. Once he even materialized before her as she was walking up the stairs at dusk. She revealed to Yasha that she loved him because his character was so like Chrabotzky's and that she had indications that Chrabotzky approved the match. She now took Yasha by both his wrists, guided him to a chair and sat him down as one would a mischievous child.

"Sit. Wait," she said.

"How long must I wait?"

"It all depends on you."

She sat down facing him, in a chaise longue. Her tearing herself away from him had been for her a physical effort. She sat, momentarily flushed as if surprised at her own lust.

They began to converse in the severed phrases of intimates who have been parted and try to bind up the broken threads. Halina had been ill two weeks ago. She, Emilia, had also had the grippe. "I wrote you that, didn't I? Well, I've forgotten . . . Yes, everything is fine now . . . Halina? Gone to the park to read. Very absorbed in books now—but such trash! God, how bad literature has become! Common, cheap . . . Wasn't this May a cold one? Snow, even . . . The theater? No, we went nowhere. Aside from the fact that tickets are exorbitant, the quality of the plays is so absurd . . . Everything translated from the French, and poorly translated at that. The eternal triangle . . . But wouldn't you rather talk about yourself? Where did you wander all these weeks? When you leave everything seems unreal. It all seems like a dream to me. But when a letter comes, the world is all right again. Well, and all of a sudden Halina comes running in all excited—you've been mentioned in the *Courier* . . . What? Some sort of a write-up. Halina is convinced that anyone whose name is mentioned in the newspapers is a demi-god, even if it is because the person has been struck by an omnibus . . . And how are you? You're looking well. You don't appear to have missed us. What do I really know about you? You always were and you still are, an enigma. The more you talk about yourself, the less I can figure you out. You have women all over Poland. You drag yourself around in a covered wagon like a gypsy. It's really amusing. A person with your talent and so unadvanced. Often I think that your entire conduct is a joke on yourself and the world. . . . What's that? About us I certainly couldn't tell you a thing. All our plans are suspended in the air. I'm afraid that everything will drag on like this until we're both old and gray. . . ."

"I've come to you now and we won't be separated again!" he said, amazed at his own words. Until just now he had not yet made a decision.

"What's that?—Well, that's what I've been waiting for. This is what I've wanted to hear!"

And her eyes grew moist. She turned her face aside and he saw her in profile. Presently she rose to tell Yadwiga to serve the coffee. The woman had already brewed it, unbidden. She had ground it herself in a coffee-grinder according to old Polish tradition. The aroma permeated the drawing-room. Yasha was left alone. Well, everything is fate, he mumbled to himself. He was seized by a tremor. With those few words to Emilia, he had just about sealed his destiny. But what would become of Esther now? And Magda? And where would he get the money he needed? And was he truly capable of changing his religion? I cannot live without her! he replied to himself. He was filled suddenly with the impatience of a convict awaiting his release, every hour an eternity. He stood up. Though his heart was heavy, his feet felt uncommonly light. Right now I could turn not one but three somersaults on the tightrope! How could I have put it off this long? Yasha skipped to the window, turned aside the draperies, gazed out at the luxuriant chestnut trees in the Saxony Gardens, at all the schoolboys, young fops, governesses, and couples who strolled along its paths. For example, that young fellow with the flaxen hair and his girl in the straw hat with the cherries! They strutted like two birds, stopped, took another step, moved about in one spot, looked at each other, sniffed one another, played at the games only lovers know. They seemed to be precipitating a tussle or a kind of dance of the sexes. But what was it he saw in her? And how blue the sky was today! Pale blue like the curtain which hung in the temple during the Days of Awe.

Yasha felt a pang of doubt at the comparison. Well, God was God, whether you prayed to Him in the synagogue or in church. Emilia came back. He walked towards her.

"When she brews coffee she smells up the whole house. It's the same when she cooks."

"What will become of *her?*" he asked. "Will we take her along with us to Italy?"

Emilia pondered a moment.

"Are we at that stage already?"

"My mind is made up."

"Well, we'll require a servant too. But it's all idle chatter."

"No, Emilia, it's just as if you were my wife already."

6

The doorbell rang. Emilia excused herself and left Yasha alone once again. He remained still, as if he were in hiding and afraid to reveal his presence to someone who sought him. He had already compromised Emilia, but she still concealed him from her relatives. He had become like one who sees but is himself invisible. He sat there and stared at the furniture, at the rugs. The pendulum in the grandfather clock swung slowly. Golden flecks of sunlight glanced off the prisms of the chandelier, off the album bound in red velvet. From a neighbor's house, piano chords drifted. He had always admired the cleanliness of this apartment, the affluent tidiness. Everything was placed where it belonged. There wasn't a hint of dust anywhere. Those who lived here never seemed to accumulate dirt or anything else superfluous, no disagreeable odors, no disconcerting thoughts.

Yasha listened intently. Emilia had several distant relatives living in town. They frequently dropped in uninvited. Yasha sometimes had had to leave through the kitchen entrance. While he listened, he tried to evaluate his situation. To realize his plans he would need money, at least fifteen thousand rubles. He could only obtain that much money one way. But again, was he prepared for such a step? Being intimate with many women had transformed him into one who lived for the moment, guided himself only by impulse and inspiration. He made plans but everything remained fluid. He spoke of love, but he could not truthfully account to himself what he meant by it, nor what Emilia understood it to be. And during all his transgressions he had always sensed the hand of Providence. Hidden forces propelled him always, even during his performances. But could he expect God to lead him into theft and apostasy? Listening to the notes of the piano, he heard his own thoughts simultaneously. Before every action, a voice within him usually made itself audible, spoke clearly, commanded sternly, proposed all the details. But this time he experienced a sense of anticipation. Something else was scheduled to occur, something was still to be altered. In his notebook he had a list of banks and addresses of wealthy people who kept their money in metal strongboxes, but he had not followed up these possibilities. He had already managed to justify the deed he contemplated, for he had sworn a promise to return everything with interest, once he had won fame abroad, but he had not yet been able to appease his conscience. Fear, disgust, and self-contempt remained. He was descended from people of honor. His grandfathers, on both sides, were famous for their honesty. A great-grandfather once trailed a merchant to Lenczno to pay back a forgotten ten groschen . . .

The door opened and Halina appeared in the doorway: fair, suddenly tall for her fourteen years, with blonde pigtails, light blue eyes, a straight nose, full lips and the transparent paleness of skin peculiar to those afflicted with anemia and weak lungs. She had grown during the short time he had been away, and she seemed ashamed of it. She looked at Yasha, pleased and confused at once. Halina took after her father—she had the mind of a scientist. She yearned to understand everything: each trick that he, Yasha, performed, every word that he spoke to her mother while she, Halina, was present. She was an avid reader, collected insects, could play chess, write poetry. She was studying Italian already . . . For a moment she seemed to hesitate. Then she charged at Yasha with a childish leap and fell into his arms.

"Uncle Yasha!"

She kissed him and let herself be kissed in return.

She promptly besieged him with questions. When had he come? Had he traveled by wagon this time too? Had he seen any wild beasts in the forest? Had he been stopped by highwaymen? How was the monkey? The crow? The parrot? How were the peacocks in his yard at Lublin? And the snake? The turtle? Would he actually perform a somersault on the wire as announced in the newspapers? Was this possible? Had he missed them— her and Mama? She seemed almost full grown, yet she chattered on like a child. But there was a sense of artificiality as well as playfulness.

"You've shot up like a tree!" Yasha said.

"Everyone refers to my height!" she pouted with childish reproof. "Just as if it were my fault. I lie in bed and I feel myself growing. An imp tugs at my feet. I don't want to grow at all. I should like to remain little always. What shall I do, Uncle Yasha? Is there an exercise to make one remain small? Tell me, Uncle Yasha!" and she kissed his forehead.

So much love! So much love! Yasha mused. Aloud he said, "Yes, there is a way."

"How?"

"We'll put you in the grandfather clock and lock the door. You won't be able to grow taller than the cabinet."

Halina perked up immediately.

"He has a solution for everything! How quickly his mind works! He doesn't have to think at all! How does your brain work, Uncle Yasha?"

"Why don't you take off the lid and look inside? It's just like the mechanism of a clock."

"More clocks? That's all you have on your mind to-day—clocks. Are you working on a new trick with a clock? Have you read the *Courier?* You're famous! All Warsaw admires you. Why did you stay away so long, Uncle Yasha? I was ill and I called for you every minute. I dreamed about you, too. Mama scolded me because I talked so much about you. She is terribly jealous!" Halina said, blushing at her own words. Just then, Emilia walked in.

"So, your Uncle Yasha is here again. I can't tell you how often she asked about you."

"Don't tell him, Mama, don't tell him. He will become spoiled. He thinks that because he is a great artist and we are insignificant little people he can lord it over us. God is mightier than you, Uncle Yasha. He can perform even finer tricks."

Emilia quickly grew stern. "Do not take the Lord's name in vain. It is no subject for levity."

"I'm not joking, Mother."

"That's the latest fashion: to bring God into every senseless conversation."

Halina seemed lost in thought for a moment.

"Mama, I'm simply starved."

"Oh?"

"Yes, if I don't eat something in the next ten minutes, I'll just die."

"Oh, how you carry on. Like a child of six. Tell Yadwiga to give you something to eat."

"And you, Mama, aren't you hungry?"

"No, I manage to survive from one meal to the next."

"But you hardly eat, Mama. A glass of cocoa means breakfast to you. How about you, Uncle Yasha?"

"I could eat an elephant."

"Come on, then, let's eat him together."

7

Yasha sat down with mother and daughter and they all ate their second breakfast, all the delicacies that Yasha had brought: the sturgeon, the sardines, the swiss cheese. Yadwiga brought coffee with cream. Halina ate with gusto, praising and enjoying every mouthful. "How good this smells! It melts in your mouth!" The crusts of the freshly baked rolls crackled between her teeth. Emilia chewed in a slow ladylike way. Yasha himself ate with enjoyment. He looked forward to these snacks with Emilia and Halina. With Esther, he had little to talk about. She knew nothing beside her housewifely chores and her sewing business. Here, the conversation came easily. It turned to hypnotism. Emilia had often warned Yasha not to discuss this subject before Halina, but he could not very well avoid it. He was advertised in the newspapers as a hypnotist, and Halina was too clever and curious to be dissuaded with a word. Besides, she read adult books. Professor Chrabotzky had left an extensive library. His colleagues from the university and former pupils sent Emilia textbooks and tear-sheets from scientific journals. Halina examined everything. She was familiar with Mesmer, his theories and his trials, had read about Charcot and Janet. The Polish newspapers printed articles about the hypnotist, Feldman, who had caused a sensation in various Polish salons. He had even been permitted to demonstrate his powers in hospitals and private clinics. For the millionth time Halina asked Yasha the same question: How could one person inject his will into another? How was it possible for one person to put another to sleep by looking at him? How could someone be made to shiver with cold in the hottest weather, or in an overheated room?"

"I don't know the answer myself," Yasha said. "That's the honest truth."

"But you've done these things yourself."

"Does the spider know how it spins its web?"

"Oh—now he compares himself to a spider! I hate spiders, I despise them! You, Uncle Yasha, I adore."

"You talk too much, Halina," Emilia interrupted.

"I want to know the truth."

"Her father's daughter. She only wants the truth."

"For what other reason are we born, Mama? Why are all the books written? All for truth. Mama, I have a big favor to ask you."

"I know what it is beforehand—and the answer is *no!*"

"Mommy, I beg you on bended knees! Have pity."

"No pity. No!"

What Halina wanted was her mother's permission to have Yasha demonstrate his hypnotism right then and there. Halina was even eager to be hypnotized herself. But Emilia repeatedly denied her daughter's request. One did not trifle with such things. Emilia had read somewhere of a hypnotist who had been unable to arouse his subject. The victim had remained in a trance for days afterwards.

"Come to the theater, Halina, and then you'll see how it's done," Yasha said.

"To tell the truth, I hesitate to take her—such riff-raff go there."

"What must I do, Mother? Sit in the kitchen and pluck chickens?"

"You're still a child."

"Let him hypnotize you, then."

"I don't want any seances in my house!" Emilia said, sharply.

Yasha was silent. They are hypnotized anyway, he thought. Love is based entirely on hypnotism. When I saw her for the first time, I hypnotized her. That is why she was waiting for me that night on Marshalkowska Boulevard. They are all hypnotized: Esther, Magda, Zeftel. I possess a power, a tremendous power. But what is it? And how far does it extend? Would I be able to hypnotize a bank director into opening the vault for me?

He, Yasha, had first heard the word, hypnotism, only a few years before. He had attempted it and had succeeded immediately. He had ordered his subject to sleep and the man had fallen into a heavy slumber. He had ordered a woman to undress and she had begun to take off her clothes. He had told a girl that she would feel no pain and though he had pricked her arm with a pin, she had not cried out, nor had there been any blood. Since then Yasha had witnessed a number of demonstrations by other hypnotists, several indeed by the famous Feldman, but what this power was or how it worked, Yasha could not understand. At times it seemed to him that both hypnotist and subject were indulging in some sort of high-jinks; but nevertheless it was no sham. Perspiration cannot be simulated in cold weather nor a flow of blood prevented when a needle is jabbed into the flesh. Perhaps this was what was once labeled black magic.

"Oh, Mommy, you're so stubborn!" Halina said, munching a sardine on a roll. "Tell me what sort of power this is, Uncle Yasha, before I die of curiosity!"

"It's a force. What is electricity?"

"Yes, what *is* electricity?"

"No one knows. They flash signals here in Warsaw and the electricity carries them in one second to Petersburg or Moscow. The signals go over fields, forests, go hundreds of miles, all in one second. Now there is such a thing as a telephone! and one can hear another's voice through the wires. The time will come when you'll be able to talk from Warsaw to Paris just the way I'm talking to you now."

"But how does it work? Ah, Mama, there is so much to learn! Some people are so wise! How did they become so wise? But it's always men. Why don't women educate themselves?"

"In England there is a woman physician," Yasha said.

"Really? That's funny. I can't help laughing!"

"What's so amusing?" Emilia asked. "Women are people, too."

"Of course. But a woman doctor! How does she dress? Like George Sand?"

"What do you know about George Sand? I'll lock you out of the library!"

"Don't do it, Mommy. I love you, I love you terribly and you're so strict with me. What do I have besides my books? The girls I know are all bores. Uncle Yasha seldom comes to see us. He plays hide-and-seek with us. I can lose myself in books. Why don't the two of you get married?" Halina blurted out suddenly, amazed at her own words. She paled. Emilia blushed to the roots of her hair.

"Are you mad, or what?"

"She is right. We will be married soon," Yasha interrupted. "Everything's been decided. All three of us are going to Italy."

Halina hung her head, shamefaced. She began to toy

with the tip of her braid as if to count the hairs. Emilia lowered her eyes. She sat there helpless, ashamed, gratified by Yasha's words. The girl chattered ceaselessly, but this time her foolish prattle had been helpful. He had just then made it official. Emilia lifted her eyes.

"Halina, go to your room!"

5

Usually, Yasha began to rehearse two weeks before the opening. Just this year when he had prepared a new and difficult repertoire, he kept delaying the rehearsals from day to day. The proprietor of the Alhambra had refused to raise Yasha's salary. Wolsky, the impresario, was quietly negotiating with another summer theater, the Palace. Often during the day, when Yasha sat in the Café Lurs, sipping black coffee and leafing through a magazine, he was seized by an odd premonition—a feeling that he would not perform that season. He feared this portent and tried to banish it from his mind, mollify it, erase it—but it kept returning. Would he grow sick? Was he, God forbid, due to die? Or was it something else altogether? He placed his hands on his forehead, rubbed his scalp, his cheekbones, enveloped himself in a blind darkness. He had wound himself into too many entanglements. He had driven himself into a dilemma. He loved and desired Emilia. He even longed for Halina. But how could he inflict such an outrage against Esther? For so many years she had shown him a rare devotion. She had stood beside him through all his difficulties, helped him in every crisis; her tolerance was the kind that the pious attribute only to God. How could he repay her with a slap? She would not live through the shock, Yasha knew—she would wither and flicker out like a candle. More than once he had seen a person die of heartbreak simply because they no longer had any reason to stay alive. Some of these people had not even been sick when they died. Swiftly and without explanations the Angel of Death performs his magic.

For some time now he had been trying to prepare Magda for his departure. But she was jittery already. Each time he returned from Emilia, Magda looked at him with mute reproach. She had almost ceased speaking to him altogether and had withdrawn like a clam into her shell. In bed, she was frigid, distant, silent. Summers past, the pimples on her face would fade, but this year her complexion was a mass of them. The rash had even spread to her neck and the upper part of her breasts. She had also begun to have accidents. Plates slipped from her hands. Pots turned over on the hot stove. She had burned her foot, pricked her finger, nearly lost an eye. In this state, how could she be expected to perform somersaults, hand him his clubs and balls to juggle, or spin the barrel on her feet? Even if he, Yasha, managed to go on this season, he would probably have to engage a new assistant at the last minute. Yes, and what of poor Elzbieta? The news of his deserting Magda might kill her.

There was a partial solution to the miserable situation: money. If he could give Esther ten thousand rubles it would temper the blow somewhat. A cash settlement would certainly appease Magda and Elzbieta. In addition, he needed a large sum for himself, Emilia, and Halina. Her plan was to purchase a villa in southern Italy where the climate would benefit Halina's lungs. He, Yasha, would not be able to begin performing right away. He would first have to learn the language, engage an impresario, make contacts. He could not afford to sell his services as cheaply there as he did here in Poland. He would have to begin right at the top. But for all this he needed a backlog of at least thirty thousand lire. Emilia had confessed to him what, actually, he had already known. She owned nothing save a pile of debts which she would have to make good before she could leave town.

Ordinarily Yasha did not smoke. He had weaned himself away from a pipe in the belief that it was bad for the heart and eyes and that it interfered with his sleeping. But now he began to smoke Russian cigarets. He sucked on the tip of a cigaret, sipped black coffee from a saucer, and scanned a magazine. The smoke stung his nostrils, the coffee his palate; the magazine article made no sense. It raved about some Parisian actress, one Fifi, at whose feet all France worshiped. The writer implied that Fifi was a former demimondaine. "Why would all France glorify a tart?" Yasha wondered. "Was this France? Was this the Western Europe of which Emilia spoke with such awe? Was this the culture, the art, the aestheticism that the journals wrote about with such fervor? He threw aside the magazine, which was immediately claimed by a white-mustached gentleman. Yasha extinguished his cigaret in the coffee dregs.

All his reflections and speculations inevitably led to the one conclusion: he must get his hands on a large sum of money, if not legally, then by theft. But when should he perform this crime? Where? How? Strange that although he had been contemplating this deed for months now, he had never even entered a bank, nor familiarized himself with banking procedure; he had not even determined where the banks stored their money during closing hours, nor the type of safes or locks they employed. He had procrastinated, procrastinated. Whenever he passed a bank, he stepped quickly, averting his face. It was one thing to open a lock on the stage or before the Piask gang, another to steal into a building manned by armed guards. For that, one had to be a born thief.

Yasha tapped his spoon against the saucer to summon the waiter but the man either did not hear, or pretended not to. The café was quite full. There were almost no patrons who, like himself, were alone. Most sat in groups, circles, clusters; the men in morning coats, striped trousers, wide cravats. Some wore pointed beards, some spade beards; some had drooping mustaches, some mustaches that curled. The women wore wide-skirted dresses, and wide-brimmed hats decorated with flowers, fruits, pins, and feathers. The patriots whom the Russians had exiled to Siberia in boxcars after the uprising were dying by the hundreds. They expired from scurvy, consumption, beri-beri, but mainly from ennui and the yearning for the motherland. But the patrons in the café had apparently reconciled themselves to the Russian invader. They talked, shouted, joked, and laughed. The women fell giggling into each other's arms. Outside, a hearse rolled by, but those within ignored it as if death did not concern them. What were they jabbering about with such fervor? Yasha wondered. Why did their eyes gleam so? And that old fellow with the white wedge beard and the mossy pouches under the eyes—why had he pinned a rose in his lapel? He, Yasha, was to all appearances their equal, yet a barrier separated them. But what was it? He never found a clear explanation. Together with his ambition and lust for life, dwelt a sadness, a sense of the vanity of everything, a guilt that could neither be repaid nor forgotten. What was life's purpose if one did not know why one was born nor why one died? What sense did all the fine words about positivism, industrial reform, and progress make when it was all cancelled out in the grave? For all his drive, he, Yasha, was constantly on the brink of melancholy. As soon as he lost his craving for new tricks and new loves, doubts attacked him like locusts. Had he been brought into the world simply to turn a few somersaults and deceive a number of females? On the other hand, could he, Yasha, revere a God whom someone had invented? Could he, Yasha, sit like that Jew with ashes on his head and bewail a temple which had been destroyed two thousand years ago? And would he be able later to kneel and cross himself before that Jesus of Nazareth who, allegedly, had been born of the holy spirit and was no less a personage than God's only son?

The waiter was at the table.

"What does the gentleman wish?"

"To pay," Yasha said.

His words seemed ambiguous—as if he had intended saying: To pay for my deceitful life.

2

In the first act of the play, the husband invited Adam Povolsky to spend the summer with him at his villa, but

Adam Povolsky made excuses. He revealed a secret. He had a sweetheart, the young wife of an old nobleman. But the husband was adamant. The sweetheart could wait. He wanted Povolsky, in the course of the vacation, to instruct his daughter on the pianoforte and to give English lessons to his wife. (French had just about gone out of fashion.)

In the second act, Adam Povolsky carried on affairs with both the mother and the daughter. To get rid of the husband, all three protagonists convinced him that he was arthritic and that he must be off to Pischany to take the mud baths.

In the third act the husband discovered the deception. "I did not have to go to Pischany to wallow in mud," he exclaimed; "I have a morass right here in my house!" He called out Adam Povolsky but now the old nobleman came, the cuckold spouse of Povolsky's inamorata, and he took Povolsky back to his estate. The play ended with a lecture by the old nobleman to Adam Povolsky on the dangers of amorous entanglements.

The farce was adapted from the French. Few plays were put on in Warsaw during the summer but this particular vehicle, *Povolsky's Dilemma*, drew audiences even in the hottest weather. The laughter began with the rising of the curtain and did not cease until the end of the third act. The women muffled their giggles in handkerchiefs while drying the tears caused by uproarious laughter. Occasionally there was a laugh that seemed scarcely human. It cracked like a shot and degenerated into a whinny. Thus one cuckold laughed at another. He slapped his knee and began to topple from his seat. His wife revived him and tried to set him right in his chair. Emilia smiled and fanned herself. The gaslights intensified the heat. Yasha barely maintained an amiable expression. He had seen hundreds of similar farces. The husband was always fatuous, the wife unfaithful, the lover cunning. The moment Yasha stopped smiling, his eyebrows tensed. Who mocked whom here? The same rabble existed everywhere. They danced at weddings and wailed at funerals, swore faithfulness at the altar and corrupted the institution of marriage, wept over a forlorn, fictitious, little orphan and butchered each other in wars, pogroms, and revolutions. He held Emilia's hand but anger burned in him. He could neither desert Esther, convert, nor suddenly turn thief on account of Emilia. He glanced sideways at her. She laughed less than the others, probably to avoid appearing vulgar, but also seemed to enjoy Povolsky's serpentine antics and two-edged bons mots. Who could tell? He probably appealed to her, too. He, Yasha, was short in stature but the farceur was tall and broad-shouldered. In Italy, Yasha would be vocally inept for years to come while Emilia would communicate in French, and quickly learn Italian. While he was roaming about doing performances, risking his neck daily, she would hold a salon, invite guests, seek a match for Halina, perhaps find for herself an Italian Povolsky. They're all the same. Each of them a spider!

No, no! he cried within himself. I won't let myself be trapped. Tomorrow, I'll run away. I'll leave everything behind—Emilia, Wolsky, the Alhambra, the magic, Magda. I've been a magician long enough! I've walked the tightrope too often! He suddenly reminded himself of the new stunt he was scheduled to introduce—the somersault on the tightrope. They would recline on soft cushions while he, pushing forty as he was, would turn somersaults on the wire. And what if he fell and smashed his body? They would put him out on the threshold to beg and not one of his admirers would stoop to fling a groschen into his hat.

He took his hand away from Emilia's. She sought it again but he turned from her in the darkness, surprised at his own rebelliousness. These thoughts were not new to him. He had wrestled with these problems even before he had met Emilia. He lusted after women, yet hated them as a drunkard hates alcohol. And as he planned new stunts, he was plagued by the fear that the old ones were beyond his powers and would cause him an untimely death. He had burdened himself with too heavy a yoke even before Emilia. He supported Magda, Elzbieta, and Bolek. He paid rent for the Warsaw apartment. He roamed for months on end through the provinces, stopping at mean hotels, playing in ice-cold firehouses, traveling dangerous roads. And what did he gain from all this? The humblest farmhand enjoyed more peace of mind and less worry. Esther grumbled frequently that he worked only for the devil.

In some odd way, the farce assisted his ruminations. How much longer would he drift along like this? How many more burdens would he assume? With how many more perils and disasters would he load himself? He was revolted by the actors, the audience, by Emilia, by himself. These important ladies and gentlemen had never acknowledged him, Yasha, nor had he acknowledged them. Artfully, they had fused religion with materialism, connubiality with adultery, Christian love with worldly hate. But he, Yasha, remained a bedeviled spirit. His passions flayed him like whips. Never had he ceased to suffer regret, shame, and the fear of death. He spent agonized nights reckoning his years. How much longer would he remain young? Catastrophically, old age hovered about him. What could be more useless than an elderly magician? Sometimes in bed, unable to close his eyes, long-forgotten passages of the Scriptures would leap to his mind, prayers, his grandmother's wise proverbs, his father's stern moralization. A Yom Kippur tune would start within him:

To what can man aspire
When death will quench his fire? . . .

Thoughts of repentance enveloped him. Perhaps there was a God, after all? Perhaps all the holy sayings were true? It just didn't seem credible that the world had created itself or simply evolved out of a fog. Perhaps a Day of Reckoning really waited and a scale where good deeds were weighed against the evil? If it were so, then every minute was precious. If it were so, then he had arranged not one but two hells for himself. One in this world, a second in the other!

But what concrete solution could he now adopt? Grow a beard and sidelocks? Don a prayershawl and phylacteries and pray thrice daily? Where did it follow that the entire truth was to be found in the Jewish codex? Maybe the answers lay with the Christians, the Mohammedans, or still some other sect? They also had their sacred books, their prophets, all sorts of legends of miracles and revelations. He felt the wrangling of the forces within him, the good and the evil. After a while, he began to daydream of flying apparatuses, of new loves, new adventures, journeys, treasures, discoveries, harems.

The curtain came down at the end of the third act. The applause was deafening. Men began to shout: "Bravo! Bravo!" Someone brought two bouquets of flowers to the stage. The cast clasped hands, took bows, smiled, peered into the boxseats occupied by the wealthy. Could this be the aim of creation? Yasha asked himself. Is this what God wills? Perhaps, it would be better to commit suicide.

"What's wrong?" Emilia asked. "You seem to be in a bad mood today."

"No, it's nothing."

3

It was a just a short distance from the theater to Emilia's house on Krolevska Street, but Yasha hired a droshky for the trip. He ordered the coachman to drive slowly. It had been hot in the theater, but, outside, cool breezes blew in from the Vistula and the Praga forests. Gaslights cast a shadowy glow. The bright sky was brilliant with stars. Simply raising one's eyes heavenward calmed the spirit. Yasha knew little about astronomy but he had read several lay books on the subject. He had even seen Saturn's rings and the mountains of the moon through a telescope. Wherever the truth was to be found, one thing was sure—the sky was vast, limitless. It took thousands of years for the light to travel from the stars before it reached our eyes. Fixed stars, winking and blinking in the heavens, were suns, each with its own planets which were probably worlds themselves. That pale stain up there was perhaps the milky way, a skein of multi-millions of heavenly bodies. Yasha never passed up the astronomical nor other scientific articles in the *Courier Warshawski*. The scientists were constantly making new discoveries. The cosmos was no longer measured in miles but in light years. A mechanism had been invented capable of analyzing the chemical components of the farthest star. Bigger and bigger telescopes were constantly being constructed which revealed the secrets of space. They predicted accurately every eclipse of the moon and sun, the return of every comet. If only I'd applied myself to my education instead of my magic, Yasha mused. But now, it's already too late.

The droshky rode down the Alexander Place parallel to the Saxony Gardens. Yasha breathed deeply. In the darkness the park seemed full of mystery. Tiny flames flared within the depths. Scents wafted from the greenery. Yasha lifted Emilia's gloved hand and kissed her wrist. He felt love for her once again. He lusted for her body. Her face was shrouded in shadows. Her eyes gleamed like twin jewels, sparkled with gold, with fire, with nocturnal promise. He had bought her a rose on the way to the theater and it now exuded an intoxicating aroma. He lowered his nostrils to the rose and it was as if he breathed in the odor of the universe. If a bit of earth and water can create an aroma like this, creation cannot be bad, he decided. "I must stop brooding about such foolishness."

"What did you say, dear?"

"I said that I love you and that I can't wait until you are mine."

She waited a moment. Her knee touched his through the gown. Something like electricity coursed into him through the silk. He was overcome with desire. A tingle streaked down his spine.

"It's even more difficult for me than for you." She said "thou" to him for the first time in their relationship. She barely managed to breathe the word. He heard it more in his mind than in his ears.

They sat there quietly and the horse walked step by step. The coachman's shoulders drooped as if he were dozing. They both seemed to listen to the lust which moved from her knee to his and back again. Their bodies conversed in a wordless language of their own. "I must have you!" one knee said to the other. He was consumed with an ominous silence as when he walked the tightrope. Suddenly she bent her head to his. The brim of her straw hat made a roof over his head. Her lips touched his ear.

"I want to bear your child," she whispered.

He embraced her, bit into her lips. His mouth drank, drank. He felt as if he had stopped breathing. Esther had spoken about a child repeatedly, but years had passed since she had last brought up the subject. Magda had also requested a child several times but he had not taken her seriously. He seemed to have forgotten that element of life. But Emilia had not forgotten. She was still young enough to conceive and carry. Perhaps this is the very cause of my torment, he pondered. I am without an heir.

"Yes, a son," he said.

"When?"

And their mouths fused again. They consumed each other in a silent, bestial way. The horse stopped suddenly. The coachman seemed to come awake.

"Gee up!"

They pulled up before Emilia's house and Yasha helped her alight. She did not immediately ring the bell but stood there with him on the sidewalk before the gate. They did not speak.

"Well, it's late." And she pulled the bellcord.

Yasha could determine by the footsteps that it was

the janitor's wife, not the janitor, who came to open the gate. The courtyard was dark. Emilia went in and Yasha sidled in behind her. He did it with deftness and spontaneity. Even Emilia was not aware of what had happened. The janitress padded back to her cubicle. He took Emilia's arm in the darkness. She started.

"Who is it?"

"It is I."

"God in heaven, what did you do?" And she giggled in the darkness at his fantastic skill and daring.

They stood there as if silently deliberating.

"No, that is not the way," she whispered.

"I only want to kiss you."

"How will you get into the house? Yadwiga will open the door."

"I'll open it," he said.

He mounted the stairs with her. Several times they stopped to kiss. He made a pass at the door and it swung open. The corridor was dark. A middle-of-the-night stillness emanated from the rooms. He walked into the drawing room, pulling Emilia along with him. She seemed to be holding back. They wrangled silently. He steered her to the divan and she followed like one who is no longer mistress of herself.

"I don't want to begin our life together in sin," she whispered.

"No."

He wanted to undress her and the silken gown began to snap and shoot off sparks. The fire, which he knew to be static electricity, startled him. She was astonished herself. She clasped him by both his wrists, squeezed with such force that it hurt.

"How will you leave?"

"Through the window."

"Halina may waken."

Suddenly she pulled back and said: "No, you must go!"

6

The following day Yasha slept late. He dozed until one in the afternoon. Magda's country habits still remained with her. She could not understand how one could stay in bed until midday. But she had long accustomed herself to the fact that Yasha was not like other people. He could eat more and fast longer, he could stay up nights and sleep the whole day through. Waking from profound slumber, he could speak to her as if he had been dissembling. His brow and the veins on his temples would indicate that he was thinking waking thoughts. Who could tell? Perhaps that was how he conceived new stunts? Magda walked about on tiptoe. She served him oat grits with potatoes and mushrooms. He ate and, afterwards, fell asleep again. Magda began to mutter to herself in a peasant jargon: "Snore away your sins, you swine, you cur. Drained himself dry with that scabby duchess." Magda had one remedy for all sorrows—work. Yasha was hard on his clothes and everything needed mending. He lost his buttons, his seams sprang apart, he wore a shirt one day, then cast it aside as if it were lousy. It was always necessary to pick up after him, to wash, polish, sew. His animals also required care: the horses in the stable, the monkey, the parrot, the crow. She was everything to him: a wife, a servant, a stage assistant— and what did she get? Nothing—a crust of bread. Actually, he had nothing himself. Everyone robbed him, swindled him, deceived him. Clever as he was in the theater, hypnotizing and reading minds or when reading his books or papers, he was stupid when it came to practical matters. Also he was ruining his health. He should not go roaming about night after night. Even though he was healthy, he sometimes grew weak as a fly, fell in a faint and lay as if in a seizure.

Magda washed, scrubbed, scoured, dusted. Neighbors dropped in to borrow an onion, a clove of garlic, a drop of milk, a bit of lard with which to brown onions. Magda turned no one away. Compared to these paupers, she was affluent. Besides, she had an unsavory reputation and she was forced to curry favor with her neighbors. She was officially registered with the municipal authorities as a house servant. When the neighbors were at odds with her, they called her strumpet and carrion and suggested she file for the yellow card of a prostitute. Men who were drunk tormented her when she went down to the store or the pump. Youths shouted after her, "Whore for the Jews!"

The belfry-bell of the church of the Holy John rang two o'clock. Magda went to Yasha in the alcove. He was no longer asleep but sitting up in bed and staring.

"Have a nice nap?" she asked.

"Yes, I was tired."

"When do we begin to rehearse? The opening is a week away."

"Yes. I know."

"The posters are everywhere. Your name is in gigantic letters."

"They can all go to hell."

Yasha wanted a bath and Magda promptly began to heat kettles of water for him. She soaped him down in the wooden tub, rinsed him off, massaged him. Magda, like any other woman, longed for a child. She was prepared to bear Yasha an illegitimate one. But he robbed her even of that. He, himself, wanted to be the child. Magda bathed him, petted him, caressed him. He wronged her more than her worst enemy, but when he spent a few hours with her and showed that he needed her, her love for him became more ardent than before.

He asked abruptly, "Do you have any sort of a dress for the summer?"

Instantly her tears began to flow.

"Now you remind yourself?"

"Why didn't you keep after me? You know I'm forgetful."

"I don't badger. I'll leave that to your new lady."

"I'm going to buy you a wardrobe soon. I've told you that you're locked in my heart. Whatever happens, wait for me."

"Yes, I'll wait."

"Take off your clothes. Let's bathe together."

Magda acted shocked at such a suggestion but he held and stripped her. She was not so much ashamed of her nudity as her gaunt body. Her ribs jutted out, her breastbone was flat, almost without breasts, her knees were angular, her arms lean as sticks. The rash had spread from her face to her back. She stood before him, a shame-faced skeleton. He climbed out of the tub and placed her within it. He bathed her, soaped her, fondled her. He tickled her until she had to laugh. Then afterwards he bore her into the alcove and drew the bed-curtains. He now made love to her so often and for such a long period of time that fear gripped her heart. He was clearly a warlock with the strength of the devil.

Lately he had avoided her. For days she had not heard the sound of his voice. Now he spoke to her as he used to. He questioned her about rural customs and she described the various harvest rites. She spoke of the fairies who secrete themselves in the corn and hide from the harvesters' sickles and the flails of the threshers. She told of a female dummy of straw which the boys would cast into the river, of a tree to which the old peasants prayed for rain although the priests had forbidden it, of a wooden rooster kept somewhere in the village elder's attic which, during times of drought, was doused with water as a talisman to bring rain. He heard her out and questioned her.

"Do you believe in God?" he asked.

"Yes, I believe."

"Then why did he create all this? Well, in my trousers pockets are ten rubles. Take them and go to a seamstress."

"I don't like to go through your pockets."

"Go on, take them while they're still there."

She went into the other room where he had hung his trousers and took the ten rubles. When she returned he was once more asleep. She felt like kissing his forehead but she did not want to wake him. Standing in the doorway for a long while, she gazed down at him with the painful awareness that no matter how long she knew him, she would never understand him. He was, and continued to be, an enigma to her, body and soul. Perhaps that was the very reason why she had trembled and clung to him so. Finally, she went to clean up the bath. There was a seamstress in the house, near the second gate. Magda spat on the banknote and tucked it into her bosom. The day had unexpectedly turned happy.

2

He slept the whole summer's day through. It had already rained and the sky had cleared again. He opened his eyes. The alcove was swathed in semidarkness. He smelled food cooking in the kitchen. Magda was frying potatoes with cutlets and sauerkraut. He had eaten nothing but the oat grits and awoke famished. Dressing quickly, he went into the kitchen. He kissed Magda and ate what was ready: bread with herring milt. He took a half-raw cutlet from the frying pan. Magda scolded him good-naturedly. Then she said: "I wish every day were like this one."

And as she spoke, a scratching was heard at the front door. The knob rattled, Yasha opened the door. An urchin girl stood there, wrapped in a huge shawl. She apparently knew him, for she said: "Panie Yasha, a lady is waiting for you downstairs by the gate."

"What lady?"

"Her name is Zeftel."

"Thank you. Tell her I'll be right down." And he gave the child two groschen.

No sooner did he close the door than Magda clasped both his hands. "No! You shan't go! Your supper's growing cold!"

"I can't let her wait there."

"I know who it is—it's that tart from Piask!"

She held him with such strength that he was forced to shake her loose. Instantly her face contorted, her hair bristled, her eyes flashed green and light as a cat's. He pushed her away and she nearly fell into the water barrel. It was always like this. Whenever he was kind to someone, she wanted to enslave him. He closed the door behind him and heard Magda weep, hiss like a snake, shout something unintelligible after him. He sympathized with her but he couldn't let Zeftel stand out there in the street waiting. He walked down the stairs, breathing the odors of the flats. Children wailed, the sick uttered sighs, girls sang of love. Somewhere up on the roof, cats caterwauled. He stopped for a moment in the dusk and planned a course of action.

I'll give her something and send her away, he decided. My life's complicated enough without her. Just at that second Yasha reminded himself of an appointment that he had with Emilia. He was supposed to eat dinner at her house that very evening. Those had been his parting words just before he had climbed out of her window the night before. How could I have forgotten? he wondered. Lord, I forget everything. I promised to write Esther the minute I reached Warsaw. She's probably half out of her mind with worry. What's wrong with me? Am I sick, or what? He leaned against the bannister as if then and there to take stock of his life. He'd frittered away a day just dozing and dreaming. It was as if he had simply skipped over an entire period of time. There was so much for him to do and think about that he could not allow his thoughts to linger on anything. He should have been planning his opening yet he had not even rehearsed. He never stopped thinking about

Emilia but he had not really arrived at any definite decision concerning her. I can't make my mind up about anything, he said to himself, that is what's wrong. What had occurred the day before—Emilia's change of mind at the last moment—had been a blow to him. She had resisted his hypnotic powers. Before he had gone, she had kissed him and again avowed her great love, but her voice had been tinged with a tone of triumph. Maybe it's all for the best that I've forgotten the dinner engagement, he said to himself. Why let her think I'm chasing her? Suddenly he thought: But what if this is the end? Perhaps at this very moment she had stopped loving him or become his enemy?

Absurd thoughts attacked him—he played an inner game of maybes and perhaps, just as he had when he had been a schoolboy and had speculated whether his father was the devil, his teacher a demon, the tutor a werewolf, and everything else merely illusion. The propensities and idiosyncracies of those years remained within him. If no one was about, he would not walk but would hop down the stairs like a bird and run the nail of his forefinger along the plaster wall. He was likewise afraid of the dark, he who, on a dare, had spent a night in the cemetery. Shapes still evolved from the shadows, terrifying faces with bridling manes, pointed beaks, holes instead of eyes. He constantly felt that only the thinnest of barriers separated him from those dark ones who swarmed around him, aiding him and thwarting him, playing all sorts of tricks on him. He, Yasha, had to fight them constantly or else fall from the tightrope, lose the power of speech, grow infirm and impotent.

He went down and saw Zeftel. She was standing before the gate, beneath a lamppost, a shawl draped across her shoulders. The street lamp cast a radiant yellow across her face. She seemed exactly what she was: a provincial woman, freshly arrived in Warsaw. She had arranged her hair in two buns, one on each side, an obvious attempt to appear younger. There hovered about her the transitory air of those who, having torn up their roots, feel alien even to themselves.

"So you're here?" Yasha said.

Zeftel started. "I began to think you weren't coming down."

She made a move as if to kiss him but somehow nothing came of it. A housewife walked by carrying a pail of water from the pump, sighing and mumbling to herself. She jostled against Zeftel, spilling water over her button-top shoes.

"Oh, the devil with her!" Zeftel lifted each foot in turn and wiped it dry with the edge of her shawl.

"When did you arrive?"

She thought the question over as if she had not understood it. The long trip seemed to have confused her.

"I set off and I'm here. What did you think, I took the fare from you for nothing?"

"It was a possibility."

"Piask isn't a town; it's a graveyard. I sold all my stuff. I was cheated. What can you expect of thieves? I was lucky to get out of there alive."

"Where are you staying?"

"I'm with a woman who finds servants work. She promised me a job but so far there's been nothing. The way things are there are more servants than mistresses. I've got to talk something over with you."

"My supper is waiting."

"Yashale, it was just hell, trying to find you. No one knew the street, nor the house number. How can one see the number when it's dark? Until I got that girl to call you, I nearly died. I didn't want to go up to your house. I knew the other one was up there. Two cats in one sack."

"She had just finished cooking. How about waiting another half hour?"

"Come with me now, Yashale. Where can I wait? Every minute there's another drunk. They think every girl is one of those. We'll buy something to eat. All right, you're a big-shot Warsaw magician and I'm only a girl from the country, but, as the saying goes, we are not exactly strangers. Everyone sends his regards: Blind Mechl, Berish Visoker, Chaim-Leib."

"Thanks a lot."

"Thanks for nothing. What do I need with your thanks? I talk to you and you're not even here. Have you forgotten already, or what? Yashale, it's like this," she changed her tone, "I go to this woman agent and she says, 'You came at the wrong time. Everybody is looking for domestic work and all the ladies are away in the country.' I pick up my basket and start to go out when she calls me back. 'Where you running, where?' It seems she lends money to the girls at interest. Anyway, she makes a bed for me on the floor and I lie down. Three cooks are lying next to me, snoring. One makes so much noise I don't close my eyes all night, just lie there and cry. With Leibush after all, I was my own boss. In the morning I was just going out when a man walks in, a dude with a watch on a chain and cuffs with cuff links. 'Who are you?' he asks. So I tell him everything. 'It's like this—my husband deserted me. I don't know where he's gone.' So he keeps asking questions and says, 'I know where your husband is!' 'Where is he?' I shout. Well, to make a long story short, this fellow comes from

America, but it seems it's another America. Anyway, Leibush is there. When I hear that, I begin to cry like it was Yom Kippur. 'What are you carrying on for?' he asks. 'It's a pity—your pretty eyes.' He talks so fancy you almost bust and he throws his money around and treats everybody to chocolate bars and halvah. 'Come with me,' he says to me, 'and I'll take you to your husband. He'll either take you back or divorce you.' He's going back in a couple of weeks and he's willing to lend me the ship's fare. But somehow, I'm afraid."

And Zeftel suddenly stopped talking.

Yasha whistled.

"That bird, eh?"

"You know him?"

"I don't have to know him. You know what a pimp is, don't you? He'll drag you off to—God knows where —and stick you in a brothel."

"But he speaks so nicely."

"He knows your husband like I know your great-grandmother."

They strolled towards Dluga Avenue. Zeftel grasped the edge of her shawl.

"What can I do? I've got to find a job. He put me up at his sister's. I spent last night there."

"His sister's, eh? She's his sister like I'm your great-uncle." Yasha was astonished at how quickly he'd adopted Zeftel's tone and jargon. "Most likely a madam, and they split the profits. He'll sell you somewhere—in Buenos Aires or who knows where. You'll rot there alive."

"What are you saying? He even mentioned the name of the city. Where is it again? In America?"

"Wherever it is, it doesn't mean a thing. They come

here to deal in flesh, in women—they're white slavers. They wait for dumbbells like you. The newspapers are full of it. Where does this sister live?"

"On Nizka Street."

"Well, let's go over and take a look. Why should he offer to advance you the fare? Can't you understand what kind of fellow this is?"

Zeftel paused.

"Yes, that's why I came to you. But when you're lying on the floor and the bedbugs are eating you alive, you do what you can. At his sister's it's clean. I have a bed to sleep in and linen. She feeds me, too. I offered to pay her but she said, 'Don't worry about it, we'll settle up later.'"

"It's enough. Get out of there unless you want to end up a whore in Buenos Aires."

"What are you talking about? I was a respectable girl. If only Leibush had appreciated me. I'd have made him a good wife. But he spent more time locked up than at home. Three weeks after the wedding he was already in jail. Later he ran away altogether. What could I do? I'm only flesh and blood, after all. All Piask ran after me. His best friends. But I didn't want to waste myself on them. I longed for you. Yashale, I don't want to force myself on you; I have my pride, as the saying goes, but you're here in my heart. After you left I began to long for you. Now that I'm walking next to you, I feel as if I'm flying. You haven't even kissed me yet!" she pouted reprovingly.

"I couldn't back there. Everyone sits at the windows looking out."

"Give me a kiss. I'm still the same Zeftel."

And she held open her shawl for him.

3

That's all I needed! Yasha said to himself. How odd that he had forgotten Zeftel and the fact that he had given her the fare to go to Warsaw. He had forgotten her presence completely. He marveled at his own entanglements, yet took some perverse pleasure from them, as if his life were a storybook in which the situation grows tenser and tenser until one can barely wait to turn the page. Earlier he had felt hungry, but now his hunger had left him. The night was warm, even a trifle humid, but he felt a chill across his back as if he had been sick and had gone outside prematurely. He had to stop himself from trembling. He looked for a droshky, but no droshkies came to Freta Street, and so he steered Zeftel in the direction of Franciskaner Street. I'll get rid of her and go on to Emilia's he decided. Emilia won't know what to think. It was the first time he had broken a promise to her. He was apprehensive lest she become really insulted. Everything was balanced on a hair as it was. He also regretted having run out on Magda and realized suddenly that a change had come over him. There had been times when he had carried on a half-dozen affairs simultaneously without the slightest hitch. He had deceived everyone without a second thought, and had struck out freely when necessary without feeling any qualms of conscience. Now he brooded over the most insignificant trifles, was always seeking to do the right thing. Am I becoming a saint or what? he asked himself. It was hardly worthwhile arguing with Emilia over Zeftel and Magda, and yet that pinpoint in his brain that had the last word ordered him to stay with Zeftel. For some reason he wanted to "take care" of this pimp and his alleged sister.

Freta Street was dark and narrow. But Franciskaner Street was illuminated by gas lamps and the lights from stores which remained open despite the law. Here merchants dealt in leather and dry goods, in prayer books, and feathers. Business was even being transacted in the upstairs apartments, and all sorts of factories and workshops could be glimpsed through the windows. Thread was being wound, paper bags glued, linen and parasols sewn, underwear knitted. From the courtyards came the sound of sawing and hammering, and there was a hum of machinery as at the height of the working day. Bakeries were going full-blast and the chimneys spewed out smoke and cinders. From the broad, slop-drenched gutters rose a familiar stench which was reminiscent of Piask or Lublin. Young men in long gabardines and wearing tousled sidelocks walked with Talmudic books under their arms. There was a Yeshivah located here as well as Chassidic study-houses. The few passing droshkies were loaded to capacity with packages, the passengers completely hidden. Only at the corner of Nalevki Street was Yasha able to find an empty droshky. Zeftel reeled as if she were intoxicated, overwhelmed by the clamor and congestion. She climbed into the carriage, catching the fringes of her shawl on something. Once seated, she clutched Yasha's sleeve. As the droshky turned the corner, Zeftel seemed to turn with it. "If someone had told me, today I'd be riding in a droshky with you, I would have thought it was a joke."

"I didn't expect it either."

"It's as light as day here. Light enough to shell peas."

And she squeezed Yasha's arm and drew him to her

as if the brightly illuminated thoroughfare had reawakened the love within her.

On Gensha Street night began to close in again. A hearse rolled by, the corpse unaccompanied by a single mourner, destined to enter the grave in darkness. Perhaps someone just like myself, Yasha thought. Up near Dzika Avenue, streetwalkers called out to the passers-by. Yasha pointed. "That's what he wants to make of you."

On Nizka Street it was almost completely dark. The globes of the infrequent lampposts were smoke-stained and murky. The gutters were filled with mud as if it were not summer but just after the Feast of Tabernacles, during the fall rains. Here there were several lumberyards and a few establishments maintained by tombstone carvers. The house where Zeftel was staying was not far from Smotcha Street and the Jewish cemetery. They entered through a door set in a wooden fence. The stairs of the house were on the outside. Yasha and Zeftel entered a pink kitchen, which was illuminated by a naphtha lamp covered with a fringed paper shade. Everything was fringed with paper: the stove, the cupboard, the shelves of dishes. In a chair sat a woman. She had a great sweep of yellow hair, yellow eyes, a beaked nose, a sharp chin. Her feet, in red house slippers, rested on a footstool. A cat dozed nearby. In her hand the woman held a man's sock stretched over a glass as she darned. She raised her eyes in half-surprise.

"Mrs. Miltz, this is the man from Lublin I told you about—the magician."

Mrs. Miltz stuck the needle into the sock.

"She talks about you all the time. The magician did this, the magician did that. You don't look like a magician."

"What do I look like?"

"A musician."

"I did saw away at a fiddle once."

"You did? Well, what's the difference what you do so long as you make, you know what." And she rubbed her thumb in her palm. Yasha immediately began to talk her language.

"You're not lying. Money is a thief."

"Get her, she just comes to Warsaw and already she goes everywhere." Mrs. Miltz indicated Zeftel. "How did you find him? I was afraid she'd get lost. Why did you ever move to Freta Street?" she addressed Yasha. "Only Gentiles live there."

"Gentiles don't look into strange pots."

"If you cover your pot with a lid, not even a Jew can look in."

"A Jew would lift the lid and take a sniff."

The yellow woman's eyes twinkled.

"As I live and breathe, nobody's fool this," she said half to Zeftel, half to herself. "Have a seat. Zeftel, bring a chair."

"Where is your brother?" Zeftel asked.

The woman raised her yellow eyebrows. "What is it? You want to sign a contract with him?"

"This gentleman wants to speak with him."

"He's in the back room, dressing. He has to go out soon. Why don't you take off your shawl; it's summer, after all, not winter."

After some hesitation, Zeftel removed the shawl.

"He'll have to take a droshky. Some merchants are waiting for him," Mrs. Miltz remarked, as if to herself.

"What does he trade in, cattle?" Yasha asked, astounded at his own words.

"Why cattle of all things? Where he comes from, there is no end of cattle."

"He deals in diamonds," Zeftel interjected.

"I'm an expert with diamonds, too," Yasha boasted. "Take a look at this." And he showed a ring with a large diamond on his little finger. The woman looked at it with amazement and then her expression turned to one of reproof. A bitter smile played about her mouth.

"My brother is a busy man. He has no time for idle talk."

"I want to get down to facts," Yasha said, surprised at his own brazenness.

The door opened and a man entered. He was tall, thick-set, and had yellow hair which was the same shade as the woman's. His nose was wide, his lips thick, and his round jaw was halved by a cleft. His eyes were bulging and yellow. A sickle-shaped scar disfigured his forehead. He wore no jacket, only trousers and a stiff collarless shirt; on his feet were unbuttoned, patent-leather shoes. A broad chest profusely overgrown with yellow hair showed through the gaping shirt front. Yasha saw immediately what kind of a thug this was. There was a smile on the man's face, the smile of the eavesdropper who has kept himself apprised of the conversation. He was all good nature, cunning, confident, a giant who knows himself invincible. Seeing him, the woman spoke, "Herman, this is that magician, Zeftel's friend."

"A magician? All right, so he is," Herman said amiably, his eyes glinting. "A good evening to you," and he gripped Yasha's hand. It was more a show of strength than a handshake. Yasha fell into the spirit of the contest and squeezed as hard as he could. Zeftel seated herself on the edge of the metal bed in which she slept. At last Herman released his grip.

"Where are you from?" Yasha asked.

Herman's protuberant eyes filled with laughter.

"Where am I not from? The whole world. Warsaw is Warsaw and Lodz is Lodz! They know me in Berlin and I'm no stranger in London."

"Where are you living now?"

"As it is written in the Scriptures, 'The sky is my chair and the earth is my footstool.'"

"So, you know Scriptures also."

"Oh, you know them, too?"

"I studied them once."

"Where? At a Yeshivah?"

"No, at a study-house, with a tutor."

"So help me God, I was once a student of the Talmud myself," Herman said amiably in a confidential tone. "But that was a long, long time ago. I like eating, and in the Yeshivah you could send your teeth out to storage. I thought it over and decided it was not for me. I went to Berlin to study medicine but the plusquamperfectum of their grammar wouldn't stay in my mind. The German girls appealed to me more. So I continued on to Antwerp and became a diamond polisher, but I saw that the cash was not in polishing but in selling. I like the dice and I believe in the old saying, 'No wrinkles in the belly.' One way or another, I got to Argentina. Lately, there have been a lot of Jews going there. They carry a pack on their shoulders and suddenly they're business men. We call them *quentiniks*, in German they're *hausierer*, in New York peddler, but what the hell's the difference? That agent woman—what's her name again? —has a son in Buenos Aires and he sent his regards to his mother. I met Zeftel at the agency. What is she to you, a sister?"

"No, not a sister."

"For all I care, she can be your aunt."

4

"Herman, you've got to go," the yellowish woman interrupted, "there are businessmen waiting for you."

"Let them wait. I waited plenty for them. Where I come from, no one is in a hurry. The Spaniard says to everything *mañana*—tomorrow; he is lazy and wants everything brought to him at home. There are the steppes—they call them *pampas*—where the cattle graze. When the *gaucho*, as they say, gets hungry, he's too lazy to kill a steer; he picks up a hatchet and carves himself a beefsteak from the live animal. He roasts it, hide and all, because he's too lazy even to skin it. He claims it tastes better that way. The Jews out there aren't lazy and that's how they make the *peso*—that's what they call the money. Everything would be fine except that too many men have come and there are too few of Eve's daughters. But without a woman a man is only half a body, as the Talmud says. A girl there is worth her weight in gold. I don't mean that in the bad sense. They get married and that's the end of it. If the marriage doesn't take, it's a lost cause because divorce is out of the question. It might be a snake you married, you got to stay with it—that's the way the priests want it. So what does a man do? Puts on his walking shoes and is on his way. So the wheel of fortune spins. Rather than have your sister become a maid and wash somebody's drawers, she's better off coming with me and getting what she wants there."

"She isn't my sister."

"And if she isn't, what of it? In Buenos Aires, we don't ask for pedigrees. Genealogy, we say, is only good to put on a gravestone. When you go there it's like being born again. What sort of tricks do you do?"

"All sorts."

"Do you play cards?"

"Occasionally."

"Aboard ship, there's nothing else to do. If it weren't for cards you'd go crazy. It's hot as blazes and when you cross the—what do you call it?—equator, you can suffocate. The sun is straight overhead. At night it gets even hotter. If you go on deck you roast in an oven. So what's left?—cards. On the way here some fellow tried to cheat me. I looked at him and I said, 'Brother, what's that sticking out of your sleeve? The fifth ace?' He'd have liked to jump me but I don't scare easy. Back home everybody carries a gun. If you get too smart you find yourself full of holes. So, like everybody else, I carry a gun. Would you like to have a look at an Argentinian revolver?"

"Why not? I've got a gun, too."

"What do you need it for, your tricks?"

"Possibly."

"Anyhow, he saw he wasn't dealing with some kid. He'd tried to mark the cards but I caught him. Zeftel mentioned you do card tricks. What can you do?"

"Not cheating."

"What then?"

"Fetch me a deck and I'll show you."

"Herman, you've got to go," Mrs. Miltz said impatiently.

"Wait, don't rush me, my business won't run away, and if it does, I don't give a damn. You know what? Let's go in the other room and have a snack."

"I'm not hungry," Yasha lied.

"You don't need to be hungry. The appetite, they say,

comes as you eat. Here in Poland, you people don't know how to eat properly. Noodles and chicken soup and chicken soup and noodles. What are noodles any-way?—nothing but water. You only bloat the belly. The Spaniard takes care of a three-pound beefsteak and that puts marrow in your bones. You come to a Spaniard's house and he lies down in the middle of the day and sleeps like a log. It's hot as hell there and flies suck your blood like leeches. In the summer, life begins at night. With us, if somebody has just enough money either to eat or pay for a whore, he chooses the whore. Somehow or other, nobody starves. You like vodka?"

"Occasionally."

"Come on, then, have a glass. Rytza, fetch us some-thing," Herman said to the yellowish woman. "The Spaniard dearly loves his magic. He'd sell his soul to see a good trick."

The living-room furniture consisted of a table covered with oilcloth, a sofa, and a clothes closet. Suspended from the ceiling was a naphtha lamp which had almost gone out and Herman turned up the wick. Valises, plas-tered with stickers, and piles of boxes were scattered about the room. Over a chair hung a jacket and also on the chair were a stiff collar and a silver-headed cane. The very air of the place smelt of foreign lands and distant shores. Two photographs, one of a man with a white beard, the other of a woman in a full wig, hung on the wall.

"Have a seat," Herman said. "My sister is about to bring something tempting to eat. She can afford a better apartment but, being accustomed to this place, she doesn't want to move. Back home the houses aren't this big and everything is done right in the courtyard. A *patio*, it's called. The Spaniard hates to climb stairs. He

sits outside with the family and drinks a kind of tea—
mate. Everybody takes a sip through the same straw; it
goes from mouth to mouth. Before you acquire the taste,
it's like drinking branchwater with licorice milk, but
you can get used to anything. In North America, for
example, they chew tobacco. One thing you must understand—it's the same world everywhere. They don't
eat people in Buenos Aires either. Take a look at me—
nobody's eaten me."

"Maybe you've eaten somebody."

"Eh?—That's a good one! You're nobody's fool; the
person who keeps his wits about him, skims the gravy
right off the top. You come from Piask?"

"No, Lublin."

"Zeftel said you were from Piask."

"You're a thief yourself."

Herman exploded with laughter.

"Say, you're all right. Not everyone from Piask is a
thief, no more than everyone from Chelm is a fool. It's
only hearsay. On the other hand, who doesn't steal? My
mother, may she rest in peace, used to say: 'The honest
way is not the easy way.' You can do anything, you only
need to know how. Just as I am now, I've already tasted
everything. Zeftel tells me you can spring any lock."

"That's true."

"I wouldn't have the patience. Why fool around with
a lock when you can smash the door down? What's a
door hung on? Nothing but hinges. But that's all in the
past. I've become, as the saying goes, a model citizen.
I have a wife and children. Zeftel told me her whole
story. About her husband deserting her and all the rest
of it. If she gets a divorce, she could marry the richest
man in South America."

"Who would grant her the divorce—you?"

"What's a divorce—A piece of paper. Everything is paper, my dear man, even money. I mean big money, not pocket change. Those who hold the pen—write. Moses was a man. That's why he wrote that a man could have ten wives, but if a woman looked at another man she had to be stoned. If a woman had held the pen she would have written the exact opposite. Do you follow me or not? On Stavka Street there's a scribe who's one of us, and if you give him ten rubles he'll write you a good divorce, signed by witnesses, absolutely legal. But I don't force anybody into anything. I was willing to advance her the ship's fare . . ."

Yasha suddenly raised his brows. "Panie Herman, I'm no simpleton. Leave Zeftel alone. She is not your kind of merchandise."

"What? You can take her with you this very minute. She's already cost me a couple of rubles but I'll write it off as charity."

"Don't do us any favors. How much did she cost you? I'll pay for everything."

"Take it easy, don't get your wind up. Here's the tea."

5

They drank tea and ate cookies and butter-cake. Mrs. Miltz and Zeftel joined them at the table. Herman drank his tea with jam, ate the butter-cake and from time to time took a puff on a fat cigar which rested in a saucer. He offered Yasha a cigar, too, but Yasha declined.

"You can't get a cigar like this in all Warsaw," Herman complained. "This is genuine Havana. None of your substitutes but the real stuff from Cuba. Somebody brought them from there especially for me. In Berlin you'd have to pay two marks for one. I like everything first-class, but you have to pay for everything, and when you pay, already you pay too much. What's a Havana cigar? Leaves, not gold. And what's a good-looking girl? Also flesh and blood. The Spaniard is jealous. You smile at his wife and he goes for his knife, but two blocks away he keeps a mistress and has children by her. After a while, she becomes a frump, too, and he has to go looking for a fresh piece. I read the Polish papers here and I've got to laugh. They write such nonsense! A girl goes out at night to get a jug of milk, along comes a carriage and she's caught inside. Later they take her to Buenos Aires and sell her like a calf in the market. But I've been here weeks and haven't seen any such carriage. And how can you transport such a girl across the border? What about the ship? Nonsense, foolishness. The truth is, they go of their own free will. You go to that district and you meet women from every part of the world. You want a black one—a black one it is; you want a white one—that's what you get. If a Lithuanian from Vilno or Ayshyshok is what you're after, you don't have to go looking, or if you have an urge for the Warsaw product, you'll be accommodated. As for myself, I don't go there. What do I need with it? I've got a wife and children. But the newspapers want readers. It's just as I've been saying, it depends on who holds the pen. I'll tell you one thing: Husbands themselves send their wives into the quarter. And do you know why? Because they're too lazy to go to work themselves. How about some of your tricks? Here's a deck of cards."

"Once you start with the cards you won't go anywhere," the yellowish woman said.

"Tomorrow is another day."

Herman began to shuffle the deck and Yasha saw at once that he was up against a cardsharp. The cards flowed through Herman's hands as if they had a life of their own. So . . . that's the sort of canary you are! Yasha said to himself. Well, we'll soon show you there are some smarter boys around.

Yasha allowed him to perform several tricks: the trick with the three cards, the one with the four sevens, the changed card. Yasha shook his head at this and clicked his tongue, "Tsk, tsk, tsk . . . " He almost said, I was already doing these tricks when I was a little girl.

He reminded himself that it was growing late and that if he still wanted to see Emilia he would have to leave that very minute; nevertheless, he remained seated. Since she is so virtuous, let her wait! a second voice within him said, a spiteful one. Yasha was well aware that his worst enemy was his ennui. To escape it, he had committed all of his follies. It lashed at him like so many whips. Because of it, he had loaded himself down with all sorts of burdens. But now, he did not feel bored. He took the deck from Herman. The fact that Herman left the merchants waiting to spend the time with him indicated to Yasha that the other was afflicted with the same malady as he. It was the disease that bound the underworld to decent society—the card players in a thieves' den to the gamblers at Monte Carlo; the pimp from Buenos Aires to the drawing-room Don Juan, the cutthroat to the revolutionary terrorist. As Yasha shuffled the cards, he marked them with the edge of his fingernail.

"Pick a card," he said to Herman.

Herman chose the king of clubs.

Deftly Yasha bent the deck.

"Put it back and shuffle the cards."

Herman did as directed.

"Now, I'll pick out the king of clubs for you."

And with the thumb and forefinger he took out the king of clubs.

"Let's just have a peep at your finger-nails."

Yasha showed one trick, Herman another. Herman was apparently familiar with all the tricks. His yellow eyes glistened with the slyness of the expert who had passed as an amateur. He did not have merely one deck in the house, he had a dozen.

"Looks like you've been holding a card up your sleeve," Yasha remarked.

"Cards fascinated me. But it's all over. Dead and buried!"

"You don't play any more?"

"Only a little 'sixty-six' with my Señora."

"Nevertheless, I'd like to show you something."

And Yasha picked up the deck again.

"Choose a suit."

Now Yasha performed some tricks which Herman did not seem to know. He looked at Yasha with a questioning smile. He furrowed his brow, took hold of his nose, held it a while in his large hand with the yellow hair. Mrs. Miltz opened her eyes wide as if incredulous that someone was able to outsmart Herman. Zeftel winked at Yasha, showed him the tip of her tongue. She blew him a kiss.

"Hey there, Rytza, you wouldn't have a carrot, would you?" Herman asked.

"Why a carrot, why not a radish?" she replied, sarcastically.

It was already eleven o'clock but still the men continued to show each other card tricks. Some of the stunts required saucers, cups, boxes, pieces of cardboard, as well as a ring, a watch, a flower pot. The women continued to fetch the necessary equipment. Herman grew overheated. He began to mop the sweat from his brow.

"Together, we could accomplish something."

"What, for instance?"

"We could take on the world."

Rytza brought vodka and the men clinked glasses, said "Prosit!" in cosmopolitan fashion. For Zeftel and herself, Rytza poured sweet brandy. They ate egg-cookies, black bread, swiss cheese. Herman began to speak with a clannish familiarity.

"I see your Zeftel at the agent's. She's pretty and sharp, too, but how was I to know what was what? She says her husband left her; I thought, 'Let him go in peace. I'll help her out somehow.' It was only later she told me about you. She mentioned a magician, but not all magicians are the same. Those who drag around courtyards with street-organs call themselves magicians, too. But you, Panie Yasha, you're an artist! First-class! Tip-top! But I've got a few years on you and I can tell you there isn't much you can do for yourself around here. With your skill you belong in Berlin, in Paris, even New York. London isn't a bad town, either. The Englishman loves to be fooled and he pays for the privilege, as well. Back home in South America, you'd be a God. Zeftel says that you can put people to sleep—how is it called—magnetism? What is this thing, anyway? I've heard of it, I've heard of it."

"Hypnotism."

"You know the thing?"

"Some."

"I've seen it somewhere. The subject really falls asleep?"

"Like a log."

"This means you could put Rothschild to sleep and snatch his money?"

"I'm a magician, not a criminal!"

"Yes, of course, but still . . . How do you do this?"

"I force my will upon the other."

"But how? It's a big world, all right. Always something new coming up. I once had a woman, she did everything I wanted her to. If I wanted her to be sick, she got sick. And if I wanted her to get well, she got well. When I wanted her to die, she closed her eyes."

"Ah, that's too much!" Yasha said, after a while.

"It's the God-damned truth."

"Herman, now you're talking foolishness!" Rytza said.

"She was in my way. Love is fine, but too much love is no good. She wound herself around me like a snake until I couldn't breathe. She was a couple of years older than me and trembled for fear I'd leave her. Once I was walking along the street and she was right on my tail, as usual. I felt smothered and I said, 'I can't go on like this.' 'What do you want?' she asked me, 'That I should die?' 'Just leave me alone,' I said. 'That I can't do,' she said, 'but if you want me to, I'll drop dead.' At the beginning I was afraid, but she made me so wild I felt it was either my life or hers. I began to think that . . ."

"I don't want to hear another word! I don't want to hear another word!" Rytza clapped her hands over her ears.

It was quiet for a time. They could hear the wick in the lamp sucking up the naphtha. Yasha consulted his watch. "Folks, I'm a cooked goose!"

"How late is it?"

"It's already daybreak in the town of Pinchev. Well, I've got to run along. Zeftel, stay for a few days. I'll pay for everything," Yasha said. "These people won't hurt you."

"Sure, sure, we'll settle everything," Rytza said.

"Where are you running to? Where are you running to?" Herman demanded. "Here when it grows a little late, everyone gets panicky. What is there to be afraid of? Back home in Buenos Aires we stay up all night. Winter and summer. When we go to the theater, the play ends around one o'clock. We don't go home afterwards but to a café or restaurant and first we eat a beefsteak and then the real drinking begins. By the time you get home, it's already daytime."

"When do you sleep?" Zeftel asked.

"Who needs sleep? Two hours out of the twenty-four is more than enough."

Yasha rose to take his leave. He thanked them for their hospitality. Rytza looked at him, questioningly, deliberately. It even seemed as if she were giving him a signal. She laid her finger to her lips for an instant.

"Don't be a stranger," she said, "we don't eat people here."

"When will you come?" Herman asked. "I've got something to discuss with you. The two of us have to make some sort of an agreement."

"I'll drop by.'"

"Don't forget."

Rytza picked up the lamp to light Yasha's passage down the stairs. Zeftel walked at his side. She took his arm. A childish exhilaration came over Yasha. He enjoyed speaking Yiddish, showing tricks in his shirt-sleeves. It was like Piask here, but even more exhilarating. Obviously Herman was a white slaver and Rytza his confederate. It defied comprehension but in the few hours that they had known each other, Herman had acted as if he were devoted to Yasha. Rytza, apparently, also looked on him with favor. Who could tell what amorous delights such a woman could serve a man, what bizarre words she might utter in the throes of passion? For a moment, the light from the naphtha lamp lit up the courtyard with its piles of logs and lumber. Then upstairs the door closed and it was dark once more. Zeftel snuggled up to Yasha.

"Could I go some place with you?"

"Where?—Not today."

"Yashale, I love you!"

"Just wait and leave everything to me. Whatever I tell you to do, do it."

"I want to go with you."

"You will be with me. I'll take you along when I go abroad. I'll repay everyone who has been good to me. But be prepared for anything and don't ask any questions. If I tell you to stand on your head, then stand on your head. Do you understand?"

"Yes."

"You'll do as I say?"

"Yes, everything."

"Go back upstairs."

"Where are you off to?"

"There's one more bit of nonsense I have to take care of today."

6

Nizka Street was deserted. There was no chance of hiring a droshky here. He walked on and his tread felt uncommonly light. The street was dark. Over the wooden houses with the spavined roofs hung a suburban sky, thickly seeded with stars. Yasha gazed upward. What, for instance, do they think of someone like me up there? He walked the length of Nizka Street, came out on Dzika Avenue. He had told Zeftel that there was one other item of nonsense on his agenda. But what sort was it? He had slept the whole day and he was now as fresh and alert as if it were morning. A strange desire to visit Emilia came over him. It was complete madness. She was doubtless already asleep by now. Besides, the court-yard gate would be locked. But his climbing out of her window the night before had brought home to him again that doors and gates meant nothing to him. There was a balcony in her apartment. He could scale it in a minute. Emilia complained that she was a poor sleeper. She would hear him. Moreover, he would will her into expecting him and she would open the French doors (if they weren't open anyway). He had a feeling that this day she would not offer further resistance. It was as if he had miraculously put on seven league boots, for here he was on Dzika Avenue; a few minutes more and he was walking down Rimarska Street. He glanced at the bank. The pillars seemed to guard the building like giant watchmen. The gate was shut, all the windows dark. Somewhere nearby were the basement vaults where treasures were stored. But where? The edifice was as huge as a city. To be properly done, the job would re-quire a long winter's night. Then Yasha recalled what Yadwiga, Emilia's servant, had told him about an elderly landowner, one Kazimierz Zaruski, who had sold his estate years before and now kept his money in an iron safe in his apartment. He lived on Marshalkowska Boule-vard, near Prozna Street, alone except for a deaf serv-ant girl who was a friend of Yadwiga. When Yadwiga had told him this story, Yasha had not even bothered to write down the man's address. He had not entertained such notions and certainly none involving a household which Yadwiga visited. But now it all came back to him. I must do something tonight, he said to himself. Tonight I have the power.

From Nizka to Krolevska Street was quite a distance, but Yasha covered the several *versts* in twenty minutes. Warsaw slept, with only here and there a night watchman testing a lock or pounding his staff on the sidewalk as if to reassure himself that no one was tunneling in the ground underneath. They are forever watching but nothing can be kept safe, Yasha said to himself. Neither their women nor their possessions. Who could tell? Maybe at times even Esther was unfaithful to him? His thoughts wandered idly. What if he should sneak into Emilia's bedroom and find her with a lover? Such things did happen. He stood now beneath her window and looked up. The thought of climbing to the balcony, which only a few minutes before he had regarded as not only feasible but as eminently right, seemed, now that he was there, pure absurdity. There was always the possibility that she would awake and, mistaking him for a prowler, raise an outcry. Yadwiga might overhear him or, possibly, Halina. Emilia would certainly never forgive him. The Age of Knighthood was long since past. This was the prosaic nineteenth century. Mentally, Yasha had commanded Emilia to awake and come to the window, but apparently he had not as yet mastered this facet of hypnotism. Even if it should prove effective, the process would be a slow one.

He started down Marshalkowska Boulevard towards Prozna Street. As long as it is inevitable, he said to himself, why not tonight? Evidently, it had been foreordained. How was it called?—predestination? If there was a reason for everything, as the philosophers claimed, and man was merely a machine, then it was as if everything had been written beforehand. He came to Prozna Street. There was only one occupied house on the block; across the street a building was in the process of construction. Piles of bricks lay there, mounds of sand and lime. The inhabited house consisted of a dry-goods store with two apartments, both with balconies, above it. The landowner's apartment obviously faced the front, but which of the two was it? Yasha suddenly knew that it was the one on the right. The windows in the apartment on the left were partially covered by drapes, partially by curtains; the ones on the right had shabby drapes, the kind that would hang in a miser's house. Well, it's now or never! something within Yasha urged. As long as you are here, go on. He can't take his money to the grave with him, anyway. The night won't last forever, the voice cautioned anew. Its intonations were almost that of a preacher.

Climbing the balcony was easy. A bar extended from the door of the dry-goods store and the balcony rested on the heads of three statues. The whole house was studded with figures and decorations. Yasha placed one foot on the bar, took hold of the knee of a goddess, and soon was hanging on the edge of the balcony. He swung his body upwards. It seemed to have grown weightless. He stood for an instant on the balcony and laughed. The impossible was really so possible. Opening the French doors proved more difficult; they were locked from the inside. But he tugged violently on the door and lifted the chain with the skeleton key which he always carried on his person. Better one loud sound, he theorized, than a series of fumbling noises. For a moment he paused to see if there was any outcry. Then he stepped inside and breathed the musty air of the house; here, it was clear, the windows were seldom opened.

Yes, this must be it, he exulted. You can smell the rot and mildew! It was not completely dark inside because of the light of the street lamp. He felt no fear. Yet his heart pounded like a trip hammer. He stood rooted for a moment, astonished at how swiftly thought had become deed. Strange, that the very safe that Yadwiga had described should be right next to him. It stood on end, long and black as a coffin. The powers that control man's destiny had led him directly to Zaruski's hoard.

7

I mustn't fail, he urged himself. Since I've taken the plunge, I must see it through. He cocked his ears and listened. Somewhere in the adjoining rooms Kazimierz Zaruski and his deaf servant slept. He heard no sound. What would I do if they were to awaken? he asked himself, but he could not supply the answer. He put his hand on the safe and felt the cool metal. Quickly he located the keyhole. He traced it with his forefinger to determine it's type and contour. Then, he reached into his pocket for his skeleton key which he had just had in his hand, but it wasn't there. Undoubtedly he'd tucked it away in another pocket. He began to search his pockets, but the key had vanished. Where could I have put it? The bad luck is starting already! He rummaged some more. Did I drop it on the floor? If so, it had not made a sound. The key had to be somewhere near at hand, but it hid itself from him. Again he thrust his hand into his pockets—again and again. The important thing is not to panic! he cautioned himself. Just imagine that you're doing a performance. Now he searched again, calmly and deliberately, but the skeleton key had disappeared. Demons? he whispered half in jest, half in earnest. He began to feel warm. He was about to break out into a sweat, but he kept back the perspiration and his body remained overheated. Well, I'll just have to find something else. He knelt and unlaced one of his shoes. The shoelaces had metal tips and once Yasha had picked a lock with just such a tip. But no, it's not firm enough to open an iron safe, he decided in the midst of removing the lace. There was probably a corkscrew or a poker in the kitchen, but to grope his way to the kitchen now was to court disaster. No, I must locate the skeleton key! He stooped and only then realized that the floor was covered by a rug. He ran his palm along the rug. Was it possible that the spirits were playing with him? Did such things as spirits really exist? Suddenly, the thought came to him: a safe must have a key, and undoubtedly the old man kept it under his pillow when he slept. Yasha knew what a risky business it would be to try to get the key out from under the old landowner's pillow. He might wake. And what assurance did Yasha have that the key was really there? There were many other possible hiding places in the apartment. But now Yasha was sure that the key lay under Zaruski's pillow. He even visualized the key: the flat head, the teeth underneath. Am I dreaming? Am I going mad? he speculated. But the unseen forces which for years had held sway over him ordered him to go into the bedroom. "It will be easier this way," they prompted. "There is the door."

Yasha got up on his toes. If only the door doesn't squeak, he prayed. It stood half-open. He walked through and found himself in the bedroom. It was darker here than in the other room, for he could not determine exactly where the window was located, could only conjecture, and then his eyes began to adjust to the darkness. From the murky whirls there began to evolve the contour of a bed, bedding, a head upon a pillow—a naked head with sockets instead of eyes, like that of a skeleton. Yasha froze. Was the old man breathing? He could not hear his breath. Was he awake? Had he just at that moment expired? Was he, possibly, feigning death? Perhaps he lay there ready to rise and attack him? Old men were often extremely powerful. And then the old man suddenly snored. Yasha came closer to the bed. He heard the clang of metal and knew what it was—the skeleton key. Probably it had caught on a button. Now it had fallen to the floor. Had it wakened the old man?

Yasha stood there a moment, prepared to bolt at the first sound. I couldn't kill him! I am no murderer. But the old man had once more fallen into a deep sleep. Yasha leaned over to pick up the skeleton key—he must leave no clues behind him; but again it had disappeared. That bit of wire had engaged him in a game of hide-and-seek. Well, I see it's one of those nights, already. The evil powers have singled me out. Something within him begged him to flee since his luck had deserted him, but, instead, he moved closer to the bed. Try to get hold of his key, he said to himself obstinately.

He ran his hand over the pillow, touched the old man's face unintentionally. He pulled back his hand as if it had been burned. The miser uttered a sigh as though he had only been shamming sleep. Yasha paused. He was prepared for attack, ready to grasp Zaruski by the throat and throttle him. But no, the man was asleep, a thin piping sound coming from his nostrils. Apparently he was dreaming. Now Yasha could see better. He slipped his hand beneath the pillow, convinced that he would touch the key—but there was no key. He raised the old man's head a trifle along with the pillow on which it rested but still he could find no key. This time his instinct had failed him. There was only one course left him. Escape! something within him counseled. Everything has gone wrong! Yet, once more he began to search for the skeleton key on the floor, even though he knew he was inviting disaster. Wagered my last gulden and threw away the ace, he thought, recalling the old Yiddish proverb. The saying had come to him in much the same way as the Scriptures and lessons from cheder popped into his mind in the middle of the night. Sweat suddenly drenched him from head to toe. It was as if a basin of water had been emptied over him. He felt hot and damp as in a steam bath. But he kept looking for the skeleton key. Maybe you should just choke the old bastard! some presence, partly within and partly outside him, suggested, a portion of him which did not have the final say, but was in the habit of offering bad advice and perpetrating cruel jokes upon him just when he most needed all his faculties.

Well, it's a lost cause. I'm going now, he muttered. He rose to his feet and backed out through the half-opened door. How light it was here in comparison to the bedroom! He could see every object. Even the paintings on the walls—the frames, not the canvases. A chest of drawers seemed to rise up from the floor and on it he spied some scissors. Just what I need! He picked up the scissors and went to the safe. The keyhole was now delineated by the light from the street. He probed inside the keyhole with the tip of the scissors, calm once again, listening to the inner workings of the lock. What sort of lock was it? Not English. The blade of the scissors was too wide at the top and he could not probe very deeply. It was evident that the lock was not complicated but there was something in it that Yasha could not make out. It was like a child's puzzle, which if not solved at once eludes one for hours. He needed an instrument that could reach to the lock's vitals.

Suddenly a new idea came to him. He took his notebook from his bosom pocket, tore several pages out of it and twisted them until they formed a stiff cone. Such a tool would not do to pick a lock yet it could penetrate to its bowels. But the cone lacked the solidity and the spring of metal. He found he could not determine anything from it. Well, I'll just have to come back another time. I don't dare wait until daybreak! He glanced at the door leading to the balcony. Failure! A fiasco! For the first time in his life! It had been a terrible night. He was overcome by fear. He knew, deep inside of him, that the misfortune would not be confined to this night alone. That enemy which for years had lurked in ambush within him, whom Yasha had had, each time, to repel with force and cunning, with charms and such incantations as each individual must learn for himself, had now gained the upper hand. Yasha felt its presence—a dybbuk, a satan, an implacable adversary who would disconcert him while he was juggling, push him from the tightrope, make him impotent. Trembling he opened the balcony door. His perspiring body shivered. It was as if winter had suddenly arrived.

8

He was just about to climb down when he heard the sound of voices below. Someone was talking in Russian. It was undoubtedly a passing patrol. Quickly he drew back his head. Perhaps he'd been seen on his way up? The patrol might be waiting for him. He stood there in the darkness and listened. If they know about me, I am trapped. —But no, no one could have seen him. He had looked in all directions before making the ascent. The patrol had just happened along. He still could not forgive himself for having failed so miserably. Perhaps I should look for my skeleton key again? he thought. He walked back into the bedroom, a gambler who has lost everything, and is no longer afraid to take a chance. At the open door he stopped, horrified. The old man lay in bed, his face completely covered with blood. There was blood on the pillow case, the bedspread, the old man's nightshirt. God Almighty, what's happened? Has he been killed? Have I, thought Yasha, had the bad luck to rob a house where there has been a murder?—But I just now heard him breathe! Is there a killer here? Yasha stood numb with fear. And then he laughed. It wasn't blood at all, merely the light of the rising sun. The window faced the East.

Once more he began his search for the key, but there on the floor it remained night. The darkness enveloped everything. Yasha groped about aimlessly. A weariness came over him; he felt a weakness in his knees and his head ached. Though he was awake his mind began to weave dreams—fanciful threads which escaped capture, for no sooner did he reach out for them than they unraveled. Well, there's no chance of finding it now. The old man may wake any second. A notion that the miser was cunningly shamming sleep returned to him. He was about to rise when his fingers brushed against the skeleton key. Anyway no trace of him would remain now. Quietly he retreated to the front room, which daylight had also entered. The walls had become a paper-like gray. Ashy flecks hovered in the air. He approached the safe on shaky legs, fitted the skeleton key into the keyhole, and began to probe. But his will, strength, and ambition had been spent. His brain was heavy with sleep. He no longer had the ability to spring this antiquated lock. It was obviously a neighborhood job, put together by an ordinary locksmith. If I had some wax I could at least take an impression of this contraption. He stood there bereft of passion, not certain which was the more astonishing—his earlier greed or his present indifference. He fumbled a moment longer. He heard a snort, and realized that it had come from his own nose. The skeleton key had caught on something and he could turn it neither to one side nor the other. He became reconciled to abandoning it there, then with one try he freed it.

He stepped out onto the balcony. The patrol had disappeared. The street was deserted. Though the street lights were still lit the darkness above the rooftops was no longer that of night but more the gloom of an overcast sky, or the murkiness of twilight. The air was cool and moist. Birds had begun to twitter. Now is the moment, he said to himself with a sort of resolution and with a sense that the words possessed a double meaning. He began to descend but his feet lacked their usual sureness. He wished to support them upon the shoulders of a statue but they fell short of the goal. For a moment he hung from the edge of the balcony feeling that he was about to doze off—suspended in air. But then he wedged his foot in a depression in the wall.—Just don't jump, he warned himself, but, even as the thought came to him, he dropped and knew at once that he had landed too violently on his left foot.—That's all I need now, a week before the opening! He stood on the sidewalk testing the foot and only then did he feel the pain.

Just then he heard shouting. The voice sounded aged, rasping and alarmed. Was it the landowner? He looked up but the cries were coming from the street. He saw a watchman with a white beard running toward him, brandishing a stout cudgel. The man began to blow a whistle. He had apparently spied Yasha descending from the balcony. Yasha forgot about his injured foot; he ran swiftly and easily. The police would arrive at any second. He did not know himself in which direction he was fleeing. Judging from his speed one would have thought his foot was uninjured, but as he ran he felt a drawing in his left foot, a piercing pain below the ankle around the toes. He had either torn a ligament or broken a bone.

Where am I now?—He had sped down Prozna Street and had come into Grzybow Place. He heard no more shouting or whistling, but he still had to hide somewhere, for the police might approach from another direction. He hastened towards Gnoyne Street. Here the gutter was strewn with mud and manure. Moreover, it was dark, as if the sun had not yet risen in this neighborhood. The light of the street lamps glared and Yasha stumbled against the shaft of an unhitched wagon. This part of the city was a hodge-podge of loading yards, markets, and bakeries. The smell of smoke, oil, grease, was everywhere. He was nearly run down by a meat-wagon. So close did the horses come to him that he smelled the fetor of their muzzles. The teamster cursed him. A janitor waved his broom at him with righteous indignation. Yasha stepped up onto the sidewalk and saw the courtyard of a synagogue. The gate stood open. An elderly Jew entered, prayer-shawl bag under his arm. Yasha darted inside.—Here they will not search!

He walked past a synagogue which was, to all appearances, shut (no light could be seen through the arched windows), and came to a study-house. In the yard stood crates filled with loose pages torn from holy books. The smell of urine was overpowering. Yasha opened the door at what appeared to be both study and poorhouse. The light of a single memorial candle flickering near the cantor's lectern showed him rows of men lying on benches, some barefoot, some wearing battered old shoes, some covered with rags, others half-naked. The air stank of tallow, dust, and wax.—No, they will not search here, he repeated to himself. He moved to an empty bench and sat down. He sat there in a daze and rested his damaged foot. Bits of manure clung to his shoes and trousers. He would have shaken them loose but in this holy place that would have been a desecration. For a moment he listened to the snoring of the beggars, incredulous at what had happened. His gaze moved toward the door and he listened for the footsteps of the police coming to arrest him. It seemed to him that he heard hoofbeats, an approaching trooper, but all the while he knew it was merely his imagination. At last there came a rusty voice crying out, "Up! Up! Up with your lazy carcasses!" The beadle had arrived. The figures began to sit up, rise, stretch, yawn. A match was struck by the beadle and his red beard was momentarily illuminated. He walked over to a table and lit a naphtha lamp.

At that very moment it occurred to Yasha what sort of lock was on Zaruski's safe and how it could be opened.

9

One by one the derelicts shuffled outside. Slowly the worshipers began to assemble. In the early morning light the naphtha lamp seemed pallid. Inside the room it was neither dark nor light; a sort of pre-day twilight prevailed. Some of the worshipers had already begun to recite the introductory prayers, others simply paced back and forth. The nebulous figures reminded Yasha that corpses were said to pray during the night in synagogues. These shadows followed a fluctuating course. They droned with an unearthly chant. Who were they? Why did they rise so early? Yasha wondered. When did they sleep? He sat there like one who had had a severe blow on his head yet knew that his senses were addled. He was awake but something within him slept the deep sleep of midnight. He rested and examined his left foot. Pain coursed through it, stabbing thrusts and a drawing sensation which commenced at the big toe and traveled up past the ankle as far as the knee. Yasha reminded himself of Magda. What would he tell her when he came home? In the years that they were together, he had often been cruel to her, but he knew somehow that this time she would be hurt more than ever before. He could be sure that he could not give an opening performance if his foot were damaged, but he kept from thinking about that. He stared off somewhere in the direction of the cornice of the Holy Ark, recognizing the tablet with the Ten Commandments. He recalled that only last night (or was it still the same day?) he had told Herman he was a magician, not a thief. But soon afterwards, he had gone off to commit a burglary. He felt dull and confused, unable any longer to understand his own actions. The men put on their prayer shawls and their phylacteries, they affixed the thongs and cloaked their heads, and he watched them with astonishment as if he, Yasha, were a gentile who had never witnessed this before. The first quorum had already assembled to say the prayers. Young men in sidelocks, skullcaps, and sashes sat down at the tables to begin studying the Talmud. They bobbed their heads, gesticulated, grimaced. For a long while the congregation was silent. They were reciting the Eighteen Benedictions. Soon the cantor began to intone the high Eighteen Benedictions. Every one of his words sounded to Yasha strangely alien yet strangely familiar: "Blessed art Thou, Oh Lord our God and God of our fathers, God of Abraham, God of Jacob, and God of Isaac . . . Who bestowest lovingkindness and possessest all things. Thou sustainest the living with lovingkindness, quickenest the dead with great mercy, supportest the falling, healest the sick, loosest the bound, and keepest thy faith to them that sleep in the dust."

Yasha translated the Hebrew words and considered each one. Is it truly so? he questioned himself. Is God really that good? He was too weak to answer himself. For a while he heard the cantor no longer. He was half dozing, although his eyes remained open. Presently he roused himself, hearing the cantor say, "And to Jerusalem, Thy City, return in mercy and dwell therein as Thou hast spoken . . ."

Well, they've been saying this for two thousand years already, Yasha thought, but Jerusalem is still a wilderness. They'll undoubtedly keep on saying it for another two thousand years, nay, ten thousand.

The red-bearded beadle approached. "If you would like to pray I'll fetch you a prayer shawl and phylacteries. It will cost you one kopeck."

Yasha wanted to refuse but he immediately thrust his hand into his pocket and took out a coin. The beadle offered change, but Yasha said, "Keep it."

"Thank you."

Yasha felt an urge to run. He had not worn phylacteries in—God knows how many—years. He had never put on a prayer shawl. But before he even made the attempt to rise, the beadle was back with the prayer shawl and phylacteries. He offered a prayer book, as well.

"Do you have to say Kaddish?"

"Kaddish?—No."

He did not have the strength to rise. It was as if he had been shorn of all his powers. He was also afraid. Perhaps the police were waiting for him outside? The prayer shawl bag lay next to him on the bench. Deliberately, Yasha took out the prayer shawl. He fingered the phylacteries within. It seemed to him that everyone was looking at him and waiting to see what he would do. In his stupor it appeared to him that everything depended on what he would now do with the prayer shawl and phylacteries. If he did not handle them properly, it would be proof that he was hiding from the police . . . He began to put on the prayer shawl. He looked for the spot where the embroidery was supposed to be, or a stripe which indicated the section meant to be worn over the head, but he could find neither embroidery nor stripe. He fumbled with the ritual fringes. One fringe even lashed him across the eye. He was filled with an adolescent shame and fear. They were laughing at him. The entire assemblage was giggling behind his back. He put on the prayer shawl as best he could but it slid off his shoulders. He took out the phylacteries and could not determine which one was for the head and which for the arm. And which should one put on first? He sought clarification in the prayer book, but the print blurred before his eyes. Fiery sparks began to sway before him. I just hope I don't faint, he cautioned himself. He felt nausea. He began to plead with God: Father in

Heaven, take pity on me! Everything else, but not this! He shook off the faintness. Taking out a handkerchief, he spat into it. The sparks continued to dip before his eyes, rising and falling in seesaw motion. Some were red, some green, some blue. There was a clanging in his ears as if bells were ringing. An old man walked over to him and said, "Here, let me help you. Remove the sleeve. From the left arm, not the right . . ."

Which is my left hand? Yasha asked himself. He began to pull the sleeve from his left arm and the prayer shawl again fell from his shoulders. A group gathered around him. If Emilia were here to witness this! he thought suddenly. He was now not Yasha the magician but some fumbling lout whom others assist and make the butt of their scorn. Well, it's come, God's punishment! he said to himself in his anxiety.

He was overcome with regret and humility. Only now did he realize what he had attempted and how Heaven had thwarted him. It came over him like a revelation. He permitted the men to do with him as they pleased, as one who's suffered a fracture and lets others bandage it for him. The old man wound the thongs around Yasha's arm. He recited the blessing and Yasha repeated it after him, like a little boy. Telling Yasha to lower his head, he fixed upon it the proper phylactery. He wound the thongs around Yasha's fingers in such fashion as to form the Hebrew letters *Shadai*.

"It must be a long time since you've prayed," a young man observed.

"Very long."

"Well, it is never too late."

And the same group of Jews, who but a moment before had watched him with a sort of adult derision, now looked upon him with curiosity, respect, and affection.

Yasha distinctly sensed the love which flowed from their persons to him. They are Jews, my brethren, he said to himself. They know that I am a sinner, yet they forgive me. Again he felt shame, not because he had been clumsy, but because he had betrayed this fraternity, befouled it, stood ready to cast it aside. What's the matter with me? After all, I'm descended from generations of God-fearing Jews. My great-grandfather was a martyr for the holy name. He remembered his father who, on his deathbed, had summoned Yasha to his side and said, "Promise me that you will remain a Jew."

And he had taken his, Yasha's, hand and held it until he entered his death throes.

How could I have forgotten this? How?

The circle of Jews had dispersed and Yasha stood alone in the prayer shawl and phylacteries, prayer book in hand. He felt his left foot draw, tear, but he continued his prayers, translating the Hebrew words to himself, "Blessed be He who spake and the world existed, blessed be He who was the maker of the world in the beginning. Blessed be He who speaketh and doeth. Blessed be He who decreeth and performeth. Blessed be He who hath mercy upon the earth and payeth a good reward to them that fear Him."

Oddly enough he now believed these words: God had created the world. He does have compassion for His creatures. He does reward those who fear Him. And as Yasha intoned these words, he reflected upon his own lot. For years he had shunned the synagogues. All of a sudden, in the course of days, he had twice strayed into houses of worship; the first time on the road when he had been caught in the storm, and now again for the second time. For years he had picked the most complex locks with ease, and now a simple lock which any common safe-cracker could have sprung in a minute had stumped him. Hundreds of times he had leaped from great heights without injury, and this time he had damaged his foot jumping from a low balcony. It was obvious that those in heaven did not intend to have him turn to crime, desert Esther, convert. Maybe even his deceased parents had interceded in his behalf. Again Yasha raised his gaze to the cornice of the Holy Ark. He had broken or contemplated breaking each of the Ten Commandments! How near he had come to strangling old Zaruski! He had even lusted for Halina, already woven a net in readiness to ensnare her. He had plumbed the very depths of iniquity. How had this come about? And when? He was by nature good-hearted. In the winter he scattered crumbs outside to feed the birds. He seldom passed a beggar without offering alms. He bore eternal hate against swindlers, bankrupts, charlatans. He had always prided himself on being honest and ethical.

He stood there with bent knees and was aghast at the extent of his degradations and, what was perhaps worse, his lack of insight. He had fretted and worried and ignored the very essence of the problem. He had reduced others to dirt and did not see—pretended not to see—how he himself kept sinking deeper in the mud. Only a thread restrained him from the final plunge into the bottomless pit. But the forces which are compassionate towards man had conspired that he now stand in prayer shawl and phylacteries, prayer book in hand, amongst a group of honest Jews. He chanted "Hear O Israel" and cupped his eyes with his hand. He recited the Eighteen Benedictions, contemplating every word. The long-forgotten childhood devotion returned now, a faith that demanded no proof, an awe of God, a sense of remorse over one's transgressions. What had he learned from the worldly books? That the world had created itself. That the sun, the moon, the earth, the animals, man, had come out of mist. But where had the mist come from? And how could a mist create a man with lungs, with a heart, a stomach, brain? They ridiculed the faithful who attribute everything to God, yet they themselves attributed all sorts of wisdom and powers to an unseeing nature which was unaware of its own existence. From the phylacteries Yasha sensed a radiance that reached into his brain, unlocked compartments there, illuminated the dark places, unraveled the knots. All the prayers said the same: There was a God Who sees, Who hears, Who takes pity on man, Who contains His wrath, Who forgives sin, Who wants men to repent, Who punishes evil deeds, Who rewards good deeds in this world and—what was even more—in the other.

Yes, that there were other worlds, Yasha had always felt. He could almost see them.

I must be a Jew! he said to himself. A Jew like all the others!

7

When Yasha went outside again, Gnoyne Street was
filled with sunlight, with dray-wagons, horses, out-of-
town merchants and factors, vendors of both sexes,
hawking all sorts of wares. "Smoked herring!" they
cried, "Fresh bagels!" "Hot eggs!" "Chick peas with
sugar beans!" "Potato patties!" Through the gates rolled
wagons stocked with lumber, flour, crates, barrels,
goods covered by mats, sheets, and sacks. The shops
dealt in oil, vinegar, green soap, axle-grease. Yasha
stood at the synagogue gate and looked ahead of him.
The very Jews who a moment previously had worshiped with such fervor and had chanted, "Let the great
name be blessed for ever, Amen," had dispersed, each to
his own store, factory, or workshop. Some were em-

ployers, some employees, some masters, some handymen. It now seemed to Yasha that the street and the synagogue denied each other. If one were true, then the other was certainly false. He understood that this was the voice of evil having its say, but the piety, which had consumed him as he stood in the prayer shawl and phylacteries in the prayer-house, began to cool now and evaporate. He had decided to fast this day as if it were the Day of Atonement, but the hunger which gnawed at him had to be appeased. His foot ached. His temples throbbed. His earlier complaints against religion reasserted themselves. Why all the excitement? something within him demanded. What proof is there that a God exists Who hears your prayers? There are innumerable religions in the world, and each contradicts the other. It's true you weren't able to open Zaruski's safe and you hurt your foot into the bargain, but what does that prove? That you're unnerved, exhausted, light-headed . . . Yasha remembered that while praying he had made all sorts of resolutions and had sworn the most exacting vows, but in the few minutes he had been standing here, all their substance had vanished. Could he really live the way his father had? Could he actually forsake his magic, romantic attachments, his newspapers and books, his fashionable clothes? The vows he had made in the study-house now sounded excessive, like the phrases one whispers to a woman in the throes of passion. He raised his eyes toward the pallid sky. If You want me to serve you, Oh God, reveal Yourself, perform a miracle, let Your voice be heard, give me some sign, he said, under his breath. Just then Yasha saw a cripple approaching. He was a small man and his head, cocked to one side, appeared to be trying to tear itself loose from his neck. So also with his gnarled hands—they seemed about to crack from his wrists even while he was collecting alms. Apparently his legs had only one goal: to grow more twisted. His beard had the same contorted look and was in the act of tearing itself from his chin. Each finger was bent in a different direction, plucking, it seemed, an unseen fruit from an unseen tree. He moved in an unearthly jig, one foot in front of him, the other scraping and shuffling behind. A twisted tongue trailed from his twisted mouth, issuing between twisted teeth. Yasha took out a silver coin and sought to place it in the beggar's hand but found himself hampered by the odd contortions of the man. Another magician! he thought, and felt a revulsion, an urge to flee. He wished to throw the coin to the other as quickly as possible, but the cripple, apparently, had his own game—pushing closer, he sought to touch Yasha, like a leper determined to infect someone with his leprosy. Fiery sparks again flashed before Yasha's eyes, as if they were constantly present and only needed the opportunity to reveal themselves. He cast the coin at the beggar's feet. He wanted to run but his own feet began to tremble and twitch as if imitating the cripple's.

He spied a soup kitchen and walked inside. The floor was sprinkled with sawdust. Although it was still early, the patrons were already dining: chicken soup with noodles, fritters, stuffed derma, sweetbreads, carrot stew. The odor of food made Yasha nauseous. I mustn't eat this kind of food so early in the morning, he admonished himself. He looked back as if about to walk out but a stout woman blocked his path. "Don't run away, young man, no one is going to bite you here; our meat is freshly killed and strictly kosher."

What connection can there be between God and killing? Yasha wondered. The woman pulled up a chair and he sat down at a long table, which he shared with the other diners.

"A glass of vodka with an egg cookie?" she suggested. "Or chopped liver with white bread? Chicken soup with buckwheat?"

"Bring me whatever you please."

"Oh? You can be sure I won't poison you."

She fetched a bottle of vodka, a tumbler, a basket of egg cookies. Yasha picked up the bottle but his hand was trembling and he spilled some of the vodka on the tablecloth. Some of his fellow patrons began to shout, half in warning, half in jest. They were provincial Jews wearing patched gabardines and unbuttoned undergarments faded from the sun. One had a burst of black whiskers extending up to his eyes. Another's beard was red—like a rooster's wattles. A little further down the table sat a Jew wearing a fringed garment and a skullcap. He reminded Yasha of the teacher who had first taught him the Pentateuch. Maybe it is actually he? Yasha thought. No, he would most certainly be dead by now. Perhaps it is his son? Earlier he had felt happy being in the company of devout Jews but now he was ill at ease sitting among them. Does one say a benediction over the vodka? he wondered. He moved his lips. When he took a sip from the tumbler the bitterness cut into him; darkness swam before his eyes. His throat burned. He reached for an egg cookie but wasn't able to break off a piece. What's the matter with me? Am I sick? What is it? He felt hostile and ashamed. When the proprietress brought him liver with the white bread he knew that he should make his ablutions, but there were no facilities for washing here. He bit off a piece of the bread and the man in the fringed garment asked, "How about making your ablutions?"

"He has, already," the fellow with the black beard answered sarcastically.

Yasha sat silent, amazed at how his earlier affection had been transformed into vexation, pride, and a desire to be alone. He looked away from the others and they soon began talking about their own affairs. They discussed everything at once: commerce, Hasidism, saintly miracles.—So many miracles, yet so much poverty, sickness, epidemics, Yasha reflected. He ate the chicken soup with groats and chased away the flies. His foot continued to ache. He felt his stomach growing bloated.

What should I do now, he asked himself. See a doctor? And how could a doctor help? They have only one remedy—put on a cast. Iodine I can smear on myself. But what if it doesn't get better? You can hardly turn somersaults on the tightrope with such a foot. The more Yasha considered his situation, the graver it appeared. He was nearly penniless—injured, how could he earn his living! What could he tell Emilia? She must be frantic at his not showing up the day before. And what explanation would he make to Magda when he returned home? Where could he say he had spent the night? What was a man worth if his entire existence depended upon a foot—even his love? Now was the time to kill himself.

He paid his bill and left. Again he saw the cripple. The man was still spinning and twisting as if seeking to bore his head into an invisible wall. Doesn't he ever grow tired? Yasha thought. How can a merciful God permit a human being to suffer such torment? A wish to see Emilia rose in Yasha. He longed for her company, needed to talk to her. But he could not go to her as he was, dirty and unshaven, the cuffs of his trousers spotted with manure. He hailed a droshky and asked to be driven to Freta Street. He rested his head against the wall of the cab and tried to doze off. Let me imagine myself dead and riding to my own funeral, he thought. Through his shut eyelids he could see the daylight, pink here, cool and shaded there. He listened to the sounds coming from the streets and inhaled the acrid odors. He had to hold on with both hands to keep from falling. No, I must change. This is no life! he said to himself. I don't have a moment's peace of mind any more. I must give up magic and women. One God, one wife, like everyone else . . .

From time to time he opened his eyes slightly to see where he was. They were passing the square on which the bank stood, and the building which the day before had appeared so still and foreboding was crowded with soldiers and civilians. A wagon-load of money rolled in, escorted by armed guards sitting on the outside. When Yasha again peered through his lids he saw the new synagogue on Tlomacka Street, where the reformed Jews worshiped and the rabbis preached in Polish instead of Yiddish.

They are religious, too, Yasha reflected, but they wouldn't allow paupers to worship in there. The next time he looked he saw the old Polish arsenal the Russians had converted into a prison. Behind its bars sat Yasha's counterparts. He dismounted at Freta Street and climbed the stairs to his house. Now for the first time he felt the extent of his injury. He was forced to lean his weight on his uninjured foot and drag the other behind him. Each time that he lifted the foot he felt a sharp pain somewhere near his heel. He rapped on the door but Magda did not open it. He knocked louder. Was she as angry as that? Had she killed herself? He pounded with his fist and waited. He did not have his key with him and he placed his ear to the door; he heard the parrot scream-ing. Then he remembered the skeleton key. It would still be in his pocket but he felt a revulsion for this ob-ject which had so humiliated him. Nevertheless, he took it out and opened the door. No one was inside. The beds were made but it was impossible to tell whether they had been slept in the night before. Yasha went into the room where the animals were kept. His appearance excited them. Each seemed to be trying in its own language to say something to him. Every cage had food and water in it, so it was not that they were hungry or thirsty. The windows were open to let in the air and the sun. "Yasha! Yasha! Yasha!" the parrot shrieked, then snapped its crooked beak and looked askance with a sort of vain querulousness. It seemed to Yasha as if the bird were trying to say, "You're only hurting your-self, not me. I can always earn my few grains." The monkey leaped up and down, and the tiny face with the flattened nose and the wrinkled brown eyes was filled with the sorrow and anxiety of the man in the story book, who is a victim of a magic spell which has caused him to grow bestial. It seemed to Yasha that the monkey asked, "Haven't you learned yet that all is vanity?" The crow tried to speak but only a human-like cawing and a sort of mimicry came from its throat. Yasha fancied that the bird scolded, mocked, moralized.

He reminded himself of the mares. They were in a stall in the court. Anthony, the janitor, was tending to them but Yasha now longed to see them—Kara and Shiva—Dust and Ashes. He had wronged them, too. On a day like this they should have been grazing in a green pasture, not standing in a hot stall.

He went back to the bedroom and lay down on the

bed, fully dressed. He intended to remove his shoes and apply cold water to his foot, but he was too weary to do it. He closed his eyes and lay there as if in a trance.

2

Only when he awoke did he realize how deeply he had slept. He opened his eyes and did not know who he was, where he was, nor what had happened to him. Someone was pounding on the front door, and although Yasha heard the knocking, it did not occur to him to open the door. His foot hurt him badly, but he could not remember the reason for the pain. Everything within him seemed paralyzed but he knew that memory would soon return and he lay there, amazed at his rigidity. Again he heard the knocking and this time he understood that he must open the door. He recalled what had happened. Was this Magda? But she had a key! For a moment he lay there, his limbs numb. Then he summoned up strength enough to rise and walk to the door. He was barely able to move his left foot. Apparently the foot had abscessed for his shoe felt tight, the foot hot. He opened the door. Wolsky stood there in a light-colored suit, white shoes, and a straw hat. He appeared sallow, wrinkled, as if he had not slept. The black, semitic eyes gazed at Yasha with a sort of knowing mockery, as if aware of what Yasha had been up to the night before. Yasha promptly lost his patience.

"What's the matter? What are you laughing at?"

"I'm not laughing. I have a telegram from Ekaterinoslav."

And he took a telegram out of his pocket. Yasha noticed that Wolsky's fingers were tobacco-stained. He took the telegram and read it. It was an offer from an

Ekaterinoslav theater for twelve performances. They guaranteed a respectable fee. The director demanded immediate confirmation. Yasha and Wolsky walked into the other room. Yasha sought not to drag his foot.

"Where is Magda?"

"Out marketing."

"How come you're dressed?"

"What do you want me to be, naked?"

"You don't wear a suit and tie so early in the morning. And who tore your pants?"

Yasha seemed to have lost his power of speech. "Where are they ripped?"

"Right here. Besides you're all dirty. Were you in a fight or something?"

Yasha had not realized until now that his pants were torn at the knees and stained with lime as well. He hesitated a moment. "I was attacked by hoodlums."

"When? Where?"

"Last night, on Gensha Street."

"What were you doing on Gensha Street?"

"I went to visit someone."

"What hoodlums? How did they tear your pants?"

"They were trying to rob me."

"What time was that?"

"One in the morning."

"You promised me you'd go to bed early. Instead you stay up to all hours and get into street brawls. Kindly take a couple of steps."

Yasha bristled.

"You're neither my father nor my guardian."

"No. But you do have a name and a reputation to maintain. I've devoted myself to you as though I were your father. The moment you opened the door I could tell you were limping. Roll up your trouser leg, please, or, better still, take off your pants altogether. You'll gain nothing by deceiving me."

"Yes, I fought back."

"You were probably drunk."

"Sure, and I also killed a few people."

"Ha! Only a week before the opening. You've finally got a name. If you appear in Ekaterinoslav, all of Russia will be open to you. Instead, you roam around, God knows where, in the middle of the night. Lift your trousers higher. Your underwear, too."

Yasha did as he was bid. Beneath his left knee was a bruise, black and blue, with a large area of torn skin. There was blood on his underpants. Wolsky looked on with mute reproof.

"What did they do to you?"

"They kicked me."

"The pants are stained with lime. And what's that down there? Horse manure?"

Yasha kept silent.

"Why didn't you put something on it? Cold water at least?"

Yasha did not answer.

"Where's Magda? She never goes out at this time."

"Panie Wolsky, you're not a prosecutor nor am I, as yet, in the witness stand. Don't cross-examine me!"

"No, I'm not your father nor a prosecutor, but I *am* responsible for you. I don't wish to insult you but it's me in whom the confidence is placed, not you. When you came to me you were an ordinary magician, who performed in market-places for a few groschen. I pulled you out of the gutter. Now that we're on the brink of success, you go ahead and get drunk or the devil knows what. Last week already, you should have been rehearsing but you didn't even show up at the theater.

Posters are plastered all over Warsaw announcing that you are beyond any magician that has ever been, but you smash your leg and don't even call a doctor. You haven't taken your clothes off since yesterday. You probably jumped out of some window," Wolsky said with a change of tone.

A shudder ran down Yasha's back.

"Why a window?"

"Undoubtedly escaping from some married woman. The husband probably showed up unexpectedly. We know all about those matters. I'm an old hand at that game. Get undressed and go to bed. You're fooling no one but yourself. I'll call a doctor. It's all over the newspapers about you performing a somersault on the tightrope. It's the talk of the town. All of a sudden you do a thing like this. If you should fail now, everything is finished."

"It'll heal by the time I open."

"Maybe it will and maybe it won't. Get undressed. Since it was a jump, I'd like to examine the whole leg."

"What time is it?"

"Ten after eleven."

Yasha wanted to say something else but at that moment he heard a key turning in the lock of the door. It was Magda. She came in and Yasha's eyes opened wide. She was wearing her Sunday dress, last year's straw hat with the flowers and cherries, and high-button shoes. She resembled a country woman off to the city to go into service. Overnight she had grown thinner, swarthier, older. Sores and lesions covered her face. Seeing Wolsky, she was taken by surprise and began to retreat toward the door. Wolsky took off his hat. The hair on his scalp lay like a wrinkled wig. He nodded. His black eyes darted from Yasha to Magda with fatherly concern. His lower lip hung loose in bewilderment.

3

"Panna Magda," Wolsky resumed after a moment, in the tone of one who preaches morality but does so reluctantly. "We two made an agreement that you would look after him. He is a child. Artists are like little children and sometimes a lot worse. See what he has done to himself!"

"I beg you, Panie Wolsky, say no more!" Yasha interrupted.

Magda did not answer but looked silently at Yasha's bare foot and the wound.

"Where did you go so early in the morning?" Yasha asked. He quickly realized that these words gave away the fact that he hadn't spent the night at home, but it was too late to recall them. Magda started. Her green eyes grew light and malevolent as an angry cat's.

"I'll give you a full account later."

"What's going on between you two?" Wolsky asked, like an elderly kinsman. He did not wait for an answer but continued, "Well, I'll have to fetch a doctor. Apply cold compresses. Maybe you have some iodine in the house? If not, I'll bring some from the apothecary."

"Panie Wolsky, I don't want a doctor!" Yasha said sternly.

"Why not? You have six days until the opening. People have already bought tickets in advance. Half the theater is sold out."

"I'll be ready for the opening."

"That foot won't heal by itself that quickly. Why are you so afraid of a doctor?"

"There's somewhere I have to go today. I'll see the doctor later."

"Where do you have to go? You can't walk around with a foot like that."

"He has to run off to one of his whores!" Magda hissed. Her mouth trembled, her eyes looked off somewhere. It was the first time that Magda—the silent, the bashful—had said anything like that, and in front of a stranger. The words came out in rural accents and, although not loud, were shrill as a scream. Wolsky grimaced as if he had swallowed something.

"I have no wish to mix in your affairs. Nor even if I wished to, do I have the right. But, there is a time for everything. We've waited for years for this day. This is your chance: you'll become famous. Don't, as the saying goes, put aside your gun an hour before victory."

"I'm throwing away nothing!"

"I beg you. Let me get a doctor."

"No."

"Well, no is no. I've been an impresario nearly thirty years and I've seen how artists commit suicide. Scramble up the mountain for years but just when the summit is in view, fall and smash themselves. Why this should be, I don't know. Perhaps they have a taste for the gutter. What shall I tell Kuzarski? He asked about you. There's a conspiracy against you in the theater. And how shall I answer the director in Ekaterinoslav? I must reply to his telegram."

"I'll give you an answer tomorrow."

"When tomorrow? What will you know tomorrow you don't know now? And what's the point in you two wrangling? You've got to work together. You've got to rehearse just like every other year. If anything, this year more. Unless what you want is to please your enemies and fail with a vengeance."

"Everything will be all right."

"Well, as it is fated, so it will be. When shall I return?"

"Tomorrow."

"I'll be here tomorrow morning, but do something for your foot. Take a step—let's see. You're limping! You can't fool me. You either sprained or fractured something. Soak it in hot water. If I were in your shoes I wouldn't wait until tomorrow. The doctor might order you to put the foot in a cast. What will you do then? The rabble will storm the theater. You know what the clientele of a summer theater is. It's not the opera where the manager comes out before the curtain and announces to the honorable guests that the prima donna has a sore throat. Here they immediately start throwing rotten eggs and stones."

"I've told you, everything will be all right."

"Well, let's hope so. At times I regret not being in the herring business."

And Wolsky bowed to both Yasha and Magda. He mumbled something in the hall. Then he went out, slamming the door.

A Christian and he wails like a Jew, Yasha said to himself. He had an impulse to laugh and looked out of the corners of his eyes at Magda. She had not spent the night at home, he decided. She'd been wandering about. But where had she been? Was she capable of this sort of revenge? Jealousy and disgust mingled in him. He had an impulse to seize her by the hair and drag her along the floor. Where were you? Where? Where? Where? he wanted to say. But he restrained himself. He imagined that each second the rash on her face grew worse. He unclenched his fist, lowered his head, stared down at his naked leg. He looked angrily at Magda.

"Fetch me cold water from the pump."

"Get it yourself."

And she burst out crying. She fled from the room, slamming the door so violently that the windowpanes rattled.

I guess I'll lie down for another half-hour, Yasha said to himself.

He returned to the bedroom and stretched out on the bed. His leg had stiffened and he could barely extend it. He lay there looking out at the sky through the window. High above him a bird was in flight. It seemed as small as a berry. What would happen to such a creature should it injure its leg or wing? For it there would be only one way out—death. It was the same with man. Death was the broom which swept away all evil, all madness, all filth. He closed his eyes. His foot throbbed, pinched. He wanted to remove the shoe but the shoe-lace had become knotted. The swelling had grown! He felt the flesh on his toes becoming puffy and sponge-like. The foot might well become gangrenous. Perhaps it would have to be amputated. No! Rather death! Well, my seven years of good fortune are over! They are not to be trusted! he exclaimed, not knowing whether he meant women or gentiles, or a combination of both. Un-doubtedly, the devil dwells in Emilia also. His mind be-came vacant and he lay in that warm fatigue that pre-cedes sleep. He dreamed that it was Passover, after the Seder, and that his father was saying, "Isn't that funny? I've lost a groschen!" "Papa, what are you saying? It's Passover!" "Oh, the ceremonial wine has made me drunk."

The dream lasted only a few seconds. He awoke with

a start, and the door opened as Magda came in carrying a basin of water and a napkin to be used as a compress. She glared at him spitefully.

"Magda, I love you," he said.

"Scum! Whoremaster! Assassin!" She burst into tears again.

4

Yasha was well aware that what he contemplated was pure madness, but he had to go and see Emilia. He was like a subject who has been hypnotized and must fulfill his master's commands. Emilia was expecting him, and her expectation drew him like a magnet. Magda had gone off somewhere again. He knew that now was the moment to go. The following day might be too late. He rose resolving to ignore his foot; he needed a shave, a bath, a change of clothes. I must talk everything over with her, he said to himself; I can't leave her hanging in mid-air. When he went to shave he found his razor had vanished. Magda had a habit of hiding things. Each time she cleaned up, something else was missing. She was capable of concealing a tie in the stove, slippers under a pillow. Always the peasant! Yasha thought. He put on a fresh shirt but a cuff link fell from the sleeve and disappeared. Apparently it had rolled under the wardrobe, but he was unable to bend. He had other cuff links somewhere, but where? Magda even tucked money away in odd places where it would turn up months afterwards. Yasha stretched out on the floor and began to search under the wardrobe with his cane, but this effort produced only stabbing pains in his foot. Then his stomach began to ache also. The devils are starting already, he muttered to himself. Now there's nothing but bad luck.

Magda had returned and had removed her Sunday dress. He could see she had been shopping for she held a basket from which protruded the legs of a chicken.

"Where are you going? I was just about to prepare lunch."

"Prepare it for yourself."

"Running back to your Piask whore?"

"I'll go where I please."

"We're finished. I'm going home today. You dirty Jew!"

She seemed afraid of her own words; her mouth agape, she stood with her hand raised as if to avert a blow. Yasha blanched. "Well, that's the end!"

"Yes, the end. You bring out the devil in me!"

And she threw down her basket and intoned a peasant dirge as if she had been scourged. The chicken lay there, its bloody neck aloft, ringed by onions, beets, potatoes. Magda fled into the kitchen and then Yasha heard a rattling sound as if she were vomiting or strangling. He had risen to his feet, still gripping the cane he had used in his search for the cuff link. For some inexplicable reason he righted the chicken and covered its torn neck with a beet. He continued to search for the cuff link. He wanted to go into the kitchen to see what Magda was up to but he restrained himself. In a little while Emilia will undoubtedly call me the same name, he thought. Yes, everything is collapsing like a house of cards.

He dressed himself somehow. When he passed the corridor he heard through the closed door Magda scraping a pot with a whisk. He hobbled down the stairs, feeling pain with each step. He barely managed to reach the barber shop but there was no one on the premises. He called out, stamped his sound foot, pounded on the wall, but no one came. They just leave everything and go off! he grumbled to himself. That's Poland for you. And still they complain that the country is torn to pieces. Probably ran off to play cards, the bum! Well, I'll just have to go to her unshaven. Let her see the state I'm in. He stood waiting for a droshky, but none came. That's the kind of country this is, he mumbled; all they can do is rebel every few years and rattle the chains.

He managed to get to the Avenue Dluga, found a barber shop and walked in. The barber was busy cutting a customer's hair. "When a barrel is filled with cabbage, you can't stuff any more in," the barber was saying. "Cabbage isn't like flax; it can't be squeezed together. When the barrel's full, it's full. With dough, dear sir, it's even worse. I'm reminded of something that happened to a woman who wanted to bake a cake for her mother. She kneaded the dough, added the yeast, and all the other things. At the last minute she decided to bring the dough to her mother's house in Praga and bake it there, because the flue in her stove was blocked or the stove smoked or something like that. So she packed the dough in a basket, covered it with a cloth, and took the omnibus. It was warm in the omnibus and the dough began to rise. It crept out of the basket as if it were alive. She tried to stuff it back but dough is something that won't be pushed. When she squeezed from one side it billowed out the other. The cover flew off. The basket swelled, and bang! it burst. Anyway, I *think* it burst."

"Is dough that strong?" the man in the chair asked.

"Of course it is. A real commotion started in the omnibus. There were several smart alecks on board and. . . ."

"She must have put a lot of yeast in that dough."

"It wasn't so much the yeast as the heat. It was a hot summer day and. . . ."

Why do they go on like that? Besides, he's a liar; the basket would never have burst, Yasha thought. But my shoe will! My foot's abscessing. And why doesn't he acknowledge my presence? Maybe I'm one who sees but isn't seen!

"Is there a long wait?" he asked.

"Till I'm finished, sir," the barber said, mingling courtesy with derision. "I have just one pair of hands. I just can't cut hair with my feet and, if I could, what would I stand on? My head, perhaps? What do you think, Panie Miechislaw?"

"You're absolutely right," his customer replied. He was a short, big-headed man with a straight nape and blond, spiky hair which reminded Yasha of a pig's bristle. The man turned and looked at Yasha with contempt. His eyes were a watery blue, small and deeply set. Evidently the barber and his customer had formed an alliance.

Nevertheless he waited until the barber had finished with his customer and the tips of the man's mustache had been waxed. Suddenly the barber underwent a transformation and began to chat familiarly with Yasha.

"Lovely day, isn't it? Summer, real summer! I like the summer. What good is the winter? Frost and catarrh! Sometimes it is too hot in the summer and one sweats, but that's no tragedy. Yesterday I swam in the Vistula and someone drowned before my very eyes."

"In the bathhouse?"

"He wanted to show off and swam from the men's to the women's bathhouse. They wouldn't have let him in anyhow because the women bathe naked. So what was the sense of the whole thing? Is it worth while to give one's life for a joke? When they pulled him out he looked asleep. I couldn't believe he was dead. And for what purpose this sacrifice? Just to make an impression."

"Yes, people are mad."

5

I must decide everything today, Yasha said to himself in the droshky. Today is my Day of Reckoning. He closed his eyes, to devote himself exclusively to his thoughts. But he passed street after street without reaching a decision. Again, blindly, he heard the sounds of the city, inhaled its smells. Coachmen shouted, whips cracked, children caroused. From courtyards and bazaars warm breezes blew, rank with manure, fried onions, the sewage, and the odors of the slaughterhouse. Laborers were ripping up the wooden sidewalks, changing round cobblestones to square ones, installing gas street lights, digging ditches for sewers and telephone lines. The bowels of the city were being rearranged. Sometimes when Yasha opened his eyes it seemed to him that the droshky was about to sink into the sandy depths. The earth seemed about to collapse, toppling the buildings; all Warsaw appeared on the verge of suffering the fate of Sodom and Gomorrah. How could he decide anything now? The droshky rolled past the synagogue on Gnoyne Street. When was I here? he asked himself in confusion. Was it today? Yesterday? The two days blended into one. His praying there in prayer shawl and phylacteries, the piety which had possessed him, were alien now, dreamlike. What sort of power possessed me? My nerves must be completely shattered! The droshky pulled up to Emilia's house and Yasha handed the driver a gulden instead of the usual twenty-groschen fare. The coachman offered him change but Yasha waved it away. He's a pauper, he thought, let him keep the extra ten groschen. Every good deed would boost his standing with heaven.

Slowly he mounted the steps, his foot now causing him less discomfort. He rang the bell and Yadwiga answered the door. She smiled and said confidentially, "The mistress is expecting you, has been since yesterday."

"What's new around here?"

"Not a thing. Oh yes, there was something! Pan Yasha may remember my telling him about old Zaruski and his deaf servant-maid, the one who's my friend. Well, they had a robbery there yesterday."

Yasha's mouth became dry. "Did they steal the treasure?"

"No, the thief got panicky and ran away. Leaped from the balcony. The night watchman saw him. Don't ask what's going on over there! The old man raised a terrible fuss! It was just awful! He wanted to discharge my friend. The police came. My friend cried her heart out. Thirty years—thirty years in one household!"

She said all this with a sort of perverse pleasure. Her friend's misfortune gave Yadwiga some sort of inner satisfaction. Her eyes sparkled with a malice that Yasha had not seen in her before.

"Yes, there are no lack of thieves in Warsaw."

"Ah, there's that fortune to tempt them. Kindly go into the drawing room. I'll announce you to the Mistress!"

It seemed to Yasha that Yadwiga had grown younger. She did not walk now but almost skipped along. He went into the drawing room and seated himself on the sofa. They mustn't notice anything wrong with my foot.

If they do, I'll claim that I fell. Or perhaps it would be better for me to mention it right off. It would seem less suspicious that way. Yasha had expected Emilia to come running to him immediately, but she took longer than usual. She's repaying me for last night, he thought. At last he heard footsteps. Emilia opened the door and Yasha saw that she was once again dressed in a brightly colored gown, this one evidently new. He rose but did not go immediately to her.

"What a marvelous dress!"

"Do you like it?"

"It's splendid! Turn around, let me see it from the back!"

Emilia did as she was told and Yasha availed himself of the moment to limp closer to her.

"Yes, exquisite!"

She turned to face him.

"I was afraid it wouldn't please you. What happened to you yesterday? I didn't sleep at all last night because of you."

"What did you do, then, if you didn't sleep?"

"What can you do at such a time? I read, I walked about. Really, I was most concerned about you. I thought that you'd already . . ." Emilia broke off.

How could she have been reading when there was no light in her bedroom? Yasha thought. He wanted to confront her with this but restrained himself, aware that by such a confrontation he would give himself away. She studied him, her face expressing curiosity, resentment, devotion. Through some imperceptible power (or omen) he knew that she regretted having repulsed him the other night, and that she was now prepared to rectify her error. She wrinkled her brow as if attempting to fathom his thoughts. He studied her and it seemed to him that she had aged—not by days but by years, as sometimes happens to a person who has suffered a grave illness or a deep sorrow.

"Something bad happened yesterday," he said.

Her face blanched. "What?"

"While I was rehearsing, I fell and injured my foot."

"I sometimes wonder that you survive at all," she said reproachfully. "You undertake the superhuman. Even if you are blessed with talent, you don't have to squander it, especially at the wages you are paid. They don't appreciate you at all."

"Yes, I do give too much. But that's my nature."

"Well, it's both a curse and a blessing . . . Have you seen a doctor?"

"Not yet."

"What are you waiting for? You're opening in a few days!"

"Yes, I know that."

"Sit down. I knew there was something wrong. You were supposed to come and you didn't. I didn't know why, but I couldn't sleep. I woke at one o'clock and didn't shut my eyes again. I had this odd sensation that you were in danger . . ." she suddenly addressed him with the familiar *thou*. "I told myself that my fears were ridiculous. I didn't want to be superstitious but I couldn't rid myself of that feeling. When did it happen? At what time did you fall?"

"As a matter of fact, it was during the night."

"At one o'clock?"

"Around then."

"I knew it! Although I can't imagine how. I sat up in bed and for no reason at all began to pray for you. Halina woke up, too, and came in. There's something about that girl which defies explanation. There's a

strange sort of bond between us. When I can't sleep, she
can't either, although I am very careful not to make any
noise. What happened? Was it a jump?"

"Yes, I jumped."

"You must see a doctor immediately and if he says
not to perform you must listen to him. You can't trifle
with such things, especially in your case."

"The theater will go bankrupt."

"Let it. No one is immune to accidents. If only we
were already together, I would take care of you. You
don't look at all well. Did you get a haircut?"

"No."

"You look as if you'd had a haircut. I know you'll
think this ridiculous but for days I've had a premonition
of this. You mustn't worry, I foresaw no great tragedy,
but there was certainly something. I tried to keep my
spirits up. When I had no word from you this morning I felt simply desperate. I even thought of going to
your place. How can such things be explained?"

"You can't explain anything."

"May I see your foot?"

"Later, not now."

"All right, dearest. But there is something important I
must discuss with you."

"What is it? Tell me."

"We must make some definite plans. Perhaps what
I'm saying is in bad taste, but we are neither of us children any more. It's come to the point where I cannot endure this waiting any longer, this feeling of everything
being up in the air. The situation is making me ill. I'm
not an irresponsible person by nature. I must know exactly where I stand. Halina must resume her schooling;
she cannot afford to lose another semester. You make
thousands of promises but everything remains as before.

Now that you've revealed our intentions to Halina, she gives me no peace. She's a clever girl, but a child remains a child. I know I shouldn't be speaking like this to you when you're in pain, but I can't impress upon you too strongly just what I've been going through. In addition to everything else, I long for you terribly. The moment we say goodbye and I close the door, my torment begins. I feel strangely insecure as if I were on an icefloe which might crack at any moment and cast me into the water. I start to believe that I've grown vulgar and have lost all shame."

And Emilia ceased her flow of words. She stood there, her head bowed, trembling, her eyes cast down as if she were ashamed to her very core.

"Do you mean physically?" Yasha asked after some hesitation.

"Everything together."

"Well, we'll decide everything."

6

"You tell me each time that we'll decide. Is there so much that needs deciding? If we intend to go, I must give up my apartment and sell the furniture. I might get something for it, although it isn't worth much any more. But maybe we can send it on to Italy. Those are the practical things that we must do. Nothing will come from just talking. We should also apply for passports because the Russians make everything difficult. We should determine the exact week and day of our departure. There's also the matter of finances. I haven't discussed this with you previously because the subject is extremely distasteful to me. Whenever I have to speak of it the blood rushes to my face," (her face indeed reddened), "but we can accomplish nothing without it. We also spoke of your—well, you did promise to assume the Christian faith—I know that these things are mere formalities, one does not acquire faith by being sprinkled with water. But without it, we cannot marry. I'm saying all this to you on the assumption that your promises were given in good faith. If they were not, why continue the farce? We're no longer children."

And Emilia stopped talking.

"You know I meant every word I said."

"I know nothing. What do I know about you, anyway? There are times when I feel I don't even know myself. When I used to hear of this sort of thing I always blamed the other woman. You do have a wife, after all, although God knows you're not faithful to her and your whole conduct, generally, is that of a man who is footloose. I am sinning, too, but I am true to my church. From the Catholic point of view, when someone is converted to our faith he is reborn and all his prior relationships are nullified. I neither know your wife nor do I want to. Another thing, yours is a childless marriage. A marriage without children is like only half a marriage. I am not young any more, either, but I can still have a baby and I would like to bear your children. You'll laugh, but even Halina spoke of it. She once said, 'When you marry Uncle Yasha I should like a little brother.' A man with your talents must not die without leaving an heir. Mazur is a good Polish name."

Yasha was sitting on the sofa, Emilia opposite him in a chaise longue. He looked at her and she looked back at him. He realized suddenly that he could put things off no longer. The words that he had to say must be uttered this very instant. But he had not yet determined what to say or how to act.

"Emilia, there's something I must tell you," he began.

"Say it, I'm listening."

"Emilia, I have no money. My entire fortune consists of the house in Lublin, but I cannot take that from her."

Emilia considered this for a moment.

"Why didn't you say anything before this? Your manner implied that money was not the problem."

"I always felt that I could get it at the last minute. If the opening proved successful, there was always the possibility that I could perform abroad. There are always foreign theater owners here—"

"You'll pardon me, but our plan was something else altogether. How could you be sure you'd find employment in Italy? They might sign you for France or the United States. It would be strange if we were married and you had to be in one place and Halina and I in another. She must remain for a time in Southern Italy. A winter in England, for example, would kill her. Besides, you planned to take a year off and study European languages. If you travel about Europe without knowing the languages, they will treat you no better than they do here in Poland. You're forgetting everything that we decided. We planned to buy a house with a garden near Naples. That was our plan. I don't mean to reprove you in any way but if you wish to better your situation you must follow a precise plan. This business of living from day to day, extempore, as you theatrical people put it, has brought you nothing but trouble. You've admitted that yourself."

"Yes, it's true, but I must get my hands on some money. How much would all this cost? I mean, what's the very minimum?"

"We've gone over all that already. We would need at

least fifteen thousand rubles. Anything over would be that much better."

"I'll just have to get the money."

"How? As far as I know it doesn't rain rubles in Warsaw. It was my impression that you'd already accumulated the required capital."

"No, I have nothing."

"Well, that's that. You mustn't think my feelings towards you have changed because of this. But our plans obviously cannot remain the same. I've already notified some of the people close to me that I'm about to go abroad. Halina can't remain at home forever. A girl her age must go to school. Besides, you and I cannot be together here. It would be senseless for both of us. You have a family and who knows what else. As it is I'm losing sleep because of the sympathy I feel for your wife, but if I were to leave the country, she would seem remote. To steal a husband from a wife and take a chance that she might come crying to me would be too much!"

And she shook her head negatively, to stress her refusal. She shuddered at the same time.

"I'll get the money."

"How? Will you rob a bank?"

Halina entered.

"Ah, Uncle Yasha!"

Emilia looked up.

"How many times have I told you to knock before you come in. You're not a three-year-old."

"If I've interrupted anything, I'll go."

"You didn't interrupt a thing," Yasha said. "What a lovely dress you're wearing!"

"What's so nice about it? A dress I've outgrown. But it's white and I adore white. I should like our house in

Italy to be white. Why can't the roof be white too? Oh, it would be gorgeous—a house with a white roof!"

"Perhaps you'd like the chimney-sweep to be all in white, too?" Yasha teased.

"Why not? It's possible to make soot white. I read that when a new Pope is chosen, white smoke comes out of the chimney at the Vatican, and if the smoke is white, the soot can be white as well."

"Yes, everything will be arranged for you, but right now go back to your room. We are in the midst of discussing things!" Emilia said.

"What are you talking about? Don't frown so, Mother, I'm leaving right away. I'm terribly thirsty but that isn't important. Before I go there's only one thing that I want to say—you seem in a bad humor, Uncle Yasha. What's wrong?"

"I've lost a boatload of sour milk."

"What? What sort of comic expression is that?"

"It's a Yiddish saying!"

"I should like to know Yiddish. I would like to know all the languages: Chinese, Tataric, Turkish. It's said that animals have a language of their own, too. I once passed Grzybow Place and the Jews looked so funny with their long caftans and black beards. What's a Jew?"

"I've told you to get out of here!" Emilia's voice rose.

Halina turned to go just as there was a knock on the door. Yadwiga stood at the threshold.

"There's a man here. He wishes to speak with the Mistress."

"A man? Who is he? What does he want?"

"I don't know."

"Why didn't you ask his name?"

"He wouldn't say. He looks like he's from the Post Office or something."

"Well, another pest. One second. I'll go out to see him." And Emilia went out into the corridor.

"Who can that be?" Halina asked. "I took a book out of the school library and lost it. Actually, I didn't lose it at all, it fell into the sewer and I was too disgusted to pick it up. I was afraid to bring it home because if Mama saw me with such a filthy book she would scold me terribly. She is good, but very bad, too. Lately, she's been acting strangely. She doesn't sleep nights, and when she can't sleep, I can't sleep either. I get in bed with her and we lie there and talk like two lost souls. Occasionally she sits at a little table, puts her hands on it and waits for the table to predict her future. Oh, she is funny sometimes, but I love her madly. In the middle of the night she is so good. At times I wish it were always in the middle of the night and that you, Uncle Yasha, were together with us and we all passed the time together. Maybe you'd like to hypnotize me now? I feel a strong desire to be hypnotized."

"What do you need it for?"

"Oh, just because! Life is so dreary."

7

"Your mother doesn't want me to, and I won't do something she opposes."

"Just make it last until she returns."

"It doesn't happen that quickly, anyway you are hypnotized."

"What ever do you mean?"

"Ah, you are compelled to love me. You will always love me. You will never forget me."

"That's true. Never! I should like to talk nonsense.

May I talk nonsense? So long as Mama is out of the room?"

"Yes, go on."

"Why isn't everybody like you, Uncle Yasha? Everyone else is so pompous and full of self-importance. I love Mama, I love her terribly but there are times when I hate her. When she gets into a bad mood she takes it out on me. 'Don't go here! Don't stand there!' Once I broke a flower pot quite unintentionally, and she didn't speak to me the whole day. That night I dreamt that an omnibus—horses, conductor, passengers and all—was driving through our apartment. I was puzzled in my dream: Why would an omnibus ride through our apartment? Where were all the people bound? And how had the omnibus got through the doorway? But it just simply rode by and made stops, and I thought: When Mama comes home and sees this she will raise a terrible fuss! I had to laugh and I woke up laughing. I must laugh now too at that foolish dream. But is it my fault? I dream about you, too, Uncle Yasha, but since you are mean and won't hypnotize me, I shan't tell you about the dream."

"What do you dream about me?"

"I won't tell you. My dreams are all either comical or just plain crazy. You're liable to think I'm mad. It's just awful the thoughts that come to me. I want to drive them away, but I can't."

"What kind of thoughts?"

"I can't tell you that."

"You don't have to hide anything from me. I love you."

"Oh, you only say so. Actually, you are my enemy. Maybe you are even a devil who's assumed human form? Perhaps you have horns and a tail like the Baba Yaga?"

"Yes, I do have horns."

And Yasha put two fingers up to his head.

"Don't do that, it frightens me. I'm an awful coward. At night I'm simply terrified. I'm afraid of ghosts, evil spirits, all that sort of thing. A neighbor of ours had a six-year-old daughter, Janinka. A pretty child with blonde curls and blue eyes like a cherub. All of a sudden she caught scarlet fever and died. Mama didn't want me to find out, but I knew everything. I even saw through the window how they carried out her coffin—a tiny coffin decorated with flowers. Oh, death is horrible. I don't think about it during the day, but when it gets dark, I begin to think about it."

Emilia came in. She looked from Yasha to Halina and remarked, "Well, aren't *you* a fine pair?"

"Who was the stranger?" Yasha inquired, surprised at his audacity.

"If I told you, you would laugh—although it's no laughing matter. We have an acquaintance who lives close by, a wealthy old man named Zaruski, a usurer, a miser. He is actually not even an acquaintance but Yadwiga is friendly with his servant and because of that, he's begun to greet me. Last night someone broke into his house. The thief came by way of the balcony and a night watchman saw him descend. The watchman chased him but the man got away. He didn't manage to open the safe. It now seems he left a notebook with the addresses of other apartments he planned to rob and my address was included among them. A detective was just here to warn me. I told him plainly, 'There isn't much he can steal here.' Isn't that strange?"

Yasha's palate became dry.

"Why would he leave a list of addresses behind?"

"He apparently lost it."

"Well, you will have to be careful."

"How can anyone be careful? Warsaw has become a nest of thieves. Halina, go to your room!"

Halina rose, languorously. "All right, I'm going. What we talked about must remain a secret!" she said to Yasha.

"Yes, an eternal secret."

"Well, I'll be going. What other choice have I if I'm driven out. But you're not leaving yet, Uncle Yasha?"

"No, I'll stay awhile."

"Goodbye!"

"Goodbye!"

"Au revoir."

"Au revoir."

"Arrivederci!"

"Hurry up!" Emilia snapped.

"Well . . . I'm going," and Halina walked out.

"What secrets does she have with you?" Emilia asked, half in jest.

"Momentous secrets."

"There are times when I regret not having had a son instead of a daughter. A boy isn't home as much nor does he mix into his mother's affairs. I love her but sometimes she upsets me. You must keep in mind that she's a child, not a grownup."

"I speak to her as to a child."

"That's odd about that thief. Couldn't he find a richer household than mine? Where do people obtain their information? They evidently go through the gates and read the directories. But I'm afraid of thieves. A thief can easily be a murderer, too. The front door has a padlock, but the door leading to the balcony has only a chain."

"You're on the second floor. That's too high for prowlers."

"True. How did you know that Zaruski lived on the first floor?"

"Because I am the thief," Yasha said hoarsely, shocked himself at the words he uttered. His throat contracted. Darkness rose before his eyes, and again he saw the fiery sparks. It was as if a dybbuk had spoken within him. A tingle zigzagged down his spine. Once more he felt the nausea which precedes fainting.

Emilia paused a moment. "Well, it's a good idea. Since you can climb down from the windows, you should be able to climb up a balcony."

"I can, indeed."

"What's that? I didn't hear you."

"I said, 'I can, indeed.' "

"Well, why didn't you open the safe? Once you begin something, you ought to finish it."

"Sometimes you can't."

"Why are you speaking so softly? I can't make out what you are saying."

"I said, 'Sometimes you can't.' "

" 'If one can't, one shouldn't try,' according to the old proverb. Funny, just a short while ago I was thinking that thieves could break into his apartment. Everyone knows he keeps his money on the premises. Sooner or later, it *must* be stolen. That's the fate of all misers. Well, but the accumulation of wealth is in itself a passion."

"A sort of passion."

"What's the difference? In the absolute sense perhaps all passions are either totally foolish, or completely wise. What do any of us know?"

"No, we know nothing."

They were both quiet. And now at last she broke the silence.

"What's the matter with you? I must take a look at your foot!"

"Not now, not now."

"Why not now? How *did* you fall, tell me."

She doesn't believe me, she thinks I'm joking, Yasha thought. Well, everything's lost anyway. He looked at Emilia but he saw her as if through a mist. It was dark in the room; the windows faced to the north and were overhung by wine-colored drapes. A strange indifference came over him, the sort of indifference that comes when one is about to commit a crime or risk one's life. He knew that what he was about to say would destroy everything, but he did not care.

He heard himself saying, "I hurt my foot jumping from Zaruski's balcony."

Emilia raised her brows. "Really, this is hardly the time for jokes."

"It's the absolute truth."

8

In the silence that followed, he could hear the chirping of the birds on the other side of the window. Well, the worst is over, he said to himself. He understood his objective, now—to put a finish to the whole affair. He had taken upon himself too heavy a burden. He needed to cut himself loose from everything. He glanced towards the door as if prepared to flee without a parting word. He did not lower his eyes but looked squarely at Emilia,

not with pride but with the fear of one who cannot allow himself the luxury of fear. Emilia looked back at
him, not angrily, but with that sort of curiosity mixed
with scorn which one feels seeing the futility of all
one's endeavor. She looked as if she were restraining
herself from laughter.

"Really, I don't believe . . ."

"Yes, it's the truth. I was in front of your house last
night. I even wanted to call up to you."

"But instead you went there?"

"I didn't want to wake Halina and Yadwiga."

"I'm hoping that you are only teasing me. You know
I'm gullible. Easily taken in."

"No, I'm not teasing. I heard Yadwiga speak of him
and I thought this would be a solution to our problem.
But I panicked. I'm apparently not cut out for that sort
of thing."

"You've come to confess to me, is that it?"

"You asked me."

"What did I ask?—But it's all the same, all the same.
If this isn't one of your games, I can only pity you.
That is, both of us. If it is a joke, I have only contempt
for you."

"I didn't come here to play games."

"Who can tell what you would or wouldn't do? You
are, obviously, not a normal person."

"No."

"I just read of a woman who let herself be seduced by
a madman."

"You are the woman."

Emilia's eyes narrowed. "That is my lot. Stephan,
may he rest in peace, was likewise a psychopath. Of another type. Apparently I'm drawn to that kind of man."

"You mustn't blame yourself. You are the noblest woman I ever met."

"Whom have you met? You stem from offal and you are offal. Pardon my harsh words, but I am only stating a fact. The blame is mine alone. I was aware of everything, actually you concealed nothing, but in the Greek drama there is a sort of fate—no, it has another name—wherein a person sees everything that will befall him but must fulfill his destiny nevertheless. He sees the pit but falls into it anyhow."

"You are not yet in the pit."

"I cannot be deeper in the pit than I am. If you had one spark of manhood in you, you would have spared me this final disgrace. You could have gone and never come back. I wouldn't have sent an emissary after you. At least I would have had a memory."

"I'm sorry."

"Don't be sorry. You told me you were married. You even admitted that Magda was your mistress. You also told me that you are an atheist or however you put it. If I could accept all this, there's no reason for me to fear a thief. It's only amusing that you should prove such an inept thief." And Emilia emitted a sort of chuckle.

"I might still prove to be a good one."

"Thank you for the promise. I just don't know what to tell Halina." Emilia changed her tone. "I hope you realize you must go away and never return. And you must not write, either. As far as I'm concerned, you're dead. I, too, am dead. But the dead have their milieu, also."

"Yes, I'll go. Rest assured that I will never . . ." And Yasha made a motion as if to rise.

"Wait! I see that you can't even get up. What have

you done to yourself? Sprained your ankle? Fractured your foot?"

"I did something to it."

"Whatever it was, you won't perform any more this season. Possibly, you've crippled yourself for life. You must have some sort of covenant with God since he punished you directly on the spot."

"I'm just a bungler."

Emilia covered her face with her hands. She bent her head. She appeared to be considering something deeply. She even massaged her forehead with her fingertips. When she removed her hand, Yasha saw, to his amazement, a transformed face. In so few seconds, Emilia had changed. Pouches had appeared beneath her eyes. She resembled someone who had just awakened from a short, deep sleep. Even her hair was disarranged. He detected wrinkles in her forehead and white in her hair. As if this were a fairy tale, she had cast off some spell which had kept her eternally young. Her voice, too, had grown dull and listless. She looked at him with confusion.

"Why did you leave behind the list of addresses? And why my address of all things? Is it conceivable that . . ." and Emilia did not go on.

"I left behind no addresses."

"The detective didn't make up the story."

"I don't know. I swear before God I don't know."

"Don't swear to God. You most certainly did make a list and it fell out of your pocket. It's decent of you not to have excluded me." And she smiled wearily, the sort of smile one sometimes exhibits in the face of tragedy.

"Really, it's a mystery! I'm beginning to doubt my own reason."

"Yes, you are a sick person!"

At that moment what had happened all came back to him. He had ripped pages from his notebook and from them had fashioned a cone with which to probe the keyhole. He had apparently left the cone behind and the list had included Emilia's address. Who could tell what other addresses had been there? In that second he realized that leaving the pages had been tantamount to informing upon himself. Wolsky's address might easily have been among them, as well as addresses of impresarios, actors, theater owners, and firms from which he purchased equipment. It was not improbable that his own address was included, since he liked to amuse himself at times by writing his street and number and festooning it with hairs, appendages, tails, and flourishes. He felt no fear but something within him laughed. His very first crime and he had denounced himself. He belonged with those incompetents who steal nothing but leave enough clues to lead the police directly to them. The police and the courts dealt mercilessly with such fools. He remembered what Emilia had said about those who see the pit but nevertheless fall into it. He felt ashamed of his clumsiness. This means I dare not go home. They'll learn my address in Lublin as well. Yes, and this foot in the bargain . . .

"Well," he said, "I shan't trouble you any longer. It's all up with us." And he rose to go.

Emilia got up also.

"Where are you going? You haven't murdered anyone!"

"Forgive me if you can."

And Yasha began to limp towards the door. She began to move as if to block his path.

"Do go and see a doctor."

"Yes, thank you."

It seemed as if she wanted to say something else to him, but he quickly backed into the hallway, grabbed his hat and coat, and let himself out.

Emilia shouted something after him, but he slammed the door and, injured foot and all, began to race down the stairs.

8

Yasha remained standing for a while at the courtyard gate. Was a police agent waiting for him just outside? Suddenly, he remembered the skeleton key. No, it was not in the suit he had on. It was in the one he had worn the day before. But if his house had been searched, then the key had been discovered.—Well, it doesn't matter now. Let them lock me up! Tomorrow's newspapers will be full of me, anyhow. What will Esther say when she finds out? The Piask gang will be delighted; they will consider it a fine irony. And what about Herman? And Zeftel? And Magda—not to mention her brother! And how about Wolsky? The crowd at the Alhambra? Anyway, I'll be taken to the prison hospital. He could feel the swelling in his foot pressing on his shoe. And I've lost Emilia, as well, he said to himself. He walked through the gate but no policeman was waiting. Perhaps the man was lurking across the street? Yasha thought of entering the Saxony Gardens but he did not do so; Emilia, peering through her window, might see him. He walked in the direction of Graniczna Street, came out on Gnoyne Street again, and saw, in a watchmaker's window, that it was only ten minutes to four. God in heaven, how long this day was! It seemed like a year! He felt he must sit and he had the notion to enter the study-house again. He turned into the courtyard of the synagogue. What's happened to me, he marveled. Suddenly I've become a real synagogue Jew! In the synagogue the evening services were in progress. A Lithuanian Jew was intoning the Eighteen Benedictions. The worshipers were dressed in short coats and stiff hats. Yasha smiled. He was descended from Polish Hasidim. In Lublin there were scarcely any Lithuanian Jews but here in Warsaw there were many. They dressed differently, talked differently, prayed differently. Although it was a hot day, a chill which the sun could not dissipate came from the synagogue. He heard the cantor chant, "And to Jerusalem, Thy city, return in mercy and dwell therein as Thou hast spoken."

So? They wish to return to Jerusalem too? Yasha said to himself. From early childhood he had considered Lithuanian Jews half-Jews, an alien sect. He could barely understand their Yiddish. He saw that there were clean-shaven men among the congregation. What was the point in shaving the beard, then praying, he asked himself. Perhaps they use scissors—that would constitute a lesser sin. But as long as one believed in God and the Torah, why compromise? If there was a God and His Law was true, then He must be served night and day. How long did one survive in this rotten world? Yasha went to the study-house. It was filled with people. Men studied the Talmud. The sunlight filtered through the windows and cast oblique pillars of dust. Young men with lengthy sidelocks swayed over volumes of the Talmud, shouted, chanted, prodded one another, gesticulated. One grimaced as if his stomach ached, a second wagged his thumb, a third twirled the fringes of his sash. Their shirts were grimy, their collars loosened. Some had lost their teeth prematurely. One's beard grew in black tufts—a tuft here, a tuft there. The beard of another small fellow was as red as fire, his head shaven, and from his skull hung yellow sidelocks, long as braids. Yasha heard him cry: They sued him for wheat and he admitted barley.

Can God will it thus? Yasha asked himself. All this business about wheat and barley. This knowledge concerns only commerce. He reminded himself of the cry of the anti-semite: The Talmud only teaches the Jew to be a swindler.

This fellow probably has a little shop somewhere. If he doesn't have one now, he will someday. Yasha found an empty bench near the bookshelves. It felt good to sit down. He closed his eyes and listened to the sounds of the Torah. Shrill adolescent voices mingled with the hoarse, rattling accents of the old. The voices shouted, mumbled, chanted, enunciated single words. Yasha recalled what Wolsky had said to him once over a glass of vodka: that he, Wolsky, was no anti-semite, but that the Jew in Poland had created a bit of Bagdad in the midst of Europe. Even the Chinese and Arabs, according to Wolsky, were civilized in comparison to the Jew. On the other hand, the Jews who wore short cloaks and shaved their beards were either eager to Russianize Poland or were revolutionaries. Quite often they were both exploiting and stirring up the working classes at the same time. They were radicals, Freemasons, atheists, internationalists, seeking to seize, dominate, and befoul everything.

A silence descended upon Yasha. He could be considered one of these beardless Jews, but he found them more alien than the pious sort. From childhood on he had been surrounded by religious people. Even Esther kept a Jewish home with a kosher kitchen. Such a breed was perhaps too Asiatic, as the enlightened Jews claimed, but at least they had a faith and a spiritual homeland, a history, and a hope. In addition to their laws governing commerce, they had their Hasidic literature, and they studied their cabala and books of ethics. But what did the assimilated Jews have? Nothing of their own. In one place they spoke Polish, in another Russian, in still others, German and French. They sat around in the Café Lurs, or the Café Semodeni, or the Café Strassburger, drinking coffee, smoking cigarets, reading a variety of newspapers and magazines, and telling jokes which elicited the kind of laughter that Yasha always found unpleasant. They carried on their politics, forever planning revolutions and strikes, although the victims of these activities were always the poor Jews, their own brethren. As for their women, they gallivanted in diamonds and ostrich-plumes, arousing Christian envy.

It was odd but no sooner did Yasha find himself in a House of Prayer than he began taking stock of his soul. True, he had alienated himself from the pious but he had not gone over to the camp of the assimilated. He had lost everything: Emilia, his career, his health, his home. Emilia's words returned to him, "You must have some sort of a covenant with God since he punishes you so promptly." Yes, Heaven kept a sharp lookout over him.

Possibly it was because he had never stopped believing. But what did they want of him? Earlier that day he had known what was required—that he keep to the path of righteousness as had his father before him and his father's father before that. Now he was again a prey to doubts. Why did God need these capotes, these sidelocks, these skullcaps, these sashes? How many more generations would wrangle over the Talmud? How many more restrictions would the Jew put on himself? How much longer would they wait for the Messiah, they who had already waited two thousand years? God was one thing, these man-made dogmas another. But was one able to serve God without dogmas? How had he, Yasha, come to be in his present predicament? He most certainly would not have been involved in all these love affairs and other escapades if he had put on a fringed garment and had prayed thrice daily. A religion was like an army—to operate it required discipline. An abstract faith inevitably led to sin. The prayer house was like a barracks; there God's soldiers were mustered.

Yasha could remain there no longer. He felt hot and yet he was shivering. Obviously, he had a fever. He decided to go home. Let them arrest me, if they wish! he thought. He was reconciled to draining the cup to the last bitter dregs.

Before leaving the study-house he took down a book from the shelves at random; opening it to the middle he consulted it as his father had been in the practice of doing whenever he was uncertain of his proper course of action. The volume, he discovered, was the *Eternal Paths* by Rabbi Leib of Praga. On the right-hand page was a verse from Scripture: "He closeth his eyes not to see evil," along with the Talmudic interpretation, "Such a man is one who does not look at women while they stand at their washing." Laboriously Yasha translated the Hebrew words. He understood what they were getting at—there must be discipline. If a man did not look, he did not lust, and if he did not lust, he did not sin. But, if one broke the discipline and did look, one ended by violating the Seventh Commandment. He had opened the book and found a text concerning the very problem which was uppermost in his mind.

He put the book back; a few moments later he took it down again and kissed it. This book, at least, required something of him, Yasha. It marked out a course of action, albeit a difficult one. But mere worldly writing demanded nothing. For all such authors cared, he could kill, steal, fornicate, destroy himself and others. He had often met literary men in cafés and theaters; they busied themselves kissing women's hands, bestowing compliments upon all and sundry; were constantly ranting against publishers and critics.

He hailed a droshky and ordered the coachman to drive him to Freta Street. He knew that Magda would make a scene but he mentally rehearsed the words he would say to her: Magda dear, I am dead. Take everything I own—my gold watch and diamond ring, my few rubles—and go home. If you can, forgive me.

2

In the droshky Yasha felt a fear he had never previously experienced. He was afraid of something but did not know what it was. The weather was hot yet he felt cold. He trembled all over. His fingers had become white and shrunken, the tips shriveled like those of a mortally-ill person, or of a corpse. It was as if his heart were being crushed by a giant fist. What's wrong with me, he asked himself. Has my last hour come? Do I fear being arrested? Do I long for Emilia? He continued to tremble and was seized by a cramp; he could scarcely breathe. So desperate was his condition that he began to console himself. Well, not everything is lost yet. I can live without a leg. And perhaps I may find some solution. Even if I'm arrested, how long will they keep me in prison? After all, I only attempted burglary—I didn't do anything. He leaned against the back of the seat. He wanted to put up his coat collar but he was too embarrassed to do so on such a hot day. But he did put his fingers inside his coat to warm them. What is it? Can it be gangrene? he asked himself. He wanted to untie the lace on his shoe but when he bent over he almost fell from the seat. The driver evidently guessed that something was wrong with his passenger and kept turning around. The pedestrians were also looking at him, Yasha noticed. Some even stopped to stare. "What's wrong?" the coachman anxiously asked. "Shall I stop?"

"No, drive on."

"Shouldn't I take you to a druggist?"

"No, thank you."

The droshky stopped more often than it moved, impeded by draywagons loaded with lumber and sacks of flour and by huge moving vans. The dray horses stomped their thick legs on the cobblestones and the stones gave off sparks. At one spot they rode by, a horse had collapsed. For the third time that day Yasha passed the bank on Rimarska Street. This time he did not even glance at the building. He had given up his interest in banks and money. Now he felt not only dread, but disgust at himself. So strong was the sensation that it produced nausea. Maybe something's happened to Esther, he thought suddenly. He remembered a dream he had

had, but just as the dream began to take shape, it slipped from him without leaving a trace. What could it have been? A beast? A verse from the Scriptures? A corpse? There were times when he was tormented nightly by dreams. He dreamed of funerals, monsters, witches, lepers. He would awaken drenched with sweat. But these weeks he had dreamed little. He would fall asleep, exhausted. More than once he had awakened in the same position in which he had fallen asleep. Yet he had known that the night had not been dreamless. Asleep, he led another life, a separate existence. From time to time he would recollect some dream of flying or some such stunt contrary to nature, something childishly preposterous, based on a child's misunderstandings or perhaps even on some verbal or grammatical error. So fantastically absurd would the dream have been that the brain, when not asleep, simply could not sustain it. He would remember and forget it at the very same instant.

As soon as he got out of the droshky, he became calm. Slowly, he mounted the stairs, supporting himself on the banister. He had neither his house key nor his skeleton key with him. If Magda was not at home, he would be forced to wait in the hall. However, the janitor, Anthony, had a key. Before knocking, Yasha listened at the door. There was no sound. He began to knock but no sooner had he touched the knob than the door swung open. When he walked into the front room he beheld a horrible sight. Magda was hanging from the ceiling, an overturned chair beneath her. He knew immediately that she was dead. Instead of crying out or hurrying to cut her down, he just stood there and gaped. She had only a petticoat on; her feet were naked and had turned blue. He could not see her face, only her neck with the bun of hair. To him she looked like an oversized doll. He wanted to move, to go and cut her down but he continued to stand there as though helpless. Where was there a knife? He must summon help, he knew, but he felt ashamed to face the neighbors. At last he threw open the door and cried out, "Help!"

His cry had not been very loud and no one responded. He sought to increase the volume but could not. A childish urge to flee almost overcame him, but instead he opened the door of a neighboring apartment and called, "You must help me. Something terrible has happened!"

The apartment was full of barefoot, half-naked children. Near the kitchen stood a stout flaxen-haired gentile woman who turned her sweat-stained face to him. She had been in the act of peeling an onion. Seeing him, she asked, "What's the matter?"

"Come! I need help! Magda. . . ." And he could not speak further.

The woman followed him into his apartment and immediately began to moan. She gripped his shoulders. "Cut her down! Cut her down!" she commanded.

He wanted to do as she bid but the woman clung to him, shrieking into his ear, still holding the paring knife and the onion. Yasha's ear was almost sliced off. Soon, other occupants of the house rushed in. Yasha saw one of them fumble with the rope, lift Magda up, loosening the noose and passing it over her head. All this time he stood immobile. Now they were busy attempting to resuscitate her, rotating her arms, pulling her hair, dousing her with water. Each minute more people came in. The janitor and his wife were already there. Someone ran to fetch a policeman. Yasha could not see Magda's face, only the slack body which yielded to all treatment with the unresisting flaccidity of the dead. A woman pinched the corpse's cheeks and then crossed herself. Two old hags threw themselves into each other's arms, appeared to be conspiring silently. Only then did Yasha become aware that there was no sound from the other room. He walked into the room and found all three animals dead. Apparently Magda had strangled them. The monkey lay with eyes open. The crow, enclosed in its cage, looked as if it had been stuffed. The parrot was on its side, a drop of dry blood on its beak. Why had she done this? No doubt to prevent the creatures from crying out. Yasha tugged at someone's sleeve to show what had happened. The policeman was already in the apartment. He pulled out his notebook and wrote down what Yasha told him.

There were other arrivals: a physician, a civilian official, another policeman. Yasha expected to be arrested momentarily. He wanted to be taken to prison but the officials left, their only admonition being that the corpse was not to be touched. And now the rest of the men left and returned to their jobs—one was a cobbler, another a cooper. Only two women remained: the stout woman who had been peeling the onion and a white-haired crone with a face sprinkled with warts. The body had been placed on one of the beds and now the stout woman turned to Yasha: "She'll have to be laid out, you know. She was a Catholic."

"Do whatever's necessary."

"We must notify the parish. The Russians will want to perform an autopsy."

Then at length they left Yasha alone. He wanted to go to Magda in the bedroom but was afraid, his childhood fear of the dead returning. He threw open the windows as if to keep in touch with the courtyard, and left the front door ajar. He dared not see the animals again, though he wished to, afraid of their silence also. The stillness of death hung over the apartment, a silence pregnant with strangled screams. But in the corridor there was still a buzzing, voices whispering. Yasha stood in the center of the room and looked through the window at the pale blue sky, where a bird soared. Suddenly, he heard music. A street musician had come into the courtyard. He was playing an old Polish melody, a ballad of a girl who had been abandoned by her lover. Children gathered about the musician and, oddly enough, Yasha was grateful to the organ-grinder. His tune had banished death's silence. As long as he played, Yasha could face Magda.

He did not approach the bed immediately but remained standing at the threshold of the room. The women had covered the dead girl's face with a shawl. He hesitated a moment and then walked over and raised the shawl. He did not find Magda but an image molded of some lifeless substance, wax or paraffin—nose, mouth, features all unfamiliar. Only the high cheekbones retained some resemblance. The ears were white as bone, the eyelids were puckered, as though the eyeballs beneath had already withered. On the throat was a bluish-brown bruise from the rope. Her lips were silent and yet she was screaming—a cry such as no mortal could long endure. Swollen and cracked, the mouth shouted, Look what you have done to me! Look! Look! Yasha wanted to cover her face but his hands were paralyzed and he could not move. Presumably, this was the same Magda who had quarreled with him that very morning, had later brought him a pot of water from the pump; but that other Magda could be asked forgiveness and mollified. This one, lying here limp on the bed, had passed into eternity, cutting herself off from good or evil. She had transcended the abyss that could not be spanned by a bridge. Yasha touched her forehead. It felt neither cold nor warm but beyond temperature. Then Yasha raised one of her eyelids. The pupil seemed that of a living person, but it stared at nothing; it was not even looking into itself.

3

A hearse arrived and Magda was carried out. A huge fellow in a blue apron and wearing an oilskin cap which only partially concealed a shock of yellow hair, took her in one hand as though she were a chicken, dropped her on a stretcher, and covered her with a gunny sack. He shouted something to Yasha and handed him a document. He was assisted by a short man with a curly mustache, who likewise seemed angry at something. The assistant stank of whiskey and the odor made Yasha think of a drink. The pain and the fear had become unendurable. He listened to the two men descend the stairs. The sound of whispering came from the other side of the door. Generally, the relatives hid the corpse from the officials, seeking to avoid an autopsy. Yasha realized he should have made some sort of arrangements with a priest, but everything had happened too quickly. He had just hung around, doing nothing. The neighbors were talking about him, he knew, astounded at his odd behavior. He had not even accompanied Magda's body to the hearse; a childish shame had overwhelmed him. If there had not been people to face, he would have left, but he waited for the crowd to disperse. By this time, the apartment was almost dark. He stood staring at a spot on the door latch, feeling hemmed in on all sides by uncanny forces. Behind him the silence rustled and snorted. He was afraid to turn his head. Some shadowy form lurked nearby, ready to leap upon him and attack him with tooth and claw—something monstrous and nameless. He had been familiar with this presence from childhood. It revealed itself to him in nightmares. It was, he assured himself, a figment of his imagination, but nevertheless he could not deny its existence. He held his breath. Such terror could be endured only a few seconds.

Outside the noises had ceased and Yasha rushed to the door. He tried to pull it open but it wouldn't move. Won't they let me out? he wondered in terror. He tugged at the knob and all at once the door swung open as if blown by a gust of wind. He saw a dark form scamper away; he had nearly killed a cat. Sweat drenched his clothes. Slamming the door behind him, he dashed down the stairs as though pursued. He saw the janitor standing alone in the courtyard and he waited until the man retired to his cubicle. Yasha's heart did not beat now so much as flutter. His scalp prickled. Something was crawling down his spine. He did not feel the same terror as before, but he knew he would never return to that apartment.

The janitor closed the door to his room and Yasha sprinted through the gate. Now once again he felt the dull ache in his foot. He kept close to the walls, his greatest wish being not to be seen, or at least not to be conscious of others watching him. He reached Franciskaner Street and hurriedly turned the corner, like a boy playing truant from cheder. The events of the past twenty-four hours seemed to have made him a child again, a frightened, guilty schoolboy, plagued by fears he could not divulge and by entanglements no stranger could understand. At the same time he had the sobriety of maturity—of one who dreams and knows that he dreams.

Get drunk? Was there a tavern nearby? There were several on Freta Street but there everyone knew him. On the other hand, Franciskaner was inhabited only by Jews; here, there was no drinking. He remembered that there was a bar on Bugay Street somewhere, but how could you get there without passing Freta Street? He walked to Nowiniarska Street and came out on a street called Bolesc.* That should be the name of all streets, he said to himself. The whole world is one great agony. He had passed Bugay Street and he doubled on his tracks. Streetwalkers were already standing under the lampposts and around gates, although it was not yet evening; but none of them motioned to him. Am I so repulsive that even they aren't interested? he wondered. A tall laborer wearing a checked jacket, blue cap, and low boots, approached. He had a narrow, sunken face which had been half-eaten away and, in place of a nose, a black plaster on a string. A dwarf of a prostitute, who scarcely came up to the man's waist, walked up to him and led him off. Yasha could see his legs shaking. The girl could not have been more than fifteen. What is he afraid of? something within Yasha asked, laughingly. Syphilis?

Yasha reached Bugay Street but the tavern he remembered having beeen there had disappeared. Had it been closed? He wanted to ask of some passerby, but he was ashamed to. What's the matter with me? Why should I feel the shame of a goat in a cabbage patch? he asked himself. All the while he was searching for the tavern, he knew it was somewhere close by, eluding him. Just because he was so anxious not to be seen, everyone

* Bolesc means pain in Polish

was gaping at him. Can they know me here? he wondered. Can some of them have been to the Alhambra? No, it's not possible. They were whispering about him, laughing in his face. A small dog growled and snapped at his trousers. He was ashamed to drive away so small a creature, but the dog foamed with rage and yelped so loudly it scarcely seemed small at all. The devil who was exacting revenge upon Yasha apparently was not yet satisfied. He kept adding annoyance to annoyance. Then, suddenly, Yasha saw the tavern. He was standing right next to it. As if they had all had a hand in the joke, suddenly everyone began to laugh.

Now he no longer even wished to go into the place; he would have preferred another but he felt he could not turn around and walk away. It would indicate surrender. He went up the three steps, opened the door, and was hit by a blast of heat and steam. The stench of vodka and beer mingled with something else which was oily and musty. Someone was playing an accordion and there was a great scurrying about, swaying, clapping of hands, and dancing. Apparently here it was like one big family. His eyes became misty and for a moment he could not see. He searched for a table but there were none, not even benches. He felt blinded and as if a cane or a rope had been placed in his path to trip him. Somehow, he managed to reach the bar but could not break through the crowd of drinkers and, anyway, the bartender had walked to the other side of the bar. Yasha put his hand into his pants pocket looking for a handkerchief but he could not find one. He could move neither forward nor backward. It was as if he had been caught in a trap. Heavy beads of perspiration dripped from his forehead. His desire to drink had, in one instant, been transformed into disgust. The nausea returned and again fiery sparks danced before his eyes: two large sparks, almost as big as coals.

"What do you want?" someone asked from behind the bar.

"Me?" Yasha replied.

"Who else?"

"I'd like a glass of tea," and he, himself, was astounded at his words. The other hesitated.

"This is not a tea-room!"

"Make it vodka."

"Glass or bottle?"

"Bottle."

"Quart or pint?"

"Pint."

"Forty or sixty?"

"Sixty."

Surprisingly, no one laughed.

"Anything to eat?"

"Might as well."

"A salted roll?"

"That'll do."

"Sit down; I'll bring your order."

"Where do you sit?"

"Where do you think?"

Then Yasha spied a table. It was like demonstrations in hypnotism which he had read about in magazines and more than once had conducted himself.

4

He sat down at the table and only then sensed how weary he was. He could no longer stand the shoe on his left foot; he put his hand under the table and tried to undo the lace. He recalled a passage from the Pentateuch: "Behold, I am at the point of dying, and what profit shall this birthright give me?"

Suddenly, the fear, anxiety, embarrassment left him. He no longer cared whether he was stared at or mocked. He was unable to untangle the shoelace and he pulled at it so vigorously that he tore it. He removed the shoe and the sock gave off a noxious heat.—Yes, it's getting gangrenous, gangrenous . . . I'll join her soon! And as he felt his foot it swelled as the dough of which the barber had spoken earlier that day. What time does this place close, I wonder? Not early. He desired to do only one thing—sit and rest. He closed his eyes and enveloped himself in the darkness of his being. Where was Magda now? What was being done to her? They must have already dissected her body. Students learning anatomy. He slumped as though from the burden of the horror. What would her mother say? Her brother? So much punishment at one blow!

Someone brought him a bottle of vodka and a glass, along with a basket of salted rolls. Yasha poured himself half a glassful of the vodka and drank it down quickly, as if it were medicine. His nose burned and so did his throat and eyes. Maybe I should rub my foot with it, he thought. Alcohol is supposed to help this sort of thing. He poured some of the vodka into his hand, stooped, and massaged it into his ankle. Well, anyway, it's too late! Then he drank another glassful. The alcohol went to his head but it did not make him feel better. He imagined Magda's head being cut from her body, her stomach being split open. And only a few hours before she'd brought a chicken from the market, to prepare for his supper. Why did she do it? Why? something within him screamed. He had left her before. She had known all his secrets. She had been tolerant of him. It was almost unbelievable that at this time yesterday he had been in good health, planning to perform somersaults on the tightrope, and with Magda and Emilia still his. Catastrophe had struck him as it had Job. One misstep and he had lost everything . . . everything . . .

There was only one way out now—it was time to see what lay on the other side of the curtain. But how? Throw himself into the Vistula? But it would be dreadful for Esther. No, he could not leave her a deserted wife. The very least he could do was arrange for her to remarry . . . He could scarcely keep himself from vomiting. Yes, Death was his master. Life had cast him to the winds.

He held the bottle in his hand but could drink no more. He sat there, blind, his lids shut. The accordion did not stop playing the old Polish mazurka. The din in the tavern became ever louder. He had already resolved to die but, nevertheless, he needed a place to spend this night. Something still required thinking out. But where could he go with his injured foot? If it were only day! By now, everything had shut down. A hotel? Which one? And how could he go there with his foot in this condition? He was unlikely to find a droshky in the neighborhood. He wanted to put his shoe on, but it had vanished. He felt around for it with his toe but it wasn't there. Had someone stolen it? He opened his eyes and saw all about him in the tavern wild eyes and flushed faces. Hands waved, bodies reeled, feeble arms sought to do battle; there was much kissing and embracing. The waiters, dressed in grimy aprons, came and went, bringing food and vodka. The accordionist played, his black hair and thin mustache almost touching his instrument, his eyes screwed up tight, his expression rapturous. His body was bent close to the floor which was sprinkled with sawdust. Evidently, there was another room in the tavern, for the sound of a piano could be heard. A curl of steam circled the naphtha lamp. Opposite Yasha sat a huge man, his skin pockmarked; he had a long mustache, a short pimpled nose, and a scar cut into his forehead. He kept grimacing at Yasha. His watery, crossed eyes rolled in exaltation, the ecstasy of one on the brink of madness.

Yasha touched his shoe and stooped to get it. He tried to put it on but it would no longer fit. This made him think of the story he had learned in cheder about Nero who, hearing of his father's death, found his shoes had become too small for him; for, as it is written, "A good report maketh the bones fat." How far away all that seemed now: his teacher, Reb Moshe Godle, the children, that volume of the Talmud containing the story of the destruction of the temple which is studied before the ninth day of Ab.—Well, I can't sit here until they close! I must find a place to sleep.

He forced the shoe onto his foot but kept it unlaced, then tried to get his waiter's attention by tapping his glass against the bottle. The giant across the way from him laughed and Yasha saw a set of broken teeth. It was as if he and Yasha were involved in some great joke together. How can a man like that live? Yasha asked himself. Is he drunk or mad? Does he have anyone at all in the world? Does he work? Perhaps what I'm going through now has already happened to him. Saliva dropped from the giant's mouth; he was laughing so hard his eyes were tearing. Yet he was someone's father, husband, brother, son. Savagery was stamped upon his features. He was still in that primeval forest from which mankind was evolved. Such men die laughing, Yasha said to himself. And then finally the waiter came.

Yasha paid his bill and got to his feet. He could barely walk. Each step he took was agony.

It was very late but, nevertheless, Bugay Street remained crowded. There were women seated upon the stoops, upon stools, upon boxes. Several shoemakers had moved their benches outside and hammered by candlelight. Even the children were still awake. A sulfurous breeze blew from the Vistula. Foul odors rose from the sewers. Above the rooftops the sky glowed as if reflecting some distant fire. Yasha looked for a droshky but soon realized he would spend the whole night waiting for one. He started off down Celna Street, continued on Swietojanska Street, and came out on Castle Place. He could move only a few steps at a time. He was overwhelmed by heat, nauseated. At every gate, at every lamppost stood groups of prostitutes. All about him drunkards reeled along as though seeking someone to fall against. A woman sat at an open door underneath a balcony. She had tousled hair and eyes which were aflame with the joy of madness, and in her arms she clutched a basket stuffed with rags. Yasha bent his head; he belched and tasted an unfamiliar bitterness. I know, it's the world! Every second or third house contained a corpse. Throngs of people roamed about the streets, slept on benches, lay on the banks of the Vistula in the midst of filth. The city was surrounded by cemeteries, prisons, hospitals, insane asylums. In every street and alley lurked murderers, thieves, degenerates. Policemen were everywhere in sight.

Yasha saw a droshky and motioned at it but the driver, after looking him over, drove on. Another droshky appeared but did not stop, either. The third droshky that came along did stop, though somewhat tentatively. Yasha climbed in.

"Take me to a hotel?"

"Which?"

"Any one. Just a hotel."

"How about the Cracowsky?"

"All right—the Cracowsky."

The coachman cracked his whip and the droshky trundled off, down Podwal Street, into Mead Street, into New Senator Street. Theater Square was still crowded, filled with carriages. Apparently, there had been a special performance of the opera. Men shouted, women laughed. Not one among all these people knew that someone called Magda had hanged herself, nor that a magician from Lublin was racked by pain. The laughter and carousing will go on until they too turn to dust, Yasha said to himself. It seemed odd to him now that he had devoted his every waking thought to entertaining this rabble. What was I after? To have these dancers upon graves spare me some of their applause? Was that why I became a thief and murderer?

The droshky pulled up at the Cracowsky Hotel and at that very instant Yasha realized that the trip had been useless—he did not have his identification papers with him.

5

Yasha paid the coachman and told him to wait. He sought to coax the room clerk into renting him a room although he was without credentials, but the dwarf-like individual behind the desk was adamant.

"It can't be done. Strictly forbidden."

"Suppose a man loses his papers? Must he die?"

The clerk shrugged his shoulders. "I have my orders."

Judgments, they do not know them—something within

Yasha quoted for him. Thus had his father labeled the Russian laws.

Yasha walked outside in time to see the droshky pulling away; someone had outbid him for the vehicle. He sat down on the doorstep of a neighboring building. This was the second consecutive night he had wandered about. Things are moving swiftly, he thought; tomorrow night, perhaps, I'll be sleeping in my grave. There were streetwalkers here also. Across the way from him he saw a woman dressed in black, wearing long earrings. She looked almost like a middle-aged housewife but she gave him the glance of a prostitute. Evidently, she was one of the unregistered ones, those who offer themselves in courtyards or doorways. She looked directly at him, as though trying to hypnotize him; her gaze clung to him in entreaty. She seemed to be saying, Since we are in the same fix, why not be so together? The light of the streetlamp bathed her in yellow and Yasha could see the wrinkles on her face, the lines in her forehead, the rouge she had smeared over her cheekbones, the mascara around her large, dark eyes. He lacked even the strength for sympathy—all he could feel was amazement. So this is the way the powers that be operate, he thought; they play with a man and then cast him aside as offal. But why him in particular? Why this woman? How was she worse than those pampered ladies who sat in the boxes at the opera and looked down at the audience through their lorgnettes? Was everything chance? If so, then chance was God. But what was chance? Was the universe chance? If the universe was not, could only a part of it be chance?

He saw a droshky coming and beckoned to the driver. The droshky stopped and he climbed in. The woman across the way watched him reproachfully. Her eyes seemed to be saying to Yasha: Will you forsake me also? The coachman turned his head but Yasha could not think of what to tell him. He wanted to go to a hospital but he heard himself saying, "Nizka Street."

"What number?"

"I don't remember the number. I'll direct you."

"All right."

He knew that it was madness to visit the yellowish woman and her brother—the pimp from Buenos Aires —at this time of night, but he had no alternative. Wolsky had a wife and children; Yasha realized he could not barge in on him in this condition. Maybe I should wake Emilia? he thought. No; even Zeftel won't be pleased to see me. He played with the notion of catching a train to Lublin but decided against it. He must arrange Magda's funeral. He could not just abandon the corpse and run. Anyway, the police undoubtedly knew that it was he who had broken into Zaruski's house the night before. It would be better to be arrested here in Warsaw than in Lublin. At least Esther would be spared the sight. Besides, Bolek was waiting in Piask. Had he not warned Yasha years ago that he would kill him? The best solution would be to leave the country. Maybe go to Argentina. But not with his foot the way it was . . .

The droshky traveled along Tlomacka Street, Leshno Street, and then on to Iron Street. There it turned into Smotcha Street. Yasha did not doze off, but sat hunched up as though chilled by a fever. Now, he was more concerned about the impropriety of visiting Zeftel at this hour and about the shame of exposing his situation to her and her hosts, than with sorrow for Magda or the fear of losing his foot. He took a comb from his pocket and ran it through his hair. He adjusted his tie. The thought of his financial predicament frightened him. A funeral would cost several hundred rubles and he had nothing. He could sell his team of horses but the police were after him and would arrest him the moment he set foot in the apartment on Freta Street. The wisest course would be to surrender to the police. He would receive everything he needed: a place to sleep, medical attention. Yes, that is the only solution, he told himself. But how should he go about it? Stop a policeman? Ask to be driven to the police station? Crowded as the other streets had been with officers of the law, now there was not a single one about. The street was deserted, all the gates locked, all the windows shut. He thought of telling the driver to take him to the nearest police headquarters but he was too ashamed to do so. He would think me mad, Yasha decided. Just the fact that I limped made him suspicious. Overwhelmed though he was by anxiety, Yasha could not rid himself of his pride and vanity.—The best solution of all is death! I'll put an end to it. And perhaps this very night!

He suddenly grew calmer, his decision made. It was as if he had stopped thinking. The droshky turned into Nizka Street and headed back in an easterly direction towards the Vistula, but Yasha could not remember which was the house. He was certain it had had a boarded fence with a gate but no such courtyard was to be seen. The coachman brought the droshky to a halt.

"Maybe it's nearer Okopova Street."

"Yes, maybe."

"I can't turn around."

"Suppose I get out here and find it myself," Yasha said, aware that this was stupidity; each step he took was an effort.

"If you wish."

He paid and climbed down. His injured leg had fallen

asleep at the knee joint. Only when the droshky drove off did Yasha realize how dark it was here. There were only a few smoky streetlamps, placed at a great distance from each other. The street was unpaved, a mass of pits and mounds. Yasha looked about him but could see nothing. It was as if this were a street in some country village. Possibly this wasn't even Nizka Street? Could it be Mila or Stavka Street? He looked for matches even though he knew there were none in his pocket. He limped toward Okopova Street. His coming here had been madness. End everything? How did one do it? You couldn't hang or poison yourself in the middle of the street. Go to the Vistula?—but that was versts away. A breeze blew from the cemetery. Suddenly, he wanted to laugh. Had anyone ever been in such a dilemma? He hobbled as far as Okopova Street but the house he wanted had vanished. He raised his eyes and saw a black sky, dense with stars, interested only in its heavenly business. Who was concerned about a magician on earth who had allowed himself to be trapped? Yasha limped to the cemetery. These lives were done, their accounts settled. If he could find an open gate and an open grave, he would lie down in it, conduct a proper Jewish funeral for himself.

What else remained for him?

6

But nevertheless he returned the way he had come. He had become accustomed to the pain in his foot. Let it tear, let it burn, let it abscess! He reached Smotcha Street and continued on. Suddenly he saw the house. There it was: the fence, the entrance. He touched the gate and it swung open, revealing the stairs which led to

Herman's sister's apartment. The occupants were up; lamplight streamed through the window. Well, fate does not wish me to die yet! He was ashamed to enter uninvited, limping, disheveled, but told himself, encouragingly: after all, such things have happened before. They won't throw me out. Even if they do, Zeftel will go with me. She loves me. The lamplight shining in the darkness returned him to life. They'll do something for my foot. Perhaps it can be saved. He considered calling out to Zeftel so as to prepare them for his arrival, but decided that this would be foolish. Limping to the stairs, he began to climb. He made as much noise as he could so as to announce himself. He had already prepared his opening remark: An unexpected visitor! A very strange thing happened. But those inside were apparently too engrossed in what they were doing to notice what was going on outside. Well, one lives through everything, Yasha comforted himself. What was engraven on that goldsmith's ring?—"This too shall pass." He knocked lightly on the door but there was no answer. They were in the other room, he decided. He knocked louder but there was no sound of footsteps. He stood there, shamed, humbled, prepared to surrender the vestige of pride he had left. Let this serve as an atonement for my sins, the voice within him uttered. He knocked three more times, very loudly, but still no one came. He waited and listened. Are they asleep, or what? He turned the knob and the door opened. A lamp was burning in the kitchen. Zeftel lay on the iron bed and, beside her, was Herman. They were both asleep. Herman was snoring deeply and sonorously. All the interior voices in Yasha became silent. He stood there gaping and then moved to the side for fear one of the pair should open his eyes. Now a shame he had never felt before came over him—

a shame not for the couple but for himself, the humiliation of one who realizes that despite all his wisdom and experience, he has remained a fool.

Later, he could not recall how long he stood there: a minute? several minutes? Zeftel lay facing the wall, one breast bared, her hair in disarray, as if completely crushed by Herman's enormous bulk. Herman was not quite naked—he wore some sort of undershirt of foreign manufacture. Perhaps most remarkable of all was that the flimsy bed supported all that weight. There was a lifelessness about the faces and, had Herman not been snoring, Yasha would have thought the couple had been murdered. Two spent figures, two wornout puppets, they lay under a blanket. Where is the sister? Yasha asked himself. And why had they left the lamp burning? He wondered, and even as he did so wondered why he was wondering. He felt sorrow, emptiness, a sense of powerlessness. It was not unlike the feeling he had experienced a few hours earlier when he had discovered Magda dead. Twice in one day there had been unveiled to him things which are best concealed. He had looked on the faces of death and lechery and had seen that they were the same. And even as he stood there staring, he knew that he was undergoing some sort of transformation, that he would never again be the Yasha he had been. The last twenty-four hours were unlike any previous day he had experienced. They summed up all his previous existence, and in summing it up had put a seal upon it. He had seen the hand of God. He had reached the end of the road.

EPILOGUE

Three years had gone by. In Esther's front room she and two seamstresses were noisily putting the finishing touches to a wedding gown. The dress was so voluminous and had so long a train that it occupied the entire work table. Esther and the girls bustled about like dwarves constructing a suit of armor for a giant. One girl basted, the other sewed on tape. Esther, wielding an iron, pressed out the wrinkles between the flounces, constantly testing the iron with her finger. From time to time, she sprayed water from a jug on the spot she was about to press. Although she did not perspire easily, even in hot weather, her forehead was beaded with drops of sweat. What could be worse than burning a hole in a wedding gown? One brown stain and all the work would have been for nothing. Nevertheless, Esther's black eyes twinkled. Despite her small hand and her narrow wrist, she handled the iron firmly. She was not one to scorch a dress.

Every now and again, she glanced out of the window that looked into the courtyard. The small brick structure or, as Esther thought of it—prison—had stood there for more than a year but she still had not become accustomed to it. At times she would forget momentarily what had happened and would imagine it was the Feast of the Tabernacles—that an arbor had been erected outside. Generally she kept the curtain of this particular window drawn, but today she needed the daylight. The three years had aged Esther. The skin under her eyes had webbed and her broadening face had acquired an over-ripe, ruddy color. Her head, as always, was kerchiefed, but now those hairs that could be seen were gray rather than black. Only her eyes remained youthful and glistened like black cherries. For three years she had carried within her a heavy heart. It was no less heavy today but nevertheless she joked with her assistants, exchanged with them the usual trade banter about the bride and groom. The girls glanced at each other knowingly; theirs was no longer an ordinary workshop. Not for one moment was it possible to ignore the presence of the small, doorless house with its tiny window, behind which sat Yasha the Penitent—as he was now known.

The first appearance of this phenomenon had created great excitement in the town. The Rabbi, Reb Abraham Eiger, had summoned Yasha to him and had cautioned him against doing what he planned. True, a hermit in Lithuania had had himself bricked up, but pious Jews were opposed to that sort of thing. The world had been created for the exercise of free will and the sons of

Adam must constantly choose between good and evil. Why seal one's self in stone? The meaning of life was freedom and the abstinence from evil. Man deprived of free will was like a corpse. But Yasha was not so easily dissuaded. In the year and a half that he had been doing penance he had learned much. He had engaged a tutor to instruct him in the Mishnah, the Agadahs of the Talmud, the Midrash, even the Zohar, and produced for the Rabbi a variety of prototypes—saints who had had themselves put under restraint for fear they would be unable to resist temptation. Had not a holy man put out his eyes so that he might not look at his Roman mistress? Had not a Jew in Shebreshin sworn himself to silence for fear of uttering a word of slander? Had not a musician from Kovle feigned blindness for thirty years to avoid gazing upon another man's wife? Harsh laws were merely fences to restrain a man from sin. The young men who were present at Yasha's debates with the Rabbi still discussed them. It was hard to believe that in a year and a half this charlatan, this libertine, had absorbed so much of the Torah. The Rabbi disputed with him as with an equal. Yasha had remained firm in his resolve. Finally, the Rabbi had placed his hand upon Yasha's head and had blessed him.

"Your actions are intended for the glory of Heaven. May the Almighty help you!"

And he had presented Yasha with a copper candlestick so that he might light a candle at night or on overcast days.

In the taverns of Piask and Lublin there had been much wagering on how long Yasha would endure his living grave. Some had estimated a week, others a month. As for the municipal authorities, they had debated the legality of Yasha's actions. Even the Governor had been kept informed. Yasha had calmly seated himself in a chair and Esther's house had been overrun by hundreds of observers as the masons worked. Children had climbed trees and had sat perched on rooftops. Pious Jews had come forward to speak with Yasha and discuss his motives, and equally pious matrons had attempted to dissuade him from his course. Esther also had wept and entreated until her voice was hoarse. Then, escorted by a group of women, she had gone to the cemetery to ascertain by measuring graves what length in candles she must give to charity. Her hope had been that such a gift would influence the spirits of saints to intercede with her husband and force him to reverse his decision. He must not leave her a deserted wife, albeit one who had her spouse so close at hand. But neither the sage admonitions, nor the laments, nor the warnings, had been of any avail. The walls of the small house had grown higher hour by hour. Yasha had allowed himself a space only four cubits long and four cubits wide. He had grown a beard and sidelocks and had put on a wide fringed garment, a long gabardine, and a velvet skull cap. As the masons worked, he had sat, book in hand, mumbling prayers. There had not even been sufficient room inside for a bed. His possessions consisted of a straw pallet, a chair, a tiny table, a pelisse with which to cover himself, the copper candlestick which the Rabbi had given him, a water jug, a few holy books, and a shovel with which to bury his excrement. The higher the walls had grown, the louder had become the laments. Yasha had cried out to the women, "Why all this wailing? I'm not dead yet."

"If only you were," Esther had called back in bitterness.

So vast and tumultuous had the crowd become that

the police had ridden in on horseback and dispersed them. The town Natchalnik had commanded the laborers to work day and night to put an end to the excitement. It had taken the masons forty-eight hours to complete their task. The building had a shingled roof and a window which could be shuttered from the inside. Curiosity-seekers had continued to come until the rains began to fall, and then the number had decreased. All day the shutters of the small window remained closed. Esther had the fence around the house repaired to keep off strangers. Soon it became clear that those who had wagered that Yasha would not stay immured more than a week or a month had lost their bets. A winter passed, a summer, than another winter, but Yasha the Magician, now known as Reb Jacob the Penitent, remained in his self-ordained prison. Thrice daily Esther brought him food: bread with groats, potatoes in their skins, cold water. Thrice daily he left off his meditations and, for her sake, spoke with her for a few minutes.

2

Outside it was a sunny, hot day, but Yasha's cell was dark and cool, even though shafts of sunlight and warm breezes did manage to penetrate the shuttered window. Every now and again, Yasha would open the shutters and a butterfly or a bumblebee would fly in. Sounds came to him: the chirping of birds, the lowing of a cow, the cry of a child. There was no need for him to light a candle this midday. He sat in his chair at the small table, perusing the Two Tablets of the Covenant. That winter he had lived through days when he had wished to tear down the walls and free himself from the cold and dampness. He had developed a rasping cough. His limbs had been racked with pain. He had urinated too frequently. At night he had huddled in all his clothes under the pelisse and blanket which Esther had thrust in through the window, yet he had been unable to get warm. From the ground had risen a gnawing frost that chilled him to the bone. Often he had felt that he was already in his grave, and at times he had even wished for death. Now it was again summer. To the right of his cell grew an apple tree and he heard the rustle of its leaves. A swallow had built its nest among the branches and bustled about all day, bringing in its bill stalks and grubs for its young. Yasha managed to force his head through the window and saw before him the fields, the blue sky, the roof of the synagogue, the spire of a church. A few bricks removed and he could—he knew —wriggle through the window. But the thought that he could fight his way to freedom at any moment he chose stifled his desire to leave his cell. He knew quite well that on the other side of the wall lurked unrest, lust, the fear of coming day.

As long as he sat there, he was protected against the graver transgressions. Even his worries were different from those outside. It was as if he had become again a foetus in his mother's womb and once more the light referred to in the Talmud shone from his head, the while an angel taught him the Torah. He was free of all needs. His food cost only a few groschen a day. He required neither clothing, nor wine, nor money. When he recalled his expenses during the time he lived in Warsaw or traveled in the provinces, he laughed to himself. No matter how much he had earned in those days it had not been enough. He had kept a whole menagerie of animals. He had required closetsful of clothes. He had constantly driven himself into new expenditures and had been in debt to Wolsky; had borrowed money on interest from usurers in Warsaw and Lublin. Ceaselessly, he had been signing promissory notes, seeking out endorsers, purchasing gifts, and been in everyone's debt. Wallowing in his passions, he had found himself in a net which kept drawing tighter about him. Performing on the tightrope had not even been enough. He had kept trying to invent more and more daring stunts which were certain to destroy him. He had turned to theft—only a small mischance had prevented him from going to an actual prison. Here, in his solitude, all externalities fell away like the husks which the cabalists call the evil spirits. He had cut through the net as if with a knife. With one stroke, he had canceled all his accounts. Esther managed to earn her own living. He had settled all his debts: had given Elzbieta and her son, Bolek, the team and wagon; had left Wolsky the furniture from his Freta Street apartment, along with his equipment, costumes, and other paraphernalia. Now Yasha possessed nothing but the shirt upon his back. Yes, but was this sufficient to cleanse him of his sins? Could he atone for the evil he had done simply by reducing his burden?

Only here, in the stillness of his cell, could Yasha meditate upon the extent of his wickedness: the number of souls he had committed to torture, to madness, to death. He was no highwayman plying his trade in the forests but, nevertheless, he had murdered. What difference did it make to the victim how one killed? He could absolve himself before a mortal judge (one who was himself evil), but the Creator could neither be bought off nor deceived. He, Yasha, had destroyed, not innocently but with purpose. Magda cried out to him from the grave. Nor was this the only horror he was guilty of. Now he

acknowledged them all. Even if he remained in his cell
for a hundred years he could not atone for all his iniquity. Repentance alone did not cancel out such mortal
sin. One could only gain absolution by begging forgiveness and receiving it from the victim himself. If one
owed even half a groschen to someone who lived on the
other side of the world, he must locate his creditor
and settle the account. So it was written in the holy
books. And each day Yasha remembered some additional evil for which he had been responsible. He had
violated every law of the Torah, had broken nearly every Commandment. And yet, while doing these things,
had considered himself an upright man, capable of ac-
cusing others. How did the little discomfort he now suffered balance against the anguish he had caused? He was
still alive, in more or less good health. Even his foot had
healed without crippling him. The true punishment, he
knew, would be given only in the other world; there
must be an accounting for every deed, every word, every thought. Only one consolation remained: that God
was merciful and compassionate and that, in the final
reckoning, good must triumph over evil. But what was
evil? He had studied the literature of the cabala with his
instructors for three years: already he was aware that
evil was merely God's diminishing of Himself to create
the world, so that he might be called Creator and have
mercy toward His creatures. As a king must have his
subjects, so a Creator must create, so a benefactor have
his beneficiaries. To this extent, the Lord of the Universe had to depend upon His children. But, it was not
enough to guide them with His merciful hand. They had
to learn to cleave to the path of righteousness by themselves, of their own free will. The celestial worlds were
awaiting this. Angel and seraph longed for the sons of

Adam to be righteous, to pray with humility, give with compassion. Indeed, each good act improved the Universe, every word of the Torah braided crowns for the Godhead. Conversely, the most insignificant transgression reverberated in the most ethereal worlds, delaying the day of deliverance.

There were times, even here in his cell, when Yasha's faith wavered. As he read the sacred books, nagging thoughts came to him: How can I be sure that these speak the truth? Perhaps there is no God? The Torah may be the invention of man? Possibly I torture myself in vain? Vividly, he heard the Evil Spirit debate with him, remind him of past delights, advise him to begin again his debauchery. Yasha had to circumvent him each time differently. When pressed too hard he would seemingly agree with his opponent that he must return to the world, but then would postpone the moment of freedom. Other times he would reply in rebuttal: Let us say for the sake of argument, Satan, that God does not exist, but that the words spoken in His name are nevertheless correct. If a man's lot depends on another's misfortune, then there is good fortune for no one. If there is no God, man must behave like God. On one occasion Yasha demanded of Satan: Well, then, who created the world? Where do I come from? and you? Who makes the snow fall, the wind blow, my lungs take in air, my brain think? Where did the earth come from, the sun, the moon, the stars? This world with its eternal wisdom had to be the creation of some hand. We can perceive God's wisdom—why not then believe that behind this wisdom is concealed the mercy of the creator?

Entire days and nights were consumed by such disputes, driving Yasha to the brink of madness. Now and again Belial would withdraw and Yasha's faith would be restored and he would actually see God, feel His hand. He would begin to understand why goodness was necessary, would savor the sweetness of prayer, the delicious taste of the Torah. It would become clearer to him, day by day, that the Holy books he studied led to virtue and eternal life, that they pointed the way to the purpose of creation, while that which lay behind him was evil—all scorn, theft, murder. There was no middle road. A single step away from God plunged one into the deepest abyss.

3

The holy books cautioned Yasha not to let down his guard for an instant. Satan's attack never abates. Temptations are offered one after the other. Even as a man lies on his deathbed, Samael comes before him and attempts to win him to idolatry. It was true, Yasha discovered. For now, Esther began to seek him out almost hourly, rapping upon the shutter, lamenting, and assailing him with all her troubles. At night she would rouse him from sleep and attempt to kiss him. There was no feminine wile that leads to sin and makes of learning a mockery that she did not employ. As if this were not enough, men and women began to visit him as though he were a thaumaturgic rabbi. They sought his advice, begged him to intercede on their behalf. Yasha pleaded that he be left in peace, since he was no rabbi, not even the son of a rabbi, only an ordinary man, and, in addition, a sinner, but to no avail. Women stole into the courtyard, pounded on the shutter, even tried to smash it down by force. They wailed and shrieked and, when thwarted, cursed him. Esther complained that they disturbed her work. Yasha was overcome by fear.

He had anticipated everything but not this. He, himself, was in need of advice. According to the law, was it right for him to deny the people and cause them sorrow? Was not this, itself, a display of arrogance? But could one such as he listen to their petitions like a rabbi? Both courses were wrong. After much consideration and many wretched nights Yasha decided to write to the Lublin rabbi. He composed his letter in Yiddish, including all the particulars and promised to abide by the Rabbi's decision. The Rabbi did not take long to reply. His answer, likewise written in Yiddish, commanded Yasha to receive those who came for two hours each day, but to accept no redemption money. The Rabbi wrote: "He to whom Jews come in audience is a rabbi."

And so Yasha now received people daily from two until four in the afternoon. So as to avoid confusion, Esther wrote numbers on cardboard and distributed them, as it was done in the offices of busy physicians. But even this did not help. Those who had an invalid at home, or who had recently suffered some tragedy, demanded to be admitted first. Others sought to bribe Esther with money and presents. Before long there was talk in the city of the miracles performed by Yasha the Penitent. He only had to make a wish, it was rumored, and the sick grew well; it was said that a conscript had been pulled right out of the hands of the Russians, that a mute had regained speech, and a blind man his sight. Yasha was now addressed by the women as Holy Rabbi, Holy Saint. Against his wishes, they showered his cell with banknotes and coins which he ordered distributed to the poor. Young Hasidim, who feared lest Yasha acquire some of the adherents of their own rabbis, mocked him and composed a lampoon listing all his former sins. A copy of it was sent to Esther.

No, the temptations never ceased. Yasha had withdrawn from the world but, through the tiny window
which he had left to admit air and light, evil talk, slander, wrath, and false flattery came. It became clear to
Yasha why the ancient saints had chosen exile and had
never slept twice in the same place; had feigned blindness and deafness and muteness. One could not serve
God amongst other men, even though separated by
brick walls. He considered putting a pack upon his back
and, with staff in hand, striking out for the unknown,
but this he knew would cause Esther unendurable
grief. Who could tell? She might even become ill from
sorrow. He had noted how her health was failing. Old
age was creeping up on her. Magda, peace be with her
soul, had shown him the sort of thing that could happen.

No, peace of mind, was not to be found in this world.
There is no tomorrow without sorrow, as the philosophers say. But even more powerful than the temptations
from without were those born within man himself, in
his brain, his heart. No hour passed without Yasha's being besieged by every sort of passion. No sooner did he
forget himself for a moment than they gathered about
him: empty fancies, daydreams, repulsive desires. Emilia's face would materialize from the darkness and refuse
to be driven away. It would smile, whisper, wink at him.
He would think of new tricks to perform, new jokes
with which to entertain audiences, new illusions and
stunts with which to bewilder them. Again he danced
on the tightrope, turned somersaults on the high wire,
sailed over the rooftops of cities, trailed by a jubilant
crowd. He would chase away the fancies as diligently
as he could, but still they would return like persistent
flies. He hungered for meat, wine, vodka. He was consumed by a longing to see Warsaw again—the droshkies,

omnibuses, cafés, confectionaries. Though he suffered from the colds and rheumatism and though there was a constant burning in his stomach, his lust had not diminished. With no woman about, he thought of sinning like Onan.

He had only two defenses against these assaults from within and without—the Torah and prayers. Night and day he studied, memorizing many chapters and reciting them as he lay on his straw pallet. "Blessed is the man that walketh not in the counsel of the ungodly." "Lord, how are they increased that trouble me! Many are they that rise up against me. Many there be which say of my soul, 'There is no help for him in God.' Selah." He repeated these passages so often that his lips swelled. In his mind he compared the Evil One to a dog which both barks and never stops biting. The creature must be constantly kept off with a stick, one's injured limbs pulled from its jaws, the wounds tended with salves and plasters. The fleas from its furry hide required also an eternal vigilance. And this until one's last breath.

He would surely have died had there not been an occasional respite. The Dog of Egypt did not always bite with the same ferocity. Now and again he withdrew, slumbered. But one had to stay on guard lest he return with renewed power and insolence.

4

One after another they all came with their troubles. They spoke to Yasha the magician as if he were God: "My wife is sick. My son must go to the army. A competitor is outbidding me for a farm. My daughter has gone mad . . ." A small dried-up man had a growth the size of an apple on his forehead. A girl had been hiccuping for a week and could not stop: at night, when the moon shone, she sounded like a hound baying. Evidently, there was a dybbuk in her, for she chanted hymns and prayers with the voice of a cantor. Now and again, she spoke in Polish and Russian, languages with which she was unfamiliar, and at such times she had a desire to seek out a priest and be converted. Yasha prayed for all of them. But each time he pointed out he was no rabbi but merely an ordinary Jew and a sinner, besides. The supplicants responded by repeating their requests. A deserted wife, whose husband had been missing six years and who had been searching throughout Poland for him, screamed so loudly that Yasha had to stuff his ears. She hurled herself at the building as if determined, from sheer bitterness, to demolish the structure. Her breath stank of onions and rotting teeth. Those standing behind her on line demanded that she make her complaints briefer, but she waved her fists at them and continued shouting and wailing. Finally, she was dragged away. "Scum, whoremaster, murderer!" she shouted at Yasha.

A melancholy young man confided that demons battled with him, knotting his fringed garment, putting elf-locks into his beard, spilling out the water he had prepared for his morning ablutions, putting handfuls of salt and pepper, along with worms and goat-dung, into his food. Every time he sought to perform his bodily functions, a she-devil prevented him. The young man had letters from rabbis and other reliable witnesses to prove the truth of what he was saying. There were also learned sophisticates who sought out Yasha to discuss religion with him and asked him all sorts of impossible questions. Young idlers came to mock and discredit him with unfamiliar quotations from the Talmud, or with words in Chaldaic. He had resolved to receive people only two hours each day but, as it worked out, he stood at his window from dawn until nightfall. His legs grew so weary that he would collapse onto the straw pallet and would say the evening services sitting down.

One day Schmul the Musician, Yasha's former drinking companion, came to see him. Schmul complained that his hand ached so much it prevented him from playing his fiddle. No sooner did he lift his instrument than the pain began. The hand with which he fingered the strings had become stiff and bloodless, and he showed Yasha yellow, wrinkled fingertips. Schmul wanted to go to America. He brought greetings from the Piask thieves. Elzbieta had died. Bolek was in the Yanov prison, Chaim-Leib in the poorhouse. Blind Mechl had lost the sight in his good eye. Berish Visoker had moved to Warsaw.

"Remember Small Malka?" Schmul asked.

"Yes, how is she?"

"Her husband's passed on, too," Schmul said. "He was beaten to death in jail."

"And where is she?"

"She's married to a shoemaker from Zakelkow. Barely waited the three months."

"Is that so?"

"Perhaps you remember Zeftel? She was the girl who was married to Leibush Lekach," Schmul said slyly.

Yasha blushed. "Yes, I remember her."

"She's now a madam in Buenos Aires. Married some fellow named Herman. He left his wife for her. They own one of the biggest brothels."

Yasha paused for a moment. "How do you know?" he asked.

"Herman comes to Warsaw to take back ships full of

women. I know a musician who's on good terms with his sister. She lives on Nizka Street and runs the whole business."

"Really!"

"And what about you? Is it true that you're a rabbi?"

"No, it is not."

"Everyone's talking about you. They say you bring the dead back to life."

"Only God can do that."

"First God, then you . . ."

"Don't talk nonsense."

"I want you to say a prayer for me."

"Let the Almighty help you."

"Yashale, I see you and I don't recognize you. I can't believe it's really you."

"We grow older."

"Why did you do it? Why?"

"I could no longer breathe."

"Well, and is it any easier in there? I think of you . . . I think of you day and night."

Schmul's arrival had been in the evening. Esther, herself, had announced him. It was a warm summer night. The moon was up, the sky filled with stars. One could hear frogs croaking and now and again the cawing of a crow. Crickets chirped. The old comrades looked at each other, each from his side of the window. Yasha's beard had become almost white and there were gold flecks in his eyes. Two disheveled sidelocks trailed from beneath his skullcap. Schmul's sideburns were also threaded with gray and his face was sunken. He spoke mournfully: "I'm disgusted with everything and that's a fact. I play here, I play there. Another wedding march, another good-morning dance. The wedding jesters repeat the same old weary jokes. Sometimes right in the middle of things I feel like running away . . ."

"Where?"

"I don't know myself. Perhaps to America. Every day somebody else dies. As soon as I open my eyes I ask: 'Yentel, who died today?' Her friends bring the news first thing in the morning. Soon as I hear who it is I get a pain in my heart."

"Well, and don't people die in America?"

"I don't know so many people there."

"Only the body dies. The soul lives on. The body is like a garment. When a garment becomes soiled or threadbare, it is cast aside."

"I don't want, as they say, to irritate you, but were you ever in heaven and did you see the souls?"

"So long as God lives, everything lives. Death cannot arise from life."

"But, nevertheless, one's scared."

"Without fear, man would be worse than an animal."

"He's worse anyway."

"He could be better. It's up to him."

"How? What should we do?"

"Harm no one. Slander no one. Not even think evil."

"And what will that help?"

"If everyone conducted himself this way, even this world would be paradise."

"It will never happen."

"Each of us must do what's in his power."

"Will the Messiah come then?"

"There is no other way."

5

Immediately after the Feast of Tabernacles the rains came. Cold winds blew and the apples, fallen from the trees, rotted, the leaves withered, the grass turned from green to yellow. At daybreak birds chirped once and then remained silent the rest of the day. Yasha the Penitent was troubled by a cold. His nose was clogged and would not clear. Pains shot across his forehead and into his temples, his ears. He had become hoarse. At night Esther heard him coughing. She could not stay in bed and went to him, in robe and slippers, to plead that he foresake his self-imposed prison; but Yasha answered, "A beast must be kept in a cage."

"You're killing yourself."

"Better myself than others."

Esther went back to bed and Yasha returned to his pallet. He stayed dressed and bundled himself up in his blanket. He was no longer cold but still sleep would not come to him. He heard the sound of the rain on the shingle roof. There was a rustling in the earth as if moles were digging there or a corpse had turned in its grave. He, Yasha, had killed both Magda and her mother, had brought about the imprisonment of Bolek, had helped Zeftel become what she had. Emilia, he felt, was likewise no longer among the living. She had often said that Yasha was her last hope. No doubt she had done away with herself. And where was Halina now? He thought of them every day, every hour. Mentally, he called to the souls of the dead and begged them to give him some sign. "Where are you, Magda?" he muttered in the dark. "What has happened to your martyred soul?" Does she know I long for her and do penance? Or is it as it is said in Ecclesiastes: "And the dead know nothing." If that is so, then it has all been in vain. For a moment he imagined he saw a face in the darkness, a figure. But soon all dissolved into the dark again. God was silent. And so were the angels. So, too, the dead. Even the demons did not speak. The channels of faith had clogged up like his nose. He heard the sound of scratching—it was only a fieldmouse.

The lids of his eyes closed and he dozed. In his dreams the dead came to him but they revealed nothing, speaking only nonsense, performing insane antics. He awoke with a start. He tried to reconstruct his dreams but as he did so they misted away. One thing was certain—there was nothing to remember. His dreams had been perverse, inconsistent—the babbling of a child, or the gibberish of a madman.

To drive away his evil thoughts Yasha intoned the Treatise of Benedictions: "From what time in the evening may the Shema be recited? From the time the Priests enter the temple to eat of their heave offering . . ." As he passed from the first paragraph to the second, he lived through a new fantasy. Emilia was still alive. She had purchased an estate in Lublin and had a tunnel dug from her bedroom directly to his cell. She came and gave herself to him. Just before daybreak she hastened back. Yasha trembled. For one moment he had relaxed and fancies had burrowed through like mice or hobgoblins. They dwelled in the mind ever ready to defile him. But what were they? What was their purpose in human biology? He quickly went on to the second paragraph: "From what time in the morning may the Shema be recited? As soon as one can distinguish between blue and white. Rabbi Eliezer says 'between blue and green.'" Yasha wished to say more but lacked the strength to continue. He ran his hand over his emaciated torso, his heavy beard, his coated tongue, his teeth—most of which had already loosened. Will it be like this until the end? he wondered. Will I never rest? If so, let the end come!

He wished to turn on his other side but feared to disturb the blankets and rags with which he had covered himself. The frost was all about him, ready to penetrate to him at any moment. Once more he felt the desire to urinate but he did not yield to it. How did so much urine collect within him? He marshaled his strength and began to mumble the third paragraph: "The School of Shammai say, 'In the evening all should recline when they recite the Shema, but in the morning they should stand up, for it is written; and when *thou* liest *down* and when *thou* risest *up* . . ." He fell asleep and dreamed that he must urinate. He walked into the outhouse but Emilia was standing there. Despite his embarrassment she said with a smile, "Do what you have to."

At daybreak the rain stopped and snow began to fall —the first snow of the winter. Clouds gathered in the east but, at sunrise, the sky became pink and yellow. The flame of sunrise caught the edge of a cloud and blazed in a fiery zigzag. Yasha rose, shook off his nocturnal weariness, and the nocturnal doubts. He had once read about snowflakes and now he verified what he had learned. Each flake that fell on the window sill was hexagonal, complete with stems and horns, with designs and appendages, formed by that hidden hand which is everywhere—in the earth and in the clouds, in gold and in carrion, in the most distant star and in the heart of man. What can one call this force, if not God? Yasha asked himself. And what difference does it make if it's called nature? He reminded himself of the chapter in

Psalms: "He that planted the ear shall not hear? He that formed the eye shall not see?" He had sought a sign, yet every minute, every second, within him and outside, God signaled His presence.

Esther had already risen; he could see smoke coming from the chimney of the main house. She was preparing food for him. The snow continued to fall but nevertheless the birds sang longer than usual this day. From their hiding places these holy creatures who possessed nothing but a few feathers and an occasional crumb chirped joyfully.

Well, I've dawdled long enough! Yasha said and, removing his jacket and shirt, he began to wash himself with water from the jug. He collected snow from the window sill and rubbed it over his body. He inhaled deeply, coughing up all his phlegm. The congestion in his nose cleared as if by a miracle. Once more he filled his lungs with the cool, morning air. His throat felt better and he began to say the morning prayer in a resounding voice. "I thank Thee." "How goodly are thy tenets!" "Oh my God, the soul which Thou gavest me is pure; Thou didst create it; Thou didst form it; Thou didst breathe it into me; Thou preservest it within me; and Thou wilt take it from me, but wilt restore it unto me hereafter." Then he put on his prayer-shawl and phylacteries. Praised be God that he, Yasha, was not confined in a real prison. Here, in his cell, he could pray aloud and could study the Torah. Just a few steps away from him was his devoted wife. Worthy Jews, the grandsons of martyrs and saints, sought his advice and blessings as if he were a rabbi. Although he had sinned greatly, God in his pity had not permitted him to perish in sin. Fate had decreed that he must do penance. Could greater benevolence exist? What more could a murderer expect? How would an earthly court have judged him?

After "Hear O Israel," he offered the Eighteen Benedictions. When he came to the words, "Yea, faithful art Thou to quicken the dead," he stopped to meditate. Yes, a God who could fashion snowflakes, form a man's body from semen, control the sun, the moon, the comets, the planets, and the constellations, was also capable of reviving the dead. Only fools would deny this. God was omnipotent. From generation to generation this omnipotence grew increasingly evident. Things which once had seemed impossible for God were now performed by man. All heresy was based on the assumption that man was wise and God a fool; that man was good and God evil; that man was a living thing but the Creator dead. As soon as one left these wicked thoughts the gates of truth swung open. Yasha swayed, beat his breast, bowed his head. Opening his eyes, he saw Esther at the window. Her eyes were smiling. She carried a saucepan from which rose a cloud of steam. Since he had already said the Eighteen Benedictions, he nodded and greeted her. Every bitter thought had left him. He was again filled with love. Esther apparently detected this in his face. Man can judge, after all. He sees everything if he chooses to see.

Esther brought a letter with his food. The envelope was wrinkled. It bore Yasha's name on it, and the name of the city. There was neither street nor street number.

He put away his phylacteries and washed his hands. Esther had brought him rice with hot milk. He ate at the table, putting aside the letter which he had decided not to open until after breakfast. This half-hour belonged to Esther. She would stand there, watching him and speaking to him as he ate. It would be the same old refrain, he feared: his health, the fact that he was killing himself, ruining her life, but—no—this morning she did not indulge in her usual complaints.

Instead, she smiled at him maternally and told him of the orders she had received, gossiped about the workshop and the seamstresses, told of her plan to have the house painted for Passover. He did not want to eat all of the rice but Esther insisted, swore she would not stir until he had swallowed the last spoonful. He felt strength returning to his body. The milk he was drinking had come from his own cow, the rice had been grown somewhere in China. Thousands of hands had labored to bring the food to his mouth. Every grain of rice held within it the hidden powers of heaven and earth.

After he had finished the rice and the coffee with chickory, he tore open the envelope. He glanced quickly at the signature and his eyes misted. He felt a mingling of joy and sorrow. Emilia had written to him. So Emilia was alive! But he did not begin to read at once, first offering up his praise to God. Then, wiping his eyes with a handkerchief, he began:

My dear Pan Yasha (or should I address you as Rabbi Jacob?), This morning I opened the *Courier Poranny* and saw your name—for the first time in more than three years. It was such a surprise that I could not read further. My first thought was that you were performing again—here or abroad—but then, eagerly, I read the whole article and my being grew sad and still. I recall that we often discussed religion and you expressed opinions which I regarded as deism, a belief in God without dogma or revelations. After you left us so suddenly in that unusual fashion, I thought many times that this was proof of how little help a faith without discipline was to a person in a spiritual crisis. You went away, leaving no trace behind you. You sank out of sight, as the saying goes, like a stone in water. Often I composed letters to you in my mind. I want to tell you first of all, should this letter reach you, that I accept all of the blame. Only after you left did I realize how badly I had behaved. I knew you had a wife. I drove you to this affair, so I am morally responsible. I have wanted to tell you this time after time, but I was under the impression that you had gone away to America, or God knows where.

The story in today's paper, describing how you have imprisoned yourself in stone, how you have become a holy man, and how Jewish men and women wait at your window for your blessing, has made an indelible impression upon me. I was unable to continue reading because of my tears. I have often cried over you but these were tears of joy. Twelve hours have gone by yet as I sit here and write this letter, I am crying again: first, because you have shown such great conscience; secondly, because you are atoning for *my* sins. I myself seriously considered entering a convent but I had Halina to think of. I could not hide from her what had happened. In her own fashion she loved you too and admired you exceedingly, and it was a great blow to her. Night after night, we lay in bed together and wept. Halina, in fact, became seriously ill and I was forced to send her to a sanitorium in Zokopane, in the Tatry Mountains. I could not have managed it (you must recall my financial situation) if an angel in human form had not come to our assistance, a friend of my dear departed husband, Professor Marjan Rydzewski. What he did for us cannot be related in one letter.

Fate chose that just then his wife should pass away (she's suffered for years from asthma) and when this good man suggested I become his wife, I could not refuse. You were no longer there; Halina was in the sanitorium; I had been left alone in God's world. But I told him the whole truth, omitting nothing. He is already an old man and a pensioner, but quite active; he reads and writes the whole day long and is extremely good to me and Halina. That's as much as I can say here. Halina regained her health in Zokopane and when she returned, I could scarcely recognize her, she had grown and blossomed so. She is already in her eighteenth year and I earnestly hope that she will have more luck than her mother. Professor Rydzewski is as kind to her as a real father could be and indulges all her caprices. This new generation seems egotistical, without restrictions and with the conviction that everything the heart desires must be granted.

Well, enough about myself. It isn't easy for me to write to you. I cannot picture you with a long beard and sidelocks as the journalist describes you. Perhaps you are not even permitted to read my letter? If this is so, forgive me. All these years I've thought of you, not a day passes that I don't think of you. For some mysterious reason I sleep badly and the human brain is such a capricious organ. In my fantasies I always pictured you in America in a huge theater or circus, surrounded by luxury and beautiful women. But reality is full of surprises. I do not dare to tell you what is right or wrong, but it does seem to me that you have inflicted too severe a punishment upon yourself. Despite your strength you are a delicate person and you must not endanger your health. The fact is you've committed no crime. You always showed a good and gentle nature. The short time that I knew you was the happiest period of my life.

This letter is already too long. They speak of you once more in Warsaw, but this time only with admiration.

We have a telephone at home now and several friends who knew of our friendship have called me. Professor Rydzewski himself suggested that I write you and he sends his best wishes although he does not know you. Halina is delighted to know that you are alive and will write shortly—a long letter she tells me. May God watch over you.

Your eternally devoted,
Emilia

*Translated by Elaine Gottlieb
and Joseph Singer*